Praise for Misty Evans'
Proof of Life

"Evans takes readers on an edge-of-your-seat thriller into the secretive world of CIA operatives."

~ *RT Reviews*

"Where the drama captures you is that what you think is real isn't...the non-stop thrill ride and mystery...brought to an action-packed conclusion will only leave you wanting more."

~ *Long and Short Reviews*

"Misty Evans has a lively voice that comes right off the page."

~ *Joyfully Reviewed*

"...I can easily see [Evans] side by side with authors such as Clancy and Gerritson."

~ *The Romance Studio*

Look for these titles by
Misty Evans

Now Available:

A Tickle My Fantasy Story
Witches Anonymous

Super Agent Series
Operation Sheba (Book 1)
I'd Rather Be In Paris (Book 2)
Proof of Life (Book 3)

Print Anthology
Tickle My Fantasy

Proof of Life

Misty Evans

A SAMHAIN PUBLISHING, LTD. publication.

Samhain Publishing, Ltd.
577 Mulberry Street, Suite 1520
Macon, GA 31201
www.samhainpublishing.com

Proof of Life
Copyright © 2010 by Misty Evans
Print ISBN: 978-1-60504-793-5
Digital ISBN: 978-1-60504-806-2

Editing by Sasha Knight
Cover by Natalie Winters

First Samhain Publishing, Ltd. electronic publication: October 2009
First Samhain Publishing, Ltd. print publication: August 2010

Dedication

This book is dedicated to Mark, protector and companion on all my journeys. You're the real deal, and *I'm* the lucky one.

A branch in my family tree belongs to the Irish, so I'm using their help in saying thanks to all who contributed to this book. Hearty Irish wishes go to Sheri Humphrey for reviewing Brigit's injuries and guiding me in realistic treatments. More good wishes go to Val Pearson for supplying a name for my peace-loving Irish poet. Thanks, Val!

I don't have to look far to find a four-leaf clover with incredible kids like Sam and Ben, and invaluable friends like Nana, Angela, Donnell, Chiron, Tessy and Ree. You guys never fail to inspire, motivate and love me whether I'm laughing or grumping.

I love research and making new friends in the process. In this story Brigit would not have come to life without the help of Dr. Cynthia Clark. Thank you, Dr. Clark, for opening my eyes to endless possibilities for Brigit's work as a consultant for DHS and answering my questions with excellent care to details.

Miles and miles of Irish smiles go to my local librarian, Sue Mannix, who guided my research into the world of Irish history, religion, politics and good old-fashioned heart. The Irish are an incredible people and I'm glad I got to know them better in this process because of you.

And to my editor, Sasha, I offer never-ending thanks for your patience, understanding and ability to make me feel like the luckiest writer on the planet. I'm wishing you a beautiful rainbow, complete with an overflowing pot of gold.

Chapter One

The grandfather clock in the corner chimed, its deep baritone vibrating under a sheet of protective plastic. The antique clock, unlike the west wall of Michael Stone's home office, had escaped damage when the bullets flew. If only his chest had been as lucky.

Michael stopped sanding the section of Sheetrock in front of him to rub the scar under his shirt. For the sixth time in as many months, he was patching and sanding holes, trying to cover up the past. But just like the drywall dust that had infiltrated every corner of his office, reminders of the hostage incident infiltrated every corner of his mind.

The edge of one of the filled bullet holes was ridged. Another had sunk. He should just knock them out and start over. He should do the same with the memories.

Julia. Conrad. Raissi. The names swirled in his brain, making his gut clench and his forehead sweat. No matter how many times he cut out and patched the holes, betrayal, obligation and failure rose from the dust to mock him.

Starting on the ridged patch, he gritted his teeth as the sandpaper chewed up the dried mud and dust fell to the ground. *Time*, he told himself, as the grandfather clock chimed again. *I just need more time.*

Using his shirt sleeve to wipe the sweat from his forehead, he pushed the past behind the carefully constructed wall he'd built in his mind. He should have been at Ella's school, watching her parade around, all smiles and six-year-old self-confidence in her Wonder Woman costume instead of trying to fix something that couldn't be fixed.

Halloween had become so dangerous Ella's school had decided to put on a trunk-or-treat, complete with parade, to keep the students protected. The fact that kids had lost the freedom to enjoy trick or treating saddened Michael. It saddened him even more that he was loathe to go watch his niece enjoy the substitute version because he couldn't go anywhere in public without a battalion of security. As Deputy Director of the CIA and brother-in-law to the next president—if the pre-election day polls were accurate—his autonomy no longer existed.

These days, it didn't matter if you were an adult or a kid. Freedom was a precious commodity choked off by criminals and terrorists.

Goddamn terrorists.

Throwing the sandpaper down on the tarp at his feet, he headed for his desk. A week's worth of newspapers covered one corner. His stuffed briefcase lay next to them. The European Directorate was waiting for his signature on a dozen different projects.

Michael wheeled his office chair out and sat down hard. He booted up his laptop, drumming a staccato on the top of his desk with his fingers as he waited for the opening screen to ask for his password. Before it could flash the message, his attention was drawn back to the wall. Raissi's smirking face danced over the holes.

Adrenaline buzzed in his veins as he shut the laptop with a firm snap. No way was he getting any work done tonight. He should call Kinnick, his bodyguard and sparring partner, and hit the gym. Fighting was the only way he'd found to jack the energy and the memories from his psyche.

He'd taken up mixed martial arts which combined kickboxing with the two other phases of combat—takedowns and submission holds. Fights required all three types of skills, and knowing which phase would give you an advantage over your opponent gave you control of the fight.

Even outside the ring, control was power.

Thad Pennington, Republican candidate for U.S. President, was mere days and percentage points away from taking control of the White House. He'd already offered Michael directorship of the CIA after the election, but Michael had turned him down.

Unlike a majority of D.C.'s political pundits, he didn't want his legacy handed to him on anything other than merit.

Thad was also Ella's father. A father on the campaign trail and missing the Halloween festivities. Yet another reason Michael should have been at Ella's school. She needed a substitute father more and more while her biological one pursued the dream of power.

Across the room, Raissi's face faded into poorly patched bullet holes once again, standing out in bas-relief from the smooth surface surrounding them. A heavy, burning sensation tugged at Michael's chest. Letting out his breath, he rocked his chair back and forth, his fingers absently probing his scar.

Holes. His life was full of them. Work, social life, family. His goddamn chest. And every time he patched one, it seemed to have the opposite effect. The holes kept getting bigger, spreading like a disease.

The phone on his desk rang, jolting him out of his thoughts. A vacation from them was such a relief, he snagged the receiver without looking at the ID.

"Stone."

"Michael?"

It was only two syllables, but his sister's high-pitched voice, cracking with strain, brought him up straight. "What is it, Ruthie?"

She sobbed and the hair on the back of his neck rose. "It's Ella. She's...gone." Another sob. "Kidnapped. We don't know who's got her. Oh, Michael, what are they doing to my baby?"

The world screeched to a halt. As the next beat of his heart echoed inside his head, he rose from the chair, his body kicking into phase one of combat.

~ ✧ ~

Washington D.C. suburbs

Brigit Kent unlocked the door to her loft, dropped her overnight bag on the floor inside and flipped on the lights. After traveling nonstop in Europe for the past week, she wanted a hot shower, a pint of Cherry Garcia and a couple hours of BBC America.

On the kitchen counter she found a basket stuffed with

various fruits and chocolates, an official Department of Homeland Security ID badge with her photo and name on it, and a note from her assistant Truman Gunn.

Welcome back to your home away from home. JOE secured your assignment with DHS. I'll catch you up on all the spiffy details first thing tomorrow. White House, eight o'clock. Wear the suit.

T.

P.S. TiVo'd Mistresses *for you.*

Brigit shed her Burberry trench coat, unwrapped a Godiva and popped it in her mouth. JOE stood for Jolly Old England, Truman's nickname for her employer, Britain's Secret Intelligence Service. The Department of Homeland Security thought they were getting a freelance consultant on domestic terrorism, and they were, but while she was working for DHS, SIS had an undercover job for her.

What neither SIS nor DHS realized was Brigit had her own agenda while she was in Washington.

She pulled the Cherry Garcia from the freezer and kicked off her boots in the living room. She flipped on the TV, anxious to catch up on her favorite show. Before she could find the TiVo remote, though, a breaking story on Headline News caught her eye. Eleanor Pennington, the daughter of Republican nominee Thad Pennington, had been kidnapped.

Frowning, Brigit turned up the volume and sat on the edge of the couch. A reporter on the scene at Eleanor's school reported scant details before summoning several people nearby to give eyewitness accounts.

Gooseflesh rose on Brigit's arms as she listened. No one had actually seen the girl being kidnapped, but she had disappeared from a school function out from under the watchful eyes of adults and Secret Service agents. No contact from the kidnapper had been made except a single phone call—Eleanor's voice crying for her mother.

Proof of life.

A tremor went down Brigit's spine and the little girl in her head cried out, the old nightmare of a locked door and the fire surfacing. Her gaze darted to the photo next to the TV. She and her younger sister, Tory, were grinning at the camera, arms thrown around each other's neck in childhood abandon. A different proof of life.

As if her body had a will of its own, Brigit rose from the edge of the couch and returned the ice cream to the freezer. She slipped on her trench and slid her sore feet back into her boots before retrieving her handgun from her overnight bag and heading for the door. At the last minute, she went back to the kitchen counter and grabbed the DHS badge. That and the kidnapping had just made her assignment for SIS a slam dunk.

Leaving the lights on in the loft, she closed and locked the door behind her, slipping her handgun into the pocket of her trench coat.

Chapter Two

Ashford Heights, MD
Midnight
Ashford Heights lay on the north side of Washington, D.C., one of the many suburbs off Interstate 270 popular with up-and-coming power players who eschewed looking like players and portrayed themselves as natural-born leaders instead. Houses were modern versions of old plantations. Churches, with their lily white steeples, were beacons to a bygone time as well. Private schools had devoured the public school district, all of which had dress codes, security guards and entire wings dedicated to the next generation of Washington's elite.

Blinding lights from video cameras and media vans bounced inside Michael's car as the armor-plated Lincoln Navigator shot through the gates of Ashford's most prestigious subdivision. Security officers flanked both sides of the entrance, the SUV's headlights illuminating letters on their jackets as the driver maneuvered the vehicle up the winding drive. Along with the media, the FBI, Secret Service, state and local cops were all working the story of the year.

The Navigator stopped in front of a two-story Colonial, a modern echo of an eighteenth-century Monticello. Columns lined the veranda and potted topiaries bookended the ruby-red-colored door. Light from the front windows fell in soft sheets across the backs of white, slat-backed rocking chairs.

Michael steeled his nerves to walk up the wide plank stairs and enter the house. In his time at the CIA, he'd faced much tougher situations. Never, though, had he experienced such a crawling fear in his stomach. Never since his father had been killed had he felt such guilt.

Images of Ella flashed behind his eyes in a kaleidoscope of memories. The pink knit hat she'd worn in the hospital after her birth, the way her blue eyes had widened when she'd blown her first bubble with the gum he'd snuck to her behind her mother's back, the sound of her laughter as his dog, Pongo, had licked a scoop of ice cream off her cone.

Failure kicked him in the gut. *I should have been there for her. I could have protected her.*

He rubbed his eyes, forcing the dampness in them to retreat as he swallowed the brick in his throat. The darkness of the night mirrored the darkness in his mind.

"Deputy Director?" Brad Kinnick stared at him from the open car door.

Filling his chest with the cool fall air, Michael gave Brad a nod and slid out. The bodyguard moved aside and focused his attention on the crowd of official cars in the circular drive and security personnel stationed around the house.

After his credentials were checked at the door by a young FBI agent, Michael was ushered into the foyer. In the hours since the kidnapping, Thad had flown home from Ohio while Michael inserted himself into the police and FBI's investigation at the school, stepping on a few toes in the process. As a CIA officer he had no jurisdiction on U.S. soil. His reputation, however, and the fact that every man and woman looking for Ella understood his need as her uncle to make sure the investigation was expedient and thorough, had bought him priceless professional courtesy.

Thad grasped Michael's hand in a tight grip. Fatigue shadowed his brother-in-law's face and lined his forehead. "Anything?"

Michael wiped his shoes on the rug out of habit. His sister Ruth's penchant for cleanliness came from their mother's gene pool. Genes that entirely skipped Michael's. "No solid leads yet. Any news on this end?"

"The phone call at ten was it. She cried for Ruthie, and the connection went dead. We never heard the kidnapper's voice. No ransom demand, nothing."

Thad massaged his forehead with one hand, dropped it to his side. His eyes pleaded with Michael. "What do they want?"

Thad knew the answer to the question, but needed to hear the truth from someone else. Someone he trusted. Michael met his stare. "They want you to stop running for president."

"Why?"

That answer wasn't so pat. "Could be a hundred and one reasons."

Thad shook his head and led the way into the study. Two FBI experts sat at his massive cherry wood desk—computers, modems and tracking equipment covered the top. Behind them, two other agents examined files, talking on cell phones and looking over the seated agents' shoulders. Thad's focus dropped to a framed photo of Ella on the coffee table next to his leg. His sigh was almost inaudible. "So if I hold a press conference and announce I'm withdrawing my bid for election, whoever took her will give her back?"

The forty-nine-year-old senator didn't expect an answer this time. He simply needed to process the facts. Michael faced the fireplace and crossed his arms over his chest. "Best case, yes."

"You know I'd do anything to get my little girl back," Thad said. "But are you sure that's what they want? The FBI said they could just want money or a favor of some sort, like releasing one of their compatriots from jail."

"If the kidnappers wanted money or anything else, they would have asked for it already. This is a show of power. They want you to back down."

His brother-in-law slumped into a high-backed chair, hope draining out of him. Knowing he needed to collect his thoughts, Michael withdrew and left him alone.

At the desk, he asked the agents specific questions and watched their body language as much as he listened to their verbal answers. They were stumped. Ella had disappeared after the parade. Multiple times during the evening, she'd run out to the parking lot during the trunk-or-treat and gone back inside the school to warm up with hot cocoa and giggle with her friends.

At some point, while Ruth chatted up their mothers, Ella, Wonder Woman costume and all, had simply vanished.

Ella had escaped her adult guardians' watchful eyes and ears on several occasions before. With unrestrained zeal, she chased butterflies into wooded areas, held her breath underwater for endless seconds too long, and jumped from heights that would intimidate military operatives.

The entire school had been searched and everyone in attendance from teachers to janitors was being interviewed. All the families as well.

Four hours later, there was still hope of finding her alive, but the odds decreased with every passing minute. The single call from the kidnapper had been made from a disposable cell phone sold by dozens of discount stores in the local area. With no traceable phone, no voice imprint from the caller and no ransom request, the investigation was stalled.

Michael had little expertise with kidnappings, but he did know a few things about power and manipulation. At this point, the kidnapper was making a statement. He had the power and the skill to get what he wanted. All they could do was wait and try to figure it out.

"Where's Ruth?" Michael asked the female FBI agent.

She raised a finger and pointed at the ceiling.

Leaving the den, Michael made his way to the circular staircase at the end of the hall. His feet were ten-pound weights as he jogged up the carpeted stairs. Heading for the bedroom wing on the right, he pulled up short when he heard muffled crying from the left. Switching directions, he saw Ella's bedroom door ajar. He stopped beside it and pushed it open with his hand.

Little-girl pink saturated every wall and corner. Even if Ella's favorite color had been black, the endless ruffles, rhinestones and feather boas would have tipped him off to her penchant for all things girly.

Ruthie perched on Ella's bed, her back to the door and her face buried in her hands. Her shoulders were set but her controlled sobs gave her away. Next to her, a woman sat rubbing Ruthie's shoulder, her head bent next to his sister's as she murmured soft words of support.

Sensing Michael's presence, the woman raised her head, her round gunmetal gray eyes locking on his. Stunning black eyelashes curved around the lids, calling attention to their striking color. With her fair skin and black curl of bangs, she resembled one of the dolls sitting on Ella's bed.

Except her eyes weren't innocent like the dolls'. In their depths, they were hard, serious, cynical. Soldier's eyes. As if she'd seen and lived her share of trouble.

Her dark brows crashed together and she rose from the

bed, keeping a protective hand on Ruth's shoulder. "Yes?"

She'd combed her hair into a tight ponytail, but several sections had broken free to frame her heart-shaped face. The severity of her hairstyle was in direct contrast to her clothes. A faded T-shirt sported a green four-leaf clover between the swell of her breasts, and brown camouflage pants hung from her hips as if she'd stolen them from her older, much larger brother. Her dusty, creased work boots looked like they belonged to an archeologist who'd just come in from a dig.

Ruth dropped her hands and turned her head. "Michael!"

His sister's eyes, bloodshot from crying, flashed relief at the sight of him. She rushed into his outstretched arms and Michael embraced her, all the time keeping his focus on the stranger who continued to stare him down.

"I can't believe this is happening," she said into his chest. She was still wearing her heels, the top of her carefully coiffed blonde hair tickling his chin. As one of Virginia's members of the House of Representatives, she was as much a Washington pundit as her husband. It was yet another motive for Ella's kidnapping. "What are we going to do?"

Michael patted her back and scanned the stranger for any kind of ID badge. He'd already ruled her out as a friend of the family. Anyone who knew Ruth knew better than to wear dusty boots into her house. Her choice of clothing also ruled out police officer. "The FBI has everything under control."

The stranger gave a quiet, derisive snort. Michael narrowed his eyes at her in warning as he shifted Ruthie under one arm and stuck out his hand. "Michael Stone. And you are?"

Her gaze slid from his face to his protective arm around Ruth and back to his face. Her eyes softened and he saw a flash of emotion in them. Desire? No. The emotion in her eyes spoke of a yearning, a longing for something she wanted and couldn't have.

Ruth gave an exasperated huff, putting one hand to her cheek. "Where are my manners? Michael, this is Dr. Brigit Kent. Dr. Kent, my brother, Michael."

Dr. Kent shook his hand, her scrutiny of him as intense as his was of her. "*The* Michael Stone? Deputy Director of Central Intelligence?" The British accent was faint, the cadence of her voice so smooth it was almost lyrical. "You are...younger...than I expected."

She looked like she was all of twenty—far too young to have earned a doctorate in anything—but Michael kept the observation to himself. She wasn't the first person to be surprised the man holding his position hadn't hit forty yet.

Still as she started to take her hand back, he held onto it. A subtle show of power. "You have me at a disadvantage, I'm afraid, Dr. Kent. Is there a reason you're here in my niece's bedroom during this delicate situation?"

Ruth patted his arm. "Dr. Kent is a consultant for Homeland Security, and she lent me some of her studies for the early education initiative bill I proposed last year. She just stopped by to offer her support."

So she was smart as well as beautiful. Michael released Kent's hand, but kept his arm around Ruthie as he smoothly maneuvered her to the side to clear a path. "Thad and Ruth appreciate your support. Now if you'll excuse us, I'd like to talk to my sister alone."

Dr. Kent's pause lingered half a second. "Of course." She put a hand on Ruthie's forearm as she stepped in front of her. "You have my mobile number. Call me if you need anything."

Ruth broke from Michael's protective arm to hug her. The two exchanged goodbyes, and Dr. Kent held out her hand to him again. "Pleasure, Deputy Director."

As before, the way she enunciated each syllable made her words sound lilting. Michael accepted her handshake, noticing the expensive watch on her right wrist. Her hand snugged into his palm, and her skin was warm and soft.

But her serious eyes challenged him and something very male and completely out of place kicked in his stomach. Her tiny hand gave his much larger one a firm squeeze and a tug.

He tugged back without considering the consequences, his response not entirely a power play this time.

~ ✧ ~

Brigit stood in the shadows under the staircase, shivering under her coat. Michael Stone was formidable. Definitely not someone to mess with. He could have been her size, instead of his six feet plus, and he still would have oozed authority from every pore of his body. His massive shoulders looked like a linebacker's. His handshake had gripped her like a vise. And his

19

eyes...

Shaking her head to clear the memory of his probing stare, Brigit took a deep breath, closed her eyes and thought of Eleanor Pennington.

Four hours into the kidnapping. Where had she been at that point? What had she been feeling? Crawling through her memories, she brought up the fear, still vivid enough to raise goose bumps on her skin.

I was still panicked, but the adrenaline was wearing off. Tory was already asleep, having cried herself out. Peter was lying low, waiting, I suppose, to make sure no one was on his trail. I couldn't make sense of why he'd brought us to the bar and then upstairs. Why he'd locked us in the bathroom. I was hungry...

Voices in the den brought her back to the present. Checking that the coast was clear, she followed the hallway to the rear of the Pennington house, slowing her pace as she noticed the walls lined with family portraits. In the midst of smiling faces, one stood out.

Michael Stone, a younger version than the one upstairs but every bit as solemn in his smart Marine dress uniform, frowned down at her. The American flag in the background was as fitting a backdrop as Brigit could imagine for the Deputy Director of Central Intelligence.

His reputation within the intelligence community pegged him as a quiet, rock-solid leader. While ambitious, he appeared to be so for the right reasons. Reasons missing from Washington for centuries. He actually wanted to protect and defend his country from all threats, rather than further his political career or line his own pockets.

In the six months since he'd taken over as the second in command of the CIA, he'd brought a mole within his organization to justice, severed the Agency's ties with a dozen different lobbyists and congressmen, and restructured a struggling spy group. All after surviving a hostage standoff and being shot. It would take time to erase the organization's failing marks in the world of international espionage, but if anyone could do it, it was Michael Stone.

He seemed as protective of his family as he was his country. She'd seen it in his eyes, in the way he kept his arm around his sister. Brigit's heart pinched with envy. Never had

Peter sought to protect his two younger half-sisters. Instead he had used her and Tory as weapons against their parents, against their government. *If only I hadn't killed Mum that night...*

Blinking away the tears that suddenly sprang to her eyes, Brigit clamped her jaw tight. If she was going to help Ella, she had to keep that part of the past in the past.

She also had to avoid any further confrontations with Michael Stone.

Ten minutes with Senator Pennington had given her a solid profile workup for SIS. Another fifteen with Ruth had filled in the few remaining holes. That job was done and there was no reason to seek the answers she wanted about the kidnapping from Thad or the FBI agents hovering around him. While the officials started at ground zero and systematically worked their way out, Brigit preferred to start on the fringes and work her way in. Parents and family members would give a glossier view of the little girl than folks who knew her but were outside the bond of love.

Her first target to talk to was at the back of the house, out of the limelight and hopefully much easier to squeeze for accurate information. Swinging through the unlit kitchen, she found the back door.

Outside, a stalwart Secret Service agent stood guard over the impressive grounds. A large patio, a pool—covered now because of the season—and an orchard surrounded the backside of the Pennington estate.

The agent, a man the size and breadth of a black bear, looked her up and down under the faint light from the windows above. He'd left the outside light off, Brigit guessed, so as not to make himself an easy target in case the kidnapper or anyone else was planning another attack on the Pennington family. She didn't blame him for being careful or edgy.

Giving him the impression she was officially working the case, she flashed her DHS security badge. He nodded and resumed his predatory stance, sweeping the grounds with a critical, observant attentiveness. A walkie-talkie buzzed softly on his belt with normal activity.

"How many Secret Service personnel does the senator and his wife use?" she asked.

The man's baritone voice answered in a reserved manner. "Five on a daily basis. An extra detail for speaking arrangements or fundraisers."

"Have you worked for them long?"

The agent slewed his eyes to her, then back to the landscape. "Since Senator Pennington's nomination."

"Did you know Ella?"

"Yes, ma'am."

"Would she willingly go off with someone she didn't know?"

Again the eye slide. "The child is precocious but intelligent. She's been schooled for years on personal-safety issues."

"So either she left the parking lot against her will or she knew the person who kidnapped her?"

"She might have been drugged."

True enough. Ella probably trusted the kidnapper right up to the point he slipped her a piece of drugged candy and dumped her in his trunk.

Just like I trusted Peter.

Timing and opportunity were crucial to any kidnapper. The Pennington's employed a housekeeper, a part-time nanny and various services for their lawn, landscaping and pool maintenance. No doubt the FBI would be interviewing everyone associated with the couple. Ella probably trusted all of them to some extent, but who had the motive and the expertise to kidnap her at a social function? And why?

There were hundreds of motives because of the Pennington's political careers and the FBI would focus on those. To Brigit, though, political motivation seemed too cliché. *This feels personal, just like my* favor *for President Jeffries.*

Her BlackBerry rang and she dug it out of her pocket. Caller ID showed it was Truman.

"Still up?" he asked, much too chipper for that time of night. "I figured you'd crashed in front of the TV already."

"Not yet. I'm working on a case." *Working on a case* was her code words for *can't talk now.*

"I see. Well, our Arab friends are getting together later tonight for a gift exchange. Thought you'd want to know."

"Where?"

The address he listed was unfamiliar to her, but as always, Truman was the perfect assistant. "I'll send you directions. Want company?"

Without warning, light from the kitchen windows showered

her and the Secret Service agent. Someone was in the kitchen. Glancing through the closest window, she caught sight of a familiar blond head, massive build and sour scowl heading toward the back door. "No. I'll just do a drive-by. If I need your help, I'll call."

She disconnected and shoved the phone back in her pocket. "Must run," she told the Secret Service agent. "Thanks a bunch for your help."

As she hurried off the back porch and into the shadows of the yard, she prayed a gun-happy FBI agent didn't shoot her and a pissed-off Michael Stone didn't catch her.

Chapter Three

Arlington, an hour later

The bed jiggled and Conrad Flynn slit one eye open to watch the half-naked woman and love of his life slip out from under the sheets. In the pale moonlit room, he watched her long brown hair slide across the pale skin of her shoulders as she crept, silent as death, across the carpeting to the spot where the jeans he'd peeled off her earlier lay in a heap.

Lying on his stomach, he kept his face partially buried in the pillow and feigned sleep as she tiptoed past his side of the bed on her way out of the room. Wherever Julia was going, he didn't want to stop her. Nor did he want her to know he knew she was sneaking out again.

Several times in the past week, his wife had risen in the early hours of the morning and left their apartment. For what purpose he didn't know, but his gut tightened every time he thought about the possibilities. As an FBI agent, she worked many assignments. Was this an undercover job she couldn't share details about? Was her life in danger?

Even though she was experienced and more than capable of handling anything the FBI threw at her, he still worried about her every time she put on her navy blue jacket and went to work.

Her training was impeccable. Under his tutelage, he'd taken her through the CIA's Farm and then through his own brand of spy craft. As a rookie Feebie, she'd spent hundreds of hours at the gun range and in hand-to-hand combat. Add to that her calculating mind and quick reflexes and she was a priceless weapon no matter whom she worked for.

But beyond all her training and experience in and out of

the field, Julia's gut instincts were spot on every time. Like she had a sixth sense about danger, she knew when to take one more risk or pull out of the game. If only she still called Langley home. What he wouldn't do to have her under him in his group of super agents as well as in his bed.

Conrad had been promoted—if you called leaving the field of operations behind for a desk job at CIA headquarters a promotion—when he'd faked his death to flush out a mole in the organization with his best friends, Smitty and Ace. Julia had been there too, working beside him but not fully trusting his actions or his words until the end. Riding the high of his success, however, he'd whisked her away to an island and proposed marriage. She'd accepted.

What once he feared would be a living hell, marriage had actually been more like heaven. *Because I married Julia. She made my dreams come true.*

He knew her like he knew the internal components of his gun, and just like the Beretta fit in his hand, Julia fit in his heart.

But for the past week, it felt like he'd married a stranger. She was hiding something. Something big. Her focus was off and she'd been riding a rollercoaster of moods. One minute she was laughing at Conrad's teasing, the next she was slamming doors because he'd left the toilet seat up and changed the station settings on the kitchen radio.

A soft rustle whispered from the kitchen. Julia was putting on her FBI windbreaker. If she followed her normal pattern, she'd be back in the apartment by dawn, humming in the kitchen as she boiled eggs and toasted bagels for breakfast. Her face would light up when he joined her at the sink, as if she truly loved him. As if he were the Prince Charming of her Happily Ever After, even if she wanted to kill him for leaving the toilet seat up again. Conrad knew it was too good to be true. Nobody in his world ever got the happily ever after, but somehow he'd scored the lottery in that department.

He'd almost stopped her and demanded an explanation for her secretive behavior the last time she snuck out in the wee hours of the morning, but an old paranoia had gripped him hard. If she *was* hiding something, Conrad wasn't sure he wanted to know...or should know. Her job was hers alone. He had no say over what she was working on, and he had to have faith that she could handle whatever it was. Still, he couldn't control the flip of his heart or the unease in his stomach. If she was keeping the details of her assignment a close hold, it meant the assignment was dangerous.

He sensed more than heard her close the front door as she slipped into the Arlington night. In one fluid motion, he threw back the sheet, grabbed his own jeans and tugged them on. Tonight he would tail her and find out exactly where she was going, who she was meeting, just for peace of mind. Sweeping both his personal cell phone and his work cell from the nightstand, he hoped for the best and steeled his gut for the worst. Never in his life had he loved a woman like he loved Julia.

Jogging to the front door, Conrad picked up his running shoes. Outside, the sidewalk was cool and gritty under his bare feet. Before he could throw his shoes into the passenger seat of his Jeep, one of his phones rang. "What now?" he muttered. One good thing about pretending to be dead had been that no one demanded his attention.

Now, in his new position as Director of Operations, he was constantly getting calls from field operators, section managers and other CIA directors at all times of the day and night. He no longer had the option of laying low under the radar. If anything, he was the center of everyone's target these days and he hated it. Michael Stone, the deputy director and his boss, had painted a neon green bull's-eye on Conrad's forehead just because Julia had picked him over Stone after the battle to oust the mole. Stone had been in love with her, but in the end, lost her to the better man. Conrad grinned at the thought as he fumbled with his work phone. He stared at it a second, hitting the connect button twice, before realizing his personal cell was still buzzing maniacally in his jeans pocket. He pulled it out, looked at the LCD screen and frowned at the ID. *Big Mike.*

With that nickname, clearly Ace, his coroner-turned-spy friend, had been playing personal assistant again with Con's phone.

The phone buzzed in his hand like a giant wasp. What could Stone want at this time of night?

Julia.

Con's heart thudded hard. Jamming the phone into the crook of his neck, he started the Jeep, his eyes scanning the road for the taillights of a certain white Audi. "Yeah?"

Stone's voice was clear and commanding, like always. "Meet me at my place in half an hour."

Conrad concentrated on wheeling the Jeep in the direction he'd seen her disappear. "Why?"

"I have an assignment for you."

"It's after midnight if you haven't noticed. Go to bed. You might have to act like you know what you're doing tomorrow."

"My house, Flynn, or you won't have a job tomorrow."

The boss card again. He shifted and pushed the gas pedal into the floor, imagining the man's face under his foot. "Does this have anything to do with Julia?"

"Julia?" Stone's voice dropped a notch. "Is she okay?"

"Forget I mentioned her." He snapped the phone shut and dropped it on top of his running shoes. His eyes caught the red flash of brake lights and his gut tightened in response. While he'd done his best to ignore the jealousy Stone triggered in him, it was always there in the background, haunting him like his tattered past as a renegade spy.

His gut didn't release until two miles south of Arlington when the Audi left the interstate and pulled into a Perkins restaurant. A giant American flag waved its shadow over Julia's petite figure as she exited her car and walked inside.

There were no FBI initials on the back of her pink Roxy jacket.

Conrad huffed out a sigh. No undercover work, just a pie run. She'd recently had a jones for the strawberry pie the restaurant served twenty-four hours a day. He'd seen her eat a piece for breakfast the previous morning and another after their lovemaking last night.

As Conrad steered the Jeep back to the interstate, his heart thudded afresh, but with a different intensity to it. An intensity that hinted at fear. Strawberry pie wasn't pickles and ice cream, but then Julia was no ordinary woman.

~ ✧ ~

Pongo, Michael's Rottweiler, barked as Flynn entered via the back door. From the den, Michael heard Flynn try to sweet talk the dog. Pongo's reply—a throaty growl—made Michael feel a touch of smug relief.

Flynn got along with almost everybody. He did not, however, get along with Michael, inside or outside CIA headquarters. Skimming the surface, it was because of their vastly different work philosophies. Plunging deeper, they stomped on each other's backsides because of Julia. Every time Michael looked at Flynn, he saw her, but damned if he'd let Flynn know.

"Call off the dog," Flynn yelled from the mudroom.

Michael gave a short whistle and Pongo came trotting into the den, Flynn following a few footsteps behind him.

"Sit," Michael said, motioning to a chair across from the desk.

"Me or the dog?"

Locking his jaw, he gave Flynn his usual *stop fucking around* look.

As he passed the west wall, Flynn eyed the patch job. "You should hire a professional, or at least let me and Ace help you."

"You're not touching my wall."

Knowing he'd hit a sore spot, Flynn smiled as he dropped into the chair.

His gaze fell on Michael's shiny new leather briefcase—a congratulations-on-your-promotion gift from Julia, Smitty and Ace—and quickly glanced away. Michael knew Julia had forged Conrad's signature on the accompanying card. Tit for tat on hitting sore spots.

"Don't you ever sleep?" Flynn asked.

Michael tapped his thumb against the coffee cup in his hand. "Not this week."

Without looking at him, Flynn pointed a finger at the obvious culprit for most folks' insomnia. "You might try laying off the jet fuel."

"Can't. Too much going on."

Michael released the coffee cup and removed a file from his briefcase. He slid it to Flynn's side of the desk. "You familiar with Dr. Brigit Kent?"

Flynn narrowed his eyes as he noticed the green stripe down the side of the folder. The information was coded for someone with much higher clearance than Flynn. Higher clearance than even Michael, which Flynn surmised without missing a beat. "How'd you get that?"

"I asked for it."

Flynn didn't hold his surprise in check, shaking his head and snorting. "Never heard of her."

"She's got her nose in the Pennington kidnapping. I want to know why."

"Your brother-in-law's been kidnapped?"

"Not my brother-in-law, you idiot. My niece. Tonight—last night." He rubbed a hand over his face. "Don't you watch the news or read the memos in your inbox?"

"Your niece? Christ." His dislike of Michael was instantly supplanted with what appeared to be empathy. "I'm sorry, man. FBI got any leads?"

"No." Michael told him the whole story. When he described the phone call, about Ella's terrified voice crying for her mom, Flynn went completely still. The usual smart-assed look in his eyes flattened.

"I found Dr. Kent hanging out with Ruthie like she's a member of our family or a close friend," Michael said. "Her interest...bothers me."

"You think she's got an ulterior motive?"

"She's on the DHS payroll as a consultant, supposedly on domestic terrorism."

Flynn frowned. "Since when do we need another expert on that?"

"There's no formal training in domestic terrorism on her resumé. She's a psychotherapist, works mostly with kids, but she has experience as a code breaker too."

Flipping the file open, Flynn studied the colored eight-by-ten photo of the woman's head and face. After a few seconds of breezing through the fact sheet and background info, he closed the folder. "Can I offer her a job?"

Michael gave Flynn his trademarked look again.

"What? She's thirty-three, beautiful, educated and skilled. A regular Swiss Army Knife. Perfect for my army."

Flynn's Army was a covert group of the best spies the CIA had. In the world of espionage, they equated to Navy SEALs or the Marines' Delta Force. And just like their counterparts in the military, they often performed black ops. "No."

Flynn made a noise in his throat that Michael took for

rebellious consent. He sat back in his chair. "She's been selling herself and her skills to foreign intelligence agencies off and on since nine-eleven but she's never worked with the FBI on any kidnappings and she barely knows Ruth, even if she's pretending otherwise."

"So where do I fit in?"

"Contact sources you have here in the States and see what they know. Outside of that, follow her and find out what you can."

"What do you want to know about her that isn't in this file?"

"Where she goes and who she meets. Who her connections are in DHS, the FBI, anyone here in Washington."

"You want to run an investigation within the borders of the U.S., a total breach of your precious by-the-book mentality. How's that going to resolve the kidnapping?"

"Let me worry about that."

"Not good enough. You're putting both our careers on the line if I investigate her and get caught. I want a reason."

Michael dropped his gaze to the file and toyed with his coffee cup. In that split second, he gave himself away.

Flynn pounced. "You got a personal interest in the doctor?"

"I simply want a guarantee she's one hundred percent on our team."

"What makes you think she isn't?"

Michael couldn't control the kidnappers, but he still needed to control something about the kidnapping. "Nothing I can put my finger on, but the encounter I had with her tonight makes me think she's working a personal angle. I want to know what it is." He squeezed the coffee cup.

His director of operations nodded, seeming to understand his *nobody messes with my family* reaction. "But she passed her background check with flying colors and has a security clearance higher than mine."

"You and I both know security clearance doesn't mean jack shit and background checks miss stuff not marked with a bull's-eye." Michael sipped his cold coffee without tasting it. "When I asked for her file, my source told me Brigit's seen a therapist off and on since she was a kid, but there's nothing in her folder about it. I want to know why. I want to know what secrets she's keeping."

If anyone knew about secret lives, it was Flynn. "If I get caught, I'm blaming it all on you. You are the boss after all."

Michael handed him a small jump drive fashioned like a Lego piece. "All the information in the file is contained on this. A few other items of information as well. Don't lose it."

Flynn slid the folder back to him, took the Lego brick and checked his watch, suddenly antsy to leave. "I'll start on this when I get into the office."

"Start now," Michael said. "Brigit's in your neck of the woods. I followed her to a bar just outside Arlington's city limits, called Sail Away. It's off the interstate past Perkins. She drives a green Ford rental car. On your way home, see if she's still there and tail her. If she's gone, her U.S. residence is listed in her file."

"Well, I'll be damned. The deputy director of the CIA did personal surveillance on a suspect. Why didn't you hang around the bar and find out who she snuggled up to?"

"She knows me now after meeting me at Ruth's. I can't get too close. You can."

"And I'm still the best field operator you've got."

"I'm handing you this job because you owe me. Big time."

Flynn tapped the desk with a finger. "I don't owe you squat. Julia chose me."

"Your debt has nothing to do with Julia. You betrayed my confidence in you as a spy when you faked your death two years ago." He jammed the folder back into his briefcase. "Earn it back."

Flynn rose, his hands clenched into fists. "You're setting me up to take a risk that could end my career and embarrass me in front of the entire intelligence community. That has everything to do with Julia."

In the past six months, Michael's dislike of Flynn had mellowed, mostly because his feelings for Julia had done the same. She was happy with the asshole, and he cared about her enough to want that for her, even if it meant she was married to someone else.

Besides that, Flynn was a damn good head of Operations. Better than Michael had been. Even with the budget cutbacks and a gutted army of field operatives, Flynn had manipulated the European and Middle East playing field with the tenacity and patience of a chess master. He'd been quietly building his secret army of spies who put their Cold War predecessors to shame. Multiple terrorist cells in Germany had been picked apart, two different attacks in Italy and Spain had been derailed. All because of Conrad Flynn.

"I'm asking for your help," Michael admitted, as much to himself as to Flynn, "because you're the only person I trust with Ella's life."

The fists relaxed. Flynn took a deep breath and eyed the wall on his way out. "I'll see what I can do."

Chapter Four

Construction site southwest of Perkins

Dull yellow light from overhead construction lamps fell on dump trucks and piles of lumber, casting eerie shadows and turning the faces of three men in the open space sallow. Their low male voices bounced like a hum between the bricks and made it difficult for Brigit to hear what they were saying from the front seat of her rental car, but she didn't need to. The exchange between two Israeli terrorists and two unknown subjects was nearing its conclusion. The terrorists had produced a woman, a cloth bag over her head and her hands bound behind her back, from their vehicle, while their redheaded counterpart yanked a gym bag from the backseat of his rusty Volvo.

As one of the Israelis rifled through the bag of money, the redheaded unsub assisted his ransomed friend toward the Volvo. Another player, smaller and wearing a knit hat, emerged from the passenger side of the car and guided the woman into the backseat. The hair on Brigit's arms rose at the sight.

Truman's instincts about Tory were spot on. There was no good reason for her to be in the States even though she was a U.S. citizen. No good reason for her to be at this construction site exchanging money for a hostage. No good reason, except for one.

Both parties satisfied, the sound of slamming car doors echoed through the site. The deal was over. The Israelis pulled out first, never looking back.

Brigit threw her binoculars into the passenger seat and shifted her car into gear. The Volvo had gone less than thirty feet when she rounded the corner, rocks flying, and cut it off.

The Volvo's front end dived as the driver hit the brakes. Brigit threw her rental into park and grabbed her gun, pointing it at the driver as she exited the car.

The cold night air smelled like upturned dirt, metal pipes and cooling concrete. Her voice carried, sounding calm and assertive even though her hands were shaking. "Get out."

The passenger door opened instead and Tory stepped out. Under the weird light, Brigit made out the dark eyes, familiar nose and full lips identical to her own. The younger mirror image she hadn't seen in years sent a wave of sadness flooding through her. It was her fault Tory was here, just like everything that had happened since the night their mother died in the fire.

Tory stayed behind the door, using it as a partial shield. "Brigit. Long time no see, sister of mine."

In the now-silent construction area, the slight Irish brogue in her sister's voice sounded soft and still childlike. Brigit's heart contracted. In her chest of memories, she heard Tory's cries as the kitchen burned, their mother trapped inside. If only she could rewind time and find a way to keep her family together.

But she and Tory weren't kids anymore. Their innocence had been stripped away at a too-young age and there was no going back. Tamping down her emotions, Brigit kept her gun aimed on the car's driver just in case he got any ideas. "What are you doing here making an exchange with Israeli terrorists?"

"'By ballot or gun, our day will come.'"

"Quoting Peter now?" Brigit laughed, from nerves and false disbelief. Bottom line, she didn't want to talk about revolutionaries. God help her, but she wanted to talk about what normal sisters talked about—reality TV, bad hair days, the shoe sale at Macy's. Unfortunately, that language was foreign to Tory. "The Troubles are over, in case he didn't tell you. Besides, this is America, not Ireland."

"Ireland, America, Afghanistan, Palestine, it's a global war." Tory tilted her head at the backseat of the Volvo. "We are international brothers and sisters in arms now, fighting against governments who would press us under their heel." She shut the door and took a step toward Brigit. "Our identity, the new nation we're building, is about family, religion and tradition. Peter peeled away all the Protestant garbage you and Da filled my head with and showed me the truth."

"Truth?" Brigit's voice dropped a decibel and she shook her head in resignation, but she didn't lower the gun. As much as she wanted to, she wasn't that stupid. "Where's Peter? Did he send you after that package you just put in the car?"

"You got close to him in London last week. Spooked him. He went underground." Tory took another step and like a compass needle finding due north, Brigit shifted the gun to point it at her. Tory stared down the barrel and chuckled. "You won't shoot me. I'm your sister."

The sound of the gun cocking reverberated across the yard. "You'd be surprised at what I'll do when it comes to Peter's war."

Without warning, Tory brushed the gun aside and embraced Brigit in a hug.

Stunned, Brigit held her breath. She'd dreamed of this moment, held it in her hand and examined it from all sides like a beautiful glass ball. Except in her dream, Tory was embracing her because she'd left Peter and returned to Brigit. In her world, dreams did not come true.

So instead of the relief and love she expected to feel spreading through her body, her skin itched, especially where Tory's heavy weight pressed against her. Tory released her and patted one of her cheeks. "We mean you no harm. Let Peter be. Let us all be."

Tory turned her back on Brigit and climbed into the car, and the glass ball fell and shattered at Brigit's feet. A few seconds later, the driver wheeled around her, where she was still frozen in place, and the Volvo disappeared into the night.

The gun suddenly felt too heavy in Brigit's hand. The cords of tension holding her together gave way and she slumped against the car, dropping her head and mentally kicking herself. For the first time in years, she'd been face-to-face with her younger sister and failed to tell her what was in her heart. Failed to make Tory see the light about Peter and his cause.

Failed to hug her back.

How could she be such a success with her career and such a miserable failure at everything else?

A noise from behind a pile of bricks brought Brigit's head up. She scanned the area over her right shoulder and saw a woman emerge from the stack, flashing a badge at her.

"FBI," she said, raising the hand with the gun. "Put your

weapon down."

Brigit drew in a deep breath and let out a heavy sigh. She tossed the gun into the car through the open window and raised both hands. Just her luck the FBI was here. She'd figured since the U.S. was in bed with the Israelis, the Feds might be focusing on groups that worried them more, and she hadn't seen any evidence they were there.

Brigit pointedly scanned the woman's pink jacket. "Who are you? Agent Barbie?"

The dark-haired, dark-eyed woman fought a smile. "Agent Julia Torrison actually."

An FBI agent doing *Pretty in Pink* while keeping tabs on Israeli terrorists? If Truman had been with her, he would have been clapping. "I have a badge in my coat pocket."

"I figured you did." Torrison drew closer. "Cop?"

Brigit caught sight of a second agent, this one blonde and every bit as Barbie-gorgeous, off to her side. She tucked what looked like a camera into her coat and held her stomach as she approached.

Torrison spoke to her without taking her eyes off Brigit. "I told you, I've got this, Zara. Go sit down before you get sick again."

The blonde shook her head as she circled Brigit's rental, and up close, Brigit could see she had circles under her eyes and a flush to her skin. "I'm fine." She met Brigit's gaze. "Who do we have here?"

Brigit played difficult because she didn't feel like being nice. "Department of Homeland Security."

The Barbie twosome exchanged a look, neither of them pleased. Torrison took one hand off the butt of her gun and rippled the ends of her fingers at Brigit. "Show us."

Brigit eased her hand into her trench, removed her badge and handed it to Blonde Barbie.

The woman looked it over and nodded at Julia as she handed it back. "Dr. Brigit Kent, DHS." She held out the badge. "Zara Morgan."

Torrison lowered the gun. "Sorry about that. We didn't know DHS was involved with this."

Brigit snapped the badge out of Morgan's hand and tossed it in the car on top of her gun before opening the door. Time to cover Tory's backside. Again. "Are you investigating the Irish Women's League?"

The blonde shook her head as she sidled up alongside Torrison. "Palestinian Sisters of Liberation. Those were Israeli terrorists handing over the hostage to your sister. Your sister affiliated with IWL as well?"

So they'd heard enough to uncover her link to a terrorist organization. Brigit glanced away. She wouldn't tell an outright lie, but then usually she didn't need to. "I would appreciate your discretion about what you saw here tonight, ladies. Neither the hostage exchange you witnessed nor my sister involves the FBI at this point. When it does, we'll talk."

She dropped into the car seat and gunned the motor. Morgan took a step forward to try and stop her, but Torrison grabbed her arm.

As Brigit backed up to turn her car around, Morgan suddenly grabbed her stomach and bent over. Brigit glanced in her rearview once and saw Torrison rubbing her partner's back as the woman threw up.

From his vantage point a hundred yards away, Conrad swore under his breath and lowered his miniature, nonreflective night-vision binoculars as Julia walked Zara into the shadows. If there were two women in his life who could screw everything up, it was these two.

Zara, a counterespionage operative in his secret army of spies, had been tracking members of the SOL in London and must have followed one or all of them to the States.

As an operative working for the CIA, she had no jurisdiction within her home country, but if she turned her mission over to the overworked and underfunded FBI, it would get put on the back burner unless there was imminent danger to American citizens.

Zara wasn't the type to work her ass off on a mission just to see it lost in the bureaucratic mess of homeland intelligence. Hence the reason, Conrad knew, she'd called in a favor from Julia the minute the SOL group set foot on U.S. soil.

Julia. She was supposed to be home, safe and sound, getting ready to tell him he was going to be a father.

He didn't know where Kent should be, but his gut told him she didn't belong at this construction site waving a Glock around any more than she belonged sniffing around the Pennington kidnapping. Add a wild card like her to the Julia-Zara mix and his career could easily be over before the Macy's Thanksgiving Day Parade.

Dread knotted its fingers into his chest. He tapped his thumbs against the steering wheel of the Jeep and wondered which bomb he should trip first.

Chapter Five

D.C. suburbs

Brigit sipped a cup of Earl Grey and stared out the window of her apartment, watching the first pink rays of sun streak the gray sky. A garbage truck clanged and banged on the street below as it lumbered from one corner to the next. Pigeons pecked at crumbs, happy to own the sidewalk for a few more minutes before the morning rush convened.

Except for the pigeons, Washington D.C. was very different from New York City, where she'd lived for the past five years. Fashion and real estate were all anyone cared about there. Two hundred miles south, power was the name of the game.

Why does the kidnapper want power over the Penningtons? She glanced at her watch. It had been more than ten hours since Ella's kidnapping. *What was I thinking the morning after Peter tricked us into the bathroom? What was I feeling?*

Scared. Abandoned. Still hungry. *We drank water from the sink, but Tory and I nearly starved to death before Mum came and rescued us.*

Tory. The thought of her sister sent a familiar wave of anger and grief washing over her.

During the seventy-two hours of their capture, Brigit had entertained Tory by playing games. Tory's favorite had been a hand-squeezing game. Creating their own childlike version of Morse code, they assigned letters and common phrases different types of squeezes. One short squeeze meant yes, two, no. A long squeeze meant stop. Three short squeezes meant I love you. As the hours wore on and Tory became bored with the hand squeezing, Brigit had changed the code to taps. They tapped on the countertop, the wooden planks, the mirror and tub, creating musical notes as well as coded messages.

When Tory had hugged her at the construction site, she'd tapped Brigit's back three short taps right between her shoulder blades. *I love you.*

Her sister was playing her again. All these years, all the heart-breaking betrayals, Tory still wanted Brigit to believe in—and look the other way because of—their blood bond.

After their mother's death, Brigit traded in the carefree thoughts and dreams of childhood for gut-wrenching sorrow and overwhelming guilt. She tried to protect Tory and become a mother to her, but everything she did after the fire only made the situation with Tory worse. While her father reassured Brigit her mother's death was Peter's fault, Tory tortured her with her version of the truth. *You killed her. You caused the fire. She burned to death because of you.*

Brigit drew into herself in order to deal with the grief and guilt, and Tory acted out in order to do the same.

Once their father accepted a new post with the British government and moved them to America, he insisted both girls see a psychotherapist. The woman's impartial air and kind eyes breathed life back into Brigit's soul, but when the therapist's office burned to the ground by an arsonist, Brigit stopped going. *It was Peter. He did it.*

She had no proof, and now, with the logic of an adult, Brigit could chastise herself for jumping to that sort of conclusion. Deep in her psyche though, she still believed the fire was Peter's handiwork.

The same illogical but nevertheless deep conviction that Peter was behind the Pennington girl's kidnapping drove her now. Finding Tory last night at the scene of the hostage exchange confirmed Brigit's fears. Peter and his group would never let the war die. Some of his followers still craved the conflict between English and Irish, Protestant and Catholic, but most just wanted something to fight against, to fight for. They needed the drug of pride and patriotism to give their life meaning. They found it in Peter's words.

His lies were monumental, but most of his followers didn't care. Clear thinking went out the door when a man with Peter's abilities to inspire spoke about blood and bullets, God and tradition.

The alarm on Brigit's watch beeped softly. Twelve hours

since Ella's kidnapping.

She grabbed her mobile and rang up Truman. "What's the latest?" she asked when he answered.

"Good morning to you too." His impatience at the interruption of his morning routine rang clearly through the connection. "Another call from the kidnappers." Brigit could see him standing in his bathroom, only a towel around his waist as he examined himself in the mirror, tousling his wet hair with one hand and holding his mobile with the other. "Only the kid again. She claims she's not hurt, only hungry."

"No demands?"

"Nope. No ransom either."

But proof of life. And proof to Brigit that Peter or one of his lieutenants was behind the kidnapping. Just like a hand squeeze or the tap of a fist between her shoulder blades, the two calls were a code. A code that could help her save Ella.

"I'm sending a car for you," Truman said. "I'll pick you up in twenty minutes."

"I can drive myself."

"This is Washington, Gidget. Nobody who's anybody drives themselves to the White House. Besides, I don't want you to be late."

"Stop calling me Gidget."

"You're right, you're no Gidget. She was much nicer. See you in twenty."

She hung up and thumbed through the files stored on her BlackBerry. Buckets of information existed about Thad and Ruth Pennington, and luckily Truman had cut out most of the common knowledge facts before sending her the rest.

On the surface, most of it was textbook, pre-politician type stuff. Law degrees, Rhodes scholarships, city government stepping stones. Combing through even the more unusual details had not caused Brigit's mind to lift an eyebrow in question. It was all too neat, too pat, just like the supposed political motivation behind the kidnapping. But Ruth Pennington had shown up on Brigit's radar screen when she was still Ruth Stone. Otherwise, Brigit would have missed the barest thread of a link to Peter.

Her watch alarm sounded again. Fifteen minutes until she had to leave. Setting the BlackBerry down, she went into her bedroom closet and pulled out her single dress suit. Powder gray, it was the only item in her closet she hated with a passion besides the matching sensible gray heels.

Suck it up, she reprimanded herself. *You don't meet the president of the United States dressed in chinos and a Green Day tee.*

Chapter Six

Still reeling from Ella's kidnapping, Michael nodded to the Secret Service agents and presidential staff as he made his way through the West Wing on auto pilot. President Jeffries took his breakfast in the small dining room adjacent to his office every morning where he reviewed the PDB, or President's Daily Brief, a Cliff Notes version of current intelligence situations around the world. This morning, instead of a junior director delivering the PDB, Michael was answering the president's invitation to deliver it in person.

The president had been on the road campaigning to extend his squatting rights at the White House for another four years. Today, however, he'd suspended his public campaign in deference to his opponent's family situation. The kidnapping was probably one of the only things that could possibly stop the politicking. Michael knew the president's campaign advisors hadn't stopped working behind the scenes, but no one wanted an unsympathetic president who would use such a tragedy to further his run for the Oval Office. The moment they found Ella, however, all bets were off. Even while Thad and Ruth went crazy with worry, Jeffries was sure to use the situation to his advantage. Before the day was over, the president would hold a press conference and make sure the world knew he and Thad were both strong family men.

On the first floor, Michael entered the dining room under the concerned eye of President Jeffries' executive assistant. Helena asked about Ella, Thad and Ruth. Michael gave her the vague answer he'd been repeating to himself all night. "The

FBI's on top of things. They'll break the case today."

Helena got him seated and poured him a glass of orange juice from a nearby service cart. "Would you like breakfast?"

Michael sipped the juice and shook his head.

Jeffries always made him feel comfortable, even though his archrival, Michael's brother-in-law, was a Republican. The president subscribed to the old adage of keeping his friends close and his enemies closer. To this day, Michael didn't know where Jeffries had pigeonholed him.

To Michael, people were complex, and dividing them with labels like Democrat or Republican couldn't encompass such complexity. However, that morning, he suspected the president had ulterior motives for the invitation.

The door to the private quarters opened and Jeffries entered. A balding man in his sixties, his massive bulk dwarfed his height. Even with the expensive jacket and tie he wore loose around his neck, he appeared more suited to a boxing ring than the Oval Office. "Michael, you look like hell."

Rising from his seat, he accepted the president's handshake. "Feel like it too."

"That's understandable." Jeffries removed his jacket, tossing it on an empty chair while ordering breakfast from Helena. "Any news about Ella?"

This was the reason the president had asked Michael to deliver the PDB. A hard, rough pit of anxiety for his niece lodged in his stomach. When Ruth had called him at four a.m. to tell him about the second phone call, the pit had grown to a boulder. Now, explaining the latest to the president, the juice in Michael's stomach turned to pure acid.

The president asked more questions and said a few words of sympathy before his breakfast arrived. "I've told the FBI and the local police to do whatever it takes to get Ella back safe and sound."

He was generally a kind man, if still a politician to his core, and Michael respected sincere kindness. "Thank you, sir."

"If you'd like some time off to spend with your family, Titus can arrange it."

Titus Allen, the head of the CIA, had already made the same offer. Michael toyed with his half-empty glass of juice. "At this point, I'd prefer to keep working."

Jeffries nodded. "When you get Ella back, I'm ordering you

to take a long weekend, agreed? They're only young for a little while, you know, and national security is always here."

Michael forced a smile and hoped he'd get to take him up on his offer. In his mind, he pictured Ella at the park, laughing at his attempts to get a kite into the air. At the zoo, commanding him to make strange noises and wake up a sleeping polar bear so she could talk to it. "Yes, sir."

While the president ate, Michael briefed him on the overnight workings of two terrorist groups causing trouble in China, a possible nuclear reactor the North Koreans had buried under a children's hospital, and an ongoing conflict between Russia and one of its neighbors.

Jeffries pushed his plate away. He took the papers of the PDB and riffled through them. "That's it?"

The briefing had truly been brief. The president wasn't used to a short list. "Ripples from our domestic financial crisis have now reached the major terror networks." Michael shrugged. "They're as broke as everyone else."

Jeffries frowned at the papers, but mimicked Michael's shrug. "I guess that's a good day for us, then?"

For the intelligence world, yes. Michael wasn't sure when the last time was he'd had a good day, personally or professionally. However, it was never prudent to disagree with the president of the country to his face. "Yes, sir."

A knock on the door interrupted them. Helena stuck her head inside. "Your eight o'clock has arrived, Mr. President."

Michael gathered the loose papers hurriedly and returned them to the PDB pouch. At the end of the day, the papers would be shredded. It was an antiquated way of disseminating information, but sending the briefs via internet, fax or phone was still too dangerous.

"Keep me posted about Ella," Jeffries said. "And tell Thad and Ruthie they're in my prayers."

"Why don't you call them, sir?" The words were out before Michael could rein in his candid thought.

A slight flush rose in the president's cheeks, and he chuckled. "I thought about it, but figured that rascal Thad would tell everyone I conceded the election ahead of time."

Michael accepted the joke with a nod and shook the president's hand. The political fight for the presidency had been ugly, as most usually were, but the president was off the mark to think Thad so underhanded. "I'll convey your thoughts to them."

"Remember what I said about taking some time off. As the PDB proves this morning, you've earned it. It's a good day for you career-wise. Enjoy it."

On his way to the door, Michael considered his commander and chief's order. The results of hard work and dedication were paying off, but the work of securing a nation was an ongoing and ever-growing job. The moment you let your guard down—the moment you enjoyed your success—some unlikely and unforeseen enemy would blow it all away. Literally.

As he tucked the pouch with the PDB under his arm and stepped into the reception room, Helena spoke to the president's next appointment. A woman in a gray suit and matching heels stood at the window, a trench coat draped over her arm.

She answered Helena over her shoulder, stopping in mid-sentence when her gaze landed on Michael.

Just like the night before, his instincts went on high alert. The change in her appearance sent a jolt of unease through his stomach. Brigit Kent was not who she claimed to be, he'd bet the PDB on it. "Good Morning, Dr. Kent." He gave her a nod.

She looked him over from head to toe and returned a small, forced smile. Her lipstick was the color of good burgundy and emphasized the white of her teeth. "Deputy Director Stone. We meet again."

He wondered how late she'd been out, and if Flynn had caught up with her. "You took off so suddenly last night, I didn't have a chance to talk to you."

She took a couple of careful steps toward him, as if she were tentative to get too close. "I believe you kicked me out."

He had, but until he figured out the puzzle standing before him, it was better to befriend her than push her away again. "My apologies. You caught me at the end of a long and stressful day." He gave her a smile that had charmed everyone from the Duchess of York to his mother. "The situation has me on edge. I'm sure you understand."

She studied the smile, studied the sincerity he willed into his eyes. Relaxed a bit. "Of course. If I overstepped my boundaries with your family, forgive me. I'd like to help if I can."

She didn't realize it, but she'd just opened the door for him to keep an eye on her. "Ruthie could use someone to talk to. A friend."

A faint quirk of her lips let him know she was pleased. "Ruth is a good person. I'll call her when I'm done here and try to stop by this evening if she's up to having company."

As Helena ushered Dr. Kent into the dining room, Michael tapped the PDB under his arm. Unlikely enemies were everywhere, and apparently conspiring with the president.

Brigit entered the dining room, flushed from Michael's apparent change of heart. She wasn't fooled by his sudden friendliness, his smoldering Clooney eyes or the flashy smile, but, jeez he was hard to resist when he turned on the charm.

She greeted the president and turned down the coffee Helena offered her. Trying not to teeter on her heels, she snagged the first chair she reached at the table, even though it was enough distance from President Jeffries to cause him to raise an eyebrow. She motioned at the newspapers and files fanned out before him. "At it already, I see."

He winked at her. "No rest for the wicked."

Like most men in power, Jeffries probably had wickedness on tap, to be served up whenever necessary. His good-guy persona wasn't completely false, but Brigit didn't trust him any more than she would trust a cobra swaying stealthily in front of her.

However, as his personal consultant—a job even his wife didn't realize Brigit held—Jeffries demanded her loyalty like a pet dog on a leash. "So what did you bring me on my enemies today, Doctor?"

Brigit pulled the BlackBerry from her jacket's hip pocket and punched several buttons. As the file she wanted emerged on the screen, Michael Stone's smile flashed across her mind. Blinking it away, she also tamped down the tiny flare of betrayal in her stomach. "Would you like to start with Thad Pennington," she asked the president, "or Ruth?"

Chapter Seven

Maryland

Peter Donovan had known deep passion in his life. Cutting pain as well. He'd sold his soul as a young man for a cause people believed was past history. A bloody, pointless war buried in political correctness these days and discussed in university studies as a *conflict.*

Even back home in Belfast, the cause he'd prayed for, bled for and killed for had been reduced to the *Bombs and Bullets Tour* given by taxi drivers who escorted tourists from the Protestant side of town to the Catholic side and back again. They gawked and snapped photos of monuments and murals depicting the two most prevalent objects in most wars...crosses and guns.

Fingering the tiny gold cross in his right earlobe, Peter repeated the only prayer he ever said anymore. *Know thy enemy. Know thyself.* While he still fought the Catholic tradition, he no longer believed in a merciful or just God. God had deserted him too many times. Left him to bleed and suffer the betrayals of his family, his friends and his conscience. After all the fighting, all the struggles, he now believed only in the truth.

Before exiting the delivery van he was driving, he slipped a pair of leather gloves on his hands and pulled the brim of his painter's cap down until it touched the frame of his sunglasses.

The side of the van was labeled Conglomerate Painting Services. It claimed the company did interior and exterior painting. A toll-free number, long ago disconnected, was stenciled under the lettering.

Behind the sunglasses, Peter scanned the residential

neighborhood as he walked around the van to the sidewalk. Pedestrian traffic was minimal, but starting to pick up. Car traffic was too, as people exited their townhouses and condos and jumped in high-end SUVs for work.

Dry leaves scattered around his feet, and he flipped the collar of his paint-splattered coveralls up against the cool wind rushing by. As he pushed a button on the key fob, the van's side door opened to reveal a collection of tarps, paint cans and tools. Hoisting a rolled-up canvas onto his shoulder, he stepped back and hit the key fob button again. The side door slid shut.

Jogging up the front stairs of the duplex, he kept his head down and whistled softly under his breath. The door was unlocked. Stepping inside, the smell of freshly sawn wood and primer filled his nose. He knocked the brim of his cap up with his knuckles and lowered his sunglasses to glance around. The duplex was undergoing a complete remodel. One that had already taken months longer and thousands of dollars more than the owners had ever dreamed. After today, however, their ailing budget and mounting impatience would dissolve in a heartbeat when the pull of a trigger from the top floor of the duplex sent a message to the world.

Taking the inside stairs with a purposeful, if slower, gait, Peter mentally reviewed the day's plan. Like a 3D topographer's map, all the important physical details of the assassination rose in his mind. The location of ground zero, the obstructions, like cars, trees and nearby buildings, the placement of his sniper— he could zoom in on each quarter of the kill zone and then efficiently pull back a degree and again review the physical details.

Cormac O'Bern, a famous modern Irish poet and an American poet laureate, would be honored for his body of written work as well as his international peace-promoting propaganda in a library renaming a quarter mile northeast of the duplex. The ex-IRA member had always had the gift of leadership and a love of Hollywood. Now he traveled the world with an entourage worthy of a movie star and spoke the words rock stars to politicians wanted to believe about attaining worldwide peace. All they had to do, Cormac claimed, was believe.

Peter scoffed at such juvenile ideas. Peace was an imaginary friend to human beings, no matter their socioeconomic status, religion or nation. The figurative image of peace helped them sleep at night. Like the image of God, it gave them hope in the face of tragedy, illness and loss. But it would never materialize, no matter how badly they wanted it to because it only existed in their mind.

War was real. Struggle was real. Peter didn't believe in peace any more than he believed in the leprechauns his mother had claimed lived in the woods behind his childhood home. His mother had believed in everything...God, peace, four-leaf clovers. She'd reached for hope in any element available. When Peter's father died in a retaliation bombing outside a pub in Belfast, Roberta had blamed bad luck and unrepentant sin.

Peter had blamed peace.

Roberta then turned her back on Irish Nationalism, betraying her dead spouse and her son. Five years after burying Peter's father, she married his archenemy, a parliament member with secretive ties to the British spy group MI5. She bore William Kent two daughters.

On the third floor, Peter entered a cramped room gutted to squeeze out floor space for a small home gym. As he moved toward a tall, skinny window where he could look across the neighborhood and nearby park, he caught sight of the barricades already erected near the library. Traffic was being diverted around the block. From this distance the black and white police cruisers lining the street looked like Matchbox cars and the large green sign over the library's entrance was clearly visible but unreadable.

He unrolled the canvas, uncovering a tripod and rifle. Carefully, he spread the canvas flat and snapped the tripod into a standing position. As he anchored the rifle to the tripod, the leather gloves hindered his fingers, slowing down his usual efficiency. Even though they were snug-fitting stretch leather, he couldn't get a good feel for the metal under them.

Grunting, he removed one of the gray gloves and threw it to the floor in frustration. The leather made a soft smacking sound, the glove landing palm up as if in defeat. Peter took a deep breath, yanked the ball cap off his head and ran his forearm over his sweating forehead.

The gloves were a necessity. A fingerprint was too easy to leave behind. No matter how carefully a person wiped off surfaces they knew they'd touched, the chance at leaving behind an errant fingerprint was high. Forcing patience into his fingers, he also forced it into his mind. He could not afford to leave behind such blatant evidence. He returned the cap to his bald head—there would be no hair fibers left behind either—and slid the glove back on his hand.

Once he attached the rifle to the tripod, he removed a scope from inside his overalls, fastening it to the top. He peered through the scope, adjusted the coordinates and read the library sign. *Cormac O'Bern. The Power of Peace.*

Cormac and Peter had been inseparable during their teenage years. Cormac, a few years older and wiser, had drawn Peter in like a magnet to steel. While Cormac persuaded people to their cause with his smooth rhetoric and winning smile, Peter carried out guerilla war tactics to spotlight their continuing war.

But then Cormac betrayed him, just like his mother. Just like Brigit.

Love, like peace, was an illusion. An imaginary friend.

Adjusting the range of the scope, Peter again referred to the three-dimensional map in his mind. From memory, he pulled up Cormac's handsome face, its long nose, dark hair and fair skin, and set the scope's hairs on the spot between his bushy eyebrows. Peter pressed the trigger on the rifle and mentally heard the report, absorbed the kick of the gun, and watched in slow motion as Cormac slumped out of the scope's range, crumpling to the ground of the stage.

Today, Cormac would be reminded, if only for the briefest of seconds, that his life, his promise of peace, was a joke.

A voice from behind him startled Peter from his daydream. The accent was thick with Palestinian genes. "You would like to do this job yourself?"

Peter removed his eye from the scope but didn't turn to face her. Of course he wanted to pull the trigger himself, but he wasn't stupid or careless. He was not the professional assassin like the woman standing behind him, and today, a professional was needed. That's why he'd paid her ransom to the Israelis and sent Tory to pick her up.

He glanced at his watch. "In two hours fifty-three minutes, the dedication will take place. The FBI and local law enforcement are already strained to the breaking point by the kidnapping and the presence of a dozen rich and famous attending the event. Your escape after Cormac's murder should be the smoothest you've ever encountered."

"Ah, yes, the kidnapping. How is the girl doing?"

Peter turned to Moira Raphael. Her dark auburn hair was pulled tight in a high ponytail. Her brown eyes were rimmed with black and her lips shone with thick, red gloss. A bruise on her left cheek, provided by her captors, was still visible under the layers of her makeup. "The Pennington child is a sniveling runt but still an effective tool to help us."

The right side of Moira's mouth tilted up in a smirk. "There is no us, Peter, you know that." She waited for him to contradict her. He didn't and she shrugged. "I've recently been in the same predicament as the child. Cold, hungry, abused and alone in the dark. It's quite terrifying, even for someone like me."

"She hasn't been abused."

"But knowing you, she has been neglected. Perhaps if you fed her, she would stop crying."

Peter tightened his hands into fists. The child was the least of their concerns. "I don't tell you how to kill people."

The left side of her mouth joined the right. She walked to the rifle, shouldered him out of the way so she could double check his work with her own gloved hands. "After this, my debt to you is paid."

Removing a brown envelope from the inside pocket of his overalls, Peter watched her adjust the scope. "When the job is done, head to Canada. I'll meet up with you as soon as I'm done here."

She raised her gaze from the scope and studied his face. "There's more at stake here than my usual jobs. No matter what measures you have taken, leaving the country will be difficult. This job is an even trade for the ransom."

Peter handed her the envelope. "You won't encounter trouble leaving the country unless you fail to follow my orders."

Moira considered his words in silence. He could see caution warring with her independent nature in her eyes. "Canada it is then."

Leaving her with the gun and envelope, Peter descended the stairs and returned to the van. He knew Moira would run when the job was done, just like she had before. If he hadn't been in love with her, been in love with what she did so flawlessly, he'd have let her go years ago. But he *was* in love with her, as in love as he could ever be.

He told himself it was simply the amazing sex they had that kept him tracking her down, chasing her like a fox after a rabbit. Deep in his gut, though, he knew it was more. The sexy assassin meant far more to him than a good fuck. Her ability to take a human life without a moment's regret matched his own. However, with Moira, there was no agenda, no mission, no loyalty to anyone or anything. He envied her that. His own mission was so ingrained in the cells of his body, he couldn't imagine a life without such passion.

Possessing Moira had become as much his passion as his homeland's nationalism. A part of him believed he could dissect her and when he did, he'd finally have the antidote to emotion. Only then, when he no longer felt anything for anyone, would he find the guts to pull the trigger on his friends as well as his enemies.

Back in the van, Peter pawed through a grocery sack and pulled out a Snickers candy bar. He'd give it to the Pennington girl when he got back to the room he'd rented. Contrary to what Moira thought, he was not a monster like the Israelis. The girl was warm and dry, and Tory had given her a doll she'd picked up at a nearby convenience store.

I even left a nightlight on for her so she wouldn't be afraid of the dark.

Chapter Eight

Arlington

Julia tossed her car keys on the kitchen counter and shrugged out of her jacket. Conrad sat at the table with a laptop, a cup of coffee and a spread of papers. He didn't glance up from the screen when he spoke. "Explain."

She didn't want to explain and even if she had, his demanding tone raised her hackles. "Business meeting."

He pecked at the keyboard. "Since when does my London operative work a case inside the States with you?"

So he knew. She hadn't fooled him at all. Now she had to find a way out of this confrontation without making things worse for Zara.

Tired and in need of a serious jolt of caffeine, all Julia could think about was how nice it would be to have a hot shower and an understanding husband. Noting the set of Con's jaw, she knew the last item on her wish list was a pipedream. As long as she was this deep in shit, she might as well ignore his question. "Zara's in the hospital. She's dehydrated and her electrolytes are messed up. The doctor's running some blood tests, but he suspects she has a serious case of influenza."

"What case are you working, Jules?"

She wasn't sure if it was his tone or the fact he wouldn't look at her that made anger bite low in her stomach. "Don't you care Zara's sick? That she's in the hospital?"

His gaze left the computer screen and crawled up her body to her face. "Of course I care about Zara. I also care about my wife. You're both walking a dangerous high wire right now, and maybe neither of you realized it, but if you get caught, I'm the asshole who's going to meet the firing squad. I have a right to know what you're involved in."

She hated it when he was right. "Zara is your espionage operative, but what I do on my off hours has no reflection on you as Director of Operations."

"Wrong." He rose from the chair and tamped his finger on the table. "Everything you do reflects on me, like it or not. A caveat of being married, Mrs. Flynn."

Julia's heart plunged. The few times Con had referred to their marriage over the last six months, he'd always made it sound constraining, damning almost. He was still annoyed she hadn't taken his name, as evidenced by the way he constantly used the term *Mrs. Flynn* like a challenge.

Julia understood the political workings of Washington as well as anyone. Through the years as a CIA analyst and then an operative, she'd broken rules and challenged authority on a regular basis. Always, though, with the complete understanding that her butt, and only hers, was on the line. Marriage to Conrad changed that. Now if she went outside the borders of her job, it would reflect badly on him.

Like Michael, Con had enemies in Washington. Enemies waiting to ambush him, to implicate him in illegal or immoral activities if it served their purpose. He'd been a rogue agent once and the shadow hung over his head. These days, he had to go above and beyond proper protocol or be suspected again.

Acknowledging the truth in his statement with a nod, she still refused to give in. "I'll tell you what we were doing if you promise not to reprimand Zara."

He drew in a deep breath, as if reining in his impatience. "Why are you so damned protective of my spy?"

"She's been kidnapped by a Mafia drug lord, held at gunpoint by a psychotic terrorist and injected with a deadly virus all in the span of the past four months. Being one of your secret army has hardly been a walk in the park for her."

"Well, if you don't come clean about your covert activities, Zara will lose her secret decoder ring before the day's over. Maybe you can put in a good word for her with your boss. Get her a job with FBI. Oh, wait." He snapped his fingers. "If you're involved with what she's doing, you'll lose your job too."

"Are you threatening me?"

"Hell, yes, I'm threatening you."

Julia kept all emotion off her face and locked her mental

energy with his. This was the problem with their marriage. Neither of them was ever willing to concede. "Clichéd as it sounds, we're trying to save the world," she said. "Save innocent people from dying."

Conrad crossed his arms over his chest as he appeared to analyze her tone and body language for sarcasm. Finding none, he said, "I applaud that. But vigilante antics will only get you fired. Who you gonna help then?"

After all his reckless behavior, it sounded funny to hear Con preach following the rules. Once again, however, Julia had to admit he was right. She glanced out the patio doors, watched a bird peck at some seeds that had fallen from the bird feeder onto the railing. "Zara followed three members of the Sisters of Liberation group from London to D.C. She turned the mission over to me unofficially so she could continue to track them and uncover what they're up to."

"The woman you met at the construction site. You know who she is?"

Julia's defenses shifted. She didn't know why, but she sensed the need to tread carefully. "Her ID said Brigit Kent. DHS."

Conrad resumed his seat, shuffling the scattered papers into a neater pile. "So our government claims. Whoever and whatever she is, though, you and Zara both need to keep your distance." He closed the laptop and pulled a flash drive in the shape of a Lego brick from a USB port. "Got it?"

"Why?"

He smirked at her, standing up again to shove the zip drive into his pants pocket. "If I told you, I'd have to kill you."

The old spy joke. Now Con was being the evasive one.

Like a cold breeze brushing against her skin, Julia's instincts told her Brigit Kent was involved in something important. Something important to Conrad.

She glanced at the pile of papers next to his laptop, then made a production out of checking her watch. "I've got to get a shower. I have duty for the O'Bern ceremony today."

As she walked out of the kitchen to head to the bedroom for fresh clothes, Conrad followed her. "I thought you might offer to work the Pennington kidnapping."

Julia stalled at the dresser. Michael's niece was a top priority case at the moment, and she would have given anything to be part of it. She still respected and admired him immensely. Somehow, though, she'd known how inappropriate it would have been to ask for the assignment. She wouldn't have gotten it anyway. "Kidnappings are outside the scope of my training."

Con was silent as she tugged at the dresser drawer and snagged a pair of underwear. She chanced a glance at him as she crossed to the closet.

"That the only reason?" he asked.

Facing him, she saw the uncertainty in his eyes. She shook her head. "If I thought I could save that little girl, Con, I'd have taken the assignment in a heartbeat, but it would have been for Ella, not Michael."

He nodded and left the doorway. Reappeared a moment later. "Want me to pick up some strawberry pie for tonight?"

Julia smiled at him, crossing the room to kiss his lips. "I'd love some."

He smiled back and dipped his head for another kiss. "You okay?"

"I didn't get enough sleep last night, but I'm fine."

"No queasiness? Dizziness? You don't have Zara's *flu* bug?"

Julia shook her head, again remembering her very sick friend. "I should stop back by the hospital after the ceremony. You should track down Lawson and let him know Zara's in the hospital. They won't let her use her cell, and he may be trying to reach her."

"I'll let him know."

They kissed again, and as Con left the apartment, Julia jumped in the shower. No matter how foolish it was, she was going after Brigit Kent like a flea after a dog.

Chapter Nine

Washington D.C.

Brigit sank into the cushy backseat of the limo and accepted a bottle of water from Truman. She kicked off the pumps, flexed her toes and took a sip of water. Under her clothes, she trembled.

Truman eyed her with interest, ending a phone call and removing the Bluetooth from his ear. "Did the Great and Mighty Oz grab your ass or something? You look like you're going to throw a whitey."

The way her stomach churned, she just might throw up. Sliding down even further into the leather, Brigit pushed the button to close the motorized privacy panel between them and the chauffeur, giving Truman a warning glance. The last thing she needed was a scandal involving the president of the United States bringing her into the spotlight. "This sucks the big one, as you always say."

"Literally? You gave the big guy head?"

As an assistant, Truman's organizational skills and willingness to abide by her confidentiality protocol on all cases were extraordinary. His attitude and snarkiness when he was alone with her, however, was always a test of her patience. "Don't be crude. I was referring to the situation with the Penningtons and the president."

"You have to take the kidnapping out of the picture. It's making you emo."

"Emo?"

"Emotional. Whiny. " He pushed buttons on his phone and replaced the earpiece. "I sent today's itinerary to your crackberry. We'll hit the office first for a meeting with Roz, then do the O'Bern dedication and reception. At two, you're sitting in on the Ethics Committee hearing at the Capitol."

Brigit held up a hand. "The O'Bern dedication?"

"Cormac O'Bern. Poet laureate and famed peace monger?" Truman shuffled in his man bag and brought out a book. *Dreams of Peace* by Cormac O'Bern. "There's a dedication and outside reception at the Randolph library today. Your invitation came while you were in London. I RSVP'd for you and a friend. I'm the friend, by the way. Total Cormy cult member. Hope you don't mind."

She reached out for the book, flipped through the pages absently. Cormac O'Bern was in town. Like Tetris blocks dropping into a grid to form a straight row, Ella's kidnapping and Tory's appearance snapped into the *ah-ha* grid in Brigit's mind. Peter and Cormac, the inseparable troublemakers. Everything became so clear.

She shut the book with a snap. "Reschedule the meeting with Roz. I need to go home and change my clothes."

Truman's call must have gone through, because he greeted the person on the other end before covering the mouthpiece and frowning at her. "You have to wear the prison guard suit all day. No exceptions."

He returned to his call. Nausea cramped her stomach. Again, her brain ran through the past twenty-four hours and a row of blocks formed, flashed and blinked out. She buzzed the chauffeur. "Change of plans. Take me back to my loft."

Truman threw his hands up in disgust but continued speaking to his phone companion without missing a beat.

Brigit watched the landscape as the driver began making the necessary lane changes and turns to follow his new route. It was a beautiful fall day. Crystal blue sky as far as you could see. Sunshine brightening the few leaves still left on trees. The library board had chosen a perfect day for Cormac O'Bern's dedication and reception.

Grabbing the book in her lap, she flipped through the stanzas of poetry and examined the back cover. While he looked older, the crisp, terse words of poetry he used in his verses still rang with authority. There was nothing warm or fuzzy about Cormac O'Bern's preachings, on paper or in person. He was a man of passion and strength, only these days he used his gift to promote peace instead of war.

If only Peter had chosen the same path. Her half-brother possessed the same type of character as Cormac. The two had been inseparable during their teens. While Cormac had gone on to college, Peter had joined a splinter group of the Real IRA. Each found his place in the new generation of Catholic versus Protestant war. Cormac ended up in jail with a group of his college buddies for inciting riots on campus. Peter had ended up there at the same time with his own comrades for similar antics in downtown Belfast. In jail, the two groups joined arms and went on a hunger strike.

Brigit's mother had begged her father to pull political strings to get Peter and Cormac released. He'd refused. "They aren't boys anymore," he'd told her. "They've committed crimes and now they have to pay the price."

As Peter and Cormac wasted away in jail, Roberta had sent them boxes of books, mainstream bestsellers to military history. One day, the books were returned. "I have my Bible and God," a note from Peter stated. "I need nothing, and no one, else."

Roberta had cried.

To Peter, Roberta's marriage to William Kent cut their blood ties. When Peter was finally freed from jail, he was fifteen pounds lighter and his heart was hardened against his mother and her husband. During the hunger strike, one of the boys died and several others were hospitalized. Upon their release, Peter and Cormac struck a bargain. All for one and all against the British.

In retaliation against his British stepfather and his traitor of a mother, Peter kidnapped Brigit and Tory. As the new leader of his freedom fighters, he'd planned to use the two girls as a weapon...to trade them for money to buy guns and bomb-making supplies for his new army.

His plan failed when Roberta, who knew her son well, found the girls and in the end died saving them. Peter disappeared and William, along with certain friends in the government, covered the incident up. Fearing he couldn't protect his daughters, William moved them to America, far away from the continuing unrest between the Irish and the British, Catholics and Protestants.

Only years later, after Brigit had undergone intensive therapy, did she understand the depths of Peter's extremist personality. The human psyche was a fascinating puzzle to her.

She'd been a psychologist for nearly eight years, but she'd been studying people her whole life. Long before she'd received her doctorate, her aptitude for code breaking had emerged.

Human beings were one giant code from their DNA to their personality triggers. Once you understood the code, you could dissect it and rebuild it for better purposes, or exploit it for negative ones. Either way, Brigit's in-depth studies and experiments had received attention from every government on the planet.

Every few years, a kidnapping occurred fitting the parameters she was interested in. The young son or daughter of a dignitary, a drug company president or a financial guru would go missing, usually from a public arena. Local law enforcement would immediately tag it a kidnapping. Leads would be nonexistent. There would be no ransom demand. A call would be placed, and the child's anxious, often hysterical voice would ask for mom or dad. Proof of life would continue to be offered over a period of forty-eight to seventy-two hours without any logical reason why. The child would turn up hungry and terrified, but otherwise unharmed, in another public venue. The kidnapper or kidnappers would remain at large.

To the untrained eye, it seemed random, more like a sport than a calculated crime. With time, the case would grow cold, the traumatized child and family would move on, and the public would forget.

To Brigit, these kidnappings were not random. Each one served a purpose...a distraction, a drain of resources, or even to make a point.

If the pieces of the puzzle snapping together did indeed form a solid row, the Pennington kidnapping was all three. Peter's fingerprints were all over it and yet, she realized with a start, she couldn't prove a thing. *You've never been able to pin any of the previous kidnappings on him. Why should this time be any different?*

Like usual, there was no hard evidence and she had no starting point to hand to the FBI. She'd already talked to an agent and asked him to check into Peter's whereabouts but had come back with information he was living and working in Argentina under an assumed name.

Brigit's resources were only slightly more accurate than the FBI's, but she knew Peter had never visited Argentina, much less lived there. And while she carried a lot of weight with everyone from the president of Microsoft to the president of the United States, the FBI regarded her as little more than an overpaid, independent profiler. A profiler who could hand them nothing more than wild speculation.

With this case, she wouldn't blame them for blowing her off. All she had were suspicions and an intangible code ingrained in her body from a terrifying couple of days spent long ago in a bathroom over a pub on the outskirts of Belfast. Who would believe her? Who could possibly find Peter, the man who moved like a ghost in the night?

"Earth to Gidget."

Truman was staring at her again, his call complete.

Brigit closed her eyes for a second before shifting gears. "What did I miss this time?"

"By the cut of that jacket, I'd say the last decade. You look like Hillary, pre-Monica."

Hillary Clinton. Now there was a psychological code Brigit would have loved to break. "You know this is the only suit I own."

"A high-powered psycho-babbler should live in Chanel, not Gap."

"Gap is more comfortable."

Truman rolled his eyes and handed her a sheet of paper. "Since you're skipping the meeting with Roz, who won't be happy, you know, because you *are* the meeting, I'll fax your analysis of the top three domestic groups to her. She can share with the rest of the taskforce."

The domestic terrorism taskforce was the least of Brigit's worries at the moment. A growing sense of dread pulsed under her skin. While Cormac had changed and embraced peace as his life's work, if he and Peter were in both in D.C. at the same time, nothing but trouble could be brewing. Where was Peter? And what was he planning?

And why did it involve Ella Pennington?

Brigit placed a call to Special Agent Edmonds, the FBI profiler in charge of the kidnapping. She got his voice mail and left him a message, asking him to check into Peter Donovan's background. Explained her idea about his possible involvement with the kidnapping. Even to her own ears, her reasoning sounded weak, implausible.

She disconnected the call and rubbed her temples. Truman was staring at her, but she avoided meeting his gaze. What should she do? The O'Bern dedication was less than two hours away. If Peter was planning something, what would it be? Would he try to scare Cormac? Take him out? Would it be a public display or something more subtle, after the show?

Would Special Agent Edmonds follow up on her call? Even if he did, it could be hours, or even days before he and his group uncovered anything concrete. By then, the dedication, and possibly the kidnapping, would be over.

In her heart, Brigit knew they didn't have hours or days to piece it all together. Something was going down today. Knowing Peter, it would be something big.

There was one possible person who would listen to her theory and cut her a tad of slack. One person with superior intelligence and a knack for understanding terrorists. A person who carried enough weight in Washington and the intelligence community to make Edmonds and his team follow up on her theory with speed and efficiency.

If nothing else, her wild speculations might receive a fair shake from him based solely on the fact that no one, including Ruth Pennington's overprotective brother, had any other lead to follow.

"Fax the info to Roz and find out Michael Stone's whereabouts. Immediately."

"Stone? Of the CIA?" Truman looked perplexed. "What for?"

The car pulled up to the curb in front of Brigit's apartment. She buzzed the driver. "Wait here. I'll be back in ten minutes." She released the call button and said to Truman, "What do I wear to CIA headquarters?"

Truman stared at her, seemingly at a loss for words, which was an alien concept. Brigit snapped her fingers in front of his eyes. "Earth to Capote."

He blinked once and raised his chin, miffed at the Capote reference. If he could call her Gidget, it seemed only fair she could call him names too. He looked down his nose at her. "Do you want to be taken seriously?"

Brigit sighed and shoved her sore feet back into the pumps. "Yes, but I can't carry myself in these shoes, and the skirt makes me look like I have watermelons for hips."

"Keep the jacket, switch to black trousers and go with a

lower heel."

She leaned over and planted a kiss on his cheek. "Thanks. I'll be right back."

Stunned into silence again, Truman only nodded.

Inside, Brigit switched her clothes and shoes at the speed of a racehorse, more so out of fear she would change her mind about going to see Stone than out of guilt for keeping Truman and her driver waiting.

Stopping at her bedroom window, she scanned the near-perfect blue sky. *Right is right. If Peter is involved in this little girl's kidnapping, he has to be stopped.*

Her gaze fell to the park nearby where several mothers sat on a bench and chatted while two small children tried out the slide and one sat in a pile of woodchips, throwing them like confetti into the air. *If only childhood could be innocent and fun for all kids.*

As if someone was watching her, bumps rose all over her arms. She lifted her gaze and scanned the area. Under a group of maples in the far corner of the park, a man stood alone and immobile with feet spread and arms hanging at his side. The shade was dense under the orange and yellow leaves, keeping him in shadows.

Brigit took a step closer to the window, squinting to try to bring him into focus. He wore a cap and what looked like a one-piece coverall. None of his features were visible and yet Brigit's stomach churned. He was so still, so hidden in the shadows. If it hadn't been for the beautiful day and the oblivious mothers and children, it could have been a scene from a horror movie.

Peter, Brigit's brain screamed.

Stumbling back from the window, she sat down hard on the bed when the backs of her knees hit the mattress. A band tightened around her rib cage and she could barely breathe.

Truman's voice behind her made her jump back up. "JOE wants you to keep a low pro— Whoa, you look like you just saw Howard Stern naked. What's wrong?"

Brigit took a deep breath and smoothed shaking hands down her shirt. "What are you doing up here?"

He lifted a set of files in his hand. "You still had these files and I need to return them to Halden's secretary before she misses them. They were on your kitchen counter." His eyes scanned her face. "You're so damn pale, Brigit. Put on some blush."

A cold had seeped into her bones. "I don't own blush."

"Of course you don't. Where's your lipstick?"

She needed a minute to compose herself. Slow down her pounding heart. She pointed at the bathroom. "There's a drawerful in there."

Truman took off for the bathroom and Brigit spun back around to the window. In the park below, the scene was the same. Children careened down slides and flung themselves from monkey bars. Mothers laughed and chatted. The man under the tree had disappeared as if he'd never been there.

"Wicked Woman?" Truman walked back into the bedroom and held up a tube of lipstick. "Drama Diva? Professional Pink? Brickhouse? Where on earth do you find these crazy colors?"

"The Rimmel beauty counter."

"Have you ever worn any of them?"

Not often. Mostly she bought them for their names. They made her believe if she did wear them, they'd provide whatever their name promised.

She crossed the room and plucked the lipstick tubes from his fingers. "Professional Pink is for the office. Brickhouse is for state dinners."

Truman cocked a brow at her and dangled one of the tubes in front of her face. "And Wicked Woman?"

Brigit snatched it from his hand. "Clubbing, of course."

"Clubbing. Uh-huh." Truman knew she preferred her free nights at home with a Steven Pinker book about cognitive science over a club filled with hip-grinding music and sweating bodies. "Right."

Chapter Ten

Langley

Michael slid his keycard through the door lock of his office, absently registering the green light and soft beep before opening the door. Nine o'clock and he was already late for his third meeting of the morning. Remnants of the last one still irritated the synapses in his brain. Illogical people were taking over the world, he was sure of it. While he lived and breathed the bloodless world of logic to make decisions and solve problems, most people seemed to ignore it, preferring emotions and drama instead. While he understood human nature well, he would never follow the thought processes of some human beings.

The door closed behind him with a soft shush. His office was dark except for a bit of daylight peeking through his closed blinds. He hadn't even had time to open them or sit at this desk and have a cup of coffee yet. Flipping on the overhead lights, he knew his foul mood couldn't be blamed on caffeine deficiency. The stress of Ella's kidnapping, lack of sleep and the incompetency of others weighed on his shoulders like an elephant. If he wasn't careful, the elephant would crush him, inch by inch, meeting by meeting.

In three steps he was at his wide mahogany desk. Piles of papers camouflaged the top, each one needing his review, and many requiring his signature. With a sigh, he scooted them out of the way, set his leather briefcase in the middle and dug around for his PDA. The briefcase had a separate pocket for his cell phone, pens and business cards, but his PDA was continuously getting swallowed up in the rest of the mess.

A voice from the corner of the room stilled his hands. "I'm glad to see you're using the briefcase. After all that happened, I wasn't sure you wouldn't burn it instead."

Michael looked up as Julia walked across the blue carpet of his office and stopped at the side of the desk. "What are you doing here?"

She smiled at him like nothing between them had changed in the past six months. Her hair was different, shorter and more professional. "Am I not allowed to pay you a visit?"

After she'd chosen to marry Flynn, Michael had used every form of logic and reason to shut down and stamp out his feelings for her. He'd only seen her a few times since and he'd known ahead of time she'd be in his proximity, so he'd prepped himself for the flood of memories, the gut-twisting loss. This morning, her presence was completely unexpected—he'd had no time to prep.

With a modicum of relief, he realized the only emotion inside him was a vague regret. He might not always understand the workings of the human mind, but he'd accepted his loss and moved on.

Tamping the regret into the mental place he reserved for all things Julia, he ignored her question in favor of his own. While no one had permission to be in his office if he wasn't in attendance, Julia had never let rules or locks stop her before. "How did you get in here?"

She pointed a slender finger at the door on his left. "Elevator."

Michael's appointment to Deputy Director of the CIA came with a host of job perks as well as endless meetings and stupid people. He had his own personal bevy of assistants, a private bathroom and a luxurious sleeper sofa, which these days saw as little action as his bed at home. If it weren't for Pongo, he'd live in this office suite without hesitation. "You evaded the cameras, violated all the security codes and rode in my personal elevator from my private garage."

He waved off the mischievous look in her eyes. Her covert skills were the best he'd ever seen. Next to Flynn anyway. "I don't want to know how you did it, just don't do it again. It will get you in trouble. *Capiche?*"

"Waltzing through the front doors and past Con would get me in trouble too," she countered. "I'm actually not here on a social call, but before I get into that, anything new on Ella?"

Michael sat in his leather chair and rubbed his forehead

where a headache was kick-starting. "I spoke to the agent in charge about an hour ago. There's been nothing more since the last call. They couldn't trace it. Ruth's close to a nervous breakdown, and Thad's seriously considering pulling the plug on his run for president."

Julia took a seat in one of the chairs across from him. "I'm so sorry, Michael. The FBI is doing everything we can."

"Yeah, I know." He let out a sigh. "So what brings you here?"

Shoving her hand in the pocket of her dark blue FBI jacket, she bit her lip before speaking. "I was working on an unofficial case last night and caught something interesting on video. I can't bring it to my bosses or pretty much anyone else because they'll ask questions I don't want to answer, so I'm bringing it to you instead."

She leaned forward and tossed a flash drive onto his desk. He eyed it with curiosity. Julia was one of the few people on the planet who was not stupid, her choice as a husband not withstanding. "Involving what?"

"Terrorists and a DHS employee. I'm not sure what's going on, but I was hoping you could look into it and pass it on if necessary without involving me."

Michael took the flash drive and stuck it in a USB port on the laptop in front of him. There was no point in chastising Julia for running outside the parameters of her job description. He was no longer her boss. Or her lover.

And if there was one thing he knew about her, besides the intimate details of their past relationship, it was never to ignore her gut instincts.

She came around the desk to his side as the seal of the CIA disappeared from the screen and a media program opened. A few seconds later, Michael watched a hostage exchange unfold on the screen. Julia's nearness made the scar on his chest tighten like he'd just bench-pressed a hundred pound weight, but he forgot it the moment the green Ford entered the picture.

When Brigit Kent emerged and pointed a gun at the rusty Volvo, he tightened his grip on the mouse. Her mouth moved but no sound came out. He clicked on the volume button. Silence continued to emanate from his speaker. "Why'd you mute the video?"

"I wasn't working alone," Julia said. "It's important my

partner not get in trouble either so I stripped the audio."

Was Flynn the partner she was protecting? After all, Michael had put Flynn on Brigit's trail. But then why was Julia bringing this video to him? Why was she avoiding her husband two floors down in the counterterrorism department?

It wasn't Flynn. Michael unclenched his jaw.

Julia pointed at the screen. "The woman with the gun is Dr. Brigit Kent. The woman in the knit cap is apparently her sister. Went by the name Tory. They discussed a man named Peter, and Tory mentioned she was involved with him and an international war. I searched the internet and found out Dr. Kent does have a sister named Tory."

"The internet? Why didn't you run Tory through the FBI databases?"

"All our databases are now connected. If the FBI runs a background on Tory, DHS will know about it. I ping anything related to Dr. Kent, somebody's going to be crawling down my throat wanting to know why. I doubt DHS would be happy to find out she's related to a woman who's running with a terrorist group, and yes I'm sure Tory and her comrades are linked to terrorists. She mentioned Ireland, Afghanistan and Palestine while she was talking to Brigit. Called them all brothers and sisters in arms."

Michael's warning bell was ringing much too loudly now to be ignored. He forced himself to show no emotion as he watched the rest of the scene play out, saw Brigit embraced by the woman in the knit cap, saw the rusty Volvo drive away and Brigit slump against her car as if the life had just left her.

As the video came to an abrupt stop, he sat back in his chair and looked at Julia. "I can't pass this on anonymously to Homeland Security without the audio. The video will certainly raise questions, but nothing Dr. Kent can't manipulate and sweep under the carpet without the audio or your testimony." He rocked his chair and held his palms up. "If you want to pursue this, you either give up the audio and your partner or you give up yourself and offer the testimony you just gave me."

Julia paced away from the desk. "You don't want me to rat out my partner, and I'm not even sure it's worth turning in. I'm not worried about Dr. Kent being a turncoat or aiding and abetting terrorists." She paced back to his desk. "I'm more interested in the man her and Tory discussed. If you could just look into their background and see if this Peter does exist and what terrorist group he's linked with..."

Her voice trailed off and Michael blew out a frustrated breath. She knew he would never do this favor for anyone but her. In his position, he could get away with asking things others couldn't. At least, up until lately, he could. "I'll see what I can do, but the environment here has changed, Julia. If I ask too many questions or try to dodge who gave me this information, my ass will be hanging out to dry with my mother's bed sheets."

Julia smiled at him as if the world would never question the Great Michael Stone. "I don't want to screw up Dr. Kent's career. I like her."

That made one of them. The phone on his desk buzzed. Probably his executive admin assistant, Irene, reminding him he was late for his nine o'clock. Michael shoved more papers aside and hit the blinking red button. "I know, Irene, I'm late. Call Max and tell him I need to reschedule. Something's come up." He glanced at Julia and shook his head in resignation. "And can you get Dr. Brigit Kent on the phone for me?"

Julia raised an eyebrow as if to say, *You're going to call her?*

He looked away. How he went about dealing with Dr. Kent and the video was now up to him. Irene's voice came over the speakerphone. "I can do you one better, Deputy Director. Dr. Kent is here in the waiting room. That's why I was buzzing you. She says she needs to speak to you. It's an emergency."

Michael locked gazes with Julia. Her eyes were wide with disbelief.

The drumming in his temples ramped up a notch. How was it he could not escape Dr. Kent even at Langley? He poked the intercom button again. "Give me a minute before you show her in."

Motioning at Julia, he pointed toward his private bathroom. "Wait in there and listen to what she says."

Her gaze zipped from him to the bathroom door and back. "You want me to eavesdrop on your conversation?"

"I may need you as a witness."

"A witness to what?"

Good question. Silence for an answer, he waved her toward the bathroom. "Go."

Julia's instincts about Dr. Kent might be right on the money, but at the moment, that didn't matter. Michael's own instincts were flaring red. His world had grown too small in the past twenty-four hours, thanks to Brigit Kent, both personally and professionally. She was trouble, and while Michael disliked trouble to his core, he never ran from it. The only way to deal with it was balls first.

Dropping the flash drive in his pencil drawer, he put on his game face and listened to the bathroom door click shut. He was about to find out just how much trouble Dr. Kent really was.

The intelligence community considered information only as reliable as its source. If the source was bogus, so was the intel.

Brigit sat in a padded chair near Michael Stone's secretary and fiddled with her BlackBerry, playing Brick Breaker to keep her mind and fingers distracted while she waited to speak to the man. It also made her look busy and important. Not that she needed to look busy and important to anyone, but the secretary—Irene, her nameplate on the desk read—was the reincarnation of the multi-armed Hindu goddess Durga, fingers flying over her keyboard, handling multiple calls with her headset, fishing through her file drawers and sipping her bottle of Sprite as if she were accustomed to deftly juggling so many tasks. Which she probably was. The CIA's secretarial pool had to be as elite as the men and women they served.

She shot Brigit a dirty look, which was due to the mobile in Brigit's hands. The little black ball on the screen careened off into BlackBerry oblivion and a message flashed on the screen. *Game over.*

Brigit sighed at the terrible score, nowhere near her high, and hoped she'd do better breaking through Director Stone's brick wall. The information she was about to lay in front of his baby blues was based on nothing more than inconclusive evidence and her own best guess. Since she wasn't on the director's Top Ten People to Trust list, she doubted she'd get far with her mission. Just like the little black ball on the screen, she was about to land in oblivion. Only, knowing her luck, she'd probably land in a special oblivion for people who repeatedly stepped on Michael Stone's Turnbull & Asser loafers.

"Deputy Director Stone will see you now," Irene said, rising from her chair like nobility and motioning for Brigit to follow her. "Remember this is a special case. It's rare anyone gets in to speak to him without an appointment."

That was the second time she'd mentioned the obvious fact the man behind the door was just as busy as his secretary. Brigit tucked her BlackBerry into her trench coat pocket, flashed Irene an insincere smile, and lifted the chain around her neck to wave the gold four-leaf clover pendant in front of the woman's glaring brown eyes. "Good thing I wore my lucky charm today then, isn't it?"

Irene's red lips thinned in a strained smile, an edge to them sharp enough to cut leather. Her eyes slid sideways in what Brigit recognized as a covert eye roll. She'd done the same thing more times than she could count during meetings and diplomatic parties when someone tried to pull lamb's wool over her eyes.

The moment the door to the inner office opened, though, all thoughts about Irene and her cutting charm evaporated. Michael Stone rose from behind his desk, wicked handsome in his black suit, the jacket now unbuttoned and showing off a beautiful sky blue silk tie she'd noticed earlier that morning in the Oval Office reception room.

"Dr. Kent," he said, moving around one end of his desk with the grace of a lion. The stiffness she'd noticed in him at the White House had disappeared and in its place was a controlled confidence. This was his domain, his lair. Here, in his suite of an office, he was totally at home.

And she was totally a nervous wreck.

As if he sensed her unease, he reached out to shake her hand and flash her a welcoming smile. "Please come in and have a seat."

She had planned to stay standing as she fed him her theory about Peter and Cormac and how Eleanor's kidnapping tied into it, but the way he guided her to a chair with a heavy, warm hand on her shoulder relaxed the unease in her stomach a notch.

Waiting for him to take his seat across from her, she drew a breath and held it deep in her lungs. Rarely did anyone shake her confidence, but the fear of confessing too much to him made her nerves twitch. She needed to be careful how she phrased her words, how she came across. She had to be a credible source in his eyes if she expected him to take her seriously. "You're a busy man, Deputy Director, and I appreciate you seeing me on such short notice."

"You happened to catch me between meetings." He leaned back in his chair and studied her face. "What can I do for you, Dr. Kent?"

"It's Brigit, and it's what I can possibly do for you. I believe I know who kidnapped Ella, but I can't prove it, and after last night I'll understand if you have trouble trusting me." She worried the four-leaf clover. "But trust is what I'm asking for."

At the mention of Ella, he sat forward, all business. "Go on."

"I believe Ella was kidnapped by Peter Donovan, also known as Peter O'Connor and a variety of other aliases. He's a terrorist who split off from the IRA in Northern Ireland in the 1990s and has been linked to car bombings and other activities, although he's only been caught and prosecuted once as a teenager."

Michael Stone's all-business face didn't change. Neither did his body. "And what does he want with my niece?"

False calm? Disbelief? She couldn't read him. Plunging forward, she laid out the important points of her theory involving Peter and Cormac O'Bern's reception. Through the whole thing, the director's affect never changed.

Finally, she explained Ella's role and watched his blue eyes harden. "She's being used as a distraction to suck resources away from the dedication ceremony today."

"You've shared this with Special Agent Edmonds?"

"I only found out Cormac O'Bern was in town less than an hour ago. I placed a call to Edmonds on the way here and left him a voice mail with the important details, but since I have no hard evidence, I doubt he'll be in any hurry to follow up. He hasn't even returned my call yet."

Director Stone remained impassive. The control of his body language was impressive. If she hadn't read his background bio while waiting to see the president, she would have thought he'd had spy training. Ruling that out, the only other cause appeared to be his God complex.

Meeting his steady gaze, she cleared her throat. "I'm bringing this to you because I know you value family above everything, even your job."

Something changed in his eyes, just for a split-second. Knowing she'd hit her mark, she continued. "If Donovan stays true to form, Ella won't be hurt, but there is a possibility innocent people attending O'Bern's reception today will be."

Again, his eyes shifted their focus. The wheels were turning. "How?"

"Donovan has been linked to multiple covert operations—taking out a target in a hotel room with a silenced gun, fiddling with brake lines to cause a target to have an accident—but he's also been linked to large, deadly operations like I mentioned. Car bombs, and also riots. With the publicity this ceremony is drawing, he'll go for something impressive. Something the news agencies will run twenty-four-seven."

"A bomb?"

Brigit gave him a tight nod and fingered her pendant again. "What I'm about to suggest goes against everything you've been trained for and all your natural instincts to protect your family." She hesitated, wishing she were standing near the door instead of sitting within reach of the director's large, strong hands. Even with his forced calm and direct manner, he still resembled a lion, ready to strike to defend his pride. "You need to tell the FBI and local police to pull off the kidnapping and double the security at the O'Bern reception."

The director blinked and let out a slow breath, drawing back into his chair. He settled an elbow on the chair's arm and tapped a finger against his desk as he stared at his laptop screen. "You want me to risk my niece's life on your speculations about Peter Donovan?"

"He won't hurt her."

Challenge sparked in his gaze as he met hers. It also echoed in his voice. "How do you know?"

Brigit ran through possible responses in her brain. Logical responses. The truth. Instead, she gripped the pendant tighter and spouted the lame one. "I just do."

He sat forward again, placing his elbows on his desk as his gaze bore into hers. The eyes darkened as if he could hypnotize her with them and reveal her deepest, darkest secret. Secrets. "I thought you were a child psychologist."

The challenge hung in the air, and Brigit let it. Michael Stone was no fool. He'd probably had her checked out before he'd left Thad and Ruth's last night. At the very least, he knew her doctorate thesis explored the minds of kidnappers.

When he got no answer, he probed deeper. "If you know so much about this Donovan, why haven't you helped put him away?"

The question caught her off guard. A vibration low in her stomach felt like she'd swallowed her BlackBerry and someone had just pinged her with an instant message.

Message received. Time to go. "Nothing will make me happier than to see Ella safely returned to your family. If Donovan's involved, I can say with ninety-nine percent certainty he'll stick to his pattern, and Ella will turn up physically fine. She'll be hungry and freaked out, and for awhile she'll experience nightmares. Maybe even suffer from post-traumatic stress. I strongly recommend therapy for a year or so to help her over the rough spots."

She stood, walked to the door and checked her watch. "O'Bern's reception starts in forty minutes. I'll be there if you have any questions or need my service."

She turned the doorknob and blew out of his office, glad she'd switched to the lower heels. The vibration had spread to the rest of her body, making her legs shake like Jell-O.

Chapter Eleven

Women were changelings. Capricious, fickle and mutable depending on the moment, their mood and their goal. They would fling themselves into the nebulous air of an idea with a courage specific to their gender and maintain equilibrium in the face of any threat. Their logic and reasoning often defied actual fact, and yet to Michael, more often than not, rang true.

He rotated his office chair to look out the window. Through the cracks in the blinds, he saw only strips of blue sky and a canopy of green leaves going to yellow and brown. The incomplete picture outside reflected the incomplete one in his mind. What Brigit had just told him troubled him on so many levels, he didn't know where to start.

Julia poked her head out of the bathroom. Seeing the room was clear, she joined him at the window, opening the blinds fully for a better view. "I believe her."

Women were as likely to be bitter enemies as they were to be indomitable sisters. Julia had no more reason to believe Brigit than he did, but the issue wasn't truth, it was trust. Julia was an ex-spy and the best counterintelligence analyst he'd ever had work for him. She trusted few and made accurate judgments in the blink of an eye. "I do too."

Glancing at her watch, she shook her head. "If there was time, I'd dig around in Brigit's past and try to tie her and her sister to this Peter Donovan, but forty minutes barely gives us enough of a window to find a recent picture of Donovan and ratchet up security. What are you going to do?"

Hate himself probably. He shifted his gaze from the striped fall landscape outside the window and looked up at her. "Go against all my natural instincts to protect my family."

Brigit pulled up short in the hallway. She'd forgotten one thing. One very important thing.

Pulling her BlackBerry out, she considered forgetting it. Phoning it in after she was outside the building. Having Truman fax it over after Cormac's dedication, just in case she was wrong. But no, she needed to give the information to Michael Stone and let him handle it. The kidnapping was truly out of her hands now. He was the only one, outside of her brother, who could shape the outcome of Eleanor Pennington's future.

Back in the waiting area, she scrolled through the application icons, found Tasks and punched it. She'd made a list of the parks and playgrounds in a five-mile radius of the Pennington home. Ella was sure to turn up at one of them in the next twenty-four hours.

Irene stared at her over her reading glasses, brows drawn together, as she continued her Durga routine. She cleared her throat after ending a call. "I already explained that cellular phones and digital devices are not to be used inside Langley without approval from the DCI himself."

Brigit ignored her and located the list. The phone couldn't receive anything inside the protected wall of Langley and it wasn't as if she were passing on secrets or anything. As she brushed past the secretary with a smile, she said, "Forgot something," and barged back into Stone's office.

Only to come to a dead halt with Irene on her heels. A woman stood next to the director, both of them facing his office window, but Stone was staring up at the woman's profile.

"Oh, Director," Irene stuttered. "I'm so sorry. I had no idea..."

As if pulled by the same string, they turned their heads in unison, and Brigit's breath caught in her throat. The woman was the FBI agent from the construction site. Where had she come from?

More importantly, what had she told Director Stone about their earlier encounter? And why had he been looking at her with such a mix of admiration and frustration?

Brigit's insides curled up like frostbitten flowers.

Director Stone waved Irene off. "It's okay, Irene."

The secretary gave Brigit a contrite look and huffed back out of the office.

Brigit glared at the woman on the other side of the desk. "Agent Barbie."

Her smile was tight. "Julia Torrison. Remember?"

As if she could have forgotten. Images of that morning's scene flashed in her brain.

Protect Tory. "If I didn't know better, I'd think you were following me, Agent Torrison, but that scenario doesn't fit, does it? You're always one step ahead of me instead of one behind."

Torrison shrugged. "Coincidence?"

While random coincidences did happen, Brigit knew this encounter was no coincidence. She glanced to her left, saw a door that had been closed before was now wide open. Inside, she could see a towel bar and the edge of a shower stall. Julia Torrison had been hiding in Deputy Director Stone's bathroom.

How interesting.

And awkward. Brigit's admiration for the good director nose-dived. She'd bet even Irene hadn't known her boss was carrying on with Agent Torrison right under her nose. To the right, Brigit noted an elevator door. Convenient for keeping trysts in his office secret.

Male personalities best suited to powerful positions drew women like pollen to bees. Keeping disgust from registering on her face, she met Director Stone's gaze with neutrality. "Forgive my interruption, but I forgot to mention that I believe Donovan will leave Ella at one of the playgrounds in the vicinity of the Pennington's home. There are three of them."

She grabbed a pen from the desktop and copied the names from her Task list to the top sheet of a square notepad. "Ella should show up at one of these spots in the next twenty-four hours. I wouldn't put surveillance on them though. Donovan will spot it and then there's no telling where he might dump her on his way out of town."

Through the whole interaction, Stone stayed quiet. Was he embarrassed to have been caught with Torrison? If so, he didn't show it. His body language and facial expressions never wavered. He was one hundred percent focused on Ella again. "Can we catch Donovan at the dedication?"

Betrayal burned inside her. Not the guilt kind like she'd experienced with the president a few hours ago. This was betrayal of another animal. An intimate one, which shocked and surprised her. How had Michael Stone gotten under her skin so fast?

But she knew the answer to that without hesitation. *He's such a family man.*

Whether Torrison had been hiding out to prevent their affair from being discovered or because Stone wanted her to eavesdrop on his conversation with Brigit, she didn't know. Bottom line, it didn't matter. The sting of the betrayal was sharp with mean-spirited candor.

Forcing it away, she reminded herself a little girl's well-being depended on her. The only real thing to worry about after that was the possibility Agent Torrison had told Director Stone about her rendezvous at the construction site with Tory.

If he did know, he seemed not to care enough to bring it up. Brigit decided to proceed likewise. "Donovan is probably the only person who knows where Ella is. You capture him and you'll seal Ella's fate."

"He'll use the information to cut a deal," Torrison said.

Peter's ability to compartmentalize his emotions and his actions as well as perpetuate the survival of an empty political formula spoke volumes about his personality.

A memory of their mother crying over returned books flashed through Brigit's mind. "Peter Donovan doesn't make deals," she said with quiet authority. "If you capture him, Ella's odds of dying will increase dramatically."

The focused but still calm energy emanating from the deputy director changed in a heartbeat. His body tensed under his jacket, and rage, raw and powerful, glinted in his eyes. "You said he wouldn't hurt her."

Before Brigit could answer, a deep male voice spoke from behind her. "Guess my invitation to the party got lost in the mail."

Torrison flinched. Stone shifted his rage back under an icy coolness. "Flynn," he said. "We have a situation."

Brigit studied the dark and dangerous-looking man in the doorway. Every hair on the back of her neck stood up. There was absolutely nothing neutral about this man. Anger radiated from his very pores. Controlled anger, but Brigit sensed he was struggling to keep it that way at the moment as he stared down Torrison. "I can see that."

"Dr. Kent." Torrison slid around the corner of the desk and motioned to the man. "This is my husband, Conrad Flynn. He's

CIA Director of Operations."

Flynn ignored Brigit, venom pouring from his gaze as he switched it from Torrison to Stone. Her worst fear confirmed, Brigit took a step back, checking the urge to flee the office. Julia's husband was about to lose it, and she didn't blame him one bit if her assumption about their affair was accurate.

Stone sat unfazed by Flynn's nonverbal death threat, and Brigit instinctively relaxed. His body language told her she had nothing to fear as he spoke to Flynn. "Dr. Kent has brought some important information to me this morning about a small-time terrorist named Peter Donovan. He may be the person behind Ella's kidnapping, and he may be planning to set off a bomb at today's Cormac O'Bern ceremony."

Flynn's death glare lessened at the mention of Ella. In the next minute, it completely evaporated as Stone laid out the nuts and bolts of Donovan's plans.

He glanced at Brigit with a perplexed expression. "Holy shit, there'll be five, six hundred people there today. Are you sure about this?"

"I'm not sure it will be a bomb, but it will be something major and will be targeted at Cormac O'Bern."

His dark eyebrows drew together. "What kind of bomb?"

Brigit and Stone spoke at the same time. "Car bomb."

Their gazes met and a ripple of something foreign and entirely too nice ran through her. She dropped her focus to her shoes, shocked again at the way he affected her.

Torrison spoke up. "The library's parking lot is roped off for the outdoor reception, but there will be dozens of cars parked up and down the streets surrounding it. Even if it's not a car bomb, we need to evacuate the area immediately, get the bomb squad and their dogs inserted, and circulate Donovan's photo to all security personnel in the area."

As Stone reached for his phone, Brigit stepped forward. "If you alert Donovan, he may disappear, thus making it nearly impossible for us to find her."

His hand stilled over the handset. He glanced at Flynn. "Options?"

Flynn set his hands on his hips, dropped his head back and stared at the ceiling without seeing it. After a few seconds, he returned his attention to Stone. "Have the Feds notify O'Bern there's been a threat on his life, but keep it quiet. Send an ambulance with a couple more Feds as the EMTs. They can take him out on a stretcher and transport him to a safe house. No O'Bern, no ceremony, no target. Everybody goes home healthy and Donovan doesn't know we're onto him. A six-year-old is trouble and he no longer needs a distraction. The worst he'll do is abandon her."

"But we don't know where she is," Torrison said. "We could still be signing her death warrant."

"Peter has never killed a child," Brigit told them. Stone, Torrison and then Flynn looked at her. Grasping at the four-leaf clover, she rubbed it hard between her finger and thumb. "It's a big risk, but I know his MO well. With a little luck, I'll be able to find her."

The silence lasted only a second. Stone nodded at her, a speck of appreciation flickering in his face. "Flynn, you and Julia head down there. We're running out of time. I'll alert Director Agouti, and then Brigit and I will follow you."

Flynn and Torrison scrambled out of the office, and Michael barked orders at Irene from his desk. Brigit moved slowly and steadily toward the still-open door.

Stone's voice brought her up short. "Skipping out now?"

"I have a car waiting at the main gate." She glanced over her shoulder. "I'll meet you there if you like."

"No." The order was voiced quietly. "You're riding with me. We need to talk."

Her limbs defying her, she waited patiently for the deputy director to show her to his personal elevator.

Chapter Twelve

Maryland

A church bell tolled a few blocks away, its baritone peals reaching far in the clear air. As he listened to the first clangs, Peter closed his eyes and saw the library in his mind, the grounds crowded with people attending the ceremony. He saw Cormac standing at the lectern at the top of the wide steps, his arms gesturing as he revved up the crowd. The library's Roman-style columns were interspersed with flags, creating a larger-than-life backdrop for the larger-than-life poet preaching world peace in front of them.

As the last echo of the church bells evaporated into the cool air outside, Peter opened his eyes and stared out the only window in the tiny apartment he hadn't boarded over. Even though the apartment was on the second story, it was too far on the outskirts of town to see anything more than the church steeple in the distance.

Although Peter looked out the window at the fall landscape, he saw the coming moments at the library from Moira's viewpoint. She insisted on doing her jobs alone. While Peter wanted to see Cormac take the bullet of death more than anything else in this world, he acquiesced to Moira's demands. Her focus, her energy, had to be harnessed and trained on the scope with no distractions. The kill had to be clean. The escape as well.

He envied her skill. His mind generated dozens of ideas a day, each one a labyrinth of details, possibilities and alternate outcomes. To keep up, his body was always in motion as well. There were far too many voices in his head to sit still and breathe like a yogi over the scope of a rifle. He preferred his statements to be loud, messy and a symbol of anarchy. A sniper kill was singular, perfect, clean.

Peter envied Moira her youth as well. Age was catching up with him, taunting him with mistakes and errors that would land him behind bars again. He would kill himself before he let it happen. The time had come to step back, return to his home, reinvent himself and his dedicated group into a legitimate political force. The idea, once repulsive, now tugged at his mind with ever-increasing demand.

This last hurrah should have been catastrophic. Instead it would be a simple exclamation point. O'Bern would be martyred and Peter would live to go on and rise as a popular figure in his place, undoing his years of peace-mongering with an effective campaign strategy to draw in youth who grew complacent and tired of peace. They were a selfish lot these days and ripe for growing seeds of dissension.

An image of Brigit's face blipped across his mind. She was in town, no doubt to see Cormac. A traitor like his old friend, she deserved to die as well.

But a quick execution was too painless for her. She deserved to suffer for killing their mother, for trying to turn Tory against him. For pretending she wasn't related to him, while at the same time following his path and trying to clean up or cover up the destruction he wrought.

She posed as an advisor, a psychiatrist. Whatever guise was needed to conceal her true past and buddy up to government officials and other power players. Peter knew all about who she really was and who she worked for. The Americans were as stupid as the British. While they watched over their shoulder for the enemy nipping at their heels, the real danger was standing in front of them, pretending to help.

After he was done with Cormac, Peter would think more about Brigit. She would be an impediment to his political career. Therefore, she would have to go.

In the bathroom, the girl stirred, and Peter turned his head to listen for a moment. Her fingernails scratched at the door like a dog. Again, Brigit's face flashed through his mind. An idea came to him and he smiled.

There would be no exclamation point for her. Brigit deserved her own personal anarchy. His mind suddenly filled with possibilities.

Chapter Thirteen

The ride to Maryland in Michael Stone's Navigator wasn't as bad as Brigit envisioned. Even though she had to face him in the split rear seating, the deputy director spent most of the ride on his cell phone, coercing the FBI and other nameless entities to trust his judgment on the impending disaster.

As Brigit and Truman sat on the leather seat across from him listening to him make high-ranking officials believe the plan he was pulling together was really their idea, Brigit guessed that in the end, if all went well and the innocent public was no more the wiser, Michael would also let those other officials take the credit.

The ability to command, rather than demand, was the true essence of power. Few men or women understood the fundamental difference. Because Michael did, he and his advice were trusted and respected from the president on down. People wanted to believe the deputy director of Central Intelligence because they believed *in* him.

He never raised his voice, never argued. He presented the facts as he knew them and requested immediate assistance with the same calm demeanor Brigit had observed in his office. If doubt was raised, he overrode it with reassurance and a smile, which conveyed his conviction even over the phone.

Everyone complied. Special units, SWAT teams and all available personnel in the giant beast of law enforcement were activated. All with a phone call from one man.

Brigit closed her eyes, awed at the control he held in the palm of his hand.

When she opened her eyes, Truman nudged her and conveyed how impressed he was with a simple lifted brow and quirk of his mouth. Brigit had to agree. Michael Stone in full-blown leader mode was damned impressive.

And sexy as hell.

He took an incoming call and she watched his body language change. His head moved but a sliver, but his stare shifted to look at her. His free hand rested on the door handle and he eased back a bit into his leather bucket seat. "What did you find out about her?"

Heat rose in Brigit's cheeks, and she fidgeted. Clearing her throat, she forced her gaze away from him and looked out the window at the passing scenery. The car had slowed to a crawl and she told herself it was the sudden delay making her antsy and not the deputy director's laser-beam gaze.

They still had to be five or six blocks from the library. How much would he discover or deduce about her in that time?

And why did she care?

Mental, emotional and physical intimacy scared her. Her secrets had to stay buried, which made friendships and relationships impossible. The few friends she had were more acquaintances then honest-to-God, go-to-lunch-and-share-your-lipstick kinds of friends. Her coworkers boiled down to Truman, who knew the deets but also loved her enough to keep them buried. Past trips down the boyfriend lane had been short and unsatisfying because she was constantly hiding her emotions, her thoughts and her past. Relationships of any kind did not fit into her complicated life.

Worrying her four-leaf clover pendant, she distracted herself from Michael and her dysfunctional life by focusing on Peter. If even one thing appeared to be off to him, even a simple slowdown in the traffic pattern, he'd abandon his plan and possibly take it out on Ella. Hurting the child would go against his code, but he had grown more reckless over the past few years. One red flag during today's event could throw him into a panic. Brigit only hoped the ambulance trick played out real enough to escape Peter's natural instincts.

Michael ended the call and Brigit's gaze automatically swung to meet his. His pause lasted just a second, but told her he wasn't happy with her. However, when he spoke, he was all business. "Ambulance is on its way with two trained SWAT members disguised as EMTs to handle O'Bern. Teams are moving in to form a staggered perimeter around the library.

Snipers are in route. Everyone's been supplied with a photo of Donovan."

Truman pushed his glasses up on his nose. "Snipers?"

"With scopes," Michael said. "To look for suspicious behavior."

Brigit nodded, peeling her attention off the sexy man across from her and back to the landscape crawling by at the pace of a snail. Even though she tried to ignore him, she could see his fixed stare from the corner of her eye. His concentrated focus, like a physical hand, roamed over her. The touch of it was warm and commanding, just like his voice had been on the phone. Her pulse tripped over itself. *Mind control*, she told herself. *He's trying to will me to confess.*

As the car came to a full stop, she cleared her throat again and rubbed her sweaty palms on her thighs. "Traffic must be bad," she said to no one in particular. "We're going to be late."

Michael's voice conveyed none of her anxiousness. "Traffic's being routed away from the area, therefore slowing normal patterns."

Truman spoke from beside Brigit. "Then how will we get through?"

"We'll get through," Michael said. His tone brokered no further questions.

Brigit wasn't sure the DD of Central Intelligence should even be in the area. "Shouldn't you be back in your office safe and sound? I mean, we're going in blind here, and it's not exactly without danger."

He clenched his teeth and a muscle in his jaw worked before he spoke. "We are quite possibly messing with the health and well-being of my niece. My place is here, dangerous or not."

Underneath the cultivated calm, he had to be struggling with mixed emotions. While the situation was seemingly out of his control, his response took a small measure of control back. He wasn't rash, but he wasn't one to play it safe either. Pursuing a safe resolution, not only to the celebration, but also to the kidnapping, helped him deal with his fear.

Being in control was a big issue in Brigit's life too. Lately it seemed the more she tried to bring order to her life and leave the past behind, the more tangled in chaos she became. Like her father's incarceration and finally catching up with Tory only to fail at being a sister to her again. Stopping Peter could change all that, but she'd have to make sure she really did stop him.

Michael was still intent on bending her mind to his will. His smoldering eyes, dark as sin inside the car, bored into her. Suddenly the big backseat seemed cramped, the air hot and weighted. She unbuttoned her trench and considered rolling down the window. Why wasn't the car moving?

She punched her BlackBerry out of sleep mode. The display window time read ten-oh-three. "We're late, and the ambulance is going to get stuck in this traffic jam too." She grabbed the door handle and gave a yank. "I'll walk the rest of the way and keep an eye on things. See if I can spot Donovan."

Jumping out of the car, she drew a breath of cold November air. Truman and Michael's voices clashed against each other as she slammed the car door shut and half-ran over to the sidewalk. If she'd been wearing her sneakers, she could have taken off at a sprint. Even though her heels were only an inch and a half, she could barely trot.

Hearing a car door slam behind her, she jogged a little faster, peeking at the people in the cars she passed. Some of them stared back. None of them were Peter.

She didn't make it to the end of the block before she heard confident, heavy footsteps closing the gap. Unable to cross because of the turning traffic, she cringed even before she heard his voice. "What the hell are you doing?"

Michael Stone stood a foot behind her. His bodyguard was two feet behind him.

Refusing to meet his eyes, she watched the cars turning in front of her, waiting for the last one so she could cross the street. "I'm going to the library to see how I can help."

A hand clamped on her wrist, whirling her around. Her left ankle wobbled and she fell into the director's chest. He righted her gently, but didn't let go. "You're not going anywhere without me, Doctor."

She pushed against the wall of muscle and straightened, staring up at his face. While he was ticked, a hint of amusement flickered in his eyes.

Her heart slammed against her ribs. "I can help look for Donovan."

Brad had gone into bodyguard mode beside them, using his body to block Michael from the eyes of those nearby as best he could. Brad was big and broad like a rugby player, but Michael was even bigger, broader. "Deputy Director, I think it would be wise to return to the car."

Michael ignored him, his attention completely on her. "You could also tip him off."

"Tip him off?" Was he saying what she thought he was saying? Did he think she was working with Peter?

Bits and pieces of ideas knocked against her brain. In a weird way, his unsaid accusation made sense. "You don't trust me."

The security officer interrupted again. "Deputy Director..."

"Hell no, I don't trust you." Michael scanned the area as if Brad's words had finally sunk in. "You show up at Ruth's hours after Ella disappears. You come to me today with this wild story about Donovan and O'Bern fifty minutes before the ceremony and tell me Ella will be okay. You suggest I pull the FBI and local police off her case to descend on this ceremony like Grant taking Richmond. And then you tell me she'll show up freaked out but otherwise unharmed at a park after this is over."

He rubbed his thumb against her racing pulse. "You know too much about Donovan, about Ella, about this ceremony, and yet you claim you're not directly tied to any of it. What else would I think? Either you're helping Peter Donovan or you're lying to me about who you really are."

Before she could reply, he began dragging her back to the car. Between his immense strength and her wobbling ankles, she didn't stand a chance against him, but she fought him anyway. By the time she landed in the backseat of the Lincoln with him beside her, they were both out of breath. Michael's hand still circled her wrist.

With her free hand, she smacked the top of his. "I never took you as someone who would manhandle a woman," she spat at him.

He released her, honest surprise breaking over his face. He sat back and shook his head. "I'm not." Regret took the place of surprise. He glanced out the window and back to Brigit. "My apologies. The stress of the situation..." His voice trailed off as the sound of an ambulance siren drew near.

She almost felt guilty about pretending to be hurt, but then once again his eyes went serious and all emotion left his face and posture. He leaned toward her. "Why do you know so much about Peter Donovan?"

Her throat closed up. Truman, loyal as always, answered for her. "Dr. Kent has done extensive research on the minds of criminal kidnappers to develop a code-based profile for intelligence services worldwide. Donovan is one of the men she studied."

Michael's gaze never left hers. The laser beam bore into her again, reaching for her mind, touching her soul. "A midlevel criminal whose heyday was fifteen years ago? He's never even been directly tied to any kidnappings. Why would you study him?"

Someone he'd spoken to on the phone had filled him in about Peter. Brigit looked away and again the well-trained Truman came to her defense. "The criminal who gets away is a more interesting research specimen than the one who gets caught."

Michael reached out and touched Brigit's wrist. "Not in my world."

~ ✦ ~

An ambulance, siren screaming, zoomed by on the street below. Moira took her eyes from the binoculars and glanced at the digital clock she'd set up on the windowsill. Ten-ten. The ceremony for Cormac O'Bern was scheduled to start at ten o'clock. Everything was in place. Her rifle and scope had been double- and triple-checked. Wind speed, velocity and humidity readouts changed constantly below the clock's time display. By now she'd expected to see O'Bern at the lectern. In America, however, nothing started on time.

Once a trained sniper for the Palestinian Authority's National Guard, Moira's superior skill depended as much on her patience level as her ability to hit the mark with deadly accuracy. As Peter Donovan's lover, she had stretched her patience level to even more extremes. A delay in the start of the ceremony did not cause her concern or anxiety. She lifted the binoculars to her eyes again and scanned the area.

A mass of people blotted out the long concrete steps of the library. Because the building couldn't handle that many people on one floor, the reading was being held outside. The reception, as well, in the roped off parking lot behind it.

Limos and other long, black, official-looking cars continued to pull up on a side street to deliver dignitaries, actors and politicians invited to the event. The majority were ushered inside, where they would watch O'Bern deliver his speech and read his poetry on TV in posh, safe quarters.

The speech would last twenty minutes. O'Bern, standing behind the lectern and gazing down on his adoring fans, would look like a king, Peter had said, on his throne.

Moira smiled to herself. The king was about to be knocked off his throne for good.

A wave went through the crowd and she lowered the binoculars to find the source. The ambulance had been let through the barricades and was easing up to the curb in front of the library's steps as it prodded the crowd to part.

Moira frowned as she watched EMTs exit the ambulance and jostle a stretcher up the steps. The crowd parted as if Moses had struck the ground with his staff, allowing the men and the stretcher to pass. They disappeared into the building.

This wasn't a contingency in her plan. Still, Moira forced herself to remain calm. Drawing in deep, even breaths, she continued her circular sweep of the grounds with her binoculars, noting where the undercover security agents had positioned themselves, extra surveillance cameras had been placed, and coming back to the library entryway.

A woman exited the library and stepped to the podium. She fiddled with the microphone for a moment. The window was open and Moira could hear the tone of the woman's voice, but not all of the actual words as they echoed and died in the distance. What she could make out was the groan of the crowd. It was a groan of disappointment.

Disappointment meant only one thing.

The king wasn't coming out.

Was he sick? For an ambulance to arrive, it had to be serious. An injury?

A flutter of anxiety pinched Moira's stomach. All the waiting, all the planning. Peter would be furious if this didn't work.

She sighed, her attention caught by a foursome passing by the podium and the woman who was still talking. Three men and a woman approached the library doors, stopping as security questioned them. Just before they were ushered in, the woman turned to look out over the crowd.

Moira's breath caught in her throat.

Brigit?

Moira's patience with Peter Donovan vanished in a heartbeat.

SIS and their spy group, MI5, had been nipping at her heels for two years. Peter had promised her he'd protect her. He'd promised her this job was a simple, straightforward assassination. He'd promised her a clean getaway.

Brigit's appearance changed everything. If MI5 was in town, Moira was dead the moment she pulled the trigger on O'Bern.

She swore under her breath and watched the EMTs reemerge from the building, the stretcher once again between them as they carried a blanketed form down the steps, flanked by security guards. Some of the crowd had already dispersed, but many of the remaining people crowded forward, gawking at the stretcher even as they were pushed back from it.

Too many people blocked her view of the stretcher, but Moira knew who they were gawking at. O'Bern wasn't giving any speeches today.

Dropping the binoculars from her eyes, she surveyed her handiwork in the upstairs room. She could leave the rifle, scope and field meter behind. She could even leave Peter behind. What she couldn't leave behind was her past or the fact Brigit was only two and half blocks away.

Her gaze fell on the rifle and an idea dawned. Moving behind the table where the tripod was secured, Moira took a deep, cleansing breath and refocused her attention through the scope. Adjusting the dial, she brought the library's entrance into view.

Patience, she told herself. *One good shot is all you need to bring her, and Peter, down.*

Chapter Fourteen

A twelve-block area around the library was secured. SWAT units were slotted. Bomb-sniffing dogs were on standby. Undercover cops, Secret Service members and all available FBI agents were milling through the still-lingering crowd outside, looking for anything suspicious. Cormac O'Bern was on his way to a safe house over the Virginia state line.

Inside the hundred-year-old building, Michael watched Brigit as she scanned the crowd and surrounding area from a window on the first floor. She was as irksome as she was sexy. God only knew why he found that so damn attractive.

As if she sensed his presence behind her, she glanced over her shoulder. "We're running out of time. Why isn't the crowd dispersing faster?"

"You think he'll still execute his plan?"

She started to speak, paused. "Taking O'Bern out of the picture changes things, but there's no guarantee. Donovan's gone to a lot of trouble to set this up."

Flynn emerged from a hallway to Michael's left, with Truman Gunn trailing after him. He nodded at Brad Kinnick as he stopped in front of Michael. "There are still four cars in the cordoned-off radius," he said. "Two within a block of here. All have valid plates and only one is registered to an out-of-state owner. Maryland PD hasn't been able to track down any of the four owners yet. SWAT tactical can send in their bomb bot or Rad sensor, but if Donovan is still watching the area, he'll know O'Bern's ambulance ride was for show."

Bomb-detecting robots were highly accurate and used by most metro police departments but hardly covert. Bomb-finding sensors—metal arms attached to a vehicle which used radiation to detect explosives—were less obvious and just as accurate, but scarce, even in the D.C. area. Getting several of them to the library would take a dozen phone calls and hours they didn't have.

"A remote bomb could be anywhere," Brigit said, talking to the window.

Flynn frowned at Michael before glaring at her back. "You said it would be a car bomb."

She did a one-eighty and stared Flynn down. "I know what I said. Now that I'm here, though, I can see how difficult it would be for him to get a car close enough to blow the front steps and take O'Bern out. The difficulty level is too high. If he was going to set off a bomb, he would've gotten closer."

She turned back to the window and began pointing out possible hiding places. "Those huge planters, the base of the flagpole, the water fountain. The garbage receptacles beside the benches in the far corner. Any or all of them are potential bomb holders."

Flynn put his hands on his hips, let out an impatient breath. "I'll alert the undercover agents outside to be on the look out for flowerpot bombs." He shook his head at Michael and walked back the way he'd come. Gunn raised an eyebrow at Brigit, and she motioned with her head for him to follow Flynn.

The entryway grew quiet again. Moving to the window next to Brigit, Michael tried not to stare at her peaches-and-cream skin, or her thick, dark hair, free of its ponytail and brushing her shoulders. He tried not to examine the way her trench coat molded to her waist and flared out at her hips, emphasizing both. Her body hummed with energy and his happily tightened in response.

Forcing his attention away from her, he stared out at the empty lectern and the large concrete pots overflowing with fall mums and ivy on either side. As he watched undercover agents dawdle on the steps, synapses fired in his brain, followed by a niggle in his gut. The crowd had thinned considerably, and the dignitaries and Hollywood stars had been evacuated from the building. Still, the niggle told him he was missing something. Something obvious.

What if it isn't a bomb?

Brigit gripped the windowsill. "Damn it. Why don't those people go home?"

He understood her frustration, born out of fear, because it crawled under his skin too. "Why would a man who was willing to kill dozens, maybe hundreds, of innocent people not kill my niece when this is over?"

She glanced at him, something unreadable in her eyes before she shut it down. "I told you, it's not his MO. He doesn't hurt the children he kidnaps."

As a psychologist who had studied the asshole, she had to know what was behind Donovan's motivation. "Why not?"

She drew in a breath and sighed, seemingly at war with herself, but her eyes were clear and steady as she spoke. "Would you think less of me if I told you I don't know?"

Actually he thought more of her. It didn't ease his fear about Ella or keep the idea at bay that this was somehow his fault for not personally keeping her safe, but at least Brigit Kent was finally telling him the truth. Admitting she wasn't perfect, or better than him, or some mysterious woman driving him to the brink of insanity. She was human. A beautiful, smart, mysterious woman. "No."

She turned her face back to the window. "That's the one thing I've never been able to figure out about Peter."

The way she said his first name made Michael's scar itch. Her connection to this guy was weird. Almost like she knew too much about him. Like she was obsessed with him.

Her gaze darted around the area outside. "He's elusive, compulsive and full of righteous certitude. A brilliant mind molded by religious beliefs and a core arrogance of superiority. He's a rocket."

"A rocket?"

She stepped back from the window and nodded once. "He's crazy, but predictably so."

Michael watched her walk away, unable to resist checking out the way her purposeful walk showcased her backside. Her scent, a vanilla and cinnamon combination that reminded him of his mother's homemade tapioca pudding, faded away with her. She pushed open one of the library's glass doors and walked out into the sunshine.

Through the window, he saw her step up to the lectern and scan the area, high and low, searching for what he didn't know. Did Donovan know her as well as she seemed to know him?

He followed her line of sight, scrutinizing nearby buildings and duplexes. So many windows. Here and there a person's face stared out from them, watching the street, the library...

The niggle in his gut jackknifed his brain and a fine-edged instinct dropped his focus to Brigit. All the hair on the back of his neck stood up like he'd been shocked.

He was running for the library door before he took his next breath. "Brigit," he yelled as he threw open the door. "Get down!"

She jerked her head around at the sound of his voice, her body shifting to the right. As if an invisible fist hit her in the left shoulder, she spun and fell, eyes going wide, just before Michael caught her.

A bullet smashed into one of the planters, sending yellow flowers shooting up in a geyser. Shouts rang out.

Bear-hugging Brigit, Michael rolled with her, moving as close as possible to the only protection they had—the lectern.

As another bullet struck, wood splintered above Michael's head. More shouts and the pounding of feet echoed over the ringing in his ears. Knowing he and Brigit were far from sheltered from the sniper's bullets, he angled his prone body over hers.

The feel of her under him, the smell of her hair where his nose was buried, the jerk of her chest under his as she tried to draw breath, tried to speak, fired his senses, awakening something deep and remote inside him. He couldn't describe it and didn't want to. He wanted, needed, to protect her.

She made a sound in her throat, a hurt sound that chilled the blood in his veins. Lifting his head a fraction to look down, he found her soldier's eyes staring back at him, blocking fear and pain. "I can't move my left arm," she murmured.

Shifting, he glanced between them and saw blood blooming like a rose on her coat sleeve. A hole was torn in the material and the blood began to drip on the ground. The chill in his blood went arctic cold.

The bastard had shot her. By the location of her wound, he'd been aiming for her heart.

Fuck. He had to get help but he couldn't move until he was sure the rain of bullets had stopped. Forcing his voice to convey calmness, he stroked her hair. "Your shoulder took a hit, but you'll be all right. Just hang tough, okay? I'll get you out of here in a minute."

She met his gaze, still struggling not to show any emotion, but it was there. Fear, shock, pain.

Nose to nose, he willed her to believe him. She swallowed hard and blinked. The fear in her eyes subsided, and she gave him a nod. The tight tug of her lips into a forced smiled conveyed gratitude.

Brad Kinnick came speeding toward them in full-blown bodyguard mode, barking orders into the radio in his watch. Still, Michael covered the length of Brigit's body with his. Until he was sure the sniper was done, he refused to move a muscle.

In the next blink of Brigit's eyes, though, he realized just how heavy his much larger and very tense body must be on top of her. She wasn't tense, but soft and warm beneath him, their legs intertwined. Her right arm was wrapped around his waist, her hand on his back beneath his jacket and radiating warmth through his shirt.

Warmth that sent a jolt right to his groin.

Just the adrenaline, he told himself, hoping Brigit didn't notice his thigh pressed between hers or his hand still stroking her soft hair as if it had a mind of its own.

Through the haze in his brain, Michael heard Brad shouting orders above him to the cops and FBI agents. It truly was over. At the sound of approaching footsteps, he forced his attention from Brigit's face and moved sideways to see Flynn racing across the open entryway to his side. Gunn was nowhere in sight.

Before Flynn could say a word, Michael eased himself off Brigit. "Get an ambulance."

Brad spoke, his gaze scanning the area as he tried to shield Michael best he could. "Three were on standby already. They're all three on the way."

"You hit?" Flynn's frowning gaze was on Michael's shoulder.

Glancing down, he saw the blood on his jacket. Brigit's blood. Looking back at her, there was suddenly too much blood. She was too still. Her eyelids fluttered, and she stared up at the blue sky, dazed.

"She's going into shock," Michael said, shrugging out of his jacket.

Flynn was one step ahead of him. He stripped off his cotton shirt and handed it to Michael. "Use this."

Michael dropped his jacket and wadded up the soft cotton,

still warm from Flynn's body, before pressing the cloth against Brigit's shoulder wound. A war of weird emotions convened inside him. It should be *his* shirt, *his* warmth, stopping Brigit's blood, not Flynn's.

"Goddammit," he swore under his breath. "How the hell did this happen?"

Flynn took Michael's jacket and laid it like a blanket over Brigit's body below her shoulders. "Maybe Donovan wasn't after O'Bern like we thought."

Brigit's gaze found Michael's and she shook her head, just a fraction. "Peter would never hurt me."

There it was again. A connection between her and Peter Donovan. Almost as if she knew him…intimately. Michael's gut plummeted into his nether regions and his mouth went dry. Had they been friends? Lovers? Accomplices?

The implications of such a relationship to Brigit's career, much less her state of mind, were serious, but he knew it wasn't the implications screwing with his gut. The reason he recoiled at the thought of her and Ella's kidnapper having once been friends or lovers was because it triggered emotions he'd buried after Julia had left him.

And if Brigit Kent could cause that kind of turmoil in him, who was he to question *her* state of mind?

Detaching himself from the anger, disappointment, and, yes, jealousy burning a hole in his stomach, he looked up at Flynn. "Where the hell's that ambulance?"

Chapter Fifteen

Brigit gritted her teeth against the pain in her shoulder as she sat on an unforgiving gurney in the ER in nothing but her bra and dress pants. Her trench and gray jacket had disappeared, and her shirt had been shredded by the EMTs to get to her wound on the way to the hospital. The injury was nothing more than a deep cut, thanks to Michael Stone. If he hadn't yelled at her, startled her so she'd turned, the bullet would have hit her in the chest. She would now be in the morgue instead of the emergency room.

She glanced at him and Truman standing in the corner. Both had grim expressions. She'd already given a statement to the police and been told a city-wide manhunt was underway. Truman's eyes were focused on his BlackBerry as he ignored hospital rules about turning off cell phones and busily typed a text message. No doubt alerting her superiors about the situation.

Michael, however, stared at her with half-lidded eyes, a tiny tic below one betraying his calm demeanor.

"You're safe now, but what about Ella?" he'd asked her as soon as the police had left.

It wasn't a question she could answer with certainty. "Someone was targeting O'Bern, and Donovan looks good as a suspect. Even though things didn't go according to his plan, we can still hope Ella turns up unharmed within the next twenty-four hours."

"Why would Donovan shoot you?"

He wouldn't, would he? Brigit shook her head. "First of all, Donovan's not a professional sniper, and secondly, he has no reason to harm me specifically."

"But somebody did."

Moira. The name flashed through her mind with the speed of a hollow-tipped slug. "The bullet was originally intended for O'Bern, I'm sure of it. Donovan probably hired a sniper. When O'Bern was carted away, perhaps the shooter became frustrated and shot at me because I just happened to step up to the lectern."

Was it her imagination or was Michael again probing her mind with his intense blue eyes? "You were trying to draw Donovan out, weren't you?"

A nurse interrupted any further questioning, relieving Brigit from answering. In a way, she *had* been trying to draw out her brother. She'd never guessed by bullet.

By ballot or bullet, our day will come. Tory's recital of the old IRA's motto rang in her head as Michael's x-ray vision burned her skin and the nurse checked her pulse. Heat rose in her cheeks, and with it an intense need to cover herself. She scanned the skinny bed and nearby cart for a sheet or her trench coat but found neither.

While Michael's gaze was in no way solicitous—in fact, at the moment she guessed she could be sitting in front of him completely naked and he wouldn't show one sign of attraction—she was exposed in ways she couldn't explain. Just like in the Navigator, he seemed to be peeling away her carefully constructed layers and infiltrating her mind.

A female doctor slapped the white curtain aside, reading Brigit's name from a chart in her hands before glancing up. "Brigit Kent?"

When Brigit nodded, the doctor scanned the chart again. Short, with dark hair and eyes, she introduced herself even as she read. "I am Dr. Lakshmi." Her attention focused on Brigit's face. "Gunshot wound, yes?"

"Yes." Brigit glanced at the layers of gauze and tape forming a fat padding over her shoulder. "Just brushed the skin. A few stitches and I should be good to go."

Michael took a step forward. "The bullet did more than brush her skin. It gouged out tissue, and since she has little fat on her arms, it probably took out muscle too."

He was right and it would hurt like a bitch for awhile. "You make it sound life-threatening." She tried to sound dismissive.

Challenge rose in Michael's gaze. "It could have been."

Dr. Lakshmi tossed the chart on the cart and grabbed a pair of latex gloves from a box. "I will judge that." Her dark brows drew down in a frown as she addressed Michael and Truman. "You gentlemen need to step outside to the waiting area."

For the first time in hours, Brigit saw the charming Michael surface. He smiled at the doctor and flashed his CIA identity badge in front of her face. The contradiction between his smile and his stiff, don't-mess-with-me body language conveyed he was a man on a mission. He would play nice...up to a point. Then he'd go Batman on everyone's ass. "We're staying. Dr. Kent may still be in danger."

The doctor studied his smile, his badge and his stance as she wrangled a glove on and snapped latex against one wrist. "Hospital policy—"

Truman ceased his texting. Her assignments always put her next to the bigwigs, but she was never, ever, to share the spotlight with them. "Hospital policy has been overruled for now by the Department of Homeland Security." He probably already had her walking papers on his PDA, but no one would know it but him. "I can get Director Halden on the phone if you have questions."

Brigit glanced between Batman and the Boy Wonder and an unexpected grin worked its way to her lips. "It's okay," she told Dr. Lakshmi, even though she hated the thought of Michael watching while she got stitched up. Watching her, period. "They can stay."

The doctor shook her head and began cutting away the padding around Brigit's shoulder. Brigit turned her head away, wincing as needle-like pain radiated down her arm and up into her neck. She'd refused pain meds other than a couple of locals near the entry and exit wounds when the nurse had cleaned them and repacked the area with gauze, but now she wished she'd taken the Percocet the nurse had offered.

No drugs, though. It was her policy. While she hated pain, she hated being out of control even more. It was her first gunshot wound, but she'd been trained to handle it. She could do it. Even with Michael Stone watching her like a guard dog.

He was so quiet. Not the calculating quiet she'd witnessed before. This quiet was the type she'd seen in her father after her mother's death. The kind of quiet she herself had known all too well.

Guilt.

As the nurse and doctor began the procedure to sew Brigit's skin back together, his energy pulled at her. She let her attention drift to him, hoping it would keep her mind off her nauseated stomach.

He was wearing his jacket again. The dark stains caused by her blood had blended into the black fabric. Remembering the sensation of being under that jacket made her shiver. The softness of the silk lining had brushed her skin and the warmth lingering from Michael's body had wrapped around her like a welcome blanket after she'd been shot. She'd just wanted to curl up under it, ignore the blood and pain, and close her eyes.

When the actual stitching began, Brigit couldn't feel the needle working its way through her skin. Yet the nurse's firm hold on her and the doctor's brusque movements caused more pain to radiate up and down her arm. Keeping her face turned away from the needle, she wished she was under Michael's jacket again. The irony struck her like a punch to her stomach. While typically attracted to power-hungry men, she was never entirely comfortable around them, and she'd certainly never wanted to hide from the world wrapped in one's jacket.

Lifting her gaze to his, she sent him a smile to tell him...what? That she was all right? That it wasn't his fault she was getting stitches? That she was grateful he'd saved her from certain death?

His gaze held hers with its usual reserve, but something flared in his eyes she recognized. Something that echoed in her blood, and suddenly she knew it wasn't his jacket she was really interested in. He stepped to her side, and without a word, took her trembling hand in his.

She forgot the throbbing in her arm and neck and closed her eyes. What the hell had she gotten herself into? Someone had deliberately tried to kill her and all she could think about was how Michael Stone's arms would feel around her instead of his jacket. How his hands would feel on her neck, her shoulders, her hips...

The pain, she could blame her pointless daydreams on the pain. Or the adrenaline crash from being shot. Or maybe she really was in shock...

Good rationalizing, she told herself. *Keep it up.*

Half an hour later, her need to bury herself in Michael's arms firmly squashed and her hand reluctantly removed from his, she was ready to walk out of the hospital with her bandaged shoulder.

Dr. Lakshmi had other ideas. "Overnight observation," she ordered.

"For what?" Brigit said.

Dr. Lakshmi set her lips as she signed a form on the clipboard. "Treatment for infection and possible shock." She eyed Michael and Truman before giving Brigit a scolding look. "And you could still be in danger. Hospital is safe."

Before Brigit could open her mouth to argue, the woman handed the clipboard to the nurse and left the small ER cubicle with a flourish, the privacy curtain swaying with her exit.

The nurse tucked the clipboard under her arm and handed Brigit a faded hospital gown. "Let's get you upstairs."

"I'm fine. I don't need to stay overnight."

Truman pocketed his phone. "Actually, it's a good idea."

The message in his eyes was clear. JOE insisted she lay low. "But really I—"

"Need to follow the doctor's orders." Michael gritted his teeth for a second, worry warring with impatience. He spoke to Truman. "I'll order a guard be put outside her door."

Truman, the traitor, nodded. The nurse opened the gown and began sliding it up Brigit's arms.

Brigit narrowed her eyes at Michael. "If you were me, with nothing more than a flesh wound, would you let the doctors keep you overnight for observation?"

"I'm not you."

"Meaning what? Because I'm female, I'm weak and can't protect myself?"

Batman bristled, hands on hips. "Being female has little to do with it. Being foolhardy does."

Foolhardy? "Please give me credit for an ounce of intelligence. I never dreamed there'd be a sniper there today, nor that said sniper would take a shot at me."

A flash of irritation made his narrowed eyes darken. She saw him mentally dig in his heels. "Intelligence is not the same thing as common sense."

Footsteps sounded near the curtain. A male voice came

from the other side. "Deputy Director? There's a phone call for you at the desk. It's the president."

"Excuse me." He nodded at Truman, some secret male message passing between them, and left the cubicle, sending one more challenging glance in Brigit's direction.

Anger burned in her veins. The nurse smiled a knowing smile at her, which only made the anger rush faster and burn deeper. "That man is gorgeous," she said in a murmured woman-to-woman voice.

Truman stepped forward as the nurse moved behind Brigit to tie the gown in place. He lowered his voice a notch. "Stay in the hospital at least for the afternoon until I decipher what happened and who was involved."

Brigit glared at him. "Bring me fresh clothes ASAP."

"Dr. Kent," he said, his voice full of warning.

"Bring me fresh clothes or I'll fire your ass."

His eyes bore into hers as he tried to go Michael on her. "Two hours, that's all I'm asking for. Take your pain meds and get some sleep."

As the nurse guided her to lie down on the gurney, Brigit winced as pain shot up her neck again. "No meds. No sleep. You have one hour to get back here with my clothes."

Truman stepped back and sighed, shifting back into his normal *I-can't-do-anything-with-you* mode. "You're the boss, Gidge."

Brigit tugged at the gown and bit her lip in frustration. *For now, anyway.*

~ ✧ ~

As Conrad hit the lock button on the Jeep's driver side door, his work cell phone rang. He shut the door and half-jogged toward the hospital's rear entrance before yanking the phone off his belt. Julia was already inside. She'd been part of the FBI team assigned to keep an eye on Brigit Kent and he'd dropped her off before returning to the library. There he'd attached himself to the FBI evidence response team.

It hadn't taken long to pinpoint the origin of the bullets fired at the lectern. The sniper's rifle was a beauty. The Mark 12 Special Purpose Rifle was built for the U.S. Navy special operations snipers to replace the SEAL recon rifle. SEALs didn't like it as well, but it had been used by both Navy and Army special op marksmen with a high success rate. Clones of the rifle had made it into the public domain and even gamers could get their hands on one in *Tom Clancy's Ghost Recon 2*. The Douglas barrel was curved to maximize efficiency and minimize weight. The semi-automatic shot 77 grain bullets, which were more effective at longer ranges than standard bullets.

The phone rang again and Conrad glanced at the readout. It wasn't Julia but his best friend and colleague, Ryan Smith. "Smitty, what's up?"

Ryan's voice sounded far away. It was. The Chief of Station was calling from London. "I found out something interesting on the party you asked me to check into."

Yes. Smitty was a true genius when it came to uncovering information. It was one of the reasons he was Chief of Station. "Knew I could count on you."

"Yeah, well, you're not gonna like it."

Conrad's hand tightened on the phone. The hospital's automatic door slid open with a swish and he ignored the posted warning about turning off cell phones. "Hit me."

"Box eight-fifty."

Conrad stopped dead in his tracks. Box eight-fifty was the code Smitty used for Britain's Secret Intelligence Service, made up of two branches—MI5 and MI6—in reference to the post office box the group had once owned. "You're shitting me."

"Not sure she's full SIS, but she is a consultant. A very pricey, well-connected consultant. Her skills are varied and much in demand."

There was that consultant crap again. "For Irish nationalism?"

"My source says she's got high-level clearance, and her meetings include everyone from the Prime Minister on down, all classified."

A passing nurse shot daggers at Conrad as he started walking again. "Turn the phone off, sir," she said.

He gave her a wave and kept talking as he rounded a corner out of her sight line. "Why would Irish republicanism be top secret?"

"You got me."

"She holds citizenship in Ireland, England and America. Anything in her past strike you as odd?"

"Nothing."

Which struck Conrad as odd. Everyone in the SIS or the CIA had something damning in their past. It's what molded their character, seasoned their personality, motivated them. His secret army was proof.

"Off topic," Smitty said. "Where's Tango? She disappeared about three days ago after leaving me a cryptic message about freedom fighters."

Tango was the nickname Conrad had given Zara after she'd danced with a nasty terrorist named Alexandrov Dmitri and managed to survive. "She's here. I'll be sending her back to you soon."

"Don't you have someone else in your army you could send me?"

"There's always Ace."

Smitty made an exaggerated choking sound on his end. "No thanks. Say hi to Julia."

Conrad disconnected and found the woman in question heading his way. "We need to talk," she said.

"Not now. I've gotta find St—"

"Now." She steered him into an empty hallway. "It's about Zara."

Zara was not high on his priority list at the moment, but the look on Julia's face made him press pause on the other stuff. She took two steps away and then paced back to him. "When the doctor releases her tomorrow, she's coming home with us."

"Why? She's got a place."

"We need to keep an eye on her. Her sister's in Europe again and I don't want Zara home alone."

Something about her tone made his skin crawl. "What aren't you telling me?"

Julia cut her eyes to the left and then to the right and Conrad's stomach dropped an inch. He knew he was about to learn something he didn't want to know. "She's pregnant."

"She's *what*?"

Julia jerked a finger to her lips and lowered her voice as she repeated, "She's pregnant."

Conrad pressed his fingers to his temples. First Julia and now Zara? "What is this, an epidemic?"

Julia's brows drew together. "What?"

Dropping his hand, he shook his head. He couldn't deal with this now. "Look, I'll deal with the Zara issue later. Right now, I've got to talk to Stone. Where is he?"

"For God's sake, being pregnant is not an *issue,* Con."

It is for me. His secret army had just decreased by one. A very valuable one. "Where is Stone? Is he still with Kent?"

Julia looked at him as if he'd just turned into an alien. "He left ten minutes ago."

Shit. He didn't have anything truly damning on Brigit Kent, but the warning bells in his head were ringing loud and clear. Her being SIS, consultant or otherwise, and being a member of Homeland Security, was a big no-no. He needed to tell Stone what Smitty had learned about her and figure out how Dr. Psych could work both sides of the Atlantic.

Julia's gaze was scalding through his skin to his very bones. First he had to keep his wife happy and make sure Zara was getting the best possible medical care available. "Smitty just called to find out how Zara's doing. I'll go check on her for him."

"You'll go check on her for yourself and tell her she's coming home with us."

"Isn't that her call?"

"I'm worried about her, okay?"

Just like he was worried about his wife. "Okay, sure. I'll see what I can talk her into, but no guarantees."

Julia's tense face relaxed. "Room 314 on the O.B. ward." She leaned forward and gave him a peck on the cheek. "Michael requested I do security at Dr. Kent's door for the afternoon. I'll see you at home tonight, okay?"

Conrad caught movement in the hallway behind her. A tall, lanky suit with heavy-rimmed glasses was typing on a BlackBerry. "Isn't that Dr. Kent's assistant?" he said under his breath.

Julia turned to look and nodded. "Truman Gunn."

An idea flashed in his brain and he patted Julia's arm. "See you at home."

Walking with long strides to the bank of elevators, he

watched Truman enter the main area to his right, heading for the exit. The elevator dinged and the doors opened. Stepping inside, Conrad punched a speed dial button on his cell phone. When Smitty answered on the other end, Conrad said, "The key to this puzzle is Truman Gunn."

Chapter Sixteen

Ashford Heights

It was just after three in the afternoon when Michael walked down the front steps of Thad and Ruth's house and slid into the backseat of the Navigator.

Conrad Flynn was waiting for him. "How they doing?" he asked.

Michael slouched down in the seat, leaned his head back against the leather and closed his eyes. It had been a long fucking day. "They're hopeful, which may be worse if Ella turns up hurt or dead."

"Nah, you did the right thing. Hope is always better than the alternative."

Michael rubbed his eyes and prayed Flynn was right. "So why are you waiting for me in the back of my car?"

"I've got something on our gal."

Pushing himself up, he fought the spurt of hope, like the one he'd just given Thad and Ruth, running under his skin. "What?"

Flynn relayed his discussion with Ryan Smith and the spurt of hope died. If anything, Brigit Kent seemed even more of a puzzle. "She's consulting for SIS *and* DHS, but she's not an agent or an operative for either intelligence service?"

"Smell the conspiracy yet?"

Michael's frustration grew. "And you're telling me she's well paid for consulting about Irish nationalism?"

Flynn shrugged. "It explains her in-depth knowledge about Donovan better than the story about her thesis."

"What's DHS doing with her? Irish terrorists are hardly on

America's top-ten watch list."

"You were right all along. There's more going on than we're privilege to."

Michael tapped a thumb against his leg and looked out the passenger window. "She met with the president this morning."

The leather squeaked quietly as Flynn shifted in his seat. "*Our* president?"

"The one and only."

Flynn whistled softly. "I followed her to a construction site after I left you at home. She drew a weapon on a car ready to leave the site. A gal jumped out, confronted her and then freakin' hugged her. I wasn't close enough to hear the exchange, but it was weird."

Michael's brain was spinning in circles but for all his logic, he couldn't pull one definitive answer about Brigit from it. "I saw what happened. Julia brought me a tape of the meeting."

"That's why she was in your office." It was a statement, not a question. "That the only reason?"

Michael met Flynn's eyes, saw the hardness in them. "Yes. She was trying to protect Zara. You might want to get a better handle on your counterintelligence operative."

"I already talked to her. She won't be doing anything stupid for awhile."

"That's what you told me when she went AWOL in Paris on the hunt for a mad scientist and the Italian Mob."

Flynn waved him off. "Julia told me Dr. Kent believes Ella will turn up at one of the local parks in the next few hours. What do you think?"

"I think I need help with surveillance."

"Consider it done." He reached for the door handle. "You take the one a block from here. I'll cover the park on Grant Avenue, and I've got Ace lined up to keep an eye on the third one over on Tremont Fairway."

"Which park has the best odds?"

Silence hung as Flynn considered the question. "Grant."

"You and I will take that one. I'll encourage the FBI to take the one up the block."

"Okay." He pushed the heavy, bulletproof door open and slid out.

"Flynn," Michael called to him.

He ducked back into the open space. "Yeah?"

"Thanks."

"Yeah."

The car door slammed shut.

Truman didn't return with her clothes until after four o'clock. Brigit was pissed. When he dropped her off at her loft and offered to hang out with her, she gave him a scorching look and slammed the car door in his too-handsome face.

Before she entered the building, she spotted an unmarked car down the block. Two men sat inside watching her. Police probably. She'd sent the FBI packing, but knowing Michael Stone, she was still under security watch.

The press would have been hanging around too, if Truman hadn't buried her personal information deep. She'd ducked the reporters at the front entrance of the hospital by using a delivery entrance at the back.

Inside, she heated water and dumped a packet of instant hot cocoa mix into a mug. While a beer appealed to her more, she didn't want the alcohol to slow her reflexes. Besides, her refrigerator was bare.

As the water boiled, Brigit's stomach growled. She hadn't eaten all day. Picking up her BlackBerry, she shuffled through the take-out menus in her head. Thai sounded good. Pressing the three on her phone, she speed dialed the local Thai restaurant and placed an order.

While she waited for her early dinner to arrive, she booted up her computer and went to work on tracking down Moira Raphael.

Three hours later, it was dark outside. Brigit had eaten, and succumbing to the exhaustion racking her body, fallen asleep on her futon.

When her BlackBerry dinged she bolted upright, scattering papers on the floor and making her shoulder throb. Biting back a curse, she grabbed up the BlackBerry and saw Truman's personal number ID'd.

"What?" she answered, pushing hair out of her face and glancing at the papers now lying on the floor.

"How's the shoulder?"

"Hurts like a son of a bitch, but it's better than being

dead."

"Agreed. Someone's snooping into your past."

Her heart did a flip. "Who?"

"Pick a name. You got a lot of people excited today, which was stupid. You should never have alerted Deputy Director Stone to Donovan's possible involvement in the kidnapping."

"Has Ella turned up?"

"Forget about Ella. Your beautiful backside is FUBARed. Do you get what I'm saying? If Stone or Jeffries or Director Halden start digging into your job history and connect you—us—with our current employer, we'll both hang."

Truman was far from innocent, but he still cared about his job. "Just keep your mouth shut and go about your business as usual. I'll handle Stone and the president, and I'll take the blame if it all goes to hell."

After ending the conversation, Brigit picked up the papers and looked at what she had on Moira. Nothing new. The ex-Palestinian army sniper, and best friend of Tory's, had been underground for the past three years.

Knowing she wouldn't be able to sleep, Brigit decided there wasn't any way to save herself after all of this, so she dug out her running clothes and went to help save Ella Pennington.

Chapter Seventeen

The park on Grant Avenue was a kid's paradise à la Steven Spielberg. A wooden castle complete with turret dominated one end. Giant insects, whose interiors were hollowed out for tunnels, appeared to roam the grounds. A mini merry-go-round with elaborately painted animals anchored the opposite end, and next to a long row of slides and swings lay a sandpit big enough for a T-Rex.

Light from decorative lamps straight from the Victorian era illuminated a curving sidewalk under large oaks surrounding the park. Since Michael had been concealed in the castle with his binoculars, several joggers had used the sidewalk, but other than those people, the insects, animals and Conrad Flynn next to him, the park was deserted.

Covert surveillance was not his specialty. It wasn't Flynn's either. Although both of them had the patience required for the act, sitting in freezing temps in cramped turrets overlooking a playground served to make them both slightly neurotic. Michael's mind was filled with thoughts of Julia, Zara, Ella and Brigit. All were worrying him.

All were worrying Flynn.

While they waited, the two of them talked in starts and stops, the darkness covering them in a blanket of familiarity if not exactly friendship.

How did you help a child you couldn't find? What did you tell a counterintelligence spy about her job options when returning to the field was too dangerous for a pregnant woman, no matter how tough and invincible she imagined herself to be? How did you convince someone to play by the rules when you never played by them yourself?

Michael dropped the binoculars from his eyes and ran a hand over his face. He liked women, respected how determined they could be and how soft and vulnerable they usually were underneath the tough exterior. He liked the way they banded together and looked out for each other. What he didn't like was their ability to outthink and outmaneuver him at almost every turn.

Movement on the path caught his attention. He didn't need the binoculars to see it was another jogger. Solitary, female, dressed for exercise in cold weather.

The cold was the least of her worries. Jogging alone after dark was asking for trouble, even in this upscale neighborhood. Maybe the woman considered herself safe here or enjoyed the feeling of taking a risk where she knew the odds were in her favor. While he admired guts in anyone, male or female, he admired common sense even more. Now he had another woman to look out for, at least as long as she was in his range of vision.

He scanned the park again while the woman stopped on the path and looked down at her feet. One of her shoestrings had come untied. As she stepped off the path and walked over to a large caterpillar, he raised the binoculars to get a better look. She must have been wearing six layers of shirts and jackets by the thickness of her shoulders. Either that or she had a stocky upper body. Bracing her foot against one the caterpillar's stomach segments, she removed her gloves and went to work on the shoelace. Her movements were awkward, though, as if her fingers were too cold to function. She lost her balance and had to put her foot down before bringing it back up for a second try.

Something about her stance tapped a warning in his brain. He watched her a moment longer, but nothing out of the ordinary happened.

A vibration in his pocket disrupted his thoughts. Shifting his hip, he fished out his cell phone and glanced at the readout. Ace was texting him.

All clear. You?

He hated trying to type on a keyboard smaller than his palm. Setting the binoculars down, he glanced around at the quiet park, noting the jogger had finished tying her shoe and was now stretching. His fingers fought to find the right keys to text back. *Mouth shut. Eyes open.*

113

A few seconds passed and then from Ace, *Balls froze.*

Michael showed the message to Flynn. Flynn smirked and typed back, *Ours too.*

Returning the cell phone to his pocket, he scanned the park. Emptiness and shadows stared back at him.

Jamming the binoculars to his eyes, he followed the path from one end to the other. The jogger had disappeared.

Brigit's shoulder was on fire. The simple task of raising her arm enough to tie her shoe had set off fireworks in her muscles. She'd downed two over-the-counter pain relievers before leaving her loft, but they were no match for the jarring of her body disguised as a jogger or the cold weather seeping under her Under Armor. *This is why I'm a consultant. I suck at fieldwork.*

While sitting in her car would have certainly been warmer, it also would have been a dead giveaway. The park sat back far enough from any of the connecting streets to be a bitch to surveil anyway. All the trees and the various pieces of high-rise playground equipment would have blocked her view.

Being on the ground, in the park, was her best bet. The inside of the caterpillar was cold but roomy. Along its abdomen, there were small holes to let in air and light during the day when kids squirmed through it. Tonight, she could use those holes to watch the perimeter of the park while remaining camouflaged.

Getting Ella back was her top priority and she'd picked the most obvious park for Peter to deliver her to. Not so close to the child's home he might be spotted and yet not so far away she would be spotted almost immediately. He wouldn't bring her until just before dawn, knowing she'd freeze overnight and not be found until morning anyway. No, he'd use the last remains of the night to do his covert drop with sunlight minutes away so the child would be found quickly.

That didn't mean Peter wouldn't be scoping the area long before then though. Precaution was second nature to him. Since the hit on O'Bern had failed, Peter would be extra cautious, which meant she had to be in place long before he showed up. She just hoped he wouldn't be so cautious he'd deviate from his normal pattern before disappearing and throw Ella to the wolves in his hurry.

Settling into her perfect hideout, Brigit adjusted her weight to ease the tension on her shoulder. It was going to be another long night.

Dawn came and Michael thought he'd crawl out of his skin if he didn't get moving. Not from the cold, but from the despair seeping into his bones. After the last jogger had disappeared, nothing had moved in the park all night except for a threesome of raccoons.

Ace had reported a similar night, and since Michael hadn't heard from the Feds, he knew they'd been screwed too.

Still, he stayed inside the castle's walls with Flynn, willing Peter Donovan to show up with Ella, even as the bright light of morning pushed through the trees and forced the shadows to disappear.

While he knew it was nearly impossible to predict what any criminal would do, he was pissed Brigit had been so wrong about Donovan. Whatever else she was, whoever she worked for, she was supposed to be the expert on this guy. So much for being an expert. She hadn't called one thing right yet.

Maybe Donovan wasn't involved at all. Julia had called to tell Flynn the ERT team had turned up nothing linking Donovan to the shooting. The rifle revealed no fingerprints. The room, not a scrap of trace evidence. All the same, the FBI had issued a be-on-the-look-out for Donovan. Nothing had materialized from the BOLO. Only Michael's refusal had kept Donovan's photo and statement saying he was wanted on suspicion from being issued to the press. Michael wanted to give him at least twenty-four hours to return Ella, and he was taking a beating for it from Jeffries on down.

Flynn was still waiting to hear from Smitty about Truman Gunn, but one way or another, they would figure out who and what Brigit Kent was and deal with her. While painfully aware of how badly he wanted to see her again, he had to shove his emotions aside. She'd made him look like a fool, and now her advice was keeping the state police and Feds from issuing an all-out manhunt for Donovan. Time was of the essence, and if Michael didn't know better, he'd think Brigit was in on the kidnapping.

Actually, he didn't know better. Maybe even the sniper taking a shot at her was all part of some bigger picture he couldn't see. He hated to believe it of her, but the facts were staring him in the face.

Using a kid as leverage was the lowest of the low. Yet, he couldn't take a chance. He had to grasp at any straw available.

The path through the park began to see some business again. More women, some walking, some jogging, cruised by. A single male, black from what Michael could tell from the small amount of the man's face showing between a knit cap and a scarf wrapped around his neck, sprinted through.

He'd just decided to wait another twenty minutes when he caught sight of a figure slipping out of the caterpillar. *Well, I'll be goddamned.* The shoe-tying jogger hadn't left the park, she'd been inside the insect all night.

Her head and face were covered by a knit face mask, but as she stretched her right arm before tentatively rubbing her left shoulder, a light bulb went off in his brain. The bulk under her outer coat was only under the left side.

Taking several stiff steps, she held her left arm with her right hand until she fell into step behind a woman pushing a stroller with big tires. As he watched her follow the path out of the park, he stretched his own stiff limbs and motioned to Flynn that he was going to tail her. Then he took the castle's fire pole down to the ground and did just that.

A block past the park's main gate, she folded herself into a green Ford.

Flynn, who had been hanging back, whistled at him. They ran through an alley and hopped into Flynn's Jeep parked in the lot of a convenience store. Making several right turns, he caught the Ford half a mile from the park.

They only followed her for another mile, hanging back in the early morning traffic, until Michael was sure she was on her way home. Then he told Flynn to take an alternative route.

She had parked and was crossing the street to her loft when they came around the corner. The knit mask was gone, and her face showed confusion as she stopped in the middle of the street and looked up. He followed her gaze and saw the cause of her surprise.

He'd been so intent on making her, he'd missed the smoke rolling out of a broken front window on the second floor. Flames shot out the window as well. Before Conrad could dial 9-1-1, Michael heard sirens.

It was still early enough there were few people out, but a

small crowd was forming on the sidewalk. Brigit stood alone in the street, watching the smoke and flames with one hand on her forehead in disbelief as a car rushed by her and honked its horn.

Flynn pulled to the curb and Michael jumped out before the Jeep stopped rolling. Without warning, Brigit's face went from dismay to terror as she continued to gaze up at the burning apartment.

She dropped her hand from her forehead, yelled "No!", and took off running. A collective gasp and then shouts from the people on the sidewalk rose as they pointed up at the upstairs windows.

As she disappeared around the side of the building, Michael took off after her, taking a second to glance upward to try and see what had spurred her into action.

Framed in a window stood a small girl, her hands pressed against the pane of glass, her face dissolved in tears. His heart jumped as her lips drew back in a cry. *Uncle Michael. Help me.*

Chapter Eighteen

The entry to Brigit's loft was on the side of the two-story building. She took the wooden stairs two at a time, her pulse so loud in her ears it drowned out the cries and yells behind her on the sidewalk.

Rational thought eluded her, but she knew without consulting logic or reason Ella was the girl in her burning loft.

She hit the entry door full force, jerking on the handle. Locked. Ignoring the terrible pain in her left shoulder, she fumbled in the pocket of her pants and found the key. Jamming in the lock, she turned the handle again.

It refused to move.

Frustration and fear drove tears into her eyes. *Get it together, Brigit. You can't fall apart now.*

Footsteps pounded up the stairs to her side. She tried the key again, wiggling it back and forth so hard the key nearly broke in half. The lock wouldn't budge.

Michael Stone appeared like a mirage at her side. He must have been the one following her in the Jeep. Without preamble, she turned to him and said, "Door's jammed. Can you kick it in?"

"It's steel," he said, wrestling the key from her hand and trying the lock himself. He threw his shoulder into the door, but nothing changed. "Other way in?"

There were no windows accessible from the landing. "Fire stairs around back go up to the roof." She took off back down the wooden stairs with the deputy director on her tail.

By the time they reached the roof, she was breathing like she'd sprinted a mile. He didn't seem to be breathing at all. He tried the fire door exit, but it too was locked from the inside.

Peter had done his homework.

"Goddammit," Michael said, throwing his shoulder against the door.

Brigit located the vent stack that corresponded to her bathroom's exhaust fan. "Here," she said, grabbing it with her right hand and giving a yank. Her left hand and arm were useless. "Help me."

Michael fell to his knees beside her and tugged on the stack until it broke free. "How's this going to help?"

"I can fit through it." A good operative always had an escape plan that didn't use doors or windows. She hadn't needed SIS training to know that, thanks to her father and the fact she'd once been locked in a bathroom with no escape.

She'd practiced escaping from this one several times from the inside out. Now she'd have to hope it worked in the opposite direction. "I'll get Ella and hand her up to you if I can't get her out the front door."

She squeezed into the hole, realizing at the last instant her extra layers and the bandage on her shoulder were too fat for her to raise her arm over her head. She sat on the lip of the roof and pulled off the jacket she was wearing, then the shirt. *Ella, hang on,* she chanted in her head. The sound of sirens drew nearer.

"Hurry," Michael said.

Down to her bra, she gripped the edge of the padded bandage and yanked as hard as she could. A small cry of pain escaped her lips as the gauze pulled free from her wound, taking flesh with it.

Blinking the tears out of her eyes, she dropped her body into the hole and fell to the bathroom floor.

Smoke was everywhere and she could hear the crackle of flames in the far room. "Ella!" she called and listened for a response. Nothing.

Ghost fingers of fear curled around her. Holy Mother Mary, she hated fire.

"Brigit." Michael's voice sounded far away. "Can you get to her?"

Slapping the fear away, she scrambled through the bedroom to the main living area where she'd seen the girl in the window. Smoke stung her nostrils and made her throat as dry as a desert. Fire burned in the path laid by some type of accelerant across the front door. No going out that way.

Ella was no longer in the window. Brigit called her name again and still heard no reply. There was already a significant lack of oxygen in the loft and her lungs strained to find the precious stuff in the midst of the smoke. She swung around in circles before running to the kitchen. The fire burned out of control there, and made her throw up her hands to protect her face and backtrack to the living room. The papers she had left scattered on the coffee table and futon were gone. The futon itself was smoking as if someone had left a cigarette burning inside its stuffing.

"Ella, my name is Brigit," she called. She sucked in smoke and coughed. When the fit passed, she called out again. "Don't be scared. I'm here to help you. Call my name so I can find you."

Through the din of the sizzling curtains and cracking wood, she thought she heard something coming from the bedroom. Not a voice, but a cough, like hers. Retracing her steps, she stopped in the doorway. "Ella, I know you're in here. Tell me where you are."

When she didn't hear anything, she threw open the closet doors, pushing aside the hanging wardrobe of blacks and other neutrals and kicking at the shoes lining the floor. Where was that girl?

Michael's voice roared from the bathroom. "Ella!"

The smoke had now invaded the bedroom to the point Brigit could barely see. She fell to her hands and knees, another coughing attack assailing her. For a second, her vision blurred and her stomach spasmed. Pushing herself forward, she crawled on the floor, her shoulder a mass of pain. She would have missed the tiny swatch of the red Wonder Woman cape peeking out from under the bed skirt if she hadn't lain her head down on the floor, searching for a breath of oxygen. "Ella?"

When she flipped the bed skirt up, a rush of relief flooded her limbs at the sight of the little girl gripping tight to a Tinker Bell doll. Her eyes were red from crying and when she saw Brigit, she started coughing. "Wendy?" she choked out.

Forcing her left arm to help her right, Brigit pulled the crying girl from under the bed, lifted her and carried her to the bathroom.

She slammed the door shut and gave Ella a quick once-over. Dirt smudged her cheeks and hands but otherwise she seemed unhurt. "I've got her," she yelled up to Michael. "She's okay."

His reply boomed down the vent. "Thank God."

"Step up on the toilet lid here," Brigit directed Ella. With her good hand, she guided her. "Now over to the vanity." Again she nudged Ella into position as she lined herself under the hole in the ceiling.

"Are you ready?" she called up to Michael.

His face was in the opening but he seemed miles away. She could tell he was lying down on his stomach as his hands reached down the exhaust fan's metal tunnel. "Go!"

"Uncle Michael?" Ella said, looking up.

"Listen to Brigit and do what she says," he told her.

Brigit addressed the child. "I want you to step over onto my shoulders, okay? Take my hand and place one foot here and the other here." She tapped each shoulder to demonstrate. "Do you think you can do that?"

The girl nodded and reached for Brigit's hand.

Balancing Ella was difficult, not because she weighed much, but because Brigit's left arm hung useless. She couldn't raise her hand to steady Ella's legs. She almost lost her once, but the girl dropped her Tinker Bell doll and grabbed her uncle's hand.

A moment later, Ella rose into the air and Brigit crumbled to the floor, exhausted.

"Come on." Michael's voice drifted down to her. In the outside room, Brigit heard glass break and wood pop from the heat. "Dr. Kent, let's go. You're out of time."

But she couldn't push herself off the floor. The opening in the ceiling was too far away. *He's right. I am out of time.*

The Tinker Bell doll lay beside her and Brigit lifted her gaze from the doll's blonde ponytail to the sink where a light burned through the smoke. *A nightlight? Where did that come from? I don't own a...*

An image of Peter and the nightlight in the locked bathroom flashed in her brain. Then an image of Moira. They made her sick to her stomach. How could they have done this to Ella? How could they be so cruel, so selfish? It was one thing to try and kill Cormac O'Bern, who'd made his bed long years ago with the company he'd kept and then betrayed, but an innocent six-year-old girl?

Bile pushed into Brigit's throat and she reached for the Tinker Bell doll. What a fool she'd been to try and stop Peter, to try and rescue Tory, to try and protect her father, to sell her soul to countless power mongers in an attempt to redeem herself for her mother's sake.

Because in the end, loving her family was destroying her.

"Brigit?" Michael's voice shot down the metal hole, sending a fresh wave of adrenaline through her.

"Is Ella okay?" she yelled up to him.

"Yes, come on."

Accepting the inner self-loathing boiling in her veins, she pushed herself into a sitting position with her right hand. The fresh wave of pain on her left side made the room spin, but she hung on until it passed.

Rising to her feet, she reached deep for her survivor instincts. She leaned on the vanity and willed the room to steady itself. The nightlight caught her attention again, glowing in the smoky haze. *Goddamn, son of a bitch.*

She'd had enough, by God. She was tired of trying to save the lost boy. Jerking it out of the socket, she smashed it against the marble countertop.

As she climbed onto the counter and raised her good arm up toward Michael's waiting hands, she silently asked for her mother's forgiveness.

Peter better pray I don't find him, she thought, as Michael gripped her by the wrist and pulled her heavenward, *because when I do, I'm putting Batman on his ass.*

Third District D.C. police station
Two hours later

Michael viewed Brigit sitting at the table in the interrogation room from behind a two-way mirror. She looked like hell, her head down on the table and her eyes closed. While her hair was pulled back in a ponytail, pieces singed by the fire had escaped. She'd tried to wipe the soot from her face, but faint traces still remained. Her clothes were covered in the black stuff as well.

But she'd saved Ella, and Michael found her beautiful. Too

bad she was the police's number one suspect in the kidnapping.

Ella was spending the night at the local children's hospital under the watchful eyes of the entire nation as well as her parents. She'd suffered smoke inhalation and appeared dehydrated, but a complete physical showed she was otherwise fine.

Brigit had been treated at the scene for smoke inhalation as well, but refused another trip to the hospital. She was lucky she hadn't suffocated or burned to death.

Flynn blew into the room, looking as worn out as Michael felt. "Shouldn't you be with your niece?"

"Ella's doing fine. Ruth called and said she ate two breakfasts this morning already and the nurses are sneaking in Jell-O and milkshakes every time she turns her back."

Flynn jutted his chin at Brigit in the adjoining room. "She makes a clean suspect."

"She was at the park with us all night. Besides, what's her angle? Why kidnap Ella and blame this Donovan character? She setting him up?"

"She knew you'd have those parks under surveillance. Someone would see her there. Makes a good alibi. I would have done the same thing."

Michael crossed his arms and studied Flynn. "I can't figure out if you'd be a better criminal or a better cop."

"Could go either way. That's why I work for you."

Michael turned back to the two-way. What was the bigger picture? "She helps Donovan kidnap Ella and then fabricates a story about O'Bern and a bomb so she can walk out to the lectern and get shot?"

"Maybe the original story she told you was right. Donovan wanted to take out O'Bern. She got cold feet, turned traitor, and he shot her for blowing his chance."

A detective entered, introduced himself and shook their hands. He was clearly uncomfortable with their presence, as well as the FBI milling around his station waiting for jurisdiction calls to be made to take the case away from him. "You guys sticking around for the interrogation?"

"Think you can get her to confess?" Michael asked.

The detective nodded. "After what you and the FBI have told me, she clearly had the means and opportunity to do this.

Not clear on her motivation, but that's not a sticking point. Just got word from the hospital. Kid ID'd her. If I can keep her from lawyering up right away, I might get her to turn on the other guy."

The urge to defend Brigit was too strong to ignore. "My niece has been through a trauma and she's only six. Her memory may be playing tricks with her."

The detective frowned as if he wondered why Michael was throwing water on the fire he was building to burn Brigit Kent. "The little girl told her momma the woman who saved her from the fire is the same woman who kept her locked in the bathroom and gave her the Tinker Bell doll. Called herself Wendy."

Michael struggled to find a solution to Ella's story, but after too many nights of no sleep, his brain was a quagmire of crap. For the first time since his father had died, he couldn't make sense of anything.

The detective nodded at a table of high-tech equipment behind them. "Everything's being recorded for posterity. Gotta tell you, though, it's an open and shut case with the kid's ID."

He left the room and entered the interrogation room, pulling out a chair and sitting down at the table. When Brigit didn't respond, the detective made a fist and started banging on the scarred wooden top.

Chapter Nineteen

Brigit woke to the sound of a railroad spike slamming next to her temple. She cracked her eyes open and realized it was a fist, knuckles knocking on the table. What a wakeup call.

With effort, she lifted her head and eyed the detective sitting across from her. His wool jacket smelled like mothballs and he sucked on his cheeks, narrowing them in a Dirty Harry impression as he glared at her. He had the Clint Eastwood balding-head thing going for him, but where Clint could nail Dirty Harry with nothing more than the gleam in his eyes, Detective Mothballs just looked like a dweeb in tweed, as Truman was fond of saying. She wished she were back in the caterpillar's stomach.

And wasn't that a sad state to be in.

He pushed a button on a digital voice recorder on the table. "State your name for the record, Sleeping Beauty."

It was obvious she was a person of interest in the kidnapping. If she'd been a civilian, she would have asked for an attorney before even stating her name. Technically, she wasn't a civilian, and because of what she was and who she worked for, asking for a lawyer wasn't prudent. She was on her own, and while she was innocent, she had to be careful how she played the game.

Miranda rights had not been read. Yet. Brigit had the feeling it was only a matter of time.

Across from the voice recorder, her BlackBerry played three notes and the detective eyed it with suspicion. "Go ahead," he said. "Answer it."

Her throat muscles clenched as she tried to speak, her esophagus raw. She swallowed, cleared her throat, and tried again. "It's an email." Hopefully from Truman telling her the cavalry was on its way. "It can wait."

"You better read it now. You won't have your phone much longer."

Yep. I've moved from a person of interest to a card-carrying suspect.

She picked up the phone, typed a three-key combo and then a password to unlock it. She hit the mailbox and brought up her email. There was one message from Truman, using the code name for their employer, JOE. No subject. One sentence. *Lie back and think of England.*

Truman wouldn't be bringing the cavalry. She was done. Axed. Terminated. *Lie back and think of England* was the Secret Intelligence Service term for *you've been burned.*

Cold sweat broke out over her body. Being burned from SIS was like being excommunicated from the Catholic Church. In their eyes, she simply ceased to exist. Except with the intelligence agency, they didn't just close their eyes and pretend you were invisible. If they were really pissed at your incompetence, they wiped out your savings, dropped your credit score in the toilet, sent you a computer virus. In other words, lie back and think of England while you're being screwed.

"You don't look so good." The detective smiled. "Bad news? Your boyfriend leaving you holding the bag?"

Brigit returned to the home screen and set down the phone. It wouldn't ring any more, wouldn't receive any more emails, text messages or calls. Just in case it might go *Mission: Impossible* on her and explode, she slid it toward the detective's side of the table.

Like a predator smelling first blood, he sucked in his cheeks and picked up the phone, turning it over and fiddling with the buttons. Brigit wasn't worried he'd find anything. The phone was encrypted and encoded with enough security it would take an accomplished hacker to figure it out. Even if one did, there was nothing criminal on it.

The detective frowned as if perplexed and set the phone back on the table. Then he began to interrogate her.

He pulled a photo from a file. Peter, bald and sporting a goatee, wearing a tie under a wool sweater. "Eleanor Pennington claims this is the man who kidnapped her. What's his name?"

Brigit pressed her lips together. Everyone from Michael to

Detective Mothballs knew Peter's name. She was too blown out to play Name That Terrorist.

Between the pain in her arm, the lack of sleep, her recent brush with smoke and fire, and the news she'd been burned, her mood mimicked a black-sucking-hole. Her brain and her body felt like she'd spent time in a blender. Topping it with the fact she'd accepted her brother did indeed intend to do her in, and she was ready to take the detective's tie and choke him with it.

And then go hunt down Peter.

The question was, could she still save Tory?

Probably not.

A wave of crushing defeat threatened to knock her to the ground. She gripped her hands in her lap and forced her body to stay upright.

After a long minute, the detective again demanded an answer. She continued her clam routine.

"Eleanor Pennington also stated you helped him keep her captive in your bathroom."

Brigit's stomach dropped. Why would Ella say that? She had never met the girl until this morning when she'd battled the fire to rescue her.

"Why did you spend the night at Grant Avenue Park?"

She took a deep breath and called on her training to keep her body frozen in place and appear calm. Refusing to answer questions didn't seem rational, but then she wasn't rational at the moment. If she answered anything, started talking at all, she might slip up and give the detective something he could use against her. Until she cleared her head, she needed to buy time.

He was unrelenting. "Anybody see you there?"

Michael and Conrad had seen her. Then they'd followed her home. Michael's bodyguard had to have been somewhere in the vicinity too. All because she'd been a suspect in the kidnapping ever since she'd opened her big mouth.

She glanced at the mirrored glass, sure a certain laser beam was firing back at her, and debated mentioning her tail. While she wanted to get the hell out of the police station, she wasn't going to spill her guts. If Michael and Conrad wanted to step forward as witnesses, they would have already. Why neither had was a mystery, but she had no plan to stick her neck out and accuse them. They could deny it and make her look even more suspect.

While the police detective continued drilling her with questions, it occurred to her that as long as she was in the suspect Twilight Zone, she might as well take a risk. Knowing SIS could toss her to the wolves at any time, she'd always hedged her bets. The president of the United States was one of them, and because of that, there was one person who might still help her. She glanced at the mirror again.

The cop finally lost his patience. "Fine. You don't want to talk and straighten things out? I'm placing you under arrest. Twenty-four hours in the hole downstairs and you'll be begging me to talk. You have the right to remain silent."

She didn't want to remain silent anymore. She had no one left to protect. No loyalty to any intelligence service. "Wait."

He raised an eyebrow and sucked in his cheeks. A gleam appeared in his eyes. He thought he'd broken her, and she was ready to spill her guts.

It takes more than a dweeb in tweed to break Brigit Kent. "I want to talk to Michael Stone, Deputy Director of the CIA."

The gleam of satisfaction disappeared. Sitting back in his chair, the detective sputtered. "You want what?"

As if she'd called him into being, Michael opened the interrogation room's door and walked in, stopping a few feet from the table. Still fiercely handsome, he looked fresh and clean, like he'd just stepped out of the shower. He smelled like it too. A light scent of aftershave and shampoo drifted to her nose. The only hint that he hadn't enjoyed a normal night's rest was the fatigue in his eyes.

His expression was torn, as if it pained him to see her this way. More likely, he hated her for bringing him into her interrogation. His gaze stayed on her as he spoke to the detective. "I'll take it from here."

A sense of security washed through her, unbidden and inexplicable. The cop started to balk, but one hard-assed look from Michael sent him on his way, grumbling under his breath.

As soon as the door shut behind him, Brigit let her guard down, melting under Michael's gaze. "How's Ella?"

His brow creased, showing surprise at her question. "Ella's fine. You, however, are not." He turned the hard-assed look on her. "What do want to tell me?"

"Not here." She struggled to her feet, dizziness rushing over her, and leaned on the table for support. "No cameras, no tape recorders. I'll tell you everything you want to know, but it has to be just you and me."

He wanted the truth and she had it. His expression told her he didn't like anyone grabbing him by the balls and forcing him to do what they wanted. Still, he wasn't about to let this opportunity pass him by. "Take the phone," was all he said before ushering her to the door.

A man's word wasn't what it used to be. Michael had to sign off on multiple forms and swear up and down to the police and the Federal agents waiting in line that Brigit would remain in custody with him in order to get her out of the station. He had no jurisdiction in her case and everybody knew it. He was, however, tied to the case and respected by most of the men and women wanting a piece of her.

As she sat in a side chair watching him perform gymnastics and tap dance around legalities, her face remained a blank slate. She'd retreated so far into herself, he wondered if he'd be able to get anything out of her.

In the Marines, he'd seen the same look on men who had lost touch with reality. Depressed, suicidal, up against a wall. CIA recruits often got the same look on their faces after Flynn had put them through The Farm. Win or lose, they had nothing left to give.

When the call from FBI Director Agouti came through, Michael took it standing up. "Give me twenty-four hours," Michael said to his old friend and even older enemy.

Out of the corner of his eye, Michael saw Brigit's assistant, Truman, slide into a seat next to her. Her face changed in an instant, lighting up and then shutting down again as Truman spoke to her.

Michael couldn't make out what Truman was saying because Agouti was speaking in his ear. "I don't understand what you're up to, but I've learned not to ask questions where you're concerned, Stone. It's four o'clock now. I'll give you to eight." He sighed. "Don't make me regret this."

Agouti meant eight p.m. Michael conveniently heard eight a.m. "You won't, Gute."

He handed the phone over to the special agent in charge so Agouti's instructions could be conveyed to the rest of the group.

As he did so, he heard Truman saying, "...destroyed. The smoke and water damaged everything the fire left."

Brigit tipped her head back and closed her eyes. "You couldn't save anything?"

"I snagged the files I could find and your laptop for security reasons, but it was all trashed." He pulled something from his pocket and handed it to her. "This was my mom's. Figured you could use a little luck."

In order to continue eavesdropping, Michael put his head down, grabbed a pen and shifted through the papers he'd already signed as if he were still working on getting Brigit released. With his back slightly turned, he appeared busy, yet could still hear and see them.

"You're all over the news," Truman said softly. "That's why they burned you."

The fine hairs on Michael's neck rose. *Burned?* Was Truman referring to the fire in her apartment or something else? In the intelligence world, a burn notice was termination. Worse than termination. It was the equivalent to being stripped naked, beaten to a pulp and left for dead.

Michael had the impression Brigit nodded. "You shouldn't be here. If you're seen with me..."

"I can take care of myself. Look"—he lowered his voice another notch—"the only way out of this is for you to tell your dirty little secret. You know it, and they know it. That's why they burned you. You walk out of here with him—" There was a brief pause and Michael knew Truman was eyeing him. He picked up a paper and pretended to read. "You're risking your life."

"What's left of it anyway." Brigit sounded like she was smiling. "Truman, thank you for the rabbit's foot. It means a lot to me."

Michael saw them embrace in his peripheral vision. He cleared his throat and made a show of facing them, glad to break up the Hallmark moment. "Ready?" he said to Brigit.

She nodded once and rose, Truman taking her by the hand and helping her. He squeezed her hand and Michael fought the urge to kick him to the door. "Let's go."

Brigit cocked her chin at Truman, signaling him to leave. The kid started to say something to Michael, thought better of it, and fled.

"There's a mass of reporters outside who'd love to put you on the evening news," he said. "Keep your head down and don't say a word or I'll let them eat you. Got it?"

Brigit scanned the room and that's when Michael noticed the glares of cops and federal agents locked on them. She spoke glumly and glanced down at the rabbit's foot in her hand. "Wolves or lions, can't decide which I'd rather be thrown to."

When she looked back up at him, her face was again a blank slate. "Got it."

Outside, Brad had the Navigator ready to go, and Flynn was on the steps ready to run interference with the reporters. Michael murmured to Brad to ride up front so he could be alone with Brigit in the back. Then he motioned for Brad to help him sandwich Brigit between them as Flynn made a path from the steps to the car.

Once inside the car, Brigit settled into the seat across from Michael like she'd done earlier that day. Her back stiff, she buckled herself in and stared at the reporters and cameras crowded around the car. When they finally broke free of the congestion, the driver buzzed the backseat intercom. "Where to, sir?"

"Home," Michael replied before thinking about it.

Brigit glanced at him, lifting one of her brows. He shrugged a shoulder as if it were a logical decision. "It's the only place I guarantee is free of listening devices and cameras."

She accepted the answer and went back to looking out the window, spine still stiff as a rod. He had to admire her stamina. She was obviously bone tired and in pain. It had been a helluva day for everyone.

Ten miles down the interstate, the rod in her back broke and she leaned her head against the door. Before another mile passed, she was asleep, her head tilted at an uncomfortable angle. Michael watched her features soften and a dark spot on her running clothes caught his eye. Blood was seeping through her jacket on the injured shoulder. She'd pulled a couple of her stitches at the fire rescuing Ella and had barely received the oxygen she needed before the cops and FBI had hauled her off to the station.

Under his seat, Michael opened the door of a storage compartment and pulled out a small pillow. It was stored there in case he wanted to sleep or rest on his many trips up and down the George Washington Parkway. He tried once or twice to relax in the car, but never found it habit-forming. Setting the pillow at the opposite end of the bench seat from Brigit, he released her seat belt and guided her onto her right side.

She resisted for a minute, seeming confused and in pain. "It's okay," Michael murmured and, a few seconds later, she burrowed down and went back to sleep, the rabbit's foot still clutched in her hand.

Her BlackBerry slid out of her pocket and landed on the floor. Michael picked it up, hit a couple of buttons and received a warning message. The handset was locked. He played with it for another minute without success. Dragging out his own digitally encrypted cell phone, he dialed his best tech support guy.

Del Hoffman, at CIA headquarters, answered on the first ring. "The Great and Mighty Michael Stone. What can I do for you today?"

"I need to hack into a BlackBerry that's been upgraded." Upgraded in Del and Michael's world meant titanium-style encoding and *007*-capabilities.

Del had once been a college student arrested for hacking into the NSA's database. When Michael had caught wind of the kid's capabilities, he'd done the required tap dance to get the charges reduced and immediately put him to work for the CIA. "Are you bringing it to me?"

"No. I want you to talk me through it."

"Uh-huh." Del seemed less enthused. "How much time we got?"

Michael checked his watch. "Thirteen minutes give or take a few depending on traffic and how long the owner stays asleep."

"O-kay." The sound of fingers hitting keys echoed in Michael's ear. "You know how I love a challenge, sir. Keyboard locked?"

"Yes."

It only took six minutes to unlock the phone and another to get past the three layers of encoding. "Pay dirt," Michael said when the email opened for him.

"Oh yeah." Michael could tell Del was air-pumping his fist. "That's a record even for me. Anything else?"

"That should do it for now. Thanks, Del."

"Anytime, Your Lordship."

Michael laid his phone on the seat as he read Brigit's last email. *Lie back and think of England.*

He glanced at her sleeping on the seat across from him. Her right hand had relaxed and the rabbit's foot had slid out of it onto the seat.

She'd been shot, had her apartment set on fire and been implicated in the kidnapping of a U.S. Senator's daughter. Her picture and story had been running on CNN and Headline News all day, half of America convinced she was a victim and the other half convinced she was a criminal.

Truman's words rang in Michael's head. *You walk out of here with him...you're risking your life.*

She'd been burned from SIS. Burned, in this case, was stripped naked and left for dead. Michael picked up the rabbit's foot and laid it back in Brigit's hand.

She was going to need all the luck she could get.

From the looks of things, he was too.

Chapter Twenty

In the dark bar, Peter stewed as his image was posted on CNN. While the volume on the TV in the corner was muted, he knew the newscaster was rattling off his vital statistics and the facts she had about his possible involvement in Brigit's shooting.

The serious brunette was replaced by a long wide-angle video taken by a press member showing Brigit at the podium. As if someone called her name, she shifted, looking behind her and then, *bam*, her body jerked and fell. A man, football-player big, hauled ass to get to her and dropped behind the podium in full-blown protection mode. A few more seconds of tape showed flowerpots exploding and other people running for cover. The brunette reporter returned to the screen, a photo of Brigit now above her shoulder next to Peter's.

He pulled the brim of his baseball cap down further on his forehead. Fifteen minutes with a razor and his quick-change kit, and he looked little like the man on the television. But every law enforcement agency in the country was looking for him because they believed he pulled the trigger. Shot one of their own, if that's what Brigit was to them.

The D.C. area was swarming with police and feds. That's why he couldn't take the chance of running. Moira had completely screwed everything up, and he had to sit tight under law enforcement's nose and wait for the right opportunity.

Another video played on the screen, this one of Brigit's apartment ablaze.

It wasn't enough Moira had tried to kill Brigit with a bullet. When she'd failed at that, she'd decided to try and burn her alive. What Moira hadn't realized was that the only person in the apartment when she'd set it on fire was a sleeping Eleanor Pennington. Because Peter knew Brigit would be looking for the girl in the vicinity of the Pennington home, he'd purposely taken Eleanor to Brigit's apartment. Setting Brigit up for the kidnapping had been worth the risk. It would have thrown suspicion on her and taken it off him.

But then Moira had done something he'd never thought possible. She let an emotion direct her actions. Her anger had taken control of her common sense. The only thing Peter wondered was who Moira really wanted to punish.

In the end, she was the one punished. He'd followed her from the apartment to a rundown gas station. When she'd disappeared into a restroom around back, he'd gone in after her.

If she lived from the beating he gave her, she'd be sure never to cross him again.

Arlington

Brigit noted three things upon entering Michael's home. It was bright, comfortable and smelled delicious. Another piece snapped into the code she'd been breaking on the man known to all as Deputy Director of Central Intelligence.

They entered through a service door from the attached garage into an ultra-modern kitchen with steel appliances and marble countertops. A muscular Rottweiler rushed forward, and Brigit froze as it lowered its head and glared, its nose quivering as it picked up her scent. Michael raised a finger and made a shushing noise and the dog sat at her feet, his stubby tail suddenly wagging.

"Will he take my hand off if I try to pet him?" she asked.

"Only on my command." Michael gave her a nod of encouragement. "His name's Pongo."

Brigit dropped her hand to let the dog smell it. She was cold and groggy after the ride, and completely, one hundred percent embarrassed. How could she have fallen asleep in front of Michael Stone of all people? "Hi, Pongo."

His stub tail wagged furiously on the tile floor, and he head-butted her hand, still sniffing. His enthusiasm made her troubles recede. She scratched behind his ear and he leaned into her fingers, making a low rumble of approval in his throat.

Michael punched buttons on the security alarm faceplate.

"He likes you."

Brigit sighed and thought of her childhood pet, Midi. "I had a dog once when I was a little girl. She was just a mutt but I loved her heart and soul."

Even in the fading light of the autumn afternoon, the tall windows invited sunshine in and it bounced off the dark wood cabinets. The kitchen's old-world details further softened the glinting steel. An arch of real earthen bricks above the sink echoed the curve of the exhaust fan over the large stove. The breakfast bar's edges were trimmed in beautifully turned wooden scrolls, like old-fashioned barbershop poles.

She had to find out what plug-in air freshener he used. The kitchen was redolent with the smell of roasted chicken and fresh baked bread. Her stomach growled. She hadn't eaten since...when?

Brad exchanged a look with Michael before shimmying past her and disappearing into the house. From the armed officer at the front gate to the dog to the motion detectors atop floodlights in the four corners of the property, there was no doubt the deputy director took security seriously. Who could blame him after he'd been held captive by terrorists earlier in the year?

Inside, the house was a security haven as well. Every window sported lithium-powered security contacts. Every door had laser receptors. She wouldn't have been surprised if there were cameras in the ceiling lights regardless of his earlier assurance there weren't.

He helped her slide off her running jacket and hung it, and his coat, on brushed silver hooks by the back door. He rubbed a hand over the bloody spot on the nylon jacket. "I'll have Marie take this to the dry cleaners tomorrow."

"Marie?"

He was now eyeing her shoulder. "My cleaning lady."

If Marie took her jacket to the cleaners, she wouldn't have anything to wear outside in the cold. All her clothes had been damaged in the fire. "Please don't impose on her. I'll just give it a rinse in the sink."

The dumbest thought struck her and was out of her mouth before she thought it through. *Tomorrow...* "I'm staying overnight?"

"Probably."

Michael gave Pongo a thorough greeting, including rubbing

his chest and patting his back. He pulled a dog treat from his jacket pocket, and Brigit couldn't help but chuckle to herself. Who knew the DD of the CIA carried dog treats in his suit coat?

"Would you like to wash up?" Michael pointed to the far side of the kitchen at an arched doorway. "There's a half bath down the hall."

Her legs were weak and she was shaking slightly, but she nodded. Cradling her left arm with her right hand, she drifted through the kitchen and found the bathroom. She shut the door behind her and sagged against it. Was she really going to spill everything to Michael Stone? Her family secret? Her status with SIS?

She knew she wasn't. She was going to come clean about a few pertinent facts to get her off the police's radar as well as the FBI's, but that was it. Family secrets weren't for outsiders. Her status with Britain's Secret Intelligence Service wasn't either.

Brigit washed her face as best she could with her right hand and ran her fingers through her hair, pushing some behind her ears and wishing she had a hairband. She needed a shower, a lot of shampoo, a few bites of food and a long rest. Then she would give Michael the facts, carefully weeded from her cache, and snag her freedom.

Freedom. An interesting lightness filled her chest. She hadn't felt it since the day her mother died. All the years of guilt about accidently killing their mom, and trying so hard to replace her for Tory's sake, had left Brigit tired and numb inside. She'd spent most of her time being whatever her dad and Tory needed and failing miserably. They didn't need a substitute. They needed Roberta.

Maybe that's all Peter had needed too. If their mother hadn't died in the fire, would Peter have changed course?

Her tired brain was too fuzzy to sort out the could-have-beens. It was shutting down on her. All she could think about was returning to the warm, delicious-smelling kitchen and throwing herself at Michael's feet in exchange for food and a few hours on his sofa.

Leaving the bathroom, she walked back toward the kitchen, taking a short detour to peek in his study. He was in the process of remodeling. Shelves of books, a flat-screen TV, a grandfather clock, and the largest mahogany desk she'd ever seen filled the room, but plastic sheeting covered most of it.

More pieces of his code snapped into place. He was a tricked-out traditionalist. A suave warrior. Her attention fell on the contents of a coffee table. He was also a Redskins fan. Even that made perfect sense.

In the kitchen, Michael was sorting through the refrigerator. His suit coat was off and his shirt sleeves were rolled up to his elbows. A tattoo on the inside of his left wrist caught her eye. It looked like a fancy compass. She perched on a stool at the expansive marble breakfast bar and dropped her chin into her hands to watch him.

Without a word, he moved around the kitchen, filling a pot with water and setting it on the stovetop. As the gas fire heated the water, he took a couple of mugs and a box of tea bags out of an overhead cabinet. "Earl Grey or English Teatime?" he asked nonchalantly, as if he served suspected felons tea at his breakfast bar on a regular basis.

"Earl Grey," Brigit answered with the same measured casualness.

A few minutes later, hot tea warming her stomach, she couldn't help but relax a smidge as Michael pulled a container from the fridge. Using a soup ladle, he transferred the contents of the container to two hefty soup mugs and popped both in a large microwave. The smell of roasted chicken intensified. Brigit couldn't help herself. "Smells delicious."

"My housekeeper is also a good cook and rather motherly." He looked a bit sheepish as he dug in a drawer and pulled out spoons. "She leaves me food all the time. Even if she was a terrible housekeeper, I'd keep her just for that."

"Smart. I would too."

They shared a smile and Brigit's pulse spiked.

She expected him to take up where the detective had left off interrogating her, so when he sat beside her at the breakfast bar and helped her with her napkin without saying anything, she gave a mental sigh. Maybe he'd at least let her eat before he started asking questions. Eating was good. If only she could figure out a way to use her right hand instead of her left. The first few tries, she seemed to spill more than she got in her mouth.

Michael watched with a bemused glint in his eye. "Would you like a straw?"

"I can't suck up the fat noodles through a straw. Give me a

minute. I just need practice."

And she did. After a couple more tries, her right hand realized it had to perform and the spoon consistently went into her mouth instead of her chin. Michael ate his soup in silence and the lightness in Brigit's chest bloomed again. A cup of tea and a bowl of homemade soup on a cold day from hell were a small form of bliss.

When they finished, Michael cleaned up the few dishes, taking his time washing the bowls and then drying them and putting them away. Brigit sat and watched, content to do so.

She should have been figuring out her game plan. How to admit her relationship with Peter without throwing more suspicion on herself. How to get her hands on some pain meds. Her arm was throbbing and now a burning pain, much like the initial bullet wound, was spreading into her muscles.

Michael returned to the stool next to hers, his blue-eyed gaze examining her shoulder as if he could feel the throbbing himself. "Looks like you need a fresh bandage. I'll be right back."

He disappeared down the hall and soon she heard footsteps above her. When he returned, his arms held a box of gauze, bandages, saline solution and a tube of antibiotic ointment.

"If I didn't know better," Brigit said, "I'd think you knew something about taking care of bullet wounds."

He stiffened and she regretted referring to his encounter with the notorious Fayez Raissi. Being taken hostage in your own home, having a block of C4 strapped to your chest and taking a bullet for your troubles was the stuff nightmares were made of. "I'm sorry. I shouldn't have referred to your...experience."

Opening a sterile gauze wrapper, he ignored her apology, which made her feel even worse. "You'll have to take your shirt off."

She saw the opportunity to lighten the moment and took it. "Most guys find it easier to get me out of my clothes if they add the word please."

The hand with the bandage paused in midair before he set it down and met her gaze. The flash of what she'd seen at the hospital was back. His eyes did that smolder thing that made her stomach freak. "I'll remember that."

Her stomach continued doing flips. Breaking eye contact,

she was suddenly self-conscious about him seeing her in nothing but her bra again. Extra self-conscious that she needed to ask for his help getting the shirt off since she could no longer lift her left arm.

Stubbornness took hold in her chest. With difficult, painful movements, she used her right hand and arm to maneuver the shirt up her belly and tug it off her left arm.

"Here," Michael said, moving so close to her his body heat warmed her inside and out. "Let me help you."

The softness of his voice, the true concern in his gentle touch, set fireworks off in her lower stomach.

A hot cup of Earl Grey on a cold day was heavenly. Michael Stone's hands on her body, his warm breath on her skin, was ecstasy.

Chapter Twenty-One

Michael clamped his back teeth down hard as he examined Brigit's wound.

Pity-blocking was a skill he'd learned after his father's death and continued to hone as an adult. He'd recently taken it to an art form after surviving his encounter with Fayez Raissi. Being at the mercy of a sociopathic prick was the epitome of loss of control.

The moment Brigit mentioned it and he'd frozen, he'd registered pity in her eyes. He could read her mind. He could hear her voice in his head. *You poor thing...*

His expression must have said it all. She'd apologized and then made a joke, almost daring him to flirt with her. Which he appreciated. He didn't have to call up one of his pity-blocking defenses and shift the conversation to safer ground.

The nightmares he'd experienced after the hostage situation were rare these days, but no less extreme when they hit. Even awake, when he looked at the den where Raissi had tried to blow him and the others sky high, the nightmares hung like phantoms in the air, toying with him. They were in the bullet holes he'd diligently patched, the blood he'd scrubbed repeatedly from the rug, and all over his desk where Raissi had sat and tormented him. The phantoms jacked memories and emotions best left alone.

That was another reason he spent so much time at Langley now. People there treated him with professionalism and respect, never mentioning the ordeal. They may have looked at him with pity early on, but never to his face. At CIA headquarters, he was Deputy Director Michael Stone, powerful and in complete control. Protector and defender of his country. Second in command of the world's premiere intelligence agency. There, in that role, he could face the world with the strength and determination he used to feel no matter where he went, where he ate, where he slept. Now, when he was home, he wanted—needed—to be back at the office and in the skin of his job.

Just thinking about Raissi made the old anger ignite in his stomach. It flared into rage over the helplessness he'd experienced against the man, the futility of wanting to raise Raissi from the dead so he could kill him all over again. Fighting terrorists these days had new meaning for Michael. Every one of them had Raissi's face.

It wasn't just his job anymore, it was his personal vendetta.

Using a wet cloth, Michael dabbed at the drying blood on Brigit's skin and she winced. "How long's it been since your last pain pill?" he asked.

Her face was turned away from him as if she didn't like the sight of blood. "I haven't had anything since they stitched me up."

No wonder she looked like hell. "Why?"

"Don't like drugs." She glanced at him, down at her shoulder and away again, blowing her tough-soldier façade. "Right now, though, I'm totally rethinking my stand on narcotics. My whole side hurts. Unfortunately, the scripts the doctor gave me for Percocet and an antibiotic went up in the fire."

She had to be in some serious pain. He rose from the barstool and rummaged through a nearby cabinet where he stored his vitamins. After finding his prescription bottle of Vicodin, he set it on the breakfast bar in front of her. "I'm out of antibiotics, but you're welcome to my pain meds."

She looked the prescription painkiller over and gave him an impish grin. "You'd share your drugs with me? Even when you think I had something to do with Ella's kidnapping? How noble."

Noble had nothing to do with it. His gut still told him Brigit was innocent—at least in the case of Ella's kidnapping.

Knowing people the way he did, especially spies, the only sure way to disarm them enough to get them talking was to pretend to be their friend. Get them to trust you.

He filled a glass of water and set it on the bar counter before fishing a pill from the bottle, admitting his concern for her well-being trumped his desire to get her to spill her guts. "You should take one now since you just ate."

An internal debate played across her face. "Will they make me sleepy?"

"Do you care?"

She took a deep breath and dropped her head so her hair screened her face. "I'm a walking zombie already, and I've got nowhere to crash. I take one of those and you'll have an overnight guest for sure."

"Like I said earlier, I planned on keeping you here anyway."

There was a pause. She spoke through clinched teeth. "Provided I tell you what you want to know."

"That was our deal."

"What about Julia?"

Michael took a step back. "What about Julia?"

Brigit shifted, looked up at him and then broke eye contact to stare at the counter. "Overstepping my boundaries again, but I assume she won't like you keeping me as an overnight guest."

Perplexed, he frowned. "I have no idea what you're talking about."

Her gaze came back to his. "You and Julia...you're not...you know? Together?"

Michael's pulse kicked under his skin. The expression on her face was almost hopeful. Usually if anyone asked, he denied there'd ever been anything between him and Julia. His gut, and his heart, rebelled when he did it, because he'd loved her deeply. "We were once. Not anymore."

Brigit's shoulders loosened and her dark lashes dipped for a second as she closed her eyes. Then she nodded and eyed the white pill in his hand.

Funny she'd pitied him after the crazy two days she'd just experienced. She'd been the target of a sniper, had spent a cold night in a giant concrete caterpillar, had her apartment burned down and been accused of a kidnapping. Truth be told, he would have a hard time kicking her out even if she didn't tell him her story.

"You're in pain, and it's only going to get worse when I sew up the wound where the sutures blew out. The doctor knotted them securely, but you must have put a lot of stress on them." He took her hand and put the pill in it. "Take the Vicodin."

"You're going to stitch me up?"

"Unless you want to take a trip back to the ER."

She shuddered and turned her face away from her shoulder and the bar top of first-aid supplies. Her voice was barely above a whisper. "Go for it."

Her skin was so pale, it was almost translucent. He could see a delicate blue vein running along her hairline. "You sure? I'm going to have to pour alcohol into the wound to cleanse it and the only needle I have is a fat little thing for sewing upholstery. It'll probably feel like an elephant pushing its way through your skin."

She slipped the pill into her mouth and swallowed it down with a gulp of water. Then she turned her head away again and squeezed her eyes shut. "Please tell me you've done this before. I really don't want a scar."

"All lacerations leave scars." He grabbed a tube of skin adhesive, pinched a glob onto a Q-tip and dotted it over the opening. "But I guarantee, my work will not leave a bigger scar." He added another layer and picked up the large sterile bandage he'd already unwrapped.

Brigit, her eyes still closed, gripped the edge of the bar with her right hand. "Tell me when you're going to start sewing."

"Okay."

"Okay, you'll tell me? Or okay you're ready to start sewing?"

He pressed the bandage onto her arm, hating her wince, and smoothed the adhesive edges. "All done."

She cracked one eye open and glanced at her shoulder. "All done?" Her other eye opened and she looked up at him, confusion evident in her features. "What about the stitching?"

He dangled the tube of skin adhesive in front of her face. "Dermabond. Needle-free."

"You said you had to stitch me up." She huffed out a breath. "I took the pain pill."

Shrugging, he kept the grin off his face as he gathered the bandage wrapper. "You pulled two sutures on the edge of the wound where it's not deep. The adhesive will hold the skin together unless you do something stupid and rip more sutures out."

Her eyes narrowed. "You tricked me."

"I did."

"Why?"

As he walked away to return his first-aid supplies to the bathroom, he wondered the same thing himself. She'd expected him to be the hard-ass, to interrogate her. Instead he'd done the opposite.

He stopped in the doorway and turned back. "It's all part of my evil plan. Feed you, doctor you and give you a place to sleep since you don't have one."

"So I'll be in your debt and at your mercy."

"Exactly." He was definitely enjoying that idea.

She mulled his confirmation over for a few seconds. "It's working."

"Yeah." He grinned. "I know."

While he was putting the bandages back in the vanity's drawer, his cell rang. Caller ID showed it was the president. Michael hadn't spoken to him since the previous day when he'd called the hospital, and the president never used anything but landlines. Curious, he hit the green talk button as he shut the bathroom door. "Stone."

"Michael, how's Ella?"

"Doing well, thank you, sir."

"Good, good." Under his usual smooth tone, the president's voice sounded tight, strained. "My sources tell me the FBI believes Brigit Kent had a hand in the kidnapping."

Since it was all over the news channels, Michael figured the president's sources were CNN and MSNBC. "I'm sure their investigation will be thorough."

"Yes, thorough..." President Jeffries's voice drifted off, and Michael's gut niggled. The president was worried about something.

An image of Brigit in her suit and heels outside the oval office flickered in his brain. As if someone clicked a hyperlink, pieces of the puzzle fell into bed with each other.

A thorough investigation into Brigit Kent might lead to the president and he was worried.

But why? What kind of relationship did they have?

Jeffries spoke again. "My sources tell me you removed her from the police station. She's in your custody?"

"Yes, sir."

"You pissed off a lot of people with that move today. Mind

explaining to me what you're doing?"

In the world of diplomacy and persuasion, explaining logic directly to people like the president never worked. Indirect speech was Michael's savior—to save face, to persuade, to escape from showing his hand. "I have knowledge a sector of international security beyond the kidnapping is at issue here. I'm duty-bound to investigate it and interrogate Dr. Kent before turning her back over to the FBI."

"I see." The clipped tone again made Michael's gut send a warning cruising through his body. "In my opinion, Dr. Kent would never be involved with anything so cruel as child kidnapping."

"I agree."

Silence reigned. Michael let it. Few people could stand forced silence. Human nature wanted to talk, to confess, to keep communication flowing.

The next words from Jeffries were calculated. "With your impeccable career, you should consider your actions carefully in this, Deputy Director."

Veiling a threat in a backhanded compliment was one of the president's linguistic specialties. Politicians as a whole often came across like Mafia wise guys offering protection in the form of concern or advice. Their soft sells were lined with a razor-edged threat, though. Ante up or say goodbye to your job, your family, your life.

Michael decided to answer more directly this time, and as was his way, he threw a giant dose of politeness on top of the pointed *back off* message. "I always consider my actions carefully, but thank you for the reminder, Mr. President."

There was a slight huff on the other end. Message received. "I expect you'll keep me posted of your findings with Dr. Kent. If international security is an issue, I want to be the first one to know the who, what, where and how. We clear?"

Abso*fucking*lutely. "Of course, sir."

The president disconnected and Michael shook his head as he stuck the phone back in its clip on his belt. What was in Brigit Kent's closet that made the president of the United States jumpy?

Time to find out. Michael opened the bathroom door and headed back to the kitchen.

Two steps down the hallway, he stopped. He had a straight

view of the breakfast bar and the empty barstools. Brigit had disappeared.

Picking up his pace, he stepped into the room, took one look around and confirmed she was gone. He checked the back entrance but the door was locked, the green light on his security dashboard near the door still on. Unless she could dematerialize like a vampire, Brigit was still in the house.

His search for her ended in the study. She'd moved the plastic cover from the couch and crashed on it, curling into a fetal position on her right side. The rabbit's foot her assistant had given her lay on the coffee table within reach.

In the deepening shadows of the approaching evening, Michael stood just inside the doorway and watched her sleep. The last people to sit on the couch had been his fellow hostages. Before them, Julia had smiled up at him from it, all the while betraying him with Flynn.

Lots of bad memories. They circled above his head, taunting him and making his stomach clench like he'd drunk Drano.

But then his eyes fell again on Brigit's sleeping form. Her dark hair lay in a mat of curls on the throw pillow. Her breathing was peaceful, the hovering phantoms invisible to her. Only Michael could see their soulless eyes, hear their demands, feel the cold muzzles of their guns skate across his skin.

He did a one-eighty and left the den, heading back to the kitchen. Leaning on the breakfast bar, he purposely slowed his breathing. Sweat beaded along his hairline and he went to the sink to splash his face with water. Once his pulse was under control again, he snagged a Sam Adams from the refrigerator and considered his options.

While he'd planned to get information out of Brigit before showing her to his guestroom, that plan was out. However, he needed to keep an eye on her. If she was indeed a spy for SIS, all his security couldn't keep her caged if she wanted to sneak off. She was sleeping like the dead right now, but when the Vicodin wore off and she'd recharged her batteries, who knew what she'd do? She hadn't been part of the kidnapping, but that didn't mean he trusted her.

Truth was, he didn't trust anyone these days.

Which was a sorry state to be in.

He hated sorry.

Taking a swig of beer, he walked back to the den. He had to do something while Brigit slept off her exhaustion and pain-medication cocktail.

He eyed his briefcase. Files and his laptop pushed at the leather to the point of breaking the zipper. He'd fallen behind in the last two days with basic paperwork, and even with everything else distracting him, it was tapping at the back of his mind like a clock alarm, dinging over and over. He didn't get sick days or vacation. Letting anything slide, even for twenty-four hours, could put the nation at risk. Bracing himself for the return trip to his study, he took another swig of beer and picked up the briefcase.

His desk sat in its temporary spot near the plasma flat screen over the fireplace and was covered with plastic. As Michael cleaned it off, he ignored the way his pulse jumped. Ignored the voices in his head and the echo of gunshots.

It's been six months. He chanted the words *six months* under his breath like a mantra. A logical mantra. Six months should have been more than enough time to get his head back on straight.

Once settled in his chair, he opened the briefcase, sorted the files into straight stacks and booted up his laptop. While it whirred and took him through several password codes and identification programs, his attention continued to stray to the couch across the room and the rise and fall of Brigit's upper body.

He envied her total surrender to sleep, yearning for a similar disconnect. When was the last time he'd slept like that? He couldn't remember, but it seemed like Julia had still been beside him.

Mesmerized by Brigit's body, he continued to watch, his own breathing slowing to match hers.

Darkness fell. When he could no longer make out her form on the couch, he forced himself to move and turn on his desk lamp. Then he picked up the receiver of his landline phone and dialed a number he never thought he'd use.

"Ace's Mortuary," a voice on the other end said. "My two-for-one special on body bags is good all month."

"Ace, this is Michael Stone."

The sound of rustling paper and something being knocked over came through the line. "Shit," Ace said under his breath.

In his mind, Michael could see the mortician fumbling to straighten what he'd knocked over. "Big Mike, how's it going, bro?"

God, he hated being called Big Mike. Hated having to go to Flynn's local source to get what he needed for Brigit. "I need antibiotics. Strong ones. And I need you to bring them to my house, ASAP."

"Uh-huh." The mortician sounded dumbfounded. "I run with the dead, you know. No call for antibiotics."

"But you have connections, and you owe me. Consider this a collection notice."

There was a long, awkward pause. A sigh of concession. "I got you, man. How many pills you need?"

"Two week supply. Leave them at the gate."

"You doping one of your spies or yourself?"

Michael glanced at Brigit. "TMI, Ace. You don't need to know."

"Uh-huh. Okay then. Give me a couple hours."

"One."

Ace's incredulousness came through even though he held back on his real thoughts. "Sure, one hour. Working miracles, that's me."

Michael hung up, stared some more at Brigit still curled in a fetal position. She looked so vulnerable, his need to protect kicked like a mule under his ribs.

The impulse was natural for him when it came to his family and his country, but it surprised him in regard to her. She'd done nothing to gain his trust, hadn't even told him what she'd promised. The impulse was so strong, though, he couldn't ignore it.

In his briefcase, he pulled out the memory stick Julia had given him. He plugged it into a USB port on his laptop and opened the single video file. As he watched Brigit leverage a gun at the woman standing next to the car, a tingling went down his spine. He leaned toward the screen.

When the woman moved in and hugged Brigit, he froze the scene. Zoomed in to get a better look at the woman's face under her knit cap. Same round eyes as Brigit, same straight nose.

Julia's words jogged through his brain. *The woman in the knit cap is apparently her sister. Went by the name Tory. They discussed a man named Peter, and Tory mentioned she was involved with him and an international war...*

Brigit Kent was protecting her sister.

Her sister who looked almost like her twin. So much so, a six-year-old under duress might confuse them.

His hunch Brigit was innocent of the kidnapping confirmed, Michael sat back and heaved a sigh of relief. It was wrong to protect her sister, who was obviously involved with terrorists, but thinking about his own family, he considered what he would do if Ruthie or Martha had gone down that path. His first impulse was always to protect the ones he loved.

Leaving his desk, he dug out an afghan blanket from an antique trunk near the fireplace and laid it over Brigit. She stirred, latching on to the blanket and pulling it up to her chin. Her eyes fluttered opened. For once they were unguarded and soft. Trusting.

Sexy.

A small smile slipped over her mouth as she looked up at him and with a sigh, she closed her eyes. He watched her slip back into the oblivion of sleep, mesmerized again by the rise and fall cadence of her breathing.

In the kitchen, he snagged another Sam from the fridge and tuned in to the ping-ponging of his pulse. This round's erratic jumping was due to the woman on his couch. He tried to bridle it and then thought, *ah, hell*, and gave in, riding it. Since Julia had left him, he'd put all feeling, except the anger and hatred directed at Raissi, on pause. When other emotions popped up, he'd dusted them like a prize fighter going after an opponent, leaving nothing but numbness in their place. For the first time in a long while, numbness or anger didn't appeal to him.

Like a photograph, an image of Brigit's trusting eyes flashed in his mind, those big baby dolls looking at him like he was the best thing since dark chocolate.

Returning to the den, he settled himself behind his desk. His gaze sought her out even though he tried to focus on the work waiting for him. Pongo lay on the floor beside her, stretched out and sleeping as hard as she was. Dumb dog, he was such a sucker for pretty women.

As the grandfather clock chimed seven o'clock, the phantoms in the room faded into the walls and the carpet. Brigit's breathing deepened. Pongo snored. A blanket of calm settled over Michael.

He pulled the first file off the stack and began to read about Peter Donovan.

Chapter Twenty-Two

Brigit woke to the sound of soft chiming. Years peeled away and she was suddenly six again, wondering why her mum had let her oversleep. The church bells were ringing. They'd be late for mass.

The chiming continued, *bong...bong...bong*, and Brigit struggled to open her eyes. The lids were heavy, refusing to cooperate. She called for her mother, nothing coming out of her throat but a raw sound. A dull ache rolled through her body and alarm ricocheted under her skin. She swallowed and tried again. "Mum?"

"You're all right, Brigit," a deep male voice said beside her. She sensed he was kneeling over her. Who was he? Not her father. Peter? Frantic, she squirmed and fought to open her eyes. Like in nightmares, the harder she tried, the heavier her lids became.

The voice murmured again, shushing her. "Hey, it's okay. You're safe."

Even though his voice was soft and kind, fear spiked in her chest. Peter wanted to hurt her. "No," she whimpered, twisting her body away from the man.

A heavy hand grasped her right arm. "Brigit, stop it. You're going to wreck your stitches."

Stitches? Suddenly, everything fell into place. Her mother was dead. This wasn't Belfast. There was no church to attend. No God or Blessed Mother to worship.

There was only her life, full of longing and charged with regret.

Her eyes flew open and she found herself staring up into Michael Stone's anxious face.

"Michael," she gasped, relief drenching her like a cascade of water. His hand was exceptionally strong and yet tender on her uninjured arm where he held her. "It's..." *Not Peter.* "...you."

"Disappointed?" He helped her sit up. A sweatshirt and nylon running pants had replaced the dress shirt and slacks. His feet were bare. "You were maybe expecting the president?"

She chuckled at the joke and then realized he wasn't making a joke. "What?"

He shrugged it off, sat on the coffee table. His knees touched hers. "How do you feel?"

Groggy, but no longer exhausted. A little achy. A lot weirded out that once again he'd been watching her sleep. She drew her left arm closer to her body, wincing as her wound bit deep into her muscle. How could a flesh wound cause so much pain? "Fine. I'm fine."

"Sure you are." He reached for a piece of white cardboard folded in half like a miniature book on the table next to him. After flipping it open, he pushed out a fat pill from a blister and handed it to her.

"More drugs?" she asked. "What does this one do? Make me confess all my sins?"

He handed her a glass of water. "Not unless you have one mean reaction to Zithromax."

He was doing a fine mother-hen impression. Brigit downed the pill while a warm sensation crept into her chest. No one had taken care of her since her dad had thrown her out of his house when she was seventeen, and his parental care had never been loving. A lump rose in her throat and she choked it back down. "Have they found Peter yet?"

"Not yet."

Disappointment sank into her bones. The odds of catching him grew slimmer with each passing hour. At least Ella was safe. "What time is it?"

"Midnight. You can have another pain pill if you need it."

Another pain pill and a few more hours of sleep sounded like heaven. A heaven she couldn't really afford. "Nah, but I'd kill for a hot shower."

Michael eyed her, speculating, she assumed, if she was sincere about the killing part. Had he found out about her mother? The truth about what had happened that night? *It was an accident. I lost my balance and knocked the candle over.*

The memory of that night spilled from the recesses of her mind. The way the candle's flame jumped to the spilled whiskey and ate the newspapers. The smoke and fire swiftly engulfing the tiny kitchen as her mother shoved Brigit and Tory past Peter toward the door. The way Tory tripped on the stairs, crying, and Brigit had to right her and keep pulling her away. Away from the fire. Away from Peter...

Michael took the glass from her suddenly shaking hand. "You feel okay? You're white as a sheet."

Brigit swallowed and nodded even though she wasn't.

He returned the glass to the table next to the rabbit's foot. "How about a bath instead of a shower. I'd have to waterproof your bandage for a shower."

"Bath it is, then," she said, standing, her voice low and rough.

He stopped her with a raised hand. Pointed to the couch as if commanding her to sit. "After you answer some questions."

Questions. There were always questions.

While the deal had slipped quietly away, and she'd been able to forget the mess she was in for a little while, it was almost a relief he was finally going to get down to business.

Just like Pongo, she responded to Michael's command, lowering herself to the couch. As she leaned her back against the soft fabric, every cell in her body screamed for her to run, to keep the secrets buried in her limbs and organs, like a good girl.

Keep your mouth shut, that was always the rule. With her father, with her sister, with SIS. Steeling herself against the alarm rippling under her skin again, she looked him straight in the eye. "Ask away."

While his face was set in deputy-director mode, his eyes were soft. "Who do you work for?"

"I'm an independent consultant. You know that."

He stared at her, saying nothing. Waiting. He was very good at waiting. She relented, childish. "I'm currently consulting with DHS on behalf of the president."

"What's the president got you doing?"

Her father's face flashed in front of her eyes. She cleared her throat. "I'm not at liberty to say."

"The only thing he cares about at the moment is getting

reelected, so I assume you're helping him with that in some way."

Denying would be futile. He would read the lie in her face no matter how hard she tried to cover it. She remained silent.

Michael took her silence for assent. Lifting her BlackBerry from the coffee table, he dangled it in midair. "Homeland Security doesn't use terms like 'lie back and think of England'. That's code. Operative language. You don't work for me, so who burned you?"

Surprise overrode caution. "You broke into my email?"

He shrugged as if it were a forgone conclusion he would do such a thing. "MI6? G2? You've been a consultant for both the British and the Irish."

The need to cover that section of her resume was gone, but the training beaten into her about it still functioned. "Does it matter? I'm on my own now. I've got nobody and nothing."

"You've still got the president."

Big plus there. Michael was right though. Consulting for DHS—a.k.a. the president—was more than nothing. She could still work something out.

He set her phone down, rested his elbows on his knees and leaned toward her, intertwining his fingers. "He called earlier to check on you. Warned me not to prod you too much."

Like in the back of the Navigator, a sudden flush of warmth spread in her veins. His big body was entirely too close. Too male. Too in control. She sputtered the first thing that sprang to mind. "He's scared of you."

A thoughtful smile thinned Michael's lips, as if she'd confirmed something he already knew. "Who are you protecting, Brigit? Your sister or the president of the United States?"

Who *wasn't* she protecting? "So you read my personnel file as well?" Her voice conveyed the incredulousness she was fighting.

"Your DHS personnel file has nothing on your family, except the fact your father was part of a political envoy Jeffries sent to Bolivia last year. He was charged with conspiring to cause a public nuisance and ended up in one of the toughest jails down there. Negotiations have failed."

Her stomach did a flip at the mention of her father being held and probably tortured for fun, but she couldn't dwell on him right now. "Then how did you know about my..." Sudden realization hit. "Julia told you about my intercepting Tory the other night."

"She and Zara videoed the whole thing."

"Shit." Brigit dropped her head back against the couch and dragged a hand through her smelly hair. A line of Oscar Wilde's poetry ran through her head, *we are each our own devil, and we make this world our hell.*

She'd certainly done a good job of building her own hell.

Michael's gaze was confident. He had her where he wanted her. The food, the medicine, the comfort he'd provided was just foreplay. Now he was ready to screw her. *Lie back and think of England...*

Family. Brigit lifted her head from the couch. He was very family-oriented. Surely he could relate to her situation. "You know how it is with your siblings. You don't always understand them but you try to love them anyway."

A spark of compassion lit his eyes. "And help them in any way you can."

Exactly. "Tory and I lost our mother when we were very young. She's always blamed me for what happened and made a lot of bad choices based on that."

"Like joining Donovan's terrorist group?"

"Yes."

"So you studied Donovan and tracked his group, but never tried to shut him down because Tory might get caught as well."

Brigit's spine stiffened. "I love my sister, but I would never jeopardize innocent people to save her. Peter is just as intelligent and clever as you and I. He's a damn good terrorist, and Tory is guilty by association, but she's never done the dirty work herself."

"But you could have arrested her the other night and you didn't."

Again, his logic was spot on. A lump rose in her throat and tears pushed against her eyelids. "I hadn't seen her in so long, and I just...I wanted to talk to her. To try and talk sense into her. For our mother's sake if nothing else."

She swallowed hard and blinked back the tears. Michael unlocked his fingers and patted the side of her knee. "She may be a terrorist, but she's still your sister."

A shock of electricity ran up her leg and she struggled to

ignore it. "Doesn't matter. I failed to do what was right. I had an inkling Peter was involved in the kidnapping. If I'd arrested her, I might have been able to break the case open sooner and saved Ella from the trauma of the fire." She met his eyes. "I'm truly, truly sorry."

"Me too," he said. "Because now I have to hunt down Tory as well as Donovan."

Brigit's throat pinched off air. She stuttered. "Hunt...hunt them down?"

"They messed with my family. I can't let either of them go."

"But the FBI—"

"The FBI and their counterparts are doing everything they can to find and capture Donovan, but the odds are they'll fail. I won't." His face, his voice, were hard and unrelenting. Batman was back. "You know why?"

Brigit shook her head.

"Because you're going to help me."

Or else. The unsaid words hovered in the space between them. "If I refuse?"

"I'll deposit your butt back at the D.C. Police Department and let Detective Hayden bring charges against you."

"Even though you know I'm innocent."

"Yes."

He, Julia and Zara were the only ones who knew about Tory, and the two agents would never take Brigit's side over Michael's. Even if Brigit offered Tory up on a silver platter to Detective Hayden, he wouldn't believe her and she could offer no proof.

But could she betray her own sister? "I don't like being blackmailed."

"Most people don't." He tapped his index finger against her knee. "If you help me, you'll get first crack at setting things straight with your sister and that's a helluva lot more than you'll get if the FBI finds her. I want justice, but I'll work on leniency for her when it's all said and done." He tapped her knee again. "If you cooperate."

Her stomach churned. "Peter Donovan is the one you want. Tory is just a confused young woman. She needs a psychiatrist, not a jail cell."

"She took part in a kidnapping. Confused or not, she's a

criminal. You can't save her from prosecution. Nor should you."

Making a deal with a man like Michael Stone was always risky, and yet she had no choice. The only way to protect Tory, get her some help, was to aid him in bringing her in.

We are each our own devil. Brigit locked her attention on Michael's large, strong hands and considered her future. She couldn't stop Peter, save Tory and rescue her father without help. A lot of help. And not the kind of carrot-dangling-in-your-face help the president kept offering. SIS and their resources were no longer at her fingertips. Her job was gone, her apartment left in smoldering ruins, and she was wanted in connection with Ella's kidnapping. No more Miss Nice Guy. It was time to pull up her big girl knickers and deal.

Lucky for her, blackmail worked both ways. "I'll help you find Peter," she said, leaning forward so her face was only inches from his. "But in the end, if we find Tory too, you'll pull the strings necessary to get her charges reduced *and* provide counseling. Deal?"

A hint of a smile danced on his lips. He tilted his head a fraction as if he were amused by her challenge. "You're not in a position to bargain, Dr. Kent."

She mirrored his smile and his head tilt. "Wanna bet?"

His lips thinned and his eyes narrowed a fraction as he mulled over her challenge. "What aren't you telling me?"

"There's something you should know about your sister and the president."

His body tensed. It was there and gone in a flash. Fear? "Spill it."

"No." She tapped his knee with her finger, refusing mercy and enjoying the way he was squirming inside even if he kept a tight lid on it. "That card is the only trump I have. I want your word you'll do whatever you can to help Tory when we find her, and I also want your word you'll help rescue my father from Bolivia. If you do all that, I'll give you the information and the proof to back it up about your sister. And then I'll help you bury it."

Doubt danced in his expression as he considered whether her claim was bogus, the convenient story of a desperate woman. It was easy enough to lay his doubts to rest. "Why do you think Jeffries warned you not to prod me?"

A minute of strained silence passed as he ground his teeth.

Finally, he let go of a controlled sigh, and his breath was warm on her face. "How do we find Peter Donovan?"

She held out her hand. "We have a deal then, Director?"

The phone on his desk rang. After a moment's pause, he slid his hand into hers. His grip was solid, his shake firm. "We have a deal."

As the realization she'd gone toe to toe with Michael Stone and won sank in, a heady satisfaction rushed through her. So did the urge to kiss him.

Whoa, back the cart up. She settled for giving his hand a tug instead.

And was rewarded when he tugged back as he rose to answer the phone.

Chapter Twenty-Three

Michael stared across his desk at the top of Brigit's head. It was bent as she studied his file on Peter Donovan. She'd bathed and her freshly washed hair hung around her face. She kept tucking sections behind her ears, but as the dark tresses dried, they formed natural waves that sprang forward like stretched rubber bands snapping back into place. Because she'd had no clean clothes to replace her smoky-smelling running attire, Michael had given her one of his T-shirts and a pair of sweats.

While she'd cleaned up in his upstairs bathroom, he'd placed the necessary calls to get the FBI chasing Tory and the charges against Brigit dropped. He'd also made sure Ella was back home safe and sound.

Brigit flipped a paper over, then pushed her hair back from her face. Keeping her eyes on the paper, she used the fingers of her right hand to make graceful sweeps through the curls, which coiled back immediately. She did it again, and Michael's concentration slipped another notch.

She glanced up. "Do you have any hairbands?"

Grabbing a section of his short hair and pulling up a whole half an inch, he cocked a brow at her.

"Right," she said. "I just thought maybe Julia or one of your other female friends might have left one here."

Her continual references to Julia did not escape notice. Even though his relationship with Julia was in the past, he liked the fact Brigit appeared threatened by her. Deciding it didn't hurt to feed Brigit's anxiety about his *other female friends*, he said, "Sorry, I haven't noticed any."

She dropped her head back, closed her eyes and let out a sigh. "I can still smell the smoke in my hair. It's driving me nuts."

All he could smell was his shampoo on her. And his soap. He liked the smell and the image of her in his bathtub washing her curves with his bath products. He blinked the image away. "Smoke is hard to get out. It may take more than one shampooing to do it."

"Especially since I'm gimped." She wiggled the fingers of her left hand, peeking out of the sling he'd given her for her arm. It was the one he'd used after his surgery. "Only having one hand, and that one being my right, I wasn't very thorough."

"You can try again in the morning."

She closed the file, setting it on his desk as she stood. "No, I won't be able to sleep. The smell brings back old nightmares. I've got to wash it again now. Mind if I do it in the kitchen sink? It might be easier."

Nightmares could be triggered by the smallest things. He'd gone around that block a time or two. Her smoke trigger could mean several different things. Either way, what did he care if she washed her hair again?

Nodding his consent, he filed the fact away and watched her walk out of the study, her hips lost in his sweatpants. She'd tugged the drawstring as tight as it would go and rolled the waistband over several times. Still, she'd had to fold cuffs into the pant legs to keep from walking on them.

A minute later, he heard her in the kitchen. He followed the sound of running water and pulled up short in the doorway. She'd removed the sling and his T-shirt, and his eyes locked on her creamy white back intersected by her bra strap as she bent to put her head under the copper faucet. The waistband of his sweatpants dipped low, revealing a shooting-star tattoo on her lower back. He sucked in air as small explosions fired in his brain.

He'd been able to keep his mind off her cleavage when it had been on display at the hospital because she'd been hurt. Now the soft pink bra strap reminded him of the cups cradling her full breasts.

Brigit's right hand snaked out to grab his bottle of shampoo on the counter and knocked it over, sending it skidding off and falling to the floor. "Damn it."

She tried to keep her dripping head over the sink as she used her foot to maneuver the bottle toward her.

Michael took three punching strides and rescued the bottle from the floor. "Let me help you."

"Oh." Her body tensed, no doubt since she was half-naked and again at his mercy. "Thanks." Her tone oozed insincerity.

Chuckling to himself, he set the bottle on the counter. "You missed a spot." With a gentle push, he eased her head back down so he could use the spray nozzle, his fingers parting her hair to make sure it was saturated. She put her good arm on the lip of the sink for support and leaned into the water.

He worked the water through her hair, enjoying the way the thick hair clung to his fingers. Grabbing the shampoo bottle, he squeezed out a coin-sized amount of the liquid and went to work massaging it into her scalp.

"Ah," she sighed, the sound warming the blood in his veins. The tension in her shoulders evaporated. The bunched muscles in her back smoothed. Her whole body relaxed.

His, however, did just the opposite. The sound of her voice, the sight of the tattoo, the memory of her luscious curves sparked a flash bang of heat low in his gut. His senses cartwheeled. A need, dormant for months, rose and spread under his skin with a fierce intensity.

He wanted the sensation to go on, but the voice inside his mind joined in the cartwheels, panic evident. Even though he was working with her to hunt down Donovan, Brigit was the enemy. She was blackmailing him. He was blackmailing her.

And while he wouldn't kid himself about the sexual attraction oozing through his veins, he wasn't into delusions either. Casual sex might be an option, but it was a damn poor one considering their current level of distrust with each other.

She moved under him, adjusting her arm position, and her hip brushed against his leg. His body stomped on his logic. What did a little innocent fantasizing hurt? He let his gaze roam over her backside, noticing how his sweats emphasized her butt while she was bent over. It was a nice butt. A really nice butt.

With an intricate tat riding it.

Damn. As he rinsed the shampoo from her hair, he let his senses soak her up while his imagination did a wheelhouse spin in the casual-sex department.

Two minutes later, he toweled her hair and forced his mind out of the erotic dreamscape in his head. His nylon sport pants were entirely too formfitting, and after he helped her put his shirt back on, he pushed her ahead of him toward the stairs.

"Where are we going?"

He adjusted his pants behind her back. "To bed."

She stopped abruptly and shot him a quizzical look over her shoulder. He righted himself and used his hand to propel her forward again. "My guestroom is all yours."

"Oh."

As they climbed, Michael couldn't stop thinking about her tattoo. "For someone who can't stomach needles, I'm surprised you'd go under one for a tat."

Again she shot him a look that questioned his roaming eyes. "I didn't. It's a temporary one. A shooting star for luck."

"Only for the person who sees it. You can't see your..." He cleared his throat. "Back there."

"Guess you're the lucky one then tonight."

Under her gaze, he faltered, a million and one comments running through his head, every last one of them completely inappropriate.

Pongo came out of nowhere and rushed up the stairs, passing them both by.

Brigit laughed, a bit of edge in the sound as if she realized what he'd been thinking, and suddenly she was bashful and eager to change the subject. "Looks like he's ready for bed too. Does he sleep in your room?"

Another quirk of hers that intrigued him. Her ability to be Miss Take No Shit one minute, a flirt the next, and then, in the blink of an eye, a self-conscious ingénue.

She glanced at him, waiting for a response. She'd asked a question. Change of subject. *Deep breath. Speak.* "Normally he sleeps outside in his kennel."

Her eyes widened a fraction. "In this cold weather?"

At the top of the stairs, he directed Brigit to the guestroom. "He likes the cold."

She visibly shivered and rubbed her injured arm as she stepped into the room.

Michael stayed in the doorway and flipped the light switch. Pongo, who'd gone to his room, trotted back out and into the guestroom. He sat down beside Brigit and looked at Michael, canting his head a fraction as if confused about the sleeping arrangements.

"There's a guest bath behind that door," Michael told Brigit. "Extra blankets are in the bottom dresser drawer."

She took the towel off and shook her hair out. "Any chance you have a blow dryer?"

He had a compact hair dryer somewhere. One of his sisters had given it to him as a Christmas gift years ago. He'd never used it, always planned to throw it out or give it to Maria. Now he was glad he'd kept it as he headed into his bathroom. It was in a drawer...

A pair of pink bikinis hanging on his shower door like a neon sign froze him in place. Brigit's sport pants and top were scattered on the window seat, but all he could focus on were the panties.

She'd washed out her underwear. Since she only had the pair she was wearing during the fire, it made perfect sense she'd do so, but seeing them sent a jolt of awareness skating through him. *Commando*, the neon sign flashed, *inside your sweats.*

His earlier mental peepshow exploded in Technicolor, and he groaned under his breath.

Her voice from the other room startled him. "Michael? Are you okay?"

No, he was not okay. He was turning into a freaking perv. "Fine," he grumbled. Jerking his attention away from the panties and concentrating on the double sink vanity, he opened the bottom drawer and dug through a bunch of miscellanea, finding the small blue Conair dryer.

Back in the guestroom, as he handed it to her, he noticed she was holding her injured arm again. "Do you need another painkiller?"

She took the dryer, fingers brushing against his. "Nah."

He checked his watch. "You can take one every four to six hours and it's after one, so you're clear if that's what you're worried about."

"I'm okay." She smiled, and he could see the lie in the strain of her face.

Sleep was the best medicine, and he wanted her fresh and ready to go in the morning. However, he couldn't make her take a pill if she didn't really want it, and she wouldn't fall for a trick this time. "I'll be downstairs for awhile if you change your mind."

"You're not going to bed?"

"I have a few things to wrap up first."

He snapped his fingers at Pongo to come. The dog took his time rising to his feet and leaving the room, as if he couldn't believe he didn't get to spend the night with Brigit. "If I'm not downstairs, I'll be in the bedroom next door."

She nodded, her drying hair already curling around her face.

At two thirty in the morning, he signed off on the last op in his file and shut down his laptop. The house was quiet except for Pongo's snores in the hallway. The dog had seemed torn between wanting to be in the den with Michael and upstairs in the guestroom with Brigit, so he'd chosen a spot in between and settled down for the night.

Michael snagged the rabbit's foot from the coffee table and examined it. The white fur under his thumb was soft, like Brigit's hair. She was a conundrum.

She had a doctorate in psychology but believed in good-luck charms. Clever and beautiful as any spy, and yet she didn't act or talk like an operative. Her reluctance to share information about the president could have been simple loyalty. Duty to a man who commanded fidelity. The way her face had blanched when Michael mentioned Jeffries, though, told him loyalty wasn't her motive.

Fear maybe.

If he had to guess, he'd bet the president was blackmailing her too. Had to be over her father's kidnapping in Bolivia. Michael squirmed, thinking he had also placed Brigit in an uncomfortable position and played on her blood bonds to get what he wanted. Was he any different from Jeffries?

Because Michael had previously been Director of Operations, in charge of the entire spy group, he didn't trust anyone, and took the Boy Scout motto to extremes. At his desk, he pulled out a tracking device the size of a lithium watch battery. He pinched off the gold metal top of the rabbit's foot and examined it. The tiny GPS fit perfectly under the cap up against a similar one already there.

So Gunn was keeping track of Brigit's whereabouts as well. Smart man. Flynn was right to put Smitty on his trail.

After attaching the unit, he set the lid back in place and used his fingers to press the flimsy metal tight to secure it.

Hitting the kitchen before he went to bed, he grabbed the bottle of Vicodin and a fresh glass of water. As he took the stairs to the second story, his steps were light and quick. He'd caught up on paperwork, emails and meeting minutes. He'd even read the file on Peter Donovan cover to cover. It hadn't taken long. There was little information about the man's childhood, but only scant details about his adult life as well, starting at the point of his first incarceration at the age of fifteen. Still, Michael figured he could throw a few resources at tracking him and find him in a week, two tops.

He peeked into the guestroom. Light sliced into the room from the bathroom's door as it stood slightly ajar. Brigit was in bed, her back to him, a pillow propped against her back to keep her left shoulder upright. Her breathing was light but rhythmic. Michael set the Vicodin, water and rabbit's foot on the nightstand. If she woke up in pain, at least she'd have the option to relieve it. If she tried to give him the slip, he'd be able to track her.

In his bathroom, he eyed the pink bikinis and hummed under his breath as he brushed his teeth.

Since it was only a few hours before he'd have to be at the office to pick up the President's Daily Brief and be on his way to the White House, he decided not to even turn down his covers. Instead he lay on top of the duvet, crossed his fingers on top of his chest and let his mind return to the ever-growing erotic images of Brigit. Since he wouldn't sleep anyway, it seemed like a nice way to pass the time.

Chapter Twenty-Four

Buzz, buzz, buzz. The pulsing ring cut through Brigit's sleep. She bolted upright into a sitting position, and her shoulder balked, sending her right back down to the bed. The slap of pain brought her fully awake, though, and she blinked at the soft light in the room, struggling to remember where she was. The ringing came again. A phone? An alarm clock?

She did a quick survey of her surroundings. As soon as her eyes lit on the pill bottle and rabbit's foot on the bedside table, the previous night's antics flooded her memory.

Michael.

She was in his house. No longer stupid from exhaustion, she stared at the pills and water, trying to reconcile the man who was blackmailing her with the man who had sealed up her wound, lent her his clothes and gently washed her hair.

The bright blue numbers on the alarm clock next to her rabbit's foot read six-oh-five. Pongo trotted into the room and whined at her as the phone rang a second time. Throwing back the covers with her good hand, she shifted her weight, balancing carefully, to swing her feet over the side of the bed. She gauged the ringing was coming from the room next door.

Why wasn't Michael answering his phone? She patted the dog and tiptoed into the hall.

His bedroom door was open and he was facedown on top of the bed's comforter. A pillow was over his head but she didn't need to see his shut eyes to know he was sleeping. His snores rumbled out of him, only slightly muffled by the pillow.

A BlackBerry in a black skin vibrated manically on the nightstand, the screen showing an unidentified number. Another ring emanated from it and after a heartbeat of internal debate, Brigit picked it up, more to stop it from waking up Michael than anything else.

She hit the green phone-receiver button and back-stepped out of the room. "Hello?"

There was a pause, long and guarded, from the caller. She frowned at Pongo, who plunked his butt down on the wooden floor and dropped his muzzle to look up at her with a *You've done it now* expression.

"May I help you?" she said, wondering if it was a wrong number or if she really had made a mistake answering it. She stepped into the guestroom and snatched up the rabbit's foot on the table. *What was I thinking, answering his phone? Why don't they say something?*

A man's gruff voice finally spoke. He sounded like he had pea gravel in his throat. "Well, well, Michael's got himself a new playmate, I see. That's good. About damn time, if you ask me. You just watch your pretty little ass and don't rain on his parade, you hear me? My deputy director's been through enough in the past six months. Now put him on the phone, honey."

New playmate? Pretty little ass? *Honey?* Brigit gritted her teeth, not sure which term irritated her more. "He's indisposed at the moment. May I relay a message?"

The man barked out a laugh. "Indisposed? At six in the morning? He's usually run ten miles, had a shower and stopped a dozen terrorists by this time. What the hell's he doing?"

Brigit made a face again, this time at the messy bed. *Never, ever should have answered the phone.* "May I tell him who's calling?"

"Titus," the man growled at her. "His boss."

Oh, God. Brigit took the phone away from her face and looked up at the ceiling, squeezing the rabbit's foot in her left hand. A dull ache set up shop in her shoulder. She put the phone back to her ear. "Shall I take a message or have him call you back, Director Allen?"

The fact she used his title and last name seemed to placate the man. Some. "Tell him I'm doing the PDB today before the president heads to Iowa. Jeffries wants to talk to me in person. About him, Michael. I don't know what he did to piss the man off, but I'll catch him afterwards and fill him in." He paused. "You got that?"

Brigit's mind whirled with the implications of what Titus had just said. "Yes, I have it."

The phone went dead.

Her legs didn't want to work as she shuffled back to Michael's bedroom. He was still snoring, so she sat in a chair near a set of patio doors which led outside to a deck. She shifted her eyes between him and the rising sun. When he wasn't pinning her with his x-ray vision or blackmailing her, he had the ability to calm her.

Pongo sat beside the chair and dropped his head into her lap, his big dark eyes expectant. He probably needed to pee, needed to be fed. Should she wake Michael or let him sleep? Why hadn't he set his alarm?

If Titus Allen was doing the president's morning briefing, what would it hurt to let Michael sleep a little while longer? She rose and motioned for Pongo to follow her. On the way past the nightstand, she set the BlackBerry down. She'd take care of the dog and wake Michael at six thirty. It was the least she could do after he'd taken such good care of her.

Back in her room, she went to slip his sweatpants on when she realized she wasn't wearing underwear. Damn, after everything last night, she'd gone and left them in his bathroom with the rest of her clothes she'd washed in the sink.

The panties were still hanging over the shower door. Brigit chastised herself like a good Catholic should even though she no longer practiced any faith. Some childhood things were hard to cast off.

Once dressed and the arm sling in place, she tucked the rabbit's foot into the pocket of the sweats and headed downstairs.

She let Pongo out and discovered the dog food container in the mudroom. Two scoops filled the bowl and she retrieved his half-empty water dish to refill it in the kitchen, absently aware of a pulsing beep as she passed the security panel. Just as she got to the sink, a loud buzz made her jump.

"Deputy Director?" a voice called through the intercom of the security panel. "Pongo's tripped the motion detectors in quadrant 2A. You might want to shut that section off."

Crap, she'd forgotten about the security system. Finding the wall panel, she pushed the talk button. "Er, sorry. The director is still sleeping and Pongo needed to go out, and, I, um…"

Another man, another voice, cut in. "He's still sleeping? But his car is waiting."

His car? Ah, crud. "He's going to the office later than usual today, so how about he calls you when he's ready for the car?"

There was another of those long, pregnant pauses. Apparently Michael adhered to a strict daily schedule. His oversleeping threw off everyone. Brigit tried to lighten the moment. "You gentlemen know where the coffee maker is?"

She got no reply. O-*kay*. "So how do I turn off the motion detector for the dog's area?"

The male voice on the other end was stern. "Yellow button, bottom right. Marked 2A."

"Right-o. Thanks."

She clicked off the speaker and slouched against the wall. She was really screwing things up for Michael. First with the president, then Titus, now even his security guards.

Tough. There was no reason for her to feel guilty about making him look bad. Her mind flashed back to their midnight talk on the couch. He was messing up her life as well, blackmailing her to find Peter and putting Tory's life in the balance. Little did he know she would have helped him hunt down her mother's true killer without any threat at all.

Brigit sank her right hand into the pocket of the sweatpants and rubbed the rabbit's foot. Suddenly, she didn't care if she got Michael in a little trouble. It would be interesting to see how he reacted, and it seemed to her he could stand to loosen up a bit.

She made her way to the study, picked up the landline and dialed Truman's number. "Gunn," he answered on the first ring. He always answered on the first ring.

"Tru, it's me. What's happening?"

"Gidget? Where are you? Still at Stone's house?"

"Yes. He's sort of holding me prisoner, but since I haven't got anywhere else to go right now, it seems like a deal."

"How's the gunshot wound?"

"Better. Listen, have you found Peter yet?"

"You on a secure line?"

"Would I call you otherwise?"

"No Peter, but I found Moira. I finally deciphered the call

that put us on Tory's ass from the other night. Peter paid the ransom for Moira to walk free."

"Damn it, I should have known. Peter and the notorious Moira Raphael."

"Poster child for beautiful deadly women everywhere."

Dropping into Michael's office chair, she closed her eyes and tried to ignore the shiver running down her spine. "Peter put up the ransom money and made Moira pay him back in blood."

"You got it, Gidge."

"Where is she now?"

"No clue. She and Peter were bedfellows once. Maybe they are again. Wouldn't be the first time they escaped together. Either way, he rescued her, and her job was to assassinate O'Bern. O'Bern disappeared on her, but you took his place. Since you've been trailing her almost as long as Peter, she must have seen it as divine intervention. An even trade."

Peter might have viewed it the same way. "Remember the last time they worked together? In Italy?"

"They escaped on a cruise ship dressed as an elderly couple."

"Better make sure all your resources are playing their A game. Peter's a master of disguise. I'll be in touch."

She returned the handset to its cradle. Her mind whirled with a dozen to-dos, but she knew it was all up to the FBI, Customs and other agents watching the airports, bus terminals and boat docks to find Peter, Tory and Moira. The problem was, had always been, finding three people out of thousands, who could use a dozen different means of escape.

Her stomach growled. Since she couldn't face the day and what it might bring on an empty stomach, she ventured back to the kitchen.

Her breakfast usually consisted of a cup of tea, but this morning she needed something stronger. She was starving and tea just wasn't gonna cut it.

In one of the cabinets, she found a fancy espresso machine that probably cost more than her entire set of kitchen appliances. Before the fire anyway. She checked the pantry and found a bag of beans and a coffee grinder. It would make a lot of noise, but if that didn't wake Michael up, he needed sleep far worse than anything else.

As the mill ground the beans into powder, Brigit brought Pongo in from his outside run. She even remembered to punch the yellow button and reactivate the backyard's motion detector.

Ten minutes later, one espresso and one cappuccino were ready. And still there was no Michael.

She carried the drinks upstairs, sipping the foam of her cappuccino.

Michael was still in the throes of deep sleep. His massive body covered the king-size bed with complete abandon. It was funny to see him so relaxed. In that moment, he was perfectly at peace. Brigit felt her own body mellow in response.

Unable to bring herself to wake him, she set the espresso on the nightstand and resumed her seat in the chair to drink her cap. She might as well return the favor of observing him while he slept.

Michael woke with a start, his heart jackhammering at his rib cage as the realization he'd overslept hit him. *Over*slept? The very idea he'd slept period shocked him.

Brigit's voice, perky and smug, came to him from the corner. "Morning," she said. "Sleep well?"

He jerked upright, glanced at her and then at his bedside clock. Why hadn't he set the alarm? "Jesus, it's seven o'clock. I'm late."

Hopping out of bed, he shot a hand through his hair and turned his back to her as he adjusted his pants around a morning erection. "How long have you been sitting there?"

"Long enough to know you talk in your sleep."

"Jesus," he said again, snatching up his phone.

"I already spoke to Director Allen, and he's handled the President's Daily Brief. I took care of Pongo and called Irene to let her know you'd be late. I think she might have stroked out."

He stopped dialing, hit the disconnect button and turned to face her, his erection much less full. "Why didn't you wake me?"

She was wearing her nylon exercise pants and top again. For some reason, he was disappointed. "What, and miss the chance to snoop through your house?" She grinned as he scowled. "By the way, there's something I want to ask you."

He slapped the phone down and picked up the white cup of

nearly black liquid. "I can hardly wait."

"Do you like your job?"

The sip of liquid choked him. It was cold and much too strong. "What?"

"I know you feel a duty and a huge responsibility as Deputy Director, but do you enjoy your position as such?"

Before his life had gone to hell six months earlier, Michael would have answered yes in a heartbeat. He'd been a good Director of Operations. Every day when he'd walked into the office, he welcomed the buzz of adrenaline in his veins. His group of spies had met the challenges of international intelligence with cunning and flexibility that had outlasted several administrations.

Since being promoted to Deputy Director of the CIA, he'd continued to be outstandingly good at his job. What he didn't experience anymore was the buzz of excitement, the thrill of meeting the endless challenges.

Nowadays, the challenges seemed like overwhelming problems. When he thought of the future, it was a black abyss. Lately, he'd caught himself daydreaming a lot. Most of them involved moving to Greece or Italy and living on a boat. Last night, he'd journeyed into sexual fantasies about Brigit.

His cock jumped and he mentally smacked himself with a dose of logic. Psych 101: everybody enjoyed escapism, especially when they had a high-stress job or had recently survived a trauma. He didn't need Brigit, or any psychiatrist, crawling around in his head to point out the obvious.

"Thanks, but no thanks to the armchair analysis. I see an agency shrink once a month as required by my position." He pointed to his head. "Cogs are all working fine."

She had the decency to blush. "I wasn't asking as a psychiatrist. I was just curious if you liked always being the responsible one, the one everybody counts on. You have a lot of pressure to be perfect, in your family and in your career. Always on time, always in control, always living up to the ideal brother, ideal leader." She shook her head. "Don't you ever want to take a break from it all? Or just be late to work once in awhile?"

Her assessment made his skin itch. He was so far from perfect on the inside, it terrified him. He couldn't take a break from life, though, not even to be late for work. The Michael Stone persona wouldn't let him.

"I'm going to jump in the shower." He held up the cup. "Think you can make plain coffee?"

"You have a top-of-the-line espresso machine and all you want is coffee." She sighed and stood up, reaching for his cup. "No further analysis necessary, but psychotherapy is advisable."

He frowned at her back as she left the room.

Chapter Twenty-Five

By noon, Brigit was stationed on a bench at the park across from her charred loft. She'd picked up the impounded Ford from the police lot and recovered her wallet before visiting The Gap for clothes and a kiosk for a new mobile phone, all under the watchful eye of the security detail Michael had assigned her. She was no longer a suspect in Ella's kidnapping and the guard had left her once she landed at the DHS headquarters on Murray Lane, where she'd promised Michael she would stay put until he called.

That morning, she'd shared some pertinent facts about Peter which were missing from his dossier so Michael and his band of merry men could start digging. That way, she looked like she was cooperating while giving herself breathing space to do her own behind-the-scenes work. The first of which was to visit her loft.

Two I-beams jutted out of the debris at opposite sides, pointing black fingers at the sky and resembling a weird jack-o-lantern grin. The lower section of the building had been damaged as well, just not as extensively. Yellow tape cordoned off half the block and the State Fire Marshall's official investigation had begun before the site had cooled.

Less than thirty hours after the fire, though, the place sat alone, abandoned. Reporters had gotten video for their stations. Gawkers had taken photos. No-trespassing signs had been posted along with the yellow tape, but no one was around, except for the occasional street patrol driving by to make sure looters weren't pilfering anything from the store or destroying potential evidence.

Brigit forced herself to stare at the I-beams and the charred half-walls. Was it Peter's fault or was it hers? He'd never harmed any of the children he'd kidnapped before. Was it her interference with O'Bern that had driven him to set her up for the kidnapping? Even so, why the fire? He had definitely wanted to drive home his point. If only she knew exactly what the point was.

She'd started the fire, albeit accidentally, that had taken his mother away from him. Maybe this was some kind of long-coming retaliation.

Low clouds rolled in from the southwest as Brigit sat wrapped in a new trench coat. A few errant raindrops heralded an approaching downpour and she was glad she'd bought an umbrella. Absently twirling it by its handle, she scanned the windows and rooftops of buildings to the north and east.

Something told her Peter had been close by, not just watching her from this park a few mornings ago, but actually living in the vicinity. He might still be there, knowing she would come back to the loft, as all victims of a fire did.

If he, Tory and Moira were still in the neighborhood, they might have front-row viewing of Brigit sitting alone, and that's exactly what she wanted. There were no cops, Feds or other undercover law enforcement anywhere in the vicinity. Because of the impending storm there wasn't even a mother-child duo in the park.

Come on, she willed one or all of them to appear. *I'm here, come get me.*

It was foolhardy, and probably pointless, to put herself out as bait. Yet she continued to sit on the bench and wait. Human motivations were typically illogical. The intensity of those motivations even more so. It was easy to grasp a motivation like Michael's because the situation involved a direct assault on a child in his family. Motivation for revenge and the intensity of his reaction were normal.

From her case studies, though, Brigit had found most people's motivations and the intensity attached to them were as ambiguous and individual as their fingerprints.

Like her hatred of nightlights. At thirty-three years old, she was still scared of the dark. Irrational, illogical, but deep-seated. The prospect of sleeping in the dark could bring on a panic attack and yet the sight of a harmless nightlight did the same.

While she wanted revenge for her mother's death and she certainly wanted to stop Peter from injecting fear into other children, her real motivation to hunt him down was to free herself from the fear of the dark. The night of the kidnapping, he'd snatched her from a warm bed and she hadn't been able to see his face in the dark room. He'd terrified her so badly she'd never again been able to survive a dark bedroom. Locked in the bathroom with Tory, she'd cried hard and long enough Peter had brought in the nightlight.

After years of therapy and nightmares, Brigit had a favorite fantasy. She shoved the nightlight down Peter's throat.

It was irrational, illogical and something in real life she would never do, no matter how much she hated him. She would not become a murderer like he was, and the very thought of such blatant personal revenge made her sweaty with guilt.

But the fantasy reoccurred after every incident she linked to Peter, and grew along with her frustration when he managed to escape police time and time again.

The day had turned dark as night and streetlights sprang to life. Rain began to fall in earnest. Brigit rose from the bench, opened her umbrella and started for her car in the lot a block down.

A torrent of rain burst loose before she took two steps. She jogged to her car, grateful she was still wearing her running shoes. Just as she slipped the key into the car door's lock, a gust of wind jerked the umbrella and she nearly lost her grip. By the time she got it under control and slid into the car, she was drenched.

She wasn't sure what fired up her instincts, but immediately she knew she wasn't alone in the small space.

Self-defense training kicked in, prodding her to get out of the car. Tamping it down and the urge to look in the rearview mirror to discover her visitor's identity, she shook her head to knock some of the rain out of her hair.

Tilting her head down, she used her right hand to lift wet strands from her neck, and wondered if her intruder meant to harm her. As she straightened her head back up, a cold gun muzzle pressed into her neck.

Harm intended.

Her gaze darted to the rearview mirror. A hooded figure with eyes rimmed in dark eyeliner stared back at her. The woman grabbed a handful of Brigit's hair and gave it a jerk, snapping Brigit's head back against the headrest. "We're going to make a deal, so listen carefully."

The accent was Palestinian. Brigit swallowed hard, but this was what she'd been hoping for. Contact. "Moira. It's been a long time."

"Put your hands on the steering wheel."

Brigit complied. "Can't keep my left arm in this position long," she said. "Thanks to you."

"I aimed for your heart."

The lump in Brigit's throat grew. "I know. What I don't know is why."

"Why?" Moira laughed without humor. "You have screwed everything up, all along, hunting Peter, hunting me. I wanted it to end. You gave me the chance when you walked to the podium."

"I don't want you, or Peter. Just Tory."

Anger made Moira's voice shake. "Yes, well now I want Peter, to kill him, and you're going to help me."

Peter must have really pissed her off. Had he double-crossed her? Promised her an easy escape and then failed to follow through?

But why? She worked for him. Knew how to pull off assassinations without leaving any trace evidence behind. Brigit suspected the woman had even tapped witnesses to Peter's misdeeds before. Moira tied up his loose ends with efficiency and mercilessness. What would make him ruin the arrangement?

The old adage about no honor among thieves was true, yet love and passion still motivated them. Thieves, terrorists, assassins...all were human at their core, and hence, prone to human vices. Moira had loved Peter once, maybe still did, and he'd risked ransoming her to take out O'Bern.

"Why do you want to kill Peter now, after all you've done for him?"

Moira pushed the hood back from her face. "Because of this."

Even in the shadows of the car, Brigit could see the fresh bruise on Moira's cheek. Her bottom lip had been split as well. An old bruise yellowed her left temple. "He beat you up? Why?"

"Because of you."

It was hard to believe Peter would get upset with Moira for trying to kill her, and yet the thought gave her pause. Did Peter still care, just a little, for her?

"Shooting you was a federal offense. I broke the rules, never kill a government agent, here, Britain, Ireland, wherever. It brings too much heat, too much need for vengeance. You hit one of their own and the police, in whatever country, want your head on a stick. Peter now has to be extra vigilant. Our escape was made ten times harder."

She should have known Peter's anger at Moira was not based on any emotion for her. "So he beat you up and left you behind as a scapegoat."

"If the authorities have me, they won't care about Peter, even though he is the one who orchestrated the assassination."

"So where is he? I can call the police and have him arrested."

"Tory is with him. You call in the cops and they'll arrest her too. Or Peter will use her as a hostage. Is that what you want?"

Brigit took a deep breath and considered her options. She didn't seem to have many again. Moira was only trying to save her own skin, but her point was still valid. Peter could use Tory as a hostage. "What's your plan?"

"Cormac O'Bern is about to leave Layton Airport on his private jet bound for Dublin."

Her brain spun through scenarios. "Peter's hijacking his plane?"

Moira snorted. "It's an easier way to get back to Ireland than his original escape plan."

Brigit stuck her key in the ignition and cranked the motor. "How much time do we have?"

Moira lowered the gun and sat back. "Less than forty minutes. Can you make it?"

As with all things in and around D.C., the answer depended on the traffic. Brigit shifted into drive, flipped on the windshield wipers and wheeled the car out of the parking spot. Pressing her foot to the accelerator, she ignored the lot's stop sign and the blare of a car horn as she pulled out in front of a gray sedan. "Of course I can."

Fifty feet away, Conrad Flynn started his Jeep to follow Brigit. Before he could put it in gear, though, Julia knocked on his window.

She had a hat on and the collar of her windbreaker up. He rolled down the window. "You following me or Kent?"

"You. We need to talk about Zara."

The green car was quickly disappearing down the street. He couldn't lose her. "Get in," he told Julia, motioning her to hurry.

She ran around the front of the Jeep and slid in, wet jacket and all. Conrad shifted into gear, one foot still on the brake. "One thing. You're in this car as my wife, not an FBI agent. Anything that happens on this run is off the record for you. You feel me, Ms. Torrison?"

Her eyes flashed annoyance but she pulled her hat off and sighed back against the seat in acceptance. "It's Mrs. Flynn to you."

Conrad grinned, releasing the brake and gunning the gas, and they shot out of the skinny alley after Brigit. He shifted on the fly, the Jeep responding like a well-tuned instrument. Julia stayed quiet until he had the green car in sight again.

"Del Hoffman called this morning," she said, shaking out her wet hair. "He told Zara her group of sisters is headed back to London. She's already booked a ticket."

"Look, I don't want her in the field any more than you do, but the doctor told her she could return to work."

"The doctor doesn't know she's a spy."

"Actually, he does. He's one of our go-to guys. She was dehydrated and anemic. He pumped her full of fluid and got her eating again."

Julia stiffened and turned to look at him. "But it's too dangerous, for her and the baby."

He agreed, but ultimately it was Zara's decision. Bottom line, Julia knew it too. She was just worried. He kept his eyes on the traffic as he changed tactics to make her realize what Zara was dealing with. "What if you were pregnant? Your job's just as dangerous. What would you do in her place?"

The pause was long enough to make Conrad glance at her from the corner of his eye. Her forehead was creased, her bottom lip skewed to the side in concentration. "I don't know. I've never thought about it."

"Maybe you should."

The crease deepened. Conrad shifted his attention back to the road. "Would you take a desk job if, you know, you were pregnant with our kid?"

She touched her stomach reflexively. "I can't get past the me-being-pregnant part to even consider what I'd do about my job."

"So you're not..."

He couldn't bring himself to say it. Part of him was in Julia's camp trying to wrap his head around her being pregnant. The other part wanted to pat her stomach too.

Her head snapped around so she could look at him again. "Pregnant? Me?"

His business cell beeped in its holder on the dash, the loud noise vibrating between them as he returned her stare. The surprise on her face and incredulous tone of her voice was the only answer he needed. "You're not pregnant."

She smiled and shook her head no. Again his feelings about a kid divided into two camps. One of relief, the other of disappointment.

The phone blared again. Caller ID registered it was Smitty. "I'll see if I can find a safe but attractive desk job for Zara," was all he could say.

Julia touched his arm as if she read the conflicting emotions in his face. "Thank you."

Shoving his mixed emotions aside, he put on his Bluetooth headset and hit the connect button. "What did you find on Gunn?"

Ryan Smith sighed. "First, tell me what's happening with Zara. She left some flippant message with my secretary about being Super Woman and returning to London tonight."

"She's Super Woman all right, but I'm pulling her off that case." He glanced at Julia who still had her hand on her stomach. "She won't be back in your camp for awhile."

"You putting her on the Kent case instead?"

The idea sparked a dozen more in Conrad's brain. If he put Zara to work on following Brigit, he could keep an eye on her. Julia could keep an eye on her. Everyone would be happy. Even Zara. "Uh, yeah. I need her to do some behind-the-scenes stuff on Kent and Donovan both. What'd'ya find out about Gunn?"

"He's a spy, definitely MI5. Why he's been paired with Dr. Kent isn't clear. On her though, I did more research and found a cold-war spy in Madrid who knew her father, might've even trained him. He was sort of purposely fuzzy on details, but he did tell me Brigit's father, William, was a senior MI5 officer running agents while pretending to be a British parliament member. After the death of his wife—a suspicious death, I might add—he uprooted Brigit and Tory and moved them to America."

"He still work for our friends?"

"Not clear, but probably. He opened a law firm in Chicago and got both girls U.S. citizenship. At seventeen, Brigit moved to London to attend Oxford. The same time Tory ran away from home."

Conrad didn't care about Tory. Finding her was Julia's job. "So Brigit followed in her daddy's footsteps and went to work for SIS after graduation."

"Actually, before her eighteenth birthday. One of their operatives recruited her and sent her to Fort Monckton for training. They put her through the usual physical and psychological bullshit. Her IQ's a hundred and nineteen so she had no trouble with the exams, but she struggled with some of the physical fitness tests. When they sent her back to campus to start cultivating agents, she sucked at it. They pulled her from their operative ranks, but paid for her postgrad education."

"In exchange for what?"

"Just like she told you, she's a consultant. She profiles psychosocial and antisocial disorders for various government organizations. In her spare time, she treats kids."

"She's a profiler."

"A very well-paid, sought-after profiler, who I'm guessing breaks down personalities and disorders of a very elite subgroup."

Kidnappers and terrorists were hardly elite. "Which is?"

"Presidents, prime ministers, queens and czars. You name it, she profiles 'em."

Brigit had hit the interstate, still acting like her ass was on fire. Conrad passed an SUV on the on ramp to keep up with her. "Why?"

"You ask that question a lot."

"That's what Stone pays me to do."

"In this day and age, dictators and elected officials alike want to know everything about their allies as well as their enemies. Brigit and Gunn have been in ten different countries in the past five years, consulting with top-level officials on a variety of projects including several kidnappings like Ella's. My guess is they were also gathering info and intel for SIS."

Conrad focused on his driving while his mind spun. "You think she's been putting a profile of Stone together?"

Julia's gaze left the road and zeroed in on him. She motioned for him to hit the speakerphone button. He did, and Smitty's voice filled the Jeep's cabin, while Conrad tossed the Bluetooth on the dash. "Michael's next in line for the CIA Director's job and Michael's brother-in-law is days away from becoming the next president."

Damn. "Good work, Smitty. I'll pass the info on."

"One other thing my asset revealed? Peter Donovan is Brigit's older half-brother."

"Holy crap," Julia said.

"Hey, Jules. Didn't know you were there."

Conrad put a finger to his lips to shush her before she could respond. "You sure?"

"Yep." Conrad could almost see Smitty nodding. "They share the same mother and there was speculation at the time Roberta Kent died in a fire that Peter had a hand in it. The British and Irish governments hushed it up, but Brigit's been trying to track Peter down and bring him to justice for years. Probably why she did her doctoral thesis on him."

"I'll be goddamned."

"Pretty sure you already are."

Julia chuckled and Conrad disconnected. Stone was going to crap a brick.

Chapter Twenty-Six

Twenty-six miles outside of D.C., the Layton private airport did a small but prestigious business. While government officials, lobbyists and high-profile company executives parked their Gulfstreams at Reagan National and Dulles, the less pretentious, though equally rich, parked their jets at Layton where the policy of the owner was discretion above all else.

Layton's security standards were as high as any public airport post 9/11. From ex-Army mechanics skilled in customized jet maintenance to ex-Air Force pilots experienced in international flights, their staff was topnotch. The airport's layout had been designed by a renowned New York architect who routinely used one of the private hangars to store his Learjet. The waiting area showcased designer chairs featured in Elle Décor magazine.

Brigit sent Moira to the café, knowing the woman would never get through security, even with her expensive fake passport. The bruises on her face alone were enough to invite suspicion.

As she ran through the private waiting area to the boarding gate, she caught sight of the Learjet on the runway. Cormac O'Bern was crossing the tarmac, the collar of his raincoat up to protect his neck. An assistant tagged along behind him with an umbrella.

Brigit waved her DHS badge at the security officer, bulldozing past the gate barrier. "I have to catch Cormac O'Bern."

The officer moved her body in front of Brigit's and ripped the badge from her hand. "Are you boarding the plane, ma'am?"

O'Bern was halfway up the stairs. "Yes, but not to leave the country. I just need to ask Mr. O'Bern a couple of questions."

Precious seconds ticked by as the officer eyed the badge and considered whether to let her through. Brigit saw O'Bern top the stairs. She pushed past the officer. "It's national security and if I don't stop that plane before it takes off, it's on your head."

Her words had the right effect. "I'll hold your badge here. Are you armed?"

"Not unless you consider an umbrella a weapon." She ran out the gate into the rain just as the jet's stairs made a mechanical grinding noise.

They began to lift off the ground as Brigit leapt onto the bottom one, grabbing the handrail. Off balance, she tripped on the stairs folding under her feet and toppled into the plane as they slammed shut behind her.

"Brigit?" Tory stood by the door dressed in a dark navy skirt and jacket just like a flight attendant. "What are you doing here?"

O'Bern's assistant was helping him get out of his wet raincoat. The poet frowned. "Who are you, and what are you doing on my plane?"

Brigit righted herself and fingered her umbrella. Her DHS badge was being held hostage back with the security officer. "Dr. Brigit Kent," she said to him, ignoring Tory. "I'm with the Department of Homeland Security, and I'm afraid there's a security issue I need to address with you."

"Wait." O'Bern pointed a finger at her. "I know you. You're the lass who got herself shot at my lecture."

Tory laid a hand on Brigit's arm and spoke softly under her breath. "Are you all right?"

Brigit nodded and answered O'Bern. "Peter Donovan is on board this plane, Mr. O'Bern."

"Peter?" The man's face paled. "On my plane?"

The assistant's gaze darted around the cabin, panic evident. "Where?"

From behind her, Brigit heard the cockpit door open. She wheeled around, raising the umbrella.

The beard had disappeared. The colored contacts, along with the pilot's uniform, worked to disguise Peter. He glanced down at the raised umbrella and back up to her face. "Give Tory the umbrella, and go sit down."

The deep nasal quality of his voice sent shivers down her spine.

"Peter?" O'Bern gripped the back of the seat in front of him. "Where's Calloway?"

Without taking his eyes off Brigit, Peter answered. "Your pilot is unharmed, as you will be if you follow my orders."

Brigit raised the umbrella a notch, but Tory moved in between it and Peter and put her hand on the tip. "Do as Peter says, Brigit, and no one will get hurt."

Brigit looked over her sister's head to keep eye contact with Peter. "Don't believe him, Mr. O'Bern. His plan all along was to kill you." She flicked her gaze to Tory and back to Peter. "What I don't understand is why you tried to hurt Ella. How could you leave an innocent girl to die in a fire?"

Tory pushed the umbrella's end toward the floor. "Peter didn't set the—"

"Tory." Peter placed a hand on Tory's shoulder. "Take the umbrella."

Brigit snapped it away from her sister's grasp, but Peter was just as quick. The dark end of a black gun appeared in front of Brigit's face.

"You always were a pain in the ass," he said, his eyes cold and merciless, his voice rumbling in his throat like a pit bull's. He cocked the gun. "Now give the goddamn umbrella to Tory."

At that moment, Brigit understood Peter would have no qualms about killing her, yet she couldn't hold back her laugh as she handed over the umbrella. "I thought you were smarter than to shoot a gun inside a fully gassed plane, but then there's the difference between you and me. I work for the good guys. They teach us basic common sense."

Enraged, Peter pushed Tory aside and tackled Brigit full force, slamming her back against the plane's interior. The cool barrel of the gun bit into her temple and his breath rushed out as he spoke. "You think I won't blow this plane to Kingdom Come with you and Tory in it?"

His breath was like a disease flooding her senses and sinking into her skin. She had to swallow bile in her throat.

Tory grabbed at Peter's arm, but he didn't budge. A flush rose up his neck and spread to his face. His nostrils flared as he gritted his teeth. "I'm not afraid to die for what I believe in."

Brigit choked back the bile, her own anger matching his. "Neither am I."

In one swift motion, Peter struck her with the butt. Pain exploded in her head, hot and white, before all went dark.

Michael hugged Ella goodbye before taking the front stairs to his waiting car. "You be good," he called to her over his shoulder.

Thad, Ruthie and Ella stood on the porch, Ella holding one of her dolls against her chest. "Mom says I have to go back to school tomorrow."

Michael frowned at Ruthie but kept his opinion Ella should have more time off to himself. Life went on. There were political campaigns to run, news conferences to hold, school.

"You'll be okay," he said, sending his niece a confident wink and a smile. "Call me if you need anything, got it?"

Ella's chin raised a fraction of an inch. She held up a tiny thumb. "Got it, Uncle Michael."

Three miles down the road, Michael's cell phone rang. It was Flynn. "Where are you?"

The tone of his voice was the same, the demanding attitude as well, and yet Michael knew something had happened. Something concerning Brigit. "What did she do?"

"She hopped a ride with Cormac O'Bern back to Ireland. Left her government ID with the security guard at the gate."

As he forced himself to breathe, he also forced his mind to consider the reasons Brigit would do such a thing. Heading to Ireland. Leaving her ID behind. Leaving *him* behind without so much as a goodbye.

Another rush of instant knowing slammed him, choking off his air. He loosened the tie at his throat and drew in a deep breath. She wouldn't leave the D.C. area right now unless she was chasing Tory. How had Tory gotten out of the country? Had that been Brigit's goal all along? To make a deal with him so he let his guard down, and then she could take off on her own to hunt for her sister?

Or help her sister get to safety?

Flynn's voice cut through his thoughts. "I followed her to Layton Air Strip. She got out of her car with another woman. I was only a minute or two behind them, but I lost her. The

187

security officer said Brigit claimed she wasn't leaving on the plane, only wanted to ask O'Bern a question, but the plane took off with Brigit still on board."

Jesus. She'd tricked him. Anger flickered low in his gut. "What happened to the woman with her?"

"Haven't seen her. She probably high-tailed it when Brigit left."

"Did you get a good look at her?"

"Better. I got a photo of her with my cell phone. Del's running it through the system. Want me to have someone pick her up when they land?"

Michael's first response was yes, but the authorities would want a solid reason and he didn't have one. Until he figured out what she was up to, he'd be better off to play things cool. "Let me think about it."

"There's more. I'm on my way to your house. Meet you there."

Dread pushed in beside anger. "Just spit it out, Flynn."

"Twenty minutes? Sounds good."

The line went dead. In the ensuing silence, Michael stared at the seat facing him where Brigit had sat less than eight hours before, her hair up in a ponytail and his T-shirt still hugging her curves under her fleece jacket. It didn't make sense. He'd been with the CIA for ten years and worked his charm on everyone from hardened politicians to infamous criminals. Most had succumbed without much of a fight. He'd read their personalities and their intentions with better accuracy than any psychiatrist or profiler and manipulated them—charmed them, as Michael preferred to call it—right out of their hardened states. Brigit Kent should have been a piece of cake compared to the rest.

There's more.

More Flynn refused to discuss over the phone.

God*damn*. Michael threw the phone at the seat.

Chapter Twenty-Seven

Conrad snagged two squat glasses in a cabinet alongside a bottle of Jack in Stone's den and poured a finger of the whiskey into each. He sat down in a leather chair and sipped the liquid as he eyed the remodeling job his boss was still doing on the south wall.

The sun was setting and a smattering of round patches of drywall mud stood out against the gray background as the waning light suffused the room. On the floor beside the wall sat a five gallon bucket of mud and several scrapers. An unopened paint can, containing the same gray-colored paint as the wall, held down one corner of the drop cloth. Drywall dust coated everything.

When Stone entered the room a few minutes later, Conrad noticed the hard set of his eyes, the rigid posture. The man was primed for a fight.

Conrad had gone a few rounds once before with him and had no desire to repeat the performance. Most men who sat at desks all day were soft, their reflexes slow. Stone wasn't most men. Even though he'd been shot and undergone surgery, when the two went fisticuffs he'd nearly kicked Conrad's ass. Since that time, he'd doubled his daily run distance and taken up kickboxing. Where once Michael Stone had been a decisive force, he was now an overwhelming one. He was lean, mean and still angry over Raissi catching him with his pants down.

Conrad stood, picked up the waiting glass and held it out like a shield. "What I'm about to tell you...remember, I'm just the messenger."

In two strides, Stone was at his desk, slamming his briefcase down on the top and shedding his wool coat. "What is it?"

"You might want to sit down."

Stone crossed his arms over his chest in his best *quit screwing me* stance.

Still holding out the glass of bourbon, Conrad took a step back. "I have reason to suspect Dr. Kent has been profiling you for The Firm."

Stone glanced at the glass and back up at Conrad's face. "That's it? That's what you refused to tell me over the phone?"

Conrad frowned as Stone sighed with what sounded like relief. "SIS has had a profile of me since I was Director of Operations. They didn't send Brigit here for me."

"You sure?"

"Yeah, I'm sure."

A new thought popped into Conrad's head. "What about your brother-in-law? Could SIS have hired Donovan to stage Ella's kidnapping in order for Brigit to profile him under a stressful situation? He's probably going to be the next president, and he's already stated he's not going to be best friends forever with Britain like his predecessors have been. Maybe they wanted him to back out of the election."

Michael dropped his arms, rubbed his eyes. "I don't have time to examine your warped conspiracy theories—" He stopped in mid-sentence. Straightened. "Our friends aren't digging into Thad's psyche, it's Jeffries."

Conrad set the glass down. "President Jeffries? Why?"

"He didn't want me questioning Brigit after Ella was rescued. She told me it had something to do with Ruthie and coerced me into a deal. If I helped Brigit get the charges against her sister reduced, she'd tell me about the secret Jeffries is keeping concerning Ruthie."

"She didn't tell you what it was?"

"No." Stone sank into his desk chair. "And now Brigit's run off to Ireland."

Conrad couldn't find the connection. "I'm lost."

Stone shook his head. "Me too."

He wasn't the king of logic like Stone was. All he knew was most people were driven by lust for power and money. On the surface, Ella's kidnapping was a diversionary tactic. Probably had nothing to do with Brigit working for Jeffries. Except for the one thing Conrad still hadn't mentioned to Stone.

He slid the glass of untouched bourbon closer to Stone's side of the desk. "Peter Donovan is Brigit's half-brother."

Stone didn't move, didn't even seem to breathe. He sat there as if this news was as inconsequential as the previous news. As if he'd just shut down.

But as Conrad relayed the information Smitty had told him, Stone started breathing again. Muscles in his jaws worked as he ground his teeth.

When Conrad stopped talking, there was a minute of complete silence. Then Stone reached out and took the bourbon and swallowed the shot whole.

As he set the glass down, Conrad's cell dinged with a message. It was from Del.

Moira Raphael. Sharpshooter for Palestinian army 2000-2004, freelance assassin since.

The list of Moira's dealings with various terrorist organizations was long. Conrad handed the phone to Stone and let him scroll through the message.

Recovering the whiskey bottle from the credenza, Conrad poured another shot for each of them.

Stone handed Conrad back his cell, ignored the second shot and pushed buttons on his landline. The man was going to need dental work the way he was grinding his teeth. A minute later, he was giving the head of the FBI Moira's name and background. "I have reason to believe she is the sniper you're looking for."

Another minute of conversation flowed before Stone ended the call. He looked at Conrad. "Why would Brigit willingly take the woman who shot her to the airport?"

"Willingly is the key word. What if she was forced?"

The office chair squeaked as Stone sat back. "Forced how?"

Conrad sipped his bourbon, shrugged. "I don't know, but if Brigit did it willingly, she's working with Moira."

Stone was a short step behind him. "Which would mean she's working with Donovan."

"Her brother."

The two sat in silence, both working out the implications. Conrad shook his head and twirled the amber liquid in his glass. "Makes no sense, because why would Moira shoot Brigit if they were both working for Donovan?"

Stone's phone rang and then Conrad's did too. The two of them exchanged a look. Something had just broken. Something big.

As the Deputy Director answered his phone with a forceful, "Michael Stone", Conrad checked caller ID and saw it was Del again. He set his glass down. "Yeah."

Del's voice vibrated with excitement. "Night crew at Layton Airport just found a body in the southwest international hangar. No ID."

"And?"

"The southwest international hangar, Hangar M, was where Cormac O'Bern's plane was stored. Body's not O'Bern. Could be his pilot."

Conrad caught Stone's eye and another round of silent communication passed between them. He'd received the same information, probably from the FBI. Stone spoke into his phone. "Someone needs to meet that plane when it lands, and find out who's on it and what's going down."

The caller said something and Stone nodded to himself. What it all meant, Conrad wasn't sure. What he was sure of was the hair on his arms stood at attention. "We need the identity confirmed ASAP," he told Del.

"The minute I know, you'll know."

Conrad disconnected, found Stone staring at him with that expressionless persona he'd perfected as Deputy Director. He was too still again, trying too hard not to show his frustration and anger. Conrad returned his cell phone to his belt and wondered how the guy kept all that hostility bottled up without going crazy.

"You want to hear my conspiracy theory now?" He didn't wait for a reply. "Peter Donovan just kidnapped the man he's trying to kill and gained himself a free ride to Dublin."

Stone was again in sync. "And he took Brigit with him."

The minute Flynn left, Michael banged his fist on the top of his desk. The glasses jumped. In the fading orangey light, he paced from his desk to the far wall to the couch and back. *Peter Donovan is Brigit's half-brother.*

As he replayed the rest of Conrad's information on Brigit,

Michael upped his pace. Brigit had lied to him and apparently everyone else to protect her sister, who was working with Donovan. Get her away from him. So why hadn't she brought the fucker to justice?

Because Tory would be implicated too.

As his brain spun in tighter and tighter circles, so did his laps around the den. Renewed anger burned in his gut. Damn terrorists. How many families had Peter Donovan torn apart, including his own, in the name of his cause? How many people had suffered because of his self-righteousness?

Early in his career, Michael had tried to understand men like Donovan. To understand what drove them to join a cause and put everything on the line for it. They believed their cause was just, moral. Because Michael believed his own cause was also just and moral, it wasn't a hard leap to grasp Donovan's motivations or convictions for standing up for what he too, believed was right. However, Michael would never condone moral absolutism.

The afghan lay half on, half off the sofa, one corner skimming the floor. The image of Brigit, sleepy and smiling at him, filled his head, and his lower half responded. So did his chest. If Donovan had killed O'Bern's pilot and kidnapped her, she was in serious trouble.

He snatched the afghan up and rubbed the soft material between his fingers. Even though she'd deceived him, he still wanted her. Wanted to touch her hair again, watch her walk across the room. Hell, he'd even drink the awful coffee she made just to have her back safe and sound in his house.

He threw the afghan down and paced to the far wall. The patches were ready for painting, but all Michael could still see were the holes the bullets had left behind. All he could feel was the cold grip of helplessness in the memory of Raissi's smile. Raissi had stripped him of control. Now Donovan had done the same.

Raissi's face morphed into Donovan's. Without thinking, Michael punched the drywall, his large fist busting a gaping hole right where the patches had been. He lowered his head and punched it again, the anger scraping along his veins. Two more punches and the skin on his knuckles cracked and started to bleed. He waited for the pain. Only numbness surfaced.

The hole wasn't big enough to match the one inside him. In

the nearby toolbox, he shuffled tools out of the way until he found his hammer. Facing the wall, he reared back and swung. The hole widened, drywall breaking, dust flying. He hammered it again and again, mindless to the damage.

What seemed like hours later, the wall lay in bits and pieces. Michael's lungs burned from inhaling the dust, and his left shoulder ached.

"Nice to see you lose your shit for once," a voice said from behind him.

He jerked to the left, bringing the hammer up at the same time like a weapon. Flynn stood in the doorway, the room's shadows almost hiding his seemingly satisfied smile. Truman Gunn stood next to him, eyebrows arched above his glasses in surprise. Both men raised their hands in self-defense.

Lowering the hammer, Michael took a deep breath and spoke to Truman. "What the hell do you want?"

"The same as you." He lowered his arms and shot his cuffs. "Stop Peter Donovan and save Dr. Kent."

"You're sure Dr. Kent needs saving?"

Truman's response was a quick nod. His lips pressed in a tight line, his jaw squared. "You may not trust her or understand her motives, but I assure you, she is in grave danger aboard that plane. As is O'Bern."

Flynn eyed the destruction of the wall. "I talked to Titus. You're due for a vacation and his Gulfstream's on the tarmac at Dulles being fueled as we speak." He changed the tone of his voice and spoke with a strong brogue. "Thought ye might wanna see a bit of me homeland."

Michael tossed the hammer onto the drop cloth and brushed at the dust on his shirt. "You were born in New York."

"Aye, but I'm Irish through and through."

Wiping the sweat off his forehead with his sleeve, Michael considered what Titus and Flynn were offering. A sense of control sparked in his gut. He toyed with the idea, found it surprisingly appealing. His hand went to his shirt above the scar and he rubbed it. "Funny, I've been craving a pint of Guinness and a pot of stew."

Flynn's smile deepened. "Then you'd be a cute whore."

Michael raised one eyebrow and glared at him. "Excuse me?"

"A cute whore," Flynn said, losing the brogue. "It's how the Irish would say you're astute, cunning." He walked over and patted Michael on the back. "We'll work on your Irish language deficit on the plane."

Chapter Twenty-Eight

Dulles International Airport

Michael climbed the steps to board Titus Allen's plane, apprehension gnawing at him. The drive to the airport had given him time to think. He shouldn't be leaving the country, no matter what Titus or the president or anyone else believed. He had responsibilities. He had...

What did he have?

A job. A dog. Nieces and nephews, but not a family of his own.

Flynn was ahead of him, Gunn and Brad behind him, forming a sandwich as if they didn't believe he'd go through with it. They were right to doubt his intentions.

He had to shift his shoulders slightly and duck to get through the plane's door. Titus stood on his left in the cockpit's opening, a navy blue pilot's cap covering his gray hair. "Welcome aboard, laddie." He slapped Michael on the back.

"You're flying the plane?" was all he could say.

Titus's fake smile fell off his wrinkled face. "Well, of course I'm flying the damn plane. You doubt my capabilities?"

As a matter of fact, he did, but it was best to choose his words carefully. "We're not allowed to take the same plane, remember? If it crashes, we could both die. Who would head the CIA?"

Titus rolled his eyes. "We'll be dead. What the hell do we care?"

Michael cringed. Flynn shot a wise-ass smile over his shoulder and started down the aisle. Before Michael could come up with an argument, he caught sight of Del Hoffman in one of the seats. Like most Gulfstreams, the bucket seats formed pairs and faced each other with skinny tables in between. Del had a thin netbook open on the table in front of him and a Bluetooth in his ear. He gave Michael a nod as he spoke into his phone.

Flynn grabbed Michael's overnight bag, opened an overhead compartment and shoved the bag in. The plane's engines came to life, and Flynn raised his voice over the noise. "Thought we might need some techie help and Del hasn't been out of the office since you hired him."

Michael set his briefcase on Del's table and sank into the blond leather bucket seat. Flynn and Gunn took seats opposite each other across the aisle.

The complete and utter absurdity of what he was doing hit him all over again. Ignoring the voice in his head, he slipped Del a piece of paper with the tracking number from the GPS chip he'd snuck into Brigit's rabbit's foot. Del terminated his call immediately and gave Michael a questioning raise of his brows. "Yes, boss?"

"GPS tracker you gave me a few months ago. Can you get a location from it?"

"Of course."

The engines revved as Del's quick fingers ran over his keyboard. "Satellite is searching...there it is." He glanced up at Michael. "It's over the Atlantic."

The plane jolted forward and everyone gripped their armrests. Gunn made haste to buckle his seat belt before raising his voice over the engine noise. "You put a tracking device on her?"

"In the rabbit's foot you gave her."

Gunn laughed. "I already had one in it."

"Yeah, I noticed."

Respect, mixed with a new awareness, flickered in Gunn's eyes. "You *are* a clever one."

"So they say."

The plane lurched again, and Del closed his laptop. His face was white and he murmured something that sounded like the Lord's Prayer.

Titus's voice came over the speaker. "This is your captain. We're second in line for takeoff. Seat belts must be fastened and trays in the upright and locked position."

His ensuing cackle echoed in the cabin and Michael caught

Flynn's eye. "How many martinis has he had?"

Flynn shrugged. "Enough to keep his hands steady."

Del's praying got louder.

In his mind, Michael joined in.

Chapter Twenty-Nine

Consciousness crept into Brigit's awareness with a steady, painful hum. The plane droned under her. The right side of her head throbbed.

Her stomach roiled at the smell of jet fuel and body sweat lingering in the air. Easing her eyes open, she saw metal chain handcuffs around her wrists and the seat belt pinning them to her lap. A bright yellow polypropylene rope cinched her upper body to the seat. Her vision swam and her head swayed side to side, heavy and unbalanced.

Night lay over the Atlantic. In the dimly lit cabin, Cormac O'Bern sat across the aisle in a similar predicament as her, but still unconscious. No doubt Peter would use O'Bern to assist his escape once they touched down.

What would Peter do with her? Brigit twisted her head and tried to see if Tory was nearby. A sharp pain jetted up her neck at the effort, and her lungs struggled to fill against the confining straps of rope.

Since she was seated next to the window and pinned to the seat, her view was limited. The pain was too much, and her eyes swam with tears. *Wimp*, she yelled at herself. *Failure*. She hung her head and closed her eyes again.

Why hadn't she, for once, asked for the help she so desperately needed and called Michael before going to the airport with Moira?

No answers came from the plane's continuing drone or her pounding head. Little pain pricks danced in her hands.

"Here, drink this."

Brigit's eyes flew open to find Tory standing beside her with a clear beverage in a plastic drink cup. The liquid fizzed, tiny bubbles rising and breaking the surface.

She opened her mouth to talk and Tory tipped the cup. Cold pop ran in her mouth. Her throat was parched and the sweet/tart drink tasted good.

As Tory continued to feed her small sips, Brigit tried to think of what to say, but it seemed impossible to understand her sister or the fact Tory would go along with Peter's cruel treatment. "You can still have a life, Tory," she spoke over the noise of the plane. "I can help you."

Tory's smile was bittersweet. "Finish your drink."

Brigit did, some pathetic part of her hoping the small gesture would endear her to Tory enough to make her sister want to be a better human. Want to stay with Brigit instead of leaving with Peter.

Tory disappeared down the aisle, and after a few minutes, Brigit's brain refused to keep thinking. Soon she fell back to sleep.

She awoke with a jolt sometime later to the sound of men's voices arguing outside. Her head was impossible to lift and her mouth was again as dry as a desert.

Where was she? Why was she tied up? As she fought the fog in her brain, one message came through loud and clear. She'd been drugged.

A familiar woman's voice, shrill and desperate, topped the men's. Tory. Bits and pieces fell into place. Brigit forced her head up and scanned the interior of the plane. Empty silence greeted her. The door was open and the stairs were down. A lone interior light brightened the plane from over the doorway.

She was in Ireland.

Outside the window, she could see shadows moving on the edge of the light's yellowy reach. Beyond it, everything was an eerie grayscale. Dark blobs, shaped like trees, fenced the area in the distance. Wherever they had landed, it was no airport.

More arguing, one man's voice pleading. Brigit flexed her hands, found they had no sensation. She worked against the rope holding her to the seat, but if anything, the rope seemed to tighten.

Taking a couple of deep breaths, she leaned her head back and stared out the window. Two of the people seemed to have gotten shorter. Were they on their knees? The largest shadow moved toward them. Peter. He raised his arm and Brigit's breath froze in her chest.

The gunshot echo reverberated through the cabin. One of the men dropped to the ground. Brigit screamed, "No!" but her weak voice was drowned out by the second gunshot.

As she struggled frantically against her bindings, she saw Peter and Tory take off at a run. Tears sprang into Brigit's eyes, and as they overflowed her lids and ran down her cheeks, she hung her head.

How was it possible Peter, a cold-blooded killer, was her brother? While they had different fathers, they still shared their mother's gene pool. It made her feel dirty, ugly. Like a monster.

Overriding that, Brigit wondered how Tory could choose life with Peter over life with her.

Shame and self-loathing burned in her chest. It always boiled down to one thing. Tory chose Peter.

Stop it. She would not go there again. For too long, she'd tortured herself with that betrayal. She had to let it go. Tory had made her choice, and she'd chosen Peter.

Time and time again.

So be it. She couldn't save someone who didn't want to be saved.

Yeah, right. How many times had she told herself the same logical fact and then jumped right back on Tory's trail, determined to make her see the light?

She was pathetic. All these years of wanting, needing her little sister to love her, and this was what she got for her trouble. Rejection. Pain. Betrayal. She was so tired of fighting. Tired of hiding the truth. Tired of trying to take care of everyone else. She wanted a life, a family.

Hell, at the moment, she'd settle for a dog like Pongo.

Michael. She wanted him too. His blue-gray eyes challenging her, his blond hair mussed from sleep, his quick wit and George Clooney smile. His power.

Power had always polarized her. Either she chased it or avoided it. Now she wondered what it might be like to do neither. What would it be like to just be friends with it? She might have a chance, if she ever got free from her bonds, to contact Michael and find out.

Her nose ran and she turned her head to rub it on her shoulder. As she shifted her arm a fraction under the rope, her hands moved and her breath snagged in her throat.

Under her hands, in her lap, lay a key.

Tory. A wave of hope crashed through her. Tory had left her the key to the cuffs. It wasn't exactly a declaration of love, but then again, maybe it was.

Analyze later. Right now she had to get the men outside medical help.

Doing the best she could with her dripping nose, she tried to make her fingers work to grasp the tiny metal key. Lack of sensation in her fingers made them move as if she were underwater. Again and again they failed to grasp it.

Flexing and releasing her hands, she ignored the painful prickling sensation, and at last got a firm grip on the key. The next few seconds passed by in a blur as she worked at maneuvering the key into the small lock of the handcuffs.

When they sprang free from her right hand, Brigit let out a proud, "Yes!"

Another minute went by as she unbuckled the seat belt and wiggled out from under the rope. She was sweating by the time she gained her freedom. Her head pounded and her arm ached. Everything ached. A seven hour flight across the Atlantic was bad enough. Bound and drugged, with a painful headache, was worse than listening to Truman do his Jonas Brothers impersonation. And if she didn't pee soon, she'd die.

Both O'Bern and his assistant lay on the ground, blood pooling from their chests. Brigit checked for pulses, found none and sent a prayer up to the heavens for each of them.

Back in the plane, the restroom was small and cramped, but she didn't care. The relief pushed all the night's atrocities from her mind for a few brief seconds.

After washing her hands, she splashed water on her face and noted the solid bruise on the side. She'd been trying to control her life since the night of her mother's death and all the time her life had been controlling her.

Leaving her ghostly image in the mirror behind, she made her way out of the plane, checking her pockets for her mobile. The only thing she found was the rabbit's foot.

She entered the cockpit and sat in one of the seats, searching for the radio. Slipping a headset on, she hit buttons and sent out a mayday when she heard static in her ear. "This is Dr. Brigit Kent, an Irish citizen. I'm in a small plane in a field and I need help."

She leaned forward and read the coordinates off a digital compass and then scanned the rest of the control panel, looking for the plane's ID. A small, green flashing light caught her attention. "Two men are dead—"

The light flashed again and Brigit's heart froze in mid-beat as realization dawned. The black numbers of a digital clock were counting down from twenty. The clock had wires running out of it into a gray block of material. Her gaze traced the wires. Duct tape secured the material to the panel and still the green light flashed in time with the descending numbers.

Ten...nine...eight...

Brigit yanked off the headset and ran.

Chapter Thirty

"Stop right there."

Peter heard the cold sound of a double-barrel locking into place and froze in his tracks, one arm rising to protect Tory.

The farmer had emerged from the shadows of a large oak. "Ya mind tellin' me what yer doin' on me land?"

The night had been one problem after another, and Peter's patience was spent. Several acres behind them, an explosion rocked the pasture. The farmer ducked and stumbled backwards, throwing up his gun as the fiery flames threw light on his wizened face.

As Tory ducked too, Peter lunged forward and disarmed the farmer in one swift motion. Stepping back, he pointed the end of the barrel at the man's head and sighted it.

"No," Tory yelled.

She gripped Peter's arm with both hands and jerked it down. Her face was a mixture of fear and grief as her gaze jumped between him and the wreckage burning behind them. "What 'ave you done, brother?"

He shrugged her hands off. "What I needed to do, just like before."

Raising the shotgun, he again took aim at the old man.

Tory stepped in front of the gun's barrel, blocking him. Tears bubbled over her bottom lids and streaked down her face. "Have you lost your mind? Blowing the plane with..."

She hiccupped and shook her head, dashed the back of her hand against her wet cheeks. Clearing her throat, she set her shoulders. "This man...he's one of us."

His half-sister's rebellion was over Brigit, not the sheep

farmer. "Brigit was not one of us," he reminded her.

Tory laid a hand on the gun and pushed the end toward the ground. "There's been enough killin' for one night, Peter."

He lowered the gun to his side and glanced behind him. Brigit was dead. O'Bern was dead. He waited for the remorse to pinch his soul. When it didn't, he tossed the gun into the tree line and took off at a jog.

The sun was rising in the east, turning the strips of fog rising from the bottoms yellow and pink. Hearing Tory's footsteps behind him, he smiled into the fading night.

He'd won.

He'd finally won.

Michael woke to the sound of a cell phone ringing. He jerked awake and sat forward, fumbling in his pockets for his phone.

Across the aisle, Gunn spoke, and Michael realized it wasn't his phone ringing. He sank back in the seat, closed his eyes and eavesdropped.

"When?" Gunn said.

His tone made Michael's stomach tense and he opened his eyes again.

After a long pause, Gunn sighed. "Both O'Bern and his assistant died by bullet?"

Michael's breath stuck in his throat. *Brigit. What about Brigit?*

Gunn glanced at him and held his gaze. Even in the dimly lit cabin, Michael could see the tense set of the man's jaw. His stomach clenched harder.

"I'm going to put the Deputy Director of the CIA on the phone and I want you to repeat what you just told me."

Gunn's eyes were watering as he handed him the phone. Michael willed his hand to reach for it.

He swallowed before identifying himself to the caller. As he listened to the words pour out of the man's mouth on the other end, his gut heaved.

O'Bern's plane had landed in sheep field outside Dublin, two people reported fleeing from the plane by a farmer. A communication from Dr. Brigit Kent was received by a local control tower, but her communication stopped at the estimated time of the explosion.

Her body had not yet been found, but the fire still burned as there was no way to reach it with equipment or fire retardant.

A cold hollowness filled his chest as Michael handed the phone back to Gunn. His brain screamed Brigit's name. *You can't be dead.*

Flynn, Del and Brad were now all awake. As Gunn disconnected, all three stared at Michael as they listened to Brigit's assistant tick off the information in a rough voice before he hung his head.

Peter Donovan was the lowest of the low. He'd kidnapped a six-year-old and left her to burn in an apartment. He'd shot and killed two men in cold blood.

He'd blown up his sister.

Vicious anger exploded in the hollowness, and Michael's mind slid into the dark shadows he'd come to know well after his encounter with Raissi. He gripped the armrests and locked his jaw tight. Peter Donovan had crossed the final line between justice and revenge in Michael's carefully preserved world.

I will hunt you down, he vowed to Peter's image, *and put you on the express train to hell.*

A loud tearing noise reverberated over the drone of the plane. He glanced down and saw the armrests in his hands, the leather ripped at the seams.

No one made a sound until Flynn coughed. "I'd suggest anger management training if I didn't know how cheap these seats were made. Titus obviously needs to upgrade."

Naturally, Flynn would reach for derisive sarcasm. For once, Michael was grateful for it.

Chapter Thirty-One

"I found 'er! Over here!"

The muffled male voice broke through Brigit's semi-lucid dreams of Tory and her mother, and she groaned.

Her head had split open, she was sure. She opened her eyes but only one seemed to be working. Through it, the world swam in streaks of green, black and blue. The other eye's lashes snagged on grass.

Snapping her eyes shut again, she drew a deep breath. She was lying on the ground, and snatches of memory swam through her brain.

The pungent smell of earth mixed with a more acrid smell. Hot metal? Burning rubber? A high-pitched ringing stung her left ear while her right was mercifully buried in the mud under her face. She raised her hand to cup the pain-filled ear, and her shoulder screamed at the movement.

God, I'm a fucking mess.

Again the muffled voice spoke, blurred and soft around the edges. "Easy, there, Miss. Help's on the way."

Help. Yes, she needed help.

Lots of it.

She tried to say thank you, but her voice wouldn't work. She popped open the eye that wasn't buried in the grass and tried to rise up on her elbows. The man had squatted down next to her and now touched her back in a controlled block. "Whoa, now. Ya best stay where ya are."

He was right. The world spun and Brigit sank back down into the grass. As the man shrugged off his blue jacket and laid it over her, she flexed her fingers and her toes. They obeyed, but when she tried to lift her head again, a hundred pound elephant was sitting on it. She stopped trying, closed her eyes and drifted...

When the emergency medical technicians arrived, they kept her conscious as they poked and prodded and talked about her. After wrapping her neck in a brace and inserting an IV in her arm, they shifted her onto a back brace as well and suddenly she was able to see the sky. Black billowing smoke covered the morning sun.

Over the background noise and the ringing in her ears, she caught snatches of the ongoing conversation around her. *Possible spinal injury...head injury...internal bleeding.*

She swallowed the bile in her throat. If she was possibly going to die, she had to tell Michael the truth about Peter. The truth about everything. Her lips were thick and rubbery. She forced them apart but her voice still refused to cooperate. "Michael," she whispered.

The man who'd found her shushed the technicians and leaned over her face. "What did ya say, Miss?"

"Mi...chael..."

"Michael? He yer husband?"

She tried to shake her head but found it immobile. "Stone."

"Stone? That yer name?"

She sighed. "Mi...chael...Stone...he's CIA..."

The man quirked his brows but nodded. "Aye, I've got it. You want me to contact 'im. Now what's your name, lass?"

"Bri...git..."

"Brigit? Now there's a hearty Irish name, it 'tis. Yer gonna be just fine, Miss Brigit." He patted her hand. "Ye've survived a rough one, but ye be in good hands now. And I'll be sure Michael Stone is contacted."

She sighed and closed her eyes. "Thank...you..."

Chapter Thirty-Two

Finding the site of the plane explosion was easy, getting up to it was impossible.

Fire trucks, police cars and Haz Mat vehicles blocked the narrow country lane. Press vans jammed the field. People by the dozens packed themselves against the police barricades, trying to get a look, take a photo and propagate gossip about why the plane had landed in a sheep field and who lay under the white sheets on the ground.

Titus stayed at the airport to refuel and store his jet. He'd had the good sense to have an armored SUV waiting to transport the others to the field south of Dublin.

The SUV got within a quarter mile of the site, and Michael jumped out and started jogging toward the crowd, the others behind him. By the time he reached the barricade and pushed his way through the gawkers, he was sweating. The temperature was only in the forties, but the heat from the wreckage permeated the air, along with the stench of burning rubber, jet fuel and hot metal.

He identified himself to a local cop, flashed his badge and grew impatient as the cop looked him over and then used a walkie-talkie to ask permission to let him pass. Permission was granted, although reluctantly.

The cop dragged the barricade open enough to let Michael and the others slip through before directing them to a knot of blue-uniformed officers.

A helicopter skimmed the still-billowing smoke from the plane. Crime-scene-recovery technicians, wearing bright orange vests, fanned out on all sides of the plane's skeleton, scanning the ground, the stone fence and the trees that formed a north-south border on one end of the field.

As Michael surveyed the surrounding area, he wondered if Donovan had purposely chosen this field because of the tree line. Even in the dark of night, it would have provided a dark parallel shadow for him to follow as he landed.

A female officer watched him approach and broke from the group of personnel to meet him and his group. Her reddish brown hair flew around her face in the breeze, dancing with the deep lines around her eyes. Her badge hung from her neck and a serious black gun sat prominently on her belt.

"State your business," she said.

Michael flashed his badge in its leather holder with one hand as he stuck out his other to her. "Michael Stone, Deputy Director of Central Intelligence. I have information about the terrorist who did this."

Another officer who'd been talking on a cell phone snapped it shut and stepped toward them as the police woman shook his hand. "Did ya say Michael Stone?"

"Yes?"

Dipping his chin in a nod, he wiped a trickle of sweat off his forehead. "Brigit, you know 'er?"

A chill went up Michael's spine. "Yes."

The man motioned for Michael to follow him down a slight embankment. He pointed to the grove of trees. "I found her along the fence, there. I don't know how close she was to the plane when it exploded, but the blast sent 'er a good ways in the air before she landed."

Michael scanned the area, looking for a third white sheet. "Where is she?"

"I hate to tell ye, but your gal looked to be in pretty bad shape. She could barely even speak, but her first words were 'Michael Stone'."

"She..." Michael paused, a lump forming in his throat. He cast a hopeful glance at Flynn standing beside him. "She's alive?"

The man dipped his chin again. "Medics took 'er to North Ridge. Good trauma unit there."

Truman clapped his hands together. "God Bless the

Queen."

Flynn slapped him on the shoulder. Michael's stomach flooded with a burning sensation, but his hope grew brighter. He turned on his heel to run back to the SUV.

The female police officer snagged the sleeve of his coat. "You said you had information about the terrorist involved in this."

He and Flynn exchanged a look. Flynn cocked his head in the direction of the SUV. "Go. Del and I'll relay the information."

Michael pulled Flynn away from the female police officer's hearing. "I want Donovan, personally, whatever it takes, and I want the word to go out Brigit Kent died in that plane."

"You think Donovan will come after her?"

"She's in the hospital and injured."

"Easy pickings."

"Exactly. Donovan's probably gone to ground, but that doesn't mean he won't send someone else after her."

"I'll barter information, see what I can do."

Michael nodded and Flynn turned back to address the female officer.

Gunn hung off to the side, waiting for him. "I'd like to go with you."

The acid in Michael's stomach flowed up into his throat. He leveled his gaze at Gunn. "She doesn't work for SIS anymore."

"She's my friend."

"That all?"

Gunn met his gaze straight on and flexed some muscle. "Brigit's been on her own since she was seventeen. She's got nobody. No family and very few close friends. For the past five years, I've looked out for her, and I don't intend to stop now."

Gunn cared about Brigit, and while the thought continued to sour Michael's stomach, he respected the man's devotion. It would be unfair to refuse him a ride to the hospital, and Michael was nothing but fair to everyone.

"Let's go."

Our Lady of Hope Medical Hospital

The ER doctor was young and cocky, with blond hair hanging in waves around his head. He looked like Michelangelo's version of an angel, but Michael was sure his

211

Irish accent was courtesy of Hollywood.

"Mild concussion. Contusion on her right temple, which she claims came from the butt of a gun and happened before the explosion." The doctor flipped through pages on a clipboard, much too willing to share information on his patient with a nonmember of Brigit's family.

Of course, Michael's ID had a way of making a lot of inexperienced Hollywood movie junkies talk, and Brigit had no available next of kin hanging around.

The man's finger ran down a list on his chart. "CT scan shows no intracranial bleeding. No broken bones, no internal bleeding, no lacerations or burns. Tox screen isn't back yet. She has two mildly bruised ribs and an older wound from a gunshot."

He glanced up, amusement lighting his pale blue eyes. "She claims she also received that prior to today's explosion. Who is she, Lara Croft?"

An image of Brigit in leather flashed through Michael's brain. He shook it off, disgusted with himself. The woman was in the hospital after her so-called brother tried to blow her up. Now was not the time to free his libido. "Can I talk to her?"

"Sure. The concussion produced echolalia so if she keeps asking you the same questions, like, 'where am I' over and over again, don't be alarmed. Echolalia is common in head-injury patients."

He flipped the papers closed. "She's refused everything but Tylenol and even as weak as she is, she's been trying to get up and leave." He pointed to a screened-off area on his right, divided by curtains into makeshift rooms. "That bruise on the side of her face is ugly and she admits she lost consciousness after she got it. I want to keep her here for observation. Four to six hours at least."

"I'll see if I can persuade her to stay on one condition."

Dr. Hollywood grinned. "Which is?"

"You keep her name from being released to the media. Her life's in danger, and this is no movie. The people who shot her and tried to blow her up will come after her. You understand what I'm saying?"

The grin fell off his face, and the pathetic Irish accent disappeared. "Yeah, no problem."

Michael insisted Gunn stay in the hallway. He wanted to

talk to Brigit first alone. When he entered the tiny, curtained-off area made into a room, she was curled on her side sleeping.

Her face was pale, even against the bleached-white sheets, and the term "ugly" was a mild description of her bruised temple. Black and purple smudges bled from her hairline toward her eye and down her cheek. As Michael drew closer, he saw an elongated welt rising in her hair.

His hands shook as he leaned his arms on the bed's guardrail to watch her. His stomach was on fire again and he clenched his fists. If Peter Donovan had been in the room, he would have punched him into a pile of raw meat.

She could barely even speak, but her first words were 'Michael Stone'.

She'd asked for him before anyone else.

Blowing out a deep breath, he tried to figure out why, even though he didn't really care. His brain had no logical answer, but his heart raced under his shirt like he'd just run a touchdown into the end zone.

Brigit's hand rested on top of the sheet. Without thinking, he reached out and placed his hand over hers. Her slender fingers disappeared under his wide ones, and she sighed in her sleep.

He stood like that for long moments, enjoying the softness of her skin and the faint rise and fall of her chest. Out in the hallway, a pan clattered to the floor. Brigit stirred.

Drawing his hand back, he straightened up as she blinked open her eyes. Her right eye was swelled and stayed half lidded as her gaze locked on him. "Are you really here or am I hallucinating?"

He smiled, swallowing the lump that seemed to form in his throat an awful lot when it came to her and her well-being. "I'm here. How do you feel?"

"Better now that you're here." She grinned, as if surprising herself at the admission, but the smile dropped off her face as she rolled over on to her back slowly, wincing. "Actually, my body feels like hell. No, worse than hell." She glanced at him from the corner of her eye. "I bet I look about as good too. Why is it you always see me at my worst? I've been gun-shot, had my hair French fried and now I've been blown up. I'd like you better if you showed up a tad earlier and saw me at my best. And maybe kept me from getting hurt. I don't like pain."

"Yet you keep throwing yourself into these situations."

"I'm not usually such a magnet for bad luck, just so you know." She stared at the ceiling and Michael could see her eyes tearing up. "That's not true, either, I guess. My mother was killed when I was seven and my father kicked me out ten years later. We had a fight over Tory, but I think the real reason we fought so much was because he got tired of seeing my face."

"I find that hard to believe."

Brigit's voice was almost a whisper. "Well, you didn't kill your mother and then have the audacity to grow up and look just like her."

"Your mother's death wasn't your fault."

She shot him a grave look. "How do you know that?" Before he could answer, though, she sighed. "Never mind. I know your skills at discovering my deepest secrets are unparalleled."

A tear trickled out of the corner of her eye and she swiped at it. "Guilt doesn't have to be directly related to fault, by the way."

"I agree."

That got her. She shifted her gaze again to look at him. "What guilt trap keeps you up at night?"

He wanted to keep her talking, partially, he admitted to himself, just to hear her voice, and a good way to do that was to offer up the truth. He hadn't ever shared it with anyone, yet the idea of telling Brigit his list seemed natural, easy to do. She would understand.

"My father's death tops the list. Five CIA operatives killed while I was Director of Operations, three men killed and another three held hostage with me last spring. Do you want me to go on?"

Something flickered in her eyes he hadn't seen before. Not pity. Something else. Camaraderie. They were in the same survivors' club. "Your father's death, what happened? How old were you?"

"I was ten. He was undercover in Germany, feeding information back to the CIA. He got caught, was arrested for spying and thrown in prison. Before the U.S. could negotiate his release, he was severely beaten by a group of fellow prisoners. They called my mother, and she didn't even take time to get a babysitter for us. She left me in charge of my siblings and took off. He died five minutes after she got there."

Brigit's expression was pained. "Oh my God, Michael. I'm so sorry."

"It wasn't my fault, and yet I've carried around guilt over it my whole life. Maybe if I'd done better in school or been a better son, things would have turned out differently."

She nodded. "I do that too. All kids do, whether their parents die or get divorced or run off and leave them." Staring again at the ceiling, she seemed to shift to a younger version of herself. "If I'd been a better little girl, maybe Peter would have left me alone," she whispered. "If he hadn't kidnapped me, I wouldn't have accidentally started the fire that killed my mother."

The world outside the room went deathly silent, as if he'd just entered a vortex. "Donovan kidnapped you as a child?"

Picking absently at the edge of the sheet, she darted a glance at him. "He's my brother. Half-brother, actually, and yes, the distinction is important to me. He kidnapped me and Tory when we were young girls, seeking revenge on our father, who Peter believed was responsible for his own father's death. When my mother tried to rescue us, I knocked over a candle, which started a fire. The fire set off some gunpowder Peter was storing in the kitchen and caused an explosion. She was killed."

When he didn't say anything, she looked away. "I know, I should have told you Peter was my half-brother sooner. You have every right to be angry."

Angry? He was furious. "You should have told me he kidnapped you."

"Three people outside of my immediate family know. You make number four. Among other embarrassing things, like the fact I'm a total klutz and failed becoming a full-fledged operative for SIS, it's not something I share on a regular basis."

"Then why tell me?"

She pressed her lips together and another tear escaped the corner of her eye. "I'm not sure, it just seems like you've...earned it."

Earning her trust shouldn't have made any difference to him, but it did. His heart took up kickboxing. It thudded so hard, he almost put his hand up to catch it when it finally broke free from his chest. *She could barely even speak, but her first words were 'Michael Stone'.* "Did Donovan give you the bruise?"

"Yes." She raised her hand and gingerly touched her hairline. "I tried to stop him from taking off, but as you can see, I'm not much of a roadblock. Another reason I didn't cut the mustard as a spy."

"But you *do* work for the Secret Intelligence Service."

"Did," she corrected. "As a legitimate consultant, just like for your government and half a dozen others, but yes, SIS was my main employer."

"And you got Gunn into meetings and places where he could do the spying for Britain."

"I see the penny's dropped," she said, smiling halfheartedly and confirming his charge. "I've also worked kidnappings, especially those that fit Peter's MO, and I treat kids who've been kidnapped. Having been an abducted child, I have firsthand knowledge of what it's like."

Michael couldn't decide if he was more pissed at Peter Donovan or more relieved Brigit had survived all the asshole had put her through. "The doctor wants to keep you awhile for observation, and I agree it's a good idea. I want you here, safe and protected. Flynn's working on keeping your name and the fact you're alive out of the media for now, and that's the best way to keep you safe from Donovan."

She struggled to sit up. "But you need me to help you find him."

He laid a hand on her arm and gently pushed her back down. "I can find Donovan on my own, and when I do, you won't have to worry about him any longer."

The old Brigit surfaced, eyes flashing with determination as she pushed against his restraining hand. "He's *my* brother. I'm the one he tried to blow up. If anyone gets to go Batman on him, it's me."

"Batman?"

She waved her hand at him. "Yeah, you know. That thing you do to anyone who gets in your way. I've been taking notes. I don't have the big shoulders you do, but I have the eye squint down pat."

He chuckled. "I would like nothing more than to see you kick his ass, but you'll have to get in line. I'm first."

Her resistance faded as fast as it had appeared. "Please let me handle this."

He patted her arm, ran a finger down to her hand, his focus

following. He wanted to imprint on his mind, in his very anatomy, how her skin felt, how she looked. "I can't. When Donovan kidnapped Ella, this became my fight." Raising his gaze to hers, he continued. "When he hurt you, it became my war. He may have started it, but I'll finish it."

Brigit's index finger came up to meet his. At her touch, Michael's racing heart skipped a beat. He took her hand in his and gave it a squeeze.

She returned it, just like she had the first time he met her. "He'll be headed to Belfast." Her voice was almost a whisper. "That's where his headquarters is. He moves it around a lot, but he never strays far from the city for long."

"I'll find him."

"We had a deal." She cleared her throat, drummed up her earlier determination. "You can't leave me behind and think I'll stay put."

She had him there. If he did try leaving her behind, she'd only check herself out and take off again. He found it easy to give in. "I have some calls to make and some red tape to work through with the Irish. I'll check back in a few hours, and if the doctor vets you clean enough to be released, we'll go to Belfast together."

She scanned his face, looking for the lie. "That was too easy. What aren't you telling me?"

"Nothing." He squeezed her hand again. "Gunn's outside waiting to see you."

"What's he doing here?"

"He cares about you."

"He cares about his job, and hanging out with me is a sure ticket to Libya. He should go back to London and get his next assignment."

A wave of relief rolled through him like warm maple syrup. "The guy gave you his mother's lucky rabbit's foot."

Brigit let loose a derisive laugh. "Yeah, and look what that got me. I nearly ended up being yet another source of global warming."

As they'd talked, he'd been leaning closer to her face. Now, he couldn't stop himself and touched his lips to her bruise. "You survived." Dropping down, he kissed her, just a brush of his lips to hers, seeking her warmth. He was so damn glad she was alive. "I'd say that's lucky."

Even her swelled eye widened at his bold move. Then she laughed again, with less derision, and sighed. A smile curved her lips. "It's about time my luck turned around."

"Mine too," he said, reaching deep for the willpower to leave her even for a short time. He released her hand in small increments and walked out of the room, ready to get to work and considering himself to be a very lucky man.

Two hours later, Brigit still cradled her hand to her chest thinking about Michael. For some reason, his presence, so solid and powerful, made her believe everything would be all right.

And it would, once she found Peter. She knew him better than anyone, and she knew he'd never let himself be taken alive. No way could she let Michael go after him in order to get revenge for her. Killing Peter would go against everything he stood for, and she couldn't let him do it and then have to live with one more item on his guilt list.

She'd dug this hole, screwed up her life all on her own, and now she was the one who had to fix it.

Truman had refused to return to London. No matter how she tried to persuade him to go back to his own life and his job, he'd told her to zip it and then changed the subject. Finally, just to get rid of him, she'd sent him shopping once again for her for some clothes. The new items sat in a bag next to the bed.

Dragging herself to a standing position, she held onto the edge of the bed until her knees stopped shaking and the room quit tipping to the left. Then she shrugged off the hospital gown and spent the next several minutes detagging and putting on the new clothes.

She'd eaten the hospital food at lunch to give her some energy and made Truman give her some cash for the vending machines before sending him off to start the process of getting her a new ID. She had ten U.S. dollars, no ID, no weapon and no phone, but she had a truckload of self-righteous fury and that had proven to be all she needed in the past.

Peter would lie low for a few days, but just like a dozen times before, he'd gotten away with murder scot-free. He'd be cocky and ready to celebrate his success with his comrades once he made it home. In Belfast, he had three bases he moved between. It wouldn't be hard to find him if she bided her time, kept herself in the shadows and didn't get distracted thinking about Tory.

There was a bedside table and she opened the top drawer to retrieve her meager possessions—her watch and the rabbit's foot.

Securing her watch on her right arm, she thought about Michael again and smiled. Her luck had definitely changed for the better.

She grabbed her dirty trench coat and tossed the rabbit's foot on the bed. Someone else could have it now.

Her bruised ribs hurt a bit, but as she walked past the nurse's station and down the hall, a lightness filled her chest. Her nerves tingled. Her headache had subsided thanks to the pain medication and the new clothes felt like a whole new identity.

As the ER doors slid shut behind her with a soft whoosh, she cinched her coat a little tighter and hailed a cab.

Thad's voice had lost its pre-election finesse as he cursed into the phone at Michael. "The election's in three days. Three. Your scandalous affair is costing me major votes. Do something."

In the backseat of the SUV, Michael avoided Flynn and Hoffman's stares as the vehicle parked in the hospital's lot. Even though Thad was on the other side of the Atlantic, his voice was loud enough to echo in the car.

"I'm not having an affair," Michael ground out between clinched teeth. "And even if I were, there would be nothing scandalous about it."

"You took Brigit Kent home with you before she was cleared of my daughter's kidnapping." Thad's voice raised yet another notch. "She's now suspected of terrorism."

"Brigit Kent is dead."

No yelling this round. Instead, startled silence. "What did you say?"

Jacking the door open, Michael slid out of the seat and started for the ER entrance. Brad fell into step beside him as a taxi pulled away from the curb. "Turn on CNN. You're not the biggest story of the hour anymore." He snapped the phone closed and shoved it in his jacket pocket.

The hospital doors opened and both he and Brad skirted an older woman in a wheelchair being pushed by an orderly. They passed the nurse's station, where Michael nodded to one of the women behind the desk. She'd been there earlier when he'd left Brigit to return to the plane site, and just like then, she barely noticed him, a phone cradled on her shoulder while she typed frantically on a computer.

His bodyguard took up post as Michael pushed aside the curtain to Brigit's ER room. The bed was a mess of sheets but there was no Brigit. An empty bag lay on the floor and the trench coat that had earlier draped the back of a chair was missing. Fear surged in Michael's veins as he circled the bed and snatched up the gown.

Truman Gunn came sailing into the small area past Brad. He glanced around, confusion contorting his features. "Where is she?"

Michael fisted the gown in his hand. "She took off. Again."

"Damn it." Truman rubbed his forehead. "I knew I shouldn't have given her any money."

Michael squinted at him. "You gave her money?"

"She has a thing about not having any money. It goes back to her days on the street after her father kicked her out."

Something on the bed caught Truman's attention and he moved to pick it up. The pale cream fur of the rabbit's foot had blended in with the sheets.

He turned it over, shaking his head. "She's gone after Peter, hasn't she?"

Michael clinched his jaw. "You know her better than I do. You tell me."

Truman sighed like he'd just lost his best friend. "She's gone after Peter."

"Then"—Michael tossed the gown back on the bed and headed for the hallway—"we go after her."

Brad fell into step beside him, and Truman brought up the rear. "But she left the GPS here."

The younger generation had relied on technology their whole lives. Michael hadn't. The ER doors flew open in his wake. "We'll find her the old-fashioned way."

"And what is that?"

As soon as Michael opened the door to the SUV, he pointed at Del Hoffman. "Get me Lawson Vaughn, and get him here yesterday."

Chapter Thirty-Three

Belfast
Two days later

The assassin's umbrella consisted of a projectile, a carbon dioxide cartridge and a spring-loaded piston. The trigger engaged the piston, driving the cartridge into the firing pin and propelling the projectile out the hollow tip of the umbrella. The projectile had to be tiny but hold enough poison to kill the intended victim.

Old-fashioned umbrellas worked best, and Brigit had found one easily enough in a resale shop. She'd pawned her Tag Heuer and bought a used digital camera, an older laptop and a pocket-size, battery-operated drill with charger.

The drilled-out hollow in the metal ball held less than a milligram of rat poison. Strychnine injected directly into the bloodstream produced serious symptoms, even in small doses. Left untreated, it could be just as deadly as if the person had ingested a larger dose.

Killing Peter wasn't her objective. Disabling him was. A slow, painful disabling.

Brigit used a plastic spoon to transfer a drop of melted wax from a nearby candle to cover the hole. Once the pellet was injected, Peter's body heat would melt the wax and release the poison.

She assembled the gun with quick, efficient movements. After all these years, her father's training still clung to her mind like an annoying song she couldn't shake.

At thirteen, he'd taught her self-defense. She'd sucked at it and the harder she tried to please him, the worse her timing and execution had grown.

At fourteen, he'd insisted on weapons training, whether it was because hand-to-hand defense would get her killed, or because it was all part of his master plan to turn her into a candidate for MI5, she didn't know, but weapons were easier to understand. Taking them apart and reassembling them was like working a puzzle, breaking a code. She understood the parts and how to put them together in order to make them work.

By her fifteenth birthday, she had acquired a cache of knowledge on maiming and killing with everything from pencils to rifles. While she never used her knowledge, her conscience acquired even more guilt.

In school, she excelled in all her classes and graduated at seventeen. Ivy League universities came calling and so did her father's employer. When she refused to consider spying as a career, they argued daily, harsh, hateful words chilling the air in their quaint suburban home.

Tory hated it, retreating constantly to her room, where she cranked R. Kelly, or tearing out of the house to crash with friends. One night she didn't come home.

William blamed Brigit for Tory running away, just like he'd blamed her for a hundred other things over the years. But when he refused to go after Tory, they argued yet again, and unable to bear the pain of all her guilt, Brigit had pushed past him, making for the door to follow Tory's footsteps. William tried to stop her, shoving her away from the door, and the self-defense training he'd ground into Brigit kicked in with precise instinct. Stunned by his bleeding nose, her father had then shoved her out the door.

He'd told her never to come back.

Homeless and devastated at her family's demise, Brigit could only focus at first on survival. Odd jobs helped her gather enough money to follow Tory to London, and when a nice businessman in spectacles offered her a job as his assistant, she accepted.

Edward turned out to be a senior officer in the British Army's shadowy Force Research Unit who had infiltrated the IRA during the height of the Troubles. Her fate was sealed from there on. Several years later she learned it was no coincidence Eddie had entered her life at that precise time. Her father had been looking out for her the only way he knew how.

Eddie, or his employer, footed the bills to send her to

university, and while she studied psychology, she also passed information between Eddie and on-campus contacts, spied on the Irish students sympathetic to the IRA, and nursed Eddie after a facial surgery to conceal his identity.

She never wanted to become a full-blown spy. Nor was she all that good at lying, and she had no stomach for killing. However, her code breaking and people-reading skills were topnotch, and her fucked-up family experience had put her light years ahead in survival of the fittest.

Funny she was still dead to the world at large. Whatever Michael had done to hide the truth had worked. For now. The advantage was hers in this game with Peter, but time was running out. First she would mess with his mind, then his body. Give him a fat dose of his own medicine.

The ruthlessness in her heart gave her pause. She'd lived for so long trying to help others, the desire to hurt someone seemed dishonest somehow. Alien. If she followed through with her plans, she would cross a distinct line in the sand. Would there be any way to go back?

A dull pain flared in her ribs as she took a deep breath, wanting to cleanse her soul as much as her lungs. Her bruises were fading and the gunshot wound itched, healing quicker than she expected. Her heart too. Both were due to Michael Stone's capable care.

As with all decisions in life, there was no going back. She'd already turned a corner, thanks to Peter's cruelty as well as Michael's intervention. The only path for her was straight ahead.

Snapping the hollowed-out end on the umbrella, she checked the clock above the door of her rented room. Peter was a block away, getting ready for his evening stop at the Roaring Cock. Ballsy, he'd fallen back into old habits with ease, and those old habits would be his undoing.

After washing her hands and donning her tourist persona, Brigit took the assassin's umbrella and slid out the door into the night.

The Irish had not outlawed smoking, and a fine shroud hung in the air with the smell of strong stout. Like many traditional pubs in the heart of Belfast, the Roaring Cock sported an ancient bar, battle-scarred from serving hundreds of hard-working Irish. While a few adventuresome tourists stopped in on occasion, the majority of patrons were natives.

Natives sympathetic, if not outright supportive, of Peter's cause.

Brigit had donned a thick farmer's jacket over her wool sweater and jeans. She'd tucked her hair under a tweed cap and now kept the brim down as she nursed a decaf coffee and read the local paper, all the while keeping a low profile in a back corner booth. A couple of men who had to be nearing eighty had given her brief attention, but she'd brushed aside their flirting and they'd left her alone. A younger man, tall and gorgeous in a leather jacket and working boots, had set eyes on her when he'd entered the bar, his tan skin tight over his cheekbones. A fisherman, she'd guessed, before averting her gaze. There were many of those in these parts as well.

The hour was late enough to ensure a packed-out place, and a championship boxing match on the semi-circle of televisions above the bar enthralled them. Every few minutes a collective whoop or groan would rise from the viewers.

Brigit was grateful for the crowd. They kept the bartender and waitress busy, so neither had time to wonder about her, and they also acted like a human screen so Peter couldn't see her from his stool at the far end. He was absorbed by the fight and surrounded by his compatriots. Around his neck, he sported a cashmere scarf in Irish colors. He'd hid his bald head under a cap that nearly matched Brigit's.

How many times had he come here after one of his crimes and went right back to a halfway normal life? The men and women in the bar were staunch Irish Catholics. Most knew Peter and treated him like family. A few had probably hidden him at one time or another in their very homes.

As several more patrons filed in, Brigit hailed the overworked waitress. When the woman stopped at her table, Brigit handed her two euro notes worth roughly fifty U.S. dollars and a folded piece of paper. "The man at the bar with the Irish scarf, supply him another Guinness and give him this with it." She tapped the folded piece of paper. "The left over change is for you."

The waitress winked at her, ecstatic about her tip. "He's a handsome one, ain't he?"

"He's my brother."

"Oh." The waitress pocketed the money and hurried away.

Brigit watched her work her way through the crowd before rising from the bench to follow her. She positioned herself behind several large, bulky patrons crowded around Peter as one of the boxers sent his tank of a fist into the other's chin. The boxer went down and the men's glasses of beer went up along with a hearty cheer.

Out of all of her skills, being calm under pressure was the one Brigit most valued. While the men bellowed a countdown with the referee and the waitress poured the drink, she bumped the man nearest her into another to start a domino effect while pressing the sharp end of the umbrella into the back of Peter's lower calf and pulling the trigger. The shove of large bodies against his back diverted his mind from the pinprick sensation.

Over in a heartbeat, Brigit slipped away from the bar as the waitress slid the glass of Guinness in front of Peter with the note. Just as she knew he would, Peter looked up from the note, bolted upright from his barstool and scanned the crowd.

As their eyes locked, Brigit touched the edge of her cap with the umbrella, saluting him as she pushed the door open and left.

Chapter Thirty-Four

The din of yelling spectators vibrated in Peter's ears. As he watched the woman disappear through the bar's entrance, the voice in his head fought for center stage over the noise. *It can't be Brigit. She's dead.*

He read the words on the paper in his hand again, the slender script conveying a familiar message. One the IRA had sent to Margaret Thatcher over twenty years prior.

You have to be lucky every day. I only have to be lucky one.

Under the handwriting, the note was signed by a dead woman.

Brigit.

Through the windows on the north side, Peter saw a red umbrella weaving and bobbing down the sidewalk. Crumpling the paper in his hand, he pushed his way past the layers of men watching the fight and took off after her.

Across the street, in a vacant apartment above a retail wool shop, Michael followed Brigit's progress down the sidewalk with his night-vision binoculars. She stopped at the entrance to a dark alley and looked both ways.

Flynn sat at the kitchenette's table with Del, listening to a small speaker as Lawson Vaughn's commentary from inside the pub came through loud and clear. "She got his attention. He's going after her."

"Damn it," Michael muttered, shoving the binoculars in his inside jacket pocket and speaking into his headset. "Go out the back and head for the alley. I'll cover the north end, you take the south. First one who can grabs Brigit."

"Copy that."

The undercover cops were only a few blocks away, waiting for Michael to pull the trigger. He tossed the headset to Del. "Call the cops."

Brigit didn't know Lawson so he'd been the one to send into the bar. Now Flynn, who'd been begging to see some action himself, rose from his seat. Michael waved at him to follow.

As their boots echoed in the long, narrow stairwell, Michael ran through scenarios in his head. Just like in his Marine days, he saw the field and the players on a giant chessboard. The king could move here, the knight here and the queen anywhere she damn well wanted.

Flynn, luckily, wasn't a player on the board. "Hang back in case I need a distraction," he said over his shoulder.

When they hit the street, Flynn peeled off to Michael's right, disappearing into the shadows.

Now to find Brigit.

Michael saw Donovan cut around a group of young kids under a streetlight, bee-lining for the alley like he was on rollerblades. Michael waited for a car to pass and jogged across the street. The cops should be there any minute. All he had to do was keep Brigit from killing Donovan.

Or vice versa.

A minute later he entered the alley. The smell of rotting garbage and old beer permeated the air. Light from the street filtered down to nothing six steps in, and Michael paused, shut his eyes for ten seconds and reopened them. A man stood in the guts of dumpsters and debris, head bowed. No one else was in sight.

Sinking his hands into his jacket pockets, Michael fingered the compact Glock hidden there as he strolled toward the shadowy figure. Sirens blared in the distance.

At the sound, Donovan's head snapped up and he turned, facing Michael. He was holding the red umbrella.

Michael did a double take. No Brigit. Had Lawson grabbed her or had she dropped the umbrella and run?

The Glock was pointed and ready to fire if necessary. It would have been so easy to drop Donovan where he stood, but over the past forty-eight hours, Michael had hit on a different plan for the asshole.

"Cops," he said, keeping his head down and his hands in his pockets as he passed Donovan. "Better disappear."

Donovan stepped in Michael's path and glared at him. "Who the hell are you?"

A police car stopped at the end of the alley, flashing lights flickering across Donovan's face in a strobe. Michael squared up with him and looked him in the eyes, wishing he could spit poison into them. "You got two choices. Run or get in the dumpster. Either way, I'll cover you."

Donovan was smart. He dropped the umbrella and ran.

Ten minutes later, Brigit shouted at him when Michael came through the door.

"You!" She jumped out of the chair like a crazed woman, her face flushed and her eyes bright. She held up her thumb and forefinger as she marched toward him. "I was this close to nailing him."

Sweet relief at seeing her alive and ready to take him on buzzed Michael's nerve endings. Kinnick, Flynn and Vaughn all moved reflexively forward to intercept her before she could take a swing, but Michael held up a hand to stop them and handed the umbrella off to Flynn.

Brigit promptly punched him in the arm. The slight sting almost made him laugh, but the sincere fury on her face kept his amusement under wraps. He rubbed the spot as if it hurt to give her some satisfaction, but couldn't hide the teasing annoyance in his tone. "You were *that close* to getting killed again. I showed up earlier like you told me to do and this is the thanks I get?"

She punched him again with more force, and he was sure it was because of his smirk. "You aren't supposed to be here, you big lout."

He gripped her elbow, steering her away from the other men's eyes and into the adjoining bedroom, lit by a single lamp. He kicked the door shut and turned her to face him.

Not done lashing out at him, she kicked his shin. "You ruined *everything*."

"Ow," he said, pushing her back out of kicking range.

She wrestled in his grip. "Peter is mine to take care of, not yours. And then you have that Lawson guy show up and kidnap me right in the middle of leading Peter into my trap. He picked me up and carted me off like a sack of potatoes. Scared me to death. And...and..."

Realizing he was smiling smugly at her attempts to break free, she stilled and narrowed her eyes at him. Took a deep breath, assessing him. "You're hurting my injured arm."

Since he was gripping her forearm and not her upper arm, he was pretty sure she was lying to get him to turn her loose. Instead of complying, he pulled her in tight, hugging her to his chest. "You put on a good show."

Being shorter by at least six inches, she had to crane her neck to meet his gaze. Frustration still darkened her eyes, or maybe it was the low light of the room, but she sounded sad when she spoke. "It's not a show. I don't want you involved in this. It's my mess. I clean it up."

She smelled like the pub...fried food, boiled onions and dark ale. The pink in her cheeks set off her doll eyes. Her lips, even set in a firm line, beckoned to him. "What if I can take care of the mess *and* get your father back?"

Brigit's pulse hopscotched under her skin. Not because Michael had mentioned her father or offered to take out most of her problems in one grand slam. It was the way he was holding her and looking down at her, like a kid with a secret so big, he was ready to burst.

In the hospital, he'd made the emotional walls between them fall like they were constructed of thin sticks. She'd confessed too much and now wondered if he felt the same way.

Yet, if there was any awkwardness, she couldn't tell from the way he was hugging her against his body. His beautiful, powerful, hard body ignited a hunger inside her. All her anger, frustration and common sense dissolved like the Irish fog when it met sunlight.

As his eyes, devilish with amusement, invited her to ask about his plan, she tried to unscramble her brain. A nanosecond later, she gave up. Forget the plan. "I think I want to kiss you."

Michael's intensity ratcheted up a notch and Brigit had to remind herself to breathe. They stared at each other for a long moment, his gaze as intimate as the hand stroking her spine. "Now that's the kind of thanks I was hoping for."

She moved on him, going up on her toes and sliding her hands up his broad shoulders and solid neck to pull his face down to hers. Without resistance, he matched her boldness, taking her mouth with the same self-confidence he did everything else.

A knock made her jump back out of his arms. Conrad Flynn's voice was muffled through the door. "We're going to get food. You coming?"

The predatory look in Michael's eyes made Brigit swallow hard and take another step backwards. The set of his jaw, the way he stalked toward her as he answered, continued to cause havoc with her pulse. "Bring us something back."

Seconds passed as the men left. Michael was nearly on top of her, and the instant the door latch clicked, he wrapped a hand around the back of her neck and brought her to him again.

Talk about crossing lines, sucking face with the Deputy Director of the CIA could only bring her more grief, but as his demanding lips parted hers, she didn't care.

For this moment, grief was far away. Guilt and responsibility too. He made her feel sexy and alive like she'd never experienced, and damn if she didn't want even more.

Enjoying his sensual lips on hers, she used her tongue to taste him. Coffee and a hint of spearmint. Power and control.

He returned the favor, meeting her tongue with his as he shifted her body around to press her against the wall. She sucked in a breath, amazed at his gracefulness, but he mistook it for pain and broke the kiss. "Is it your ribs? Did I hurt you?"

Brain muddled from an overdose of his lips, she shook her head in confusion. "My ribs?"

Michael's fingers grazed her rib cage, sending an electrical charge through her chest. "Your bruised ribs, remember?"

She giggled, the sound almost a whisper. Had she really just been sticking her tongue in his mouth? "Oh, that, no. You didn't hurt me." Touching him in the same spot, she watched his eyes darken with desire. "I'm in tiptop shape."

"You were almost blown to pieces two days ago."

Two days ago was another lifetime she didn't want to talk about. She didn't want to talk at all. She wanted his tongue back in her mouth and his body pressed up against hers, trapping her to the wall. "I'm not done thanking you for today."

With slow smugness, he smiled and slid his face so his cheek was next to hers and his mouth was by her ear. "What were you doing hunting Peter by yourself? I told you we would come to Belfast together."

His low tone, the sound of pure sex in his voice, made her shiver. How did he do that? Talking about a terrorist and undressing her with his voice at the same time?

She struggled to form coherent words. "Killing Peter would ruin your career."

He kissed a spot under her earlobe. "What about your career?"

"Gone already." Leaning her cheek against his, she breathed in his clean-smelling aftershave and hoped it would rub off on her. "No career. No family. No life."

"I told you"—he nibbled her lobe—"I'm going to get your dad back."

Sinking her fingers in his short hair, she sighed. "How?"

"Peter's the key."

"Peter will be dead soon, or at least very, very sick."

Michael's lips stopped nibbling. "How do you know?"

Shut up, she told herself. *You're ruining everything.* But she couldn't ignore his question, nor could she lie. "I poisoned him."

"What?" Michael put his face in front of hers so they were nose to nose. "How?"

She let her hands fall to his chest. His sculpted-like-a-Roman-god chest. Now she'd blown everything. "The umbrella."

Michael stepped back and held up his hands, looking at them as if they were diseased. "You put poison on the umbrella?"

"No." She shook her head in earnest. "*In* the umbrella. It's a Cold War technique. You use it like a gun to inject a poison pellet into your target."

His brows drew down and then he strode out of the room, clearly irritated, taking all his magnificence with him.

Brigit slumped against the wall, deflated. Her luck hadn't really changed after all. She didn't belong with Michael any more than she belonged with her father or her sister or anyone else. She was alone. Totally alone.

"Show me."

Her head snapped up at Michael's command. The umbrella was in his hands and he was holding it out to her.

Taking it apart, she laid each piece on the bureau and answered his questions about how it worked. Keeping her focus on the umbrella, she tried to let his annoyance roll off her back, but his obvious disappointment in her couldn't be ignored.

When his silence stretched into the painful zone, she peeked at him from the corner of her eye. He was staring at her with an unreadable expression, arms crossed over his chest. "You built this?"

Returning her attention to the umbrella, she swallowed the lump in her throat. "Yes, and I followed Peter to the bar and injected him with rat poison. Got him right in the calf."

Silence again. Unable to stand it any longer, she turned to face him. "Say something."

A light had entered his eyes. He rubbed his chin with his fingers and thumb. "I think I'm turned on."

Relief slammed through her as he grinned wide, perfect teeth showing. In an instant, she was in his arms again. She wrapped one leg around his muscled thigh as their mouths found each other, and the next second he lifted her and swung her around to sit on the top of the bureau—umbrella parts scattering—all without breaking their kiss.

Her legs instinctively parted to allow him access, and he slid her to the edge of the bureau where their hips snapped together. The bulge in his pants teased her as mercilessly as his lips.

"I didn't think you had it in you," he murmured against her mouth.

"I don't normally," she said, feeding him short, hot kisses. "But every time I think of Ella and Tory and what Peter's taken from me, I hate him. I hate him so much I want to kill him a hundred times over." She pulled back and checked his response. "Sounds terrible, doesn't it? That I hate my brother enough to kill him? Holy Virgin, I'm fucked up."

"You have every right to feel mad, Brigit. Blood doesn't mean shit in this case."

God, she loved him for saying that. Leaning into him again, she teased his lips. "Thank you."

He responded, speaking through her kisses. "Dangerous to go after him alone, though."

"I laugh in the face of danger."

One of his hands went under her sweater, raked her stomach. "Jesus, you're my kind of woman."

She arched into the thumb now rubbing her nipple through her bra's lace. He kissed her cheek, her chin, her neck. "No I'm not, but I don't care as long as you don't."

His chuckle was deep and seductive. It made her smile. He leaned his forehead against hers and cupped her breast under the sweater. "How long does Peter have?"

Wrapping her legs around his waist, she brought their already impossibly close lower halves even closer. "Why?"

His other hand slid under her sweater and over her head the wool went, landing on the floor with the umbrella's guts. "I need him alive for my plan to get your father back."

He gazed at her breasts, running his fingers over her cleavage. His touch was so soft and so opposite of the conversation they were having, Brigit's breath stuck in the back of her throat. Interrogation by seduction, that's what this was. A sweet, exquisite torture.

Two could play at that game. "Exactly what is the plan?"

"Not telling." Michael dipped a finger inside her bra and scooped out her nipple. "I don't want you running off again trying to save my career."

Damn him. Refusing to be outmaneuvered, even in her hormone-induced stupor, she undid his belt, ran the zipper down and slid her hand inside.

Contact. Hot skin, stretched to the max, met her touch and she gasped. "No knickers?" She couldn't control the giggle that escaped her mouth.

The moment she'd touched him, he'd gone still as marble. Now his voice came out strained as he scanned her face with annoyance. "You find that funny?"

Not funny at all. Just...surprising...and sexy. "I think *I'm* turned on."

He laughed, the deep, full sound echoing in the small room. Finally having the upper hand, she smiled and gave him a little squeeze. His laughter came to an abrupt halt. "But I am going with you to help with this plan, right?"

"Right." He squeezed her nipple, and it was her turn to freeze. "As long as you behave."

She released him to push his pants down over his hips, never breaking eye contact. His gun, stored in the waistband at his back, thumped to the floor. "Define *behave*."

Before she could blink her bra was unhooked. The pile on the floor grew as Michael added the flimsy piece of spandex to it. Her breasts heaved in his hands as her breath came faster. "Following my orders down to the last detail."

"Is that all?"

Again, his laughter cascaded over her. "That seems to be hard for you."

The hardest thing ever. "Try me. Right now. Give me an order."

Instantly the dangerous predator was back. "Shut up while I kiss you senseless."

I laugh in the face of danger, she reminded herself as she tipped her mouth up and parted her lips.

Chapter Thirty-Five

High-octane desire hit Michael like a wildfire as Brigit parted her lips for his kiss. He grasped her chin and tilted her face up more, catching the image of her hair cascading down her back in the bureau's mirror.

The dark waves brushed her back and contrasted deeply with her pale, flawless skin. He played up her spine with his fingertips, letting his hand disappear under her hair.

As he brought his full attention back to her face, her lashes dipped, her gaze following him in as he claimed her mouth. She wasn't bashful about what she wanted either, sucking at his tongue and teasing him with hers.

The half a synapse still firing in his brain told him this was wrong for many, many reasons, but he couldn't recall one of them, especially with Brigit unbuttoning his shirt and slipping her hands inside to stroke his chest.

Using the hand buried in her hair, he tilted her back another fraction and shifted his mouth to her exposed neck. Her moan was so soft, he wondered if he'd imagined it. As he licked the spot under her earlobe he liked, he palmed one breast, tweaking the nipple. This time he heard her moan loud and clear.

Keeping her upper half prisoner under his lips, he moved his erection to replace it with his hand, thumbing her through her pants. Her voice was hoarse as she cried his name and arched even more.

Glancing in the mirror again, he surveyed her back. He wanted to see the reflection of her fine ass there. Wanted his hands on it. "The pants have to go," he murmured in her ear as his fingers popped the top button of her pants and ran the zipper down.

She came right back at him, pushing the shirt off his shoulders. "Quid pro quo."

His shirt dropped to the floor, and he helped her off the edge of the bureau so she could get her pants off. While she slipped her feet out of her shoes and then out of the garment, she eyed his body, head to toe, over and over, constantly flicking unabashedly back to his lower center. Approval was evident on her face.

He was doing the same to her as he kicked off his shoes and pants and watched her full breasts bounce as she bent to tug the pant legs off her feet.

Swinging around to face the bureau, she eyed him in the mirror. "You're amazing."

She wasn't wearing underwear and, sweet Jesus, he might just explode right there without even touching her again. Noticing his fixation, she waggled her ass in a slow circle. "You're one of those guys who carries a condom so you're prepared for sex at the drop of a hat, right?"

"What?" The synapses fired. Condom. *Shit.* "Tell me you're on the pill."

"I'm on the pill. Aren't you concerned about disease?"

He palmed her butt cheeks and parted her legs so he could step between them. Bending his knees, he slid his erection into the end zone like a magnet drawn to steel. "We're both clean."

She wiggled again, teasing him, and raised her brows. "How do you...?" Her voice trailed off. "You read my health records too?"

"Not per se." He couldn't believe they were once again engaged in unnecessary conversation. "Your file stated your medical assessments were clean."

She gripped the edges of the bureau, bracing herself, and leaned over the top, baring herself to give him better access. "I'm not really on the pill."

He froze, his fat tip pulsing with fresh need in her hot, slick folds. "You just said you were."

"You told me to say I was, and I'm trying to follow orders."

Everything from his brain to his toes cramped. She might as well have kneed him in the balls. He couldn't even utter the curse circling the fog in his cranium. Setting his palms on either side of her hips, he bent at the waist and pulled back, slamming the thinnest coat of control down on his uncontrollable lust.

"Nice withdrawal." She giggled. "But we're safe. I get Depo shots."

Lifting his head, he met her gaze in the mirror again. Exhaled the breath he'd been holding. Straightened up. Leaned in over her so close he could touch the back of her neck with his tongue. "You did that on purpose."

The laugh started low in her belly, and as he grabbed her and aimed for home, it broke free into a half laugh, half whoop of ecstasy.

"Like I mentioned earlier," she panted. "I'm not your kind of woman."

The hell she wasn't. Driving home in a single hard thrust, he relished how tight she was. How soft. "I like...a challenge."

Her softness pillowed his hardness so completely, he was once again a virgin ready to lose it on the first stroke.

He should have taken it slow, figured out what she liked and found a place nicer than this abandoned upstairs dump of an apartment to explore it with her. There wasn't even a bed. For some insane reason, she didn't seem to care.

Instead of a slow, enjoyable lovemaking session, they were going at it like dogs. While her assertiveness might be an act, he didn't think so. She liked power, was drawn to it.

Maybe she was as sex-starved as he was, or maybe it was the adrenaline of the mission fueling their actions. Either way, her no-holes-barred approach, and the way she twisted and teased him as mercilessly as he did her, was the biggest turn-on he'd ever experienced.

They weren't making love, but it wasn't a casual fuck either. There was something between them. He just wasn't sure what.

As he rode her, he let his gaze switch between her actual body under him and her reflection in the mirror. The skin on her back was satin white. Her hair, wild and tangled, fell forward, curtaining her face, but he didn't want her hiding from him. Combing the mass away with his fingers, he held it with his hand so he could read her expression.

Her eyes were closed, lips parted, cheeks flushed. She looked...

Euphoric.

Exactly.

Dropping his mouth to her uncovered neck, he kissed and nipped and licked at her, running his tongue down her spine as he worked himself in and out, finding her rhythm, enjoying how she met his. Self-control had left the building, and if he didn't slow down, he would lose it before she did.

He was so not going that route.

Using his free hand, he slid it over her breast, down her stomach and fingered her between her legs. On contact, her eyes flew open and they locked gazes.

Her hips undulated under him, getting the most bang for her buck, he imagined, as he sandwiched her between his hips and his hand. She moved in sexy little jerks, her breath coming out in bursts and her core tightening around him like a band.

"Michael?" she whispered.

He could tell she was so close, why didn't she let go? It was as if she were trying to match him, trying not to give in until he did.

Her eyes were pleading, dark pools of desire. "Can I...can...I...?"

Damn it. She was waiting for his order. "Yes," he answered, his voice a Brillo Pad. He was lost in her eyes, in her heat. "Now."

Her eyes closed, her head fell back and she gave in, a low, guttural moan escaping her lips as she pushed into him hard. Time spun out as she peaked and then, without warning, went limp under him.

He wrapped his arms around her to keep her upright and two seconds later, with her soft folds spasming around him, the half a synapse in his brain winked out completely and his body released with a jerk.

As he held her gently trapped between him and the bureau, he laid his forehead on her back. *Hell, yes, my kind of woman...*

On the tail of that thought came *my woman.*

Chapter Thirty-Six

Brigit hung limp in Michael's arms as time came back to her in snippets. The beat of her heart, thudding in her ears. The beat of Michael's, thudding against her back, thin vibrations pulsing through her skin. Rain tickling the glass window, lulling her further into bliss.

In the mirror, her reflection was flushed. She'd just been taken over the waterfall and looked to have enjoyed it thoroughly. Which was an understatement. There'd been no bed, no romantic gestures, not even a glass of wine between them. Just carnal, demanding lust.

The voice in her head chastised her. Pricked her with guilt. An intelligent woman did not throw herself at a man she barely knew. As if he didn't already believe her to be a liar and a blackmailer, what would Michael think of her now?

Turning her head to avoid her reflection, she considered her actions. Shove a powerful man in front of her and she was a goner. Shove a drop-dead gorgeous, powerful man in front of her and she was a slut.

Well, not exactly. In her profession, she was around powerful men all the time. Some of them were wicked attractive too. And yet she'd never slept with any of them. Even the single ones who flirted with her. She'd never let her shields down. Never shared anything about her family. Never challenged or teased them like she had Michael.

So where did that leave her in her current situation?

Having the best sex of my life.

Michael's lips brushed the back of her neck. "You okay?"

Just like before, an irreverent response shot out of her mouth. "You're a little big for me, but I managed."

His soft chuckle jiggled her body against his and all her nerve endings flared hot again. "What a trooper."

He turned her around and she leaned her hips against the bureau, legs still entirely too shaky. He planted his hands on the bureau top on either side of her and gave her a gentle kiss. "Next time, we find a bed."

Next time? Her heart tap-danced like an Irish clogger in her chest. "Whatever you want."

He straightened and flexed his arms as if shaking out a cramp. "What I want is a shower and some food." As he picked up her pile of clothes, he sighed deeply. "Neither of which is going to happen at the moment."

She took her bra from his outstretched fingers and put it on. "We could go back to my place."

He handed her her pants. "And where is that?"

She stuck her legs in, heaved the pants over her hips and zipped them up. "A few blocks from here. A rented room, much like this, above a retail business."

"Any security?"

"Deadbolt on the door."

Ignoring his hard look and commentary about it being unsafe, she took her shirt from him and went to the bathroom.

The moment she was alone, she sagged against the door. Her heart continued to tap dance...*next time, next time, next time.* It drowned out the voice in her head.

She cleaned herself up best she could, a smug smile on her lips. Her nerve endings sang an opera. Her psyche was performing lazy cartwheels. She was living in the here and now. Not the past and not the future. The only rules she had to follow were Michael's.

For now, that was okay.

Leaving the bathroom, she was going to ask about the plan to get her father back, but the pile of clothes on the floor was gone and so was the man who wore them.

She trailed out to the living room. His gaze locked on her, but before either of them could say anything, the outside door opened and people started filing in.

Del Hoffman, Brad Kinnick, Conrad Flynn and Julia Torrison.

Julia.

Why was she here? As the group passed out nods and murmured greetings to her and Michael, all Brigit could do was watch Michael's face looking for any hint of...

"Thanks," he said, already opening the white bag Julia handed him to see what was inside.

"One fish. One corned beef." Julia gave Brigit a small smile. She was dressed in a rich leather jacket and form-fitting designer jeans. Her hair was flat-iron perfect, smooth and glossy as it fell over her collar. "I wasn't sure what you liked."

Michael grabbed Brigit by the hand and led her to the small table and chairs in the kitchen. The others followed, Julia bringing one of the living room candles for light.

"Where's Vaughn?" Michael asked no one in particular. "Sit," he said to her.

She sat and watched him pull the two sandwiches, chips and pickles from the bag. Conrad leaned against the sink, crossing his legs at the ankles. "He's back at the hotel with Zara."

Julia placed the candle on the counter and leaned next to him. "They needed to talk."

Michael glanced at her and something passed over his face. Sadness? Brigit's stomach cramped. But then he shifted his gaze to Conrad. "No drinks?"

From his coat pockets, the Director of Operations pulled two sodas.

Michael popped the lid of one soda and set it in front of Brigit. "Sandwich?"

She toyed with the can, skimming the cold, damp aluminum with her fingers, wishing with all her might she didn't like Julia. "I'm not hungry."

The fish sandwich instantly replaced the soda under her fingers. "Eat," Michael commanded.

Meeting his gaze, she saw concern in his face. "Please," he added.

The jealousy leaked out of her like the rain running down the window. He was taking care of her again. She took a bite of the sandwich and chewed. The concern lessened a fraction.

"Why did you let Donovan escape?" Conrad asked.

Michael worked on his sandwich, swallowed. "Didn't want the cops to end up with him."

Brigit started to ask her own question, but as soon as she opened her mouth, Michael stuck a chip in it. As the others discussed what had happened and what was going to happen, Michael continued to feed her. Every time she tried to add her opinion or disagree with an element of the plan, he shoved more chips at her or a pickle. Once he even gave her back the soda.

He was worse than Truman.

Truman. She swallowed the last of her fish. "Where's Truman? Did he go back to London?"

"I sent him back," Michael said around a mouthful of corned beef. "He's negotiating with the Bolivian government on Jeffries' behalf to turn over Donovan in exchange."

"You think you can trade Peter for my dad? Why would the Bolivian government want Peter?"

Del raised his hand from the corner. "Because I implicated Peter in the 2007 uprising between the farmers and the cocoa growers. You know the one where the factory blew up and the cokeheads lost a million pounds of pure snort?"

Brigit almost laughed in disbelief. "Do I want to know how you did that?"

Del wiggled his fingers as if typing. "Master geeks never reveal their secrets."

"Nice play on Donovan in the bar," Conrad said. He was staring at her, his dark brows hung low over his hard eyes. There was measured mischief in them though. "He shot out of there looking like he'd seen a ghost."

Suddenly everyone was staring at her, including Michael. She smiled at the group. "He did."

Conspiratorial smiles returned hers. A flush crept up her neck, over her cheeks. In the blink of an eye, she was one of them. They respected her, she could see it in their eyes. Even Julia was wearing a big *you go, girl* grin.

The sensation was heady, like Michael's arms around her, holding her up and tucked against his solid body. Remembering their earlier encounter, the flush spread over her skin. Slipping her focus to his face, she saw in his smile he was remembering the sex too.

Oh, for the love of God, she was going to giggle.

The one sure way to get her back on track was to think about Donovan.

Donovan? When did I stop thinking of him as Peter?

Everyone was still watching her. She cleared her throat. "Your plan to capture Donovan will work, but I have a better one."

Michael tensed, and he opened his mouth to say something, probably disagree, before he'd even heard her plan. But then he stopped, nodded at her. "You're the expert on him."

Another wave of confidence rolled over her. All the years she'd been without family, without roots. Wandering from one country to another, trying to fit in, blend in, find acceptance. Here in this small group, she now had it.

Because of Michael. The men and women who had come with him to Ireland had accepted her into their secret society.

Now it was time to earn their acceptance on her own merit. "O'Bern's memorial service is tomorrow. Donovan will be there. In fact, he might even try to blow something up, just to make a point. Either way, that's our best bet to catch him."

Michael crumpled the empty sandwich bag. "If he's still alive."

Confusion marked Conrad's face as he glanced between Michael and Brigit.

Michael motioned at her. "She poisoned him. In the bar."

"No way." Conrad's dark eyes assessed her with approval. "How'd'ya do that? Put something in his drink?"

Heat rose in her cheeks again. "Assassin's umbrella."

"Seriously?" Julia straightened. "You know how to build one of those?"

"Yep."

Conrad pushed away from the sink, eager as Julia. "That red umbrella?"

"Yep."

"Will you show me how it works?" Julia again.

Brigit glanced at Michael. He gave a nod of assent. "It's in the bedroom," she told the others, rising from her chair. "I'll go get it."

Chapter Thirty-Seven

The rain continued, slow and easy. Under the assassin's umbrella, with Michael's arm around her, Brigit barely noticed. The street was deserted in the early morning hour, although light from several bars and restaurants dotted their path to her rented room at the inn.

The rest of the group had gone to the hostel. Michael had wanted her to go with them, telling her it was a safer place to spend the last half of the night.

But Brigit wasn't worried. Michael's arm reassured her. His bigger-than-life presence relaxed her. And even though she loved having a new group of friends to be part of, she wanted him all to herself again.

Inside her room, she set the umbrella near the radiator to dry and flipped on a table lamp as Michael locked the door. Few words had passed between them as they'd walked, as if they'd been a couple for a long time, but now as she slipped off her trench coat and hung it on a hook near the door, self-consciousness flooded her mind. The bed in the far corner seemed suddenly too big for the space. Should she make tea? Turn on the TV? Strike up a conversation about world events?

Continuing to run options through her mind, she watched him go from window to window, checking locks. Once satisfied, he shrugged out of his jacket and threw it on the nearby chair. His blue eyes met hers and Brigit was pretty sure from their darkened, sultry appearance, tea was the last thing his mind. He moved toward her and turned off the light.

Without a word, she took him by the hand and led him to the bed. In the shadows, he kissed her, running his hands up her arms, over her shoulders and into her hair. Rising up on tiptoes, she did the same to him.

With slow movements and maintaining perfect quiet, he removed her sweater, then her bra. She helped him with her jeans, kicking off her shoes and stripping down to nothing.

His clothes went next, and then he eased her onto the bed, the box springs squeaking under them. He made love to her mouth, sucked the skin of her collarbone, worshiped each breast in an exquisite torture of lips and tongue and teeth.

Moving to her stomach, he licked her skin and kissed each hipbone. His hands parted her legs and his mouth took her, not with strength, but with gentleness. As he worked her with his lips, tongue and fingers, she cried out in the dark room, and his name echoed in the shadows as well as in her heart.

She'd been starved for so long, the orgasms came fast and hard, one right after the other. He stroked her through them, teasing them out and exhausting her. After the third one, he released her legs and pulled her close.

Bliss tingled her nerve endings. Snuggling into Michael's chest, she was content to drift and wonder how she was going to keep him around for awhile. Once they were done exacting revenge on her brother, what would hold them together?

Nothing. He was Deputy Director of the CIA and she was...a psychologist without a job. She wasn't even a consultant anymore, for the president or anyone else. In fact, if Thad Pennington found out what she'd been doing for Jeffries—she shuddered at the thought.

Michael's hand stroked her back, up and down, up and down, comforting her, and she pushed thoughts about the presidents, old and new, out of her head. In their place, an image of Michael as a small boy rose. After losing his dad and blaming himself all these years, Brigit thought he was the one who needed comforting.

She shifted her head to kiss his chest, his heartbeat strong under her lips. The hard planes of his body called to her fingers. He was a big man from his head to his feet. A hard man.

Kissing the scar above his heart, she moved her lower half languidly to find what she wanted. He sucked in his breath at her touch and she rose over him, spreading her legs. Comforting each other was done.

"You're beautiful," he murmured as his hands locked onto her hips and pulled her down. "Damn tight too."

Little by little, she eased his hot thickness into her body, wishing she could do the same with his heart. He'd already stolen hers and the thought of not having him beside her, inside her, made her eyes well with tears. For once she was glad the light was off.

She found the rhythm she wanted, bracing her hands on his gorgeous, rock-hard chest and blinking away the tears. "You're not bad yourself."

He chuckled and even though she couldn't see the details of his face, she knew what he looked like. Deciding this might be the only time she could let the raw feelings in her heart show on her face without him seeing them, she kept the rhythm steady and thought about how nice it would be to have this man, with his high-powered job, traditional house and group of friends, to make a new life with. Instant security. Instant family.

But even without that treasure chest of dreams Brigit had longed for all her life, Michael Stone was what she wanted. What she needed. He made her look to the future with hope instead of trepidation. He made her accept who she was, so she could stop pretending to be who she wasn't.

Don't go there. There was no future with him, certainly nothing long term. Just like she'd told him, she wasn't his kind of woman. Powerful men always attracted her, but they always tried to control her too. They usually saw her as a willful woman who intrigued them. A challenge.

Some played mind games with her. They always lost. Others took the me-Tarzan, you-Jane approach. They lost too. When each of them realized there was no wearing her down or breaking her spirit, she became disposable.

When Michael returned to Langley, she'd find more consulting jobs and go on with her life. She hoped to form a new relationship with her father. What she wouldn't do was hang around, waiting and hoping Michael would fall in love with her.

Even if he did, she couldn't handle his constant demands in the long run. No one told her what to do or when to do it. She wasn't necessarily a feminist, she'd just been on her own for too many years to ever play second fiddle to anyone, most especially a powerful Washington bureaucrat.

Michael still gripped her hips and now urged her to

increase the speed of her strokes. She removed his big hands from their spot and put them on her breasts. "This time, we do it my way."

He latched on to her breasts with no further encouragement. "Yes, ma'am," he said in a perfect-sounding military response. "I'm at your mercy."

Having power over Michael Stone was a Disney kind of fantasy for her. *Pretend you love me,* she wanted to command. Instead, she rode him harder. "Kiss me," she said.

He reached up and pulled her head down. "Whatever you want, Doctor."

Hot and sweet, his lips took her, and Brigit gave herself up to the power.

Morning dawned too early for Michael, even though the bubbling clouds outside hid the sun. The bed was far too small for both him and Brigit to sleep comfortably, but then they hadn't slept much anyway. Brigit had recovered relatively quickly after their first lovemaking session, sleeping for less than an hour before slipping under the covers to bring him to full attention again with her mouth. He'd found himself completely under her control and loving every minute of it.

At some point, she'd gotten up and used the tiny bathroom. When she'd returned, she'd snuggled back into his body, only to place her lips next to his ear and give him instructions on what she wanted him to do to her. Very explicit instructions. Teasing her about her language, even as he forced her onto her back, he'd laughed when she blamed her Irish roots.

Lying on his side now, facing her, he memorized the minuscule freckles on her nose, counted the lashes on her cheeks, timed the rise and fall of her chest.

He couldn't remember the last time he'd faced the morning after with a woman he hadn't already established a relationship with. One-night stands had disappeared from his routine by the time he hit thirty, and casual affairs had followed shortly after. Always, he blamed it on the job. In reality, he just wasn't interested in anything quick, casual or meaningless.

He had one more night with her, two tops, unless their plan to snatch Donovan from the memorial service failed. If they succeeded, the exchange in Bolivia would take place in twenty-four hours.

His gut tightened as if Brad had just landed one hell of a kick to his solar plexus. Outside of that, and the fact he'd had a total of three hours of sleep, he was totally juiced.

Brigit's eyelids fluttered open, revealing her sexy, beautiful eyes. She stretched, arching her back, and smiled lazily at him. "Tell me I wasn't talking in my sleep."

Her voice, husky from sleep and the night's depravity, made him instantly hard. Hello, morning after. "You might have admitted a couple of scandalous things."

She studied him for sincerity as she stifled a yawn. "What did I say?"

Stealing the muscles in his mouth so he wouldn't grin, he pushed the sheet down to reveal her breasts. Oh, yeah, they were exactly as lush and erotic as he remembered. "You said, 'Michael, take me home with you. I want to be your sex slave.'"

The sleepy look left her face as if he'd shocked with her ten volts of juice. Embarrassed horror took its place, and she glanced away. And oh, hell, his solar plexus took another hit.

She didn't want a relationship. Not even an ongoing sexual one after this. Surprised he'd read her so wrong, he mentally cursed himself, and then he mentally chastised her too. Didn't she realize it was okay to have a relationship? Didn't she just once want someone to take care of her? Love her?

Love? Whoa. He was not going down that road again any time soon.

Touching her chin with his finger, he tipped it up to make her meet his eyes. "I was kidding. The most you did while I was watching was sigh."

She looked at him now, seeing him again as he was, naked and honest. He turned on the charm and added a flirtatious smile. After a heartbeat, she took his hand in hers and held it. "I'm a loner, Michael. I'm used to being on my own, relying on myself for everything. Relationships are a challenge for me."

Her honesty took him by pleasant surprise. As long as she was telling him what she thought, he could work with it. "Hell, Brigit, they're a challenge for me too, but your independence is a strength, not a weakness. I respect it."

She ran her fingers over the healing skin of his knuckles, then stroked his index finger between hers and her thumb. Such a simple touch and yet he could hardly stand not to jump on her, spread her thighs and go for the gold. "From the look in your eyes, I think I could say just about anything at this moment and you'd swear you respect me."

Ding, ding, ding. The lady was a winner.

Her fingers tickled over his wrist at the spot of his compass tattoo. "Did you get this in the Marines?"

"No, just a few months ago."

"The intricate design must have taken hours."

Several hours and multiple visits to the tat parlor. Pain he'd embraced. "A compass, the North Star and wits were all a sailor ever needed to find his way in the world. I lifted the design from an old navigational chart that belonged to my father."

She went back to stroking his fingers. "Does it help you find your way?"

The N at the top of the compass pointed at her while her fingers slipped over his again. His breath came faster. "Yes."

She stroked his middle finger. "Cards on the table, okay?"

He couldn't do more than nod.

She took a deep breath. "We need to talk about Ruth."

The gears in his head strained to shift. They were both naked and mere inches from each other and she wanted to do a family intervention. His voice sounded weird as he spoke. "Now?"

"Yes." She moved to his ring finger. "I need to get this off my chest."

He'd move mountains to get anything she wanted off her chest. "Okay, but you better make it fast because I have the attention span of a gnat on Red Bull at the moment."

"When Ruth was in London on her Rhodes scholarship, she took weekend trips with a friend to Belfast. While there, she and Kelly met a member of the Real IRA. At first, the two simply hung out with the man and his friends, enjoying the attention. They were American girls after all. But at one point, Kelly stopped going on these weekend trips and only Ruth continued to meet with the man. They spent hours together, like lovers do, down by the wharfs, in pool halls and at his place."

She took a breath and continued full-throttle. Whether to please him or to get it over with as fast as possible, he wasn't sure. "During the following months, one of the professors at her university was killed. Shot on his way home from his last class on Friday night. A liberal group on campus promoting birth control was targeted at a fundraiser. Half a dozen students were seriously injured. A fire burnt the political science hall to the ground and the cause was ruled arson."

She paused, as if to give Michael time to catch up with what she was insinuating. He didn't need any time. "You think Ruth was involved?"

"I was watching Peter and his group. Ruth showed up on too many occasions directly before these terrorist activities to dismiss her involvement. She fed him information about the campus, the professor, the student body."

His chest hurt, and he had to take several deep breaths to slow his hyper heart rate. "Peter? The man was Peter?"

She shook her head. "One of his younger followers."

Michael pulled his hand away. "Ruth would never hurt anyone. If she did give him information, she didn't realize what she was doing."

"Maybe the first time she didn't. I certainly gave her the benefit of the doubt in the beginning. But your sister is a Rhodes Scholar, Michael. After the second and third incidents, you really think she didn't put two and two together?"

Michael sat up, scrubbed his face with his hands. He bent his knees and dropped his forearms on them. "There could have been dozens of college-aged people running information for Donovan."

"There were a few students during that time interested in antisocial movements, but Ruth was the only one coming from Cambridge and meeting with one of his compatriots."

"But she...she..." He couldn't finish.

"Wouldn't do such a thing? I told myself the same thing about Tory for years after I discovered she'd joined Peter's organization too. Peter, Cormac and many others are—were— very persuasive and charming men. Passionate men who are difficult to say no to."

Ruth and a member of the IRA. Michael could not picture his sister hooking up with a terrorist much less helping him. "Proof?"

Sitting up beside him, she tapped the side of her head. "Most of it's in here, but I have documentation of her trips and their relevant timing with each incident. I've asked Truman to make sure it goes directly to you if anything happens to me."

He stared at the far wall, not seeing it. "You never gave it to Jeffries."

"After Ella was kidnapped and I met you, I stalled him. I just couldn't do it. Ruth means everything to you and I...I couldn't follow through and give it to Jeffries, even to save my father."

Her gift touched him. Deeply. So deeply, he couldn't find the right words to say. "Thank you."

"Now the election's over," she said, tipping her head in that familiar movement that let her hair screen her face. "My timely death saved Ruth and Thad from public humiliation and quite probably from losing the White House, but the truth is still there. It could come out someday."

There was nothing coercive implied in the tone of her voice. However her words still made Michael stiffen. "Blackmail again?"

Her face jerked up, her eyes wide, hurt and indignation clear even in the soft morning light. "I have no intention of blackmailing you or your sister. I just thought you should know so you could talk to her. She and Thad will have even more enemies now they're the First Family. And I'm not one to preach, but right is right. You need to talk to her about what she did and why."

Right *was* right, of course, and he owed her. Big time. He reached up and pushed a piece of her tousled hair behind her ears. "I'm sorry. It's a lot to take in."

She grabbed his hand and held it. "Yeah, I know." Her eyes filled with sadness. "Been there."

His gut twisted and he pulled her into his arms, hugging her for all he was worth. She'd survived far worse than he had and by God he wanted to fix it all. Make her happy. "You're not alone anymore, Brigit. I'm here, and we'll get your dad back, I swear it on my honor."

Her arms went around him, and she crawled into his lap. A second later he noticed the ragged hitch of her breathing. Warm tears fell on his shoulder. Easing them both back, he held her until she stopped crying. For the first time, she melted, small and fragile, against his chest.

He would have held her like that forever, but she finally pushed away and went to the bathroom, avoiding his eyes, but picking up his shirt on the way.

Listening to the sounds of the faucet running, his brain worked on a backup plan in case Donovan eluded them at the memorial service. No matter what happened, Michael was going to reunite Brigit with her dad. And then he was going to bury his foot in her dad's backside for being such a horse's ass.

Brigit reappeared from the bathroom, Michael's shirt on but unbuttoned. His groin tightened. She had a thing about his clothes and he was damn happy she did. The sight of her in them never failed to satisfy his deep male urge to protect her.

As she reached the bed, a teasing smile on her lips, a noise by the door caught Michael's attention. A white piece of paper slipped through the crack at the bottom. Before he could blink, Brigit was moving to pick it up. "Wait," he whispered.

She froze, half bent. He grabbed his Glock off the nightstand as he rolled out of bed. Moving cautiously, he flipped the safety off and motioned her away from the door.

"It's Tory's handwriting," she said, matching his whisper as she started to pick up the paper again.

He snapped his fingers, and she glanced up. Shaking his head, he again motioned at her to move away from the door. She straightened, crossed her arms over her chest and raised one brow.

At the door, he listened for movement outside. Nothing. He checked the peephole. What he could see of the hallway was clear. With deliberate slowness, he undid the bolt and lock. With once glance back at Brigit, who was still eyeing him like he'd lost his mind, he turned the knob and pulled the door open.

Cold, empty hallway greeted him as he stepped out. Until, at least, while he leaned over the wooden railing to view the lower staircase, the renters in the room next door came out with umbrellas and guidebooks in hand.

"Oh," one said, raising her guidebook to shield her eyes.

The other openly gawked at him. "Gonna be hard to top this on our sightseeing trip."

Michael smiled and beat retreat into Brigit's room, slamming the door behind him.

An amused grin crooked her lips. "Naked and brandishing a gun. That's so hot."

She was holding the paper and now handed it to him. Michael took it and read the small printed address. A time was also noted, one hour before O'Bern's memorial service.

"Crumlin Road Courthouse and Jail," she said. "A historic symbol of the Troubles. Closed in 1996. Donovan and his group have secretly used it off and on as a meeting place."

And this was an invitation for her to join them. Donovan was herding her into a bucket, where he could take aim and be sure to kill her. Michael's knees lost their ability to lock, and he leaned against the door to keep himself upright.

Brigit eyed the paper. "Tory's on my side now. She's setting Peter up."

Michael shook his head and tapped the spot next to his right eye with the barrel end of the gun. "Blinders, Brigit. You're wearing blinders if you think Tory is helping you. She's helping Donovan. It's a trap."

"You may be right, but if he knew I was here, in this rented room, why not kill me last night? Why have Tory write and deliver the note?"

He crumpled the note in his hand and replaced the safety on the gun. He wondered the same thing. "Get dressed. We're out of here."

"But Peter doesn't know where I am. I'm sure of it."

Grabbing Brigit, he hugged her close, frustration burning in his veins. Then he steered her toward the pile of clothes on the chair. "We're not taking chances."

Her brows collided over her eyes. "You should be happy. Now we won't waste our time at the memorial service."

Michael wasn't happy at all. Donovan wanted Brigit and was probably laughing his ass off at the idea that he could have killed her in her sleep. He was toying with her, drawing her into a no-win situation. "You're not going inside that courthouse."

"Then who is?"

He pulled on his pants and stuck the gun in his waistband. Grabbing his cell phone, he called the one man who knew how to handle an Irish terrorist.

"Flynn," the best ex-spy in the business answered on the first ring.

"I need you."

Chapter Thirty-Eight

Crumlin Road Courthouse

By noon, Conrad had the whole group locked and loaded for a look at the crumbling stone courthouse and jail. Ryan Smith had ferried over from London with Truman Gunn to join the party, and Titus Allen had left his baby jet to get in on the action too.

From Conrad's lookout point on the roof of the nearby hospital, he could see the entrance to the courthouse across the street and the jail's four story, six-hundred-and-forty cell wings next door.

Even with the peeling paint and broken windows, it was easy to imagine how stunning the grand Victorian building had once been. Behind the beauty of the architecture, the horrors forced on those who passed through its courts, however, was staggering. One hundred and fifty years of Belfast's bloody political history haunted the Crum. Gerry Adams, Ian Paisley, Paddy Devlin and David Ervine had all been convicted here and marched across the street to the gaol via the underground connecting tunnel. Inside the prison, inmates were subjected to squalor, beatings, mice and cockroaches. Seventeen men had been executed and many more had died from the deplorable, primitive living conditions.

Alcatraz, in comparison, was a carnival.

Conrad had to hand it to Donovan. The place was a decent spot for a terrorist meeting. Avoiding the occasional afternoon tours must have put a cramp in his Day-Timer but he probably held his meetings at night. The wrought-iron gates with their barbed-wire tops were a deterrent to kids and vagrants, but they would hardly keep out an experienced criminal like

Donovan and his group. Once past the gates, accessing the buildings through the many broken windows and busted walls was easy. The tunnel system probably offered another simple means of access.

Certain sections of the buildings were in such bad repair, tourists were blocked from entering them. And while there were no pool tables, bars or big-screen TVs, Conrad had spotted a small satellite dish on the south edge of one of the guard towers.

If he were a criminal hiding out, he'd pick a warmer, drier place, say Caracas, but Irish criminals were an interesting lot. Bullheaded to a fault and martyrs to the last drop of whiskey. Home and the Church were never far in spirit or physical proximity.

Besides, Donovan could spit on the ground where so many of his IRA compatriots had been trapped and rouse his followers into a frenzy just by pointing out the chairs still chained to the floor, the heavy metal locks, and the names carved into seats and tables. The modern day martyrs would embrace the connection to their ancestors here, caring little about the falling plaster, rotting wood and subhuman comforts.

There was only one scheduled tour today and Conrad had pulled a Hail Mary and gotten a single ticket. An hour before O'Bern's memorial service, when the tour group entered the grounds, Michael Stone was going in with them.

Reconnaissance was a valuable skill. One Conrad had used many times in the field. However, Stone had flipped the boss card to take Conrad's fun away. Hell, it wasn't even about that. The last time Stone had been in the field in any kind of recon capacity, the first Jurassic Park movie was number one at the box office.

On the rooftop, Conrad wasn't the only one upset about Stone going in. Brigit paced along the far edge, fidgeting with her hair and biting her nails. Every couple of seconds, she'd glance at Stone from the corner of her eye. At least she was trying to be cool about it. If it had been him going in and Julia staying behind, well...he would have been getting an earful.

"Everybody over here," he said, waving the various people over to Del's makeshift computer station.

The hospital roof had two raised exits north of a small helo pad. One exit was probably stairs, the other an elevator for transporting patients on gurneys. Del had plopped his butt and his miniscule laptop between the two brick outcroppings and went to work.

As the ten people gathered around, Conrad looked his team over. "You got the work order form?" he asked Del.

The techie hit a button and the mobile printer next to his leg hummed to life. "Coming right up."

"Titus, you, Gunn and Kinnick are going in as hired security specialists. The city's still trying to turn the courthouse into a real tourist attraction, but crime's high in this area. You're here to install camera surveillance. Smitty's got uniforms and badges in the green van at the corner over there." He pointed behind him. "Once inside—"

Titus interrupted, excitement over playing spy again getting the better of him. "We know what to do, Flynn."

The printer spit out a sheet of paper and Titus nabbed it. His eyes scanned the details with careful scrutiny. Folding it, he nodded at Del. "You're good, son."

Clearly flustered, Del started pecking at his keyboard again.

Conrad handed the three men two-way radios with wireless headsets. Titus raised a white brow. "We going low-tech on this mission?"

"Without Del's storeroom of toys, it's the best I could do on short notice."

As the three inserts drifted back to try out their new toys, Lawson raised a hand. "Where do you want me?"

"Right here," Zara said. She was less pale and had kept her breakfast down, but the circles under her eyes and the way she leaned against the bricks let Conrad know she was exhausted. She shouldn't be here, but he was the idiot who'd assigned her to stay close to Kent's backside and dig into Donovan's history. "You're not going anywhere without me."

Lawson looked out over the rooftop, as if he wished to avoid the conversation, but finally met her eyes again. "Z, we talked about this. I have a job to do."

"And so do I."

Julia placed a hand on Zara's forearm. "Not a good idea in your condition."

"In my condition, I need Lawson."

Julia looked at Conrad. Shit, like Zara wasn't stubborn enough, throw in hormone-induced bullheadedness and he might as well beat his brains against the bricks. Thank God Julia wasn't pregnant too. He couldn't help being totally relieved she wasn't when he found out the FBI was sending her to Ireland to follow up on Donovan's escape and murder of O'Bern.

Handing Lawson a radio, he indicated the jail. "I want you to find us a way in. If Donovan's meeting place is anywhere, it will be inside that jail and I want to know how to get in and get out."

Zara started to balk, but snapped her lips shut when Conrad handed her another radio and headset. "I'll allow you to tag along, but you do not under any circumstances follow him onto the grounds. If I have to come in and rescue your butt, I will kick you out of my program so fast the Earth will spin backwards on its axis. You feel me?"

"I second that," Stone said from the edge of the group. "Family is important, Agent Morgan. The most important thing in the world."

It was the best kind of intervention they could have done with her, and God help him, the hormones did another dance. Her eyes went moist and she grinned at Lawson. "Family, yeah. I promise not to do anything stupid."

Stone had sauntered over and was standing behind and off to the side of Brigit. Her head was bowed as if she were counting the puddles at her feet or praying. Conrad saw Stone's gaze linger on her.

"One ticket for the tour." He pulled the ticket out of his inside jacket pocket and held it out. "Sure you don't want to stay here and orchestrate this?"

Brigit turned to Stone, now realizing he was behind her. His gaze immediately shifted to Conrad, the normal controlled expression back on his face. "Nope. My gig."

"Why?" Brigit demanded.

Stone reached for the ticket, but Brigit was half a second faster and she snatched it from Conrad's hand, putting it behind her back like a child. "Don't do this," she pleaded with him. "Please. Let someone else."

Conrad exchanged a glance with Julia. She winked at him.

Stone scrubbed his hair with a fist and walked several

paces away. "Brigit, don't start with this again. I'm not storming the place. It's a simple recon mission."

"What if something goes wrong?"

He turned and faced her. "Titus, Brad and Truman are backing me up."

"With a bogus cover that could be blown before they even get through the gate."

"Hey," Del spoke up from the sidelines. "They'll get through the gate. My work is topnotch."

Everyone ignored him.

Stone checked his watch and held out a hand for the ticket. "Look, I need to get going. Don't worry."

"Don't worry?" Her voice rang over the rooftop. Titus, Lawson, Kinnick and Zara all looked over at them. Gunn frowned and started forward, but Conrad turned slightly and made a *no go* motion with his hand.

Gunn stopped, and the rest went back to what they were doing, trying to act like they weren't listening. Del's fingers flew across his keyboard as if he might force it to open up and swallow him.

"Don't worry?" Brigit repeated, a little less loudly, but with no less emotion. "I don't know what you think we shared last night and this morning, but if anyone here has a reason to worry about you walking into that courthouse, it's me."

Stone's face gave nothing away. "This is not the time or the place to discuss what's going on between us."

Like he'd slapped her, Brigit took a step back. "You could be walking into a trap and you want me to just stand here and watch you go without a word? Is that it? You want me to be stoic and brave and all that other bullshit while you risk your life for my family?"

Conrad saw a muscle work in Stone's jaw before he spoke. "You said yourself this wasn't a trap. That Tory was on our side now."

"I know." She brought the ticket in front of her stomach and looked down at it, back up at him. "I'm having second thoughts."

Stone shut his eyes for two taps of Del's fingers and let out a terse sigh. "No time for second thoughts. I can handle this. Trust me."

She wavered, and Stone pulled the ticket from her fingers. He made it as far as the metal fire escape stairs on the south edge of the building before Brigit spoke again. She raised her voice for him to hear. "I just found you. I just found happiness for the first time in my life. Please don't take that away from me."

All motion stopped. Michael. Conrad. Del. Lawson and Zara. Titus, Kinnick, Truman. No one moved.

Except Brigit. She looked around at all of them, settled her attention back on Michael. All her frustration, fear and love threatened to jet out of her in a stream of emotional need. That was not the way to reach Michael, though. "Your group here"— she motioned at them with her hand as she met his gaze— "needs you. Your family needs you. My God, America needs you. If you go in there and something, *anything*, about this plan goes wrong, everyone loses. Every. Last. One. Loses. Do you understand?"

She drew in a shaky breath and admitted the truth. "It's not just about me and what I want. It's about you, Michael. So don't think you can walk away from me without so much as a goodbye, and tell me not to worry. If you get hurt, or God forbid, die"—her breath stuck in her throat, a solid ball of anguish—"it will be my fault, and I can't live with that. I can't live without you."

Michael hung his head and said, "Jesus Christ" under his breath.

She waited for him, her legs shaking and her fingernails biting into her palms. After a moment, when he said nothing else and made no move to argue, she knew she'd lost.

Batting back the tears burning her eyes, she raised her chin and faced the open stares of the others head on. Her gaze finally settled on Conrad. "Well, where do you want me?"

"Uh," he stuttered.

Before he could answer, Michael crossed the distance, swept her into his arms and kissed her hard.

Out of the blue, someone started clapping. Someone else wolf whistled. A few seconds later, everyone was clapping and hooting as Michael went for her tonsils.

The world went away then for a few heartbeats and Brigit poured everything—all the fear and love she was feeling—into kissing Michael back.

It was over too soon. Michael's lips left hers, but his hands stayed on her hips and his gaze rested on her face.

"All right. All right," Conrad said, waving his hands to quiet the group. Turning his back on Stone and Brigit, he whirled one finger in a circle. "Move out. Titus, you and your group get down to the van. Once you're inside the courthouse, get those bugs and cameras planted in the areas I showed you on the map. Especially down the tunnel."

As the men filed by to hit the fire escape, Titus punched Michael on the arm. Truman tapped Brigit on her good shoulder. Michael dropped his hands from her hips and stepped back. Brigit kicked at a pebble at her feet.

When he got to the ledge, he grabbed the fire escape's handrails and swung one leg over to the first step. "Hey, Doc."

Brigit looked up.

Michael dangled the left-behind rabbit's foot on a chain from one finger. "I'm not done with you yet. I promise, I'll be back."

She nodded, and Michael disappeared, taking her heart with him.

When she faced Conrad and Julia, she shrugged. "I thought for sure the part about his country needing him would work."

Julia laughed. "So did I."

"Huh, so did I," Conrad admitted, handing his binoculars to Julia. "You watch the sidewalk. Keep an eye on the tour group. You"—he pointed to Brigit—"stay here with Del. He'll be able to show you everything the cameras catch, including the feed coming in from the cell phone Stone's using."

Normally she would have balked at being on tech duty, but this job meant she could watch Michael, maybe even be his guardian angel if anything went wrong. Without a word of complaint, she went to sit with Del.

Chapter Thirty-Nine

Brigit watched fascinated as one square after another popped up on Del's tiny screen. The *security specialists* were inside the courthouse. So was the tour group, including Michael. Video and audio pieces were coming through loud and clear. So far. So good.

Twenty minutes later, Michael had managed to lose the tour group and guides. A camera set high on one of the walls showed a distorted view of the dark tunnel, the farthest point disappearing into darkness.

Brigit's breath caught in her throat when Michael appeared on screen entering the tunnel. He was moving quickly, checking back over his shoulder to make sure he wasn't followed. As his body became smaller and smaller, her heart beat faster. When he finally disappeared into the darkness at the narrowed end, she thought she would throw up.

"Here," Del said, typing in a command and pointing at a new square on his screen. "This is coming from Director Stone's cell phone. I rigged it to send a shot every three seconds."

Pixilated grays and browns appeared on the screen like a photo had been snapped. The tunnel was dark and dingy with deep shadows, making it difficult to make out much of anything. Seconds later, a new image appeared, not all that different from the previous one, but still different enough Brigit could tell Michael was moving forward.

At the end of the tunnel, enough light filtered through to add more colors, but the dinginess didn't subside. Into the jailhouse, up the steps, Michael was silent but keeping his cell phone camera moving in arcs so they could see what he was seeing. Narrow stairs with green railings, plaster debris everywhere, fallen lights. Massive locks and inch-thick metal bars. Large, gaping holes in the walls.

Brigit watched, completely enthralled with the tiny square of Michael's world. While Del kept an eye on the various other feeds and relayed information to Conrad, Brigit tuned it all out. All she cared about was Michael.

A shadow moved in the corner and Brigit leaned closer to the screen. Were her eyes playing tricks on her or was that a man's shadow? Maybe it was Michael's? But that couldn't be right. He would have to be standing on the stairs to his right to throw the shadow the camera was capturing. The next two seconds seemed to take forever.

Without warning, an explosion punched the air nearby. Brigit ducked, all her reflexes contracting as if she'd been hit. The sound reverberated through the rooftop, running over her skin and raising the hair on the back of her neck. The explosion had come from the jail.

She was up and running toward Conrad before she could form coherent thought. "What happened?"

Binoculars in one hand, a radio in the other, he ignored her. "Black King, come in."

Titus Allen's voice broke through a bunch of static. "Black King here. We're okay. What the hell was that?"

"Explosion inside the jail," Conrad answered, and a shiver ran down Brigit's spine.

"Blue Knight? You there?"

"Blue Knight here." It was Lawson. "All clear on our side. Over."

Brigit jerked on Conrad's sleeve. "What about Michael?"

"White Knight, you see anything?"

More static and then Ryan Smith's voice. "Nothing unusual. What's Del got?"

Del. Brigit left Conrad and sprinted back to Del and his laptop. "What can you see? Is Michael okay?"

The computer guru was leaning toward his screen. He said nothing, his face pale as he shifted the screen so Brigit could see the display.

The multiple squares were now only one filling the screen with a choppy, pixilated picture. The view seemed to be the ceiling with a light blob in the upper left corner. Brigit squinted.

"What is that?"

Del cleared his throat. "I think it's the director's ear."

Dropping to her knees, she stared at the screen with her heart fluttering hard in her throat. The picture stuttered as the video updated and understanding dawned on her. Michael was on his back, the cell phone camera lying beside him, next to his head.

"Oh, God." Far below, the sounds of the frightened tourists filled the air as they filed out of the courthouse. The three-second update showed a piece of Michael's arm, as he'd raised it to rub his forehead. Hope soared in her chest. She slid sideways and yelled at Conrad. "Michael's hurt."

He came running, radio still glued to his mouth as information continued to be relayed between the teams. "Stone's down, possibly injured," he told someone as he stared at the screen. "Get to him. Now."

Brigit reached to touch the screen, tears welling in her eyes. "Goddamn jerk," she whispered.

Without another word, she rose and started for the fire escape.

"Hey," Conrad said. "Where're you going?"

She didn't stop, didn't answer. Just as she put a hand on the rail, he grabbed her by the back of the coat and hauled her around. "Oh, no. You are not allowed to leave this rooftop."

Struggling against his iron grip, she forced herself to sound calm. She was anything but. "Says who?"

"Stone."

"He needs help. Let me go."

Conrad wasn't as big as Michael, but he was strong enough and fast enough to pin her arm behind her back and march her away from the edge of the roof. "Help's on the way. I need you here."

Since he had her left hand jacked behind her and pointing up at her shoulders, she couldn't ignore the pain to her still sore arm. "I don't appreciate being manhandled."

He forced her back to Del's side. "Don't try to run off and it won't happen again."

"Um," Del muttered, looking up at her and pointing at the screen. "Who's that?"

All of Brigit's senses screamed in panic. The pale face, the shaved head, the eyes like a shithouse rat. There, staring down at the phone and Michael, was the face of her childhood nightmares.

Her knees kissed the blacktop first. Her hands followed. "That's Peter Donovan," she murmured before her stomach heaved.

Chapter Forty

Michael came awake slowly, his ears ringing and his eyes burning. He would have sworn Brad had landed a kick to the back of his head.

Blinking to clear the grit from his eyes, he saw a man's face looming over him. "Well, who do we have 'ere?" the man muttered. "Yer the man from the alley."

Though he could barely make out the words over the ringing in his ears, Michael recognized the voice. The nasal tone, combined with deep-sunk eyes and days-old growth of beard, registered with a cold slap. Peter Donovan.

Rubbing his eyes and tapping his right ear—the one ringing the most—with his palm, he shifted his body to sit up. Donovan held a gun by his side and Michael saw his hand tense on the butt. Moving with slow, deliberate motions, he got to his feet. The shadows around him fuzzed out and the floor seemed to move under his feet, making him waver. The damage to his eardrum was knocking his balance off.

Nothing like being half-blind, half-deaf and dizzy as hell when facing the terrorist you planned to apprehend.

"Why'd ya blast the tunnel?" Donovan demanded. "Who're ya working for?"

His face was even paler than it had been the previous evening in the alley. Sweat beaded his forehead. The bags below his eyes spoke of sleeplessness or perhaps poisoning?

Yer the man from the alley. At least he hadn't called Michael Brigit's lover. Maybe Brigit was right and this wasn't a trap. Or at least not one orchestrated by Donovan.

Pretending to be deaf gave him time to come up with a plausible story. Michael tapped his ear again. "What? My ears are ringing. What happened?"

Donovan's cruel eyes measured him. He raised his voice a notch. "Explosion. The tunnel's caved in."

His attention dropped to the floor to Michael's left. Michael followed it and saw his cell phone lying on the tunnel's dirty floor. He moved to retrieve it, but froze when Donovan's gun came up and pointed at his chest. "Yer one of Shankill's men, aren't ye? How'd ye know I'd be 'ere?"

The flashback hit without warning. The black hole. The shiny cylinder. The feverish eyes of a madman staring down the gunsight. Michael had faced down a gun before. Raissi had pointed one at him and pulled the trigger.

What doesn't kill you makes you stronger, the old adage went. Some days Michael wasn't sure. It didn't make you stronger, only wiser. You realized you could die at the drop of a hat, the pull of a trigger, on any given day in any situation.

The old anger roared and rumbled like an animal inside his chest. His Glock was still in his waistband. The hard metal had dug into his back when he was on the ground. No way could he reach it before Donovan blew him away, though.

He raised his hands in the air in a gesture of surrender even as his mind counted the ways he could turn the tables. "I don't know who Shankill is and I'm not after you. I'm an American film producer doing a documentary on Gerry Adams. The U.K. government doesn't want to give my film crew unlimited access to the prison, so I snuck away from the tour group to do a bit of unauthorized filming." He pointed at the phone still on the ground.

Donovan seemed to consider the story. "Why'd ye help me last night in the alley?"

His voice had dropped back to its normal pitch. Michael turned his left ear to him, very aware of how easy it would be to blow his fictional cover. How tough it was one-on-one to keep the bluff in place. Flynn did this all the time, even now in the bowels of Langley. Bluffing was more of an art than Michael had realized. "What?"

"Last night in the alley. What were ye doin' there?"

Michael nodded and played another card. Sometimes the truth worked just as well. "Your picture's been all over the news in America and I thought it was you at the bar. I saw that woman get your attention and how you ran after her. When the cops came, I figured you could use some help."

Donovan's face showed nothing but gray despair. His gun, though, showed he still didn't see Michael as anything but a threat. He wiped at the sweat along his brow line. "Why'd ye blast the tunnel?"

Michael frowned, hoping to look confused. "I didn't. I was filming it."

Donovan motioned with his free hand for Michael to give him the phone.

The angry animal inside him continued to roar, wanting to lay waste to the terrorist threatening him. The terrorist who had tried to kill Brigit. Still, he moved in a careful manner to do as instructed. "I figured you'd be attending O'Bern's memorial service at the capitol today."

Donovan kept the gun and one eye trained on him while he fiddled with the phone to look at the video Michael had shot. After a minute, he shut the phone, disconnecting Michael's link to the outside. "Everyone figured the same."

Smart man. While no one but Brigit could directly tie Donovan to O'Bern's murder, many in Northern Ireland were heralding Donovan for the murderer.

"Except this Shankill character?"

"He knows me better than most and he likes bombs." Donovan started, seemingly struck by a new idea. "Either him or..." He trailed off and shook his head as if discarding the thought.

Somewhere outside the jail, a siren blared. Michael pretended not to hear it even as Donovan cocked his head a fraction, catching the sound of it too. He tossed the phone back to Michael and started to walk away from the tunnel's dilapidated entrance toward the jail. "Gotta git outta here."

"There'll be cops covering every inch of the place and Shankill and his men may be out there waiting for you."

Donovan hesitated, looked at the gun in his hand. "Perhaps. Would not surprise me if someone's waiting for me." He glanced at the gun in his hand. "Last stand has come sooner than I expected."

What had Raissi wanted as much as martyrdom? Fame. Recognition. Michael took a step toward Donovan. All he needed was to give the terrorist hope and an incentive to live.

And Flynn wasn't the only one versed in Lie-Your-Ass-Off

training. "This isn't your last stand. My crew's outside. You give us an exclusive interview on the ongoing fight for Irish nationalism for our documentary and I'll get you out."

Donovan looked over his shoulder at Michael, considering the offer. The calculating gaze was still there but something else was too. The promise of fame beyond what he'd already tasted seduced him, just like it did so many of the power hungry. "How?"

Michael smiled, mentally taming the animal inside him as well as the one five feet away. He snapped the Motorola off his belt and keyed the transmit button. "Leave that to me."

Chapter Forty-One

The clear bleep of the blue radio cut through the layers of noise floating up on the rooftop and stopped Brigit's heart. Conrad snatched the walkie-talkie from its holder and met her gaze. Was it her imagination or did the muscles in his face unclench? Her heart thudded so hard it nearly knocked her back down to her knees.

"Yeah," Conrad said into the radio.

Michael's voice erupted from the speaker. "I have a situation. A certain member of the Real IRA has agreed to an exclusive interview for our documentary, but we need to get out of here undetected."

What? Brigit frowned and started to speak but Conrad shook his head and put a warning finger to his lips to silence her. "Courthouse entrance should be avoided."

"The explosion blocked the tunnel back to the courthouse. The entity who set off the explosion may be in attendance. Put eyes on your outer perimeter. We need to get out via the jail."

We? This time the word hit her hard. Oh, God, he was bringing Donovan with him under some kind of guise about a documentary. A trembling started in her bones.

"Roger that," Conrad said. "Let me check the options and call you back. Over."

"Hurry."

Conrad grinned at her as the radio went silent. "A documentary." He shook his head in amused disbelief. "Fucking brilliant cover. He'll get Donovan walking out on his own. Never knew Stone had it in him to be so creative. I may have to recruit him for my army."

"Forget your goddamn army." Brigit's voice shot up an

octave. "You didn't even ask him if he was hurt."

"Hurt?" Conrad chuckled and picked up the radio that connected him to the others. "Stone's a jarhead. He doesn't feel pain."

An image of Michael in the hospital telling her about his father flashed across her mind. Suddenly the urge to protect him rose up like a hot spring inside her, bubbling up from her stomach, rocking through her throat.

She took a step toward Conrad and put a finger in his face. "You screw this up and he gets hurt, you'll be the one in pain."

His dark eyes glanced at her finger, back to her face, measuring her. He nodded, one dip of his head.

But even as he radioed instructions to Lawson, Smitty and Julia, he was still grinning, utterly unconcerned about her threat.

Annoyed, Brigit plopped down by Del. The computer tech looked at her over the rim of his glasses. "You're good at your job, right?"

She pressed her hands along her hairline and leaned her elbows on her bent knees. "Yes. Why?"

"I'm good at my job too."

Appraising him, she raised a brow in question. "Agreed. So what?"

Del smiled at his laptop. "Deputy Director Stone is not just good, he's a fucking god. And so are Director Flynn, my man Vaughn, Smitty and Julia and Zara. You shouldn't worry so much. It's insulting. Show a little faith."

Brigit dug deep for patience. This might be a run-of-the-mill day for members of the CIA, but it wasn't for her. She couldn't stop thinking about Michael and Peter being face-to-face. Couldn't stop thinking about how deceitful and cruel her brother could be.

Or how heroic Michael could be. "I've never been one to have faith in others."

"This group's done a lot to help you out. Might be a good time to start."

As Conrad maneuvered the white van into place according to the coordinates Lawson had given him, Julia kept watch of the area, looking for whoever might have planted the bomb that blew the tunnel. Off and on, Brigit heard the others' voices chiming in about the situation below as fire trucks and ambulances and police cars filled the streets.

They were all there, helping her like Del said, but they were doing it for Michael. He had earned their respect, not through fear and dominance, but through trust and honor. Having a small amount of faith in him and his group seemed the least she could do.

Still, the trembling inside her wouldn't stop. She needed to do something. "How can I help?" she asked Del.

He clicked keys on his keyboard and a blueprint of the jail appeared. "Who do you think planted that bomb?"

Brigit ran through various options. "Donovan's group has a dozen enemies, any of who might have figured out he'd be in the jail and planted it."

"But why this way? Why cut off the tunnel?"

"To flush him out into the jail yard?"

Del shrugged. "Your sister led us here. Is it possible she set off the explosion?" He pointed at the buildings in the distance. "Could she be on one of these rooftops with a rifle, waiting for him to appear?"

Tory, a sniper? Not hardly. "She might have built a bomb to blow the tunnel, but—"

A block snapped into place, forming a row, and flashing out of existence. Sniper.

She jumped to her feet.

Conrad paced the helo pad, radio in hand, as he gave Michael details of the evacuation plan. Brigit heard Michael's voice, solid and determined as usual, replying. She grabbed Conrad's arm to get his attention. "Moira Raphael. Was she captured back in America after I left?"

Conrad frowned at her. "I don't know."

Brigit grabbed the binoculars from his left hand and started scanning windows and rooftops. "Tell Michael to stay inside. We need to look for her."

Without hesitation, Conrad told Michael to sit tight a little bit longer and then switched radios to alert the rest of the group about Brigit's suspicions. He barked an order to Del to find out about Moira's status as well.

Del had heard her question over the sirens and was already on the job. "Got it," he said, glancing up. "She's still wanted by the FBI."

Brigit's hands shook, making her view through the binoculars blurry. What was crystal clear was the trap had been set, not for her, but for Peter.

Impatience was getting the best of him. Michael paced the first floor of the jail. He could see out the windows on the far end, but stayed back from them in case there was someone outside waiting for Donovan to make an appearance. No sense in being confused for a terrorist and getting nailed.

Outside, sirens continued to blare, but most seemed distant as if they were across the street at the Courthouse. Suited Michael fine. If the focus was on the tour group and the Courthouse, it made his job of getting Donovan out of the jail and off the grounds much easier.

Donovan stood staring down the hall toward the windows and possible freedom. Probably thinking the same thing Michael was...better to stay out of the line of sight.

Michael tapped his thumb against the two-way, waiting for Flynn to give him the go ahead. Vaughn had an opening in the fences for them, and Smitty had the van waiting on the street near the escape route. All they needed was the all-clear message.

A rat as big as his forearm skittered down the hall, seemingly in full panic mode, heading right for Michael's leg. He started to draw his gun and then stopped himself. Film producers didn't carry weapons and a gunshot would echo through the jail and bring attention down on them like the wrath of God. He stomped his foot at the rat and the ugly brown thing jumped and headed in a different direction.

Behind him, Michael heard the crunch of plaster under a boot. He turned, reflexes drawing the gun and aiming at the target.

Moira Raphael stood in the hall, a gun in each hand. One pointed at Donovan. The other pointed at Michael. Tory Kent stood beside her.

"Peter," Moira said.

Out of the corner of his eye, Michael saw Donovan pivot slowly to look at Moira. His gaze grazed the guns and landed on Tory. "Not you."

Tory said nothing. Moira parted her red lips in a smug

smile. "The Judas gene runs in your family."

Donovan's gun hung by his side. Michael wondered why he didn't raise it and at least defend himself. "What do you want?" he said to Moira.

Seemed obvious to Michael what she wanted. The two guns in her hands were a dead giveaway. Dead being the optimal word.

Tory's voice quivered when she spoke. "Ya went too far when ya tried to kill Brigit, Peter."

"You went too far when you left me behind," Moira added.

Donovan was so still, Michael wasn't sure he was breathing until he spoke, this time to Tory. "Siding with her? She done shot Brigit, or have ye forgotten?"

Moira answered him. "Under your orders."

"I never..." Donovan's voice trailed off and he narrowed his eyes at Moira. "Ah, I see what'ch'ave done. Turned 'er against me."

Moira's right hand swiveled to point a gun at Tory. "Easy enough to do."

Tory's wild gaze bounced back and forth between Moira's gun and Donovan's face.

"Leave 'er be," Donovan said.

In the next instant, Moira's smug smile returned, and she drew the gun in her right hand back around to point at her temple. "Easy enough to do."

In the blink of an eye, she pulled the trigger.

First of the gun in her left hand pointed at Donovan. Followed by the gun in her right hand.

Her head tipped to her left and she dropped. At the same instant, Donovan took his bullet right between his eyebrows, the force rocking him back on his heels before he fell as well.

Tory cried out and slammed her back against the wall. Michael trained his gun on her. "Hands up."

She did as commanded, sobbing and staring at Donovan. The man's eyes were fixed on the jail's crumbling ceiling as blood gurgled from the wound in his forehead. Michael swiftly kicked his gun away from his hand and then proceeded to do the same with Moira's guns.

He patted Tory down to be sure she was weapon-free. "We need to get out of here." He took a breath, relief flooding through him that both he and Tory were alive. "At least Brigit will be happy to see you."

A mix of emotions crossed her face, confusion the most evident. "Do not lie to me."

Satisfied she wasn't packing a gun or a bomb, he stepped back and retrieved the Motorola where he'd dropped it. The thing was beeping and Flynn's voice was calling him. "Your sister still loves you, Tory, even after the hell you've put her through."

Tory slid down the wall, burying her head in her hands.

Amazing what families did to each other and for each other. The logic defied him, even though the emotions did not.

Keeping his gun on her, Michael pushed the talk button on the radio.

On the nearby rooftop, a hole opened in Brigit's heart. Two men, two gunshots. What were the odds Michael wasn't hurt this time?

Since the echo of the first gunshot stopped her heart from beating, Conrad had been trying to raise Michael on the radio. Julia had left her post to put an arm around Brigit, but Conrad had ordered her back to keep a look out over the area.

In her mind, Brigit saw Michael's face, handsome and stoic even in death. She should have known better than to get involved with him, to fall in love with him. She was a walking curse, always damning those she loved.

So when Michael's voice answered Conrad via the radio, she thought she was hallucinating. "Donovan's dead. So is Raphael," he said. "Extraction is still necessary as planned though. Tell Doc I'm bringing her sister out with me."

Brigit heard the words, but was now sure Michael's voice wasn't a hallucination. It was a dream. A crazy dream that made her shake so hard her teeth chattered.

Conrad looked at her and then pushed the talk button again. "Are you hurt?"

A snicker came across the airwaves. "Hell no."

Her teeth parted to let a hysterical laugh pass through them. Michael wasn't dead. He wasn't hurt. He had her sister.

Suddenly, faith in Michael Stone was the best lucky charm she could imagine.

Chapter Forty-Two

Inside the plane, Brigit sat holding Tory's hand. Not an easy task since Tory's hands were cuffed together. Julia had allowed them to stay cuffed in front of her instead of behind her, though, for the ride back to the States.

Michael was on the phone, Del beside him on his laptop. The others flying back had paired off. Zara and Lawson cuddled and looked at each other with adoration while they whispered about the baby they were expecting in roughly eight months. Conrad and Julia sat across from Michael and Del, joining in the discussion with the FBI about Peter and Moira's deaths and Tory's apprehension. Brad Kinnick was up front in the cockpit with Titus Allen, getting his first flying lesson.

Ryan Smith had gone back to London to his CIA position as head of European operations. Truman had gone back to London too, and SIS. He'd hugged her tight before boarding his plane, and Brigit's heart had filled with remorse to watch him go. Good friends were hard to find.

She now snuck a look at Michael. He was back to being Deputy Director of the CIA. They hadn't had a moment to themselves yet and there was so much she wanted to say to him. How worried she'd been about him, which he would probably scoff at. How much gratitude she owed him for saving Tory. Questions zipped through her brain too. What about her father? Was there anything she could do now to rescue him?

As if Tory read her mind, she squeezed Brigit's hand. "How is Da?"

Brigit dragged her eyes away from Michael and faced her sister. They had a long flight ahead of them, which was good. There would be no rushing fifteen years worth of catching up.

There'd been no witnesses to the deaths of Donovan and Raphael except him and Tory. Michael had snapped photos of both bodies before sneaking Tory out of the jail.

Crawling through the traffic and roadblocks had been slow going, especially since Brigit wasn't in the van with him. The first thing he'd done at the airport was search her out. With the throng of people and the need to get Tory out of the country and back to the States without alerting the Irish government, though, Michael had not had a chance to do anything other than exchange a smile and a couple of words with her.

The relief at seeing her was mirrored in her own face. She was a trooper, through and through. She'd bear-hugged Tory before quietly turning her over to Julia, who placed her under arrest. Michael could see the determination in her face and body posture it took for her not to jump in and try to defend her sister.

Once they were on board the plane, Brigit had discussed options with Julia about the charges the FBI would press against Tory. While he would have found her behavior annoying before, now he only smiled to himself, knowing he would have done the same in her position. As soon as he was back home, he had to deal with his own sister.

Outside the window, night had descended. Most everyone had drawn the shades and was sleeping. The operation, the time change, the adrenaline had drained them all. He was the only one still awake.

He'd sent the pictures to the FBI and informed them Tory would be delivered to them at Dulles when the plane landed. Dancing around red tape and formal statements had put him to the test. He wasn't used to committing crimes or ignoring rules, and he'd never been more grateful for his natural charm than during the grueling interrogation he'd received from the authorities waiting for him and the others at the end of this ride. He'd cut some deals that made even Flynn smile.

Movement inside the cabin caught his attention. Brigit was shaking Del awake and asking him to move. The computer tech rose from his seat, still half asleep, and went to sit by Tory.

Brigit slid into Del's place. When she smiled at him, awe and gratitude in her doll eyes, the blood in his veins warmed and pulsed under his skin. Her sweet smell engulfed him and he wanted to touch her. Wanted her under him and on top of him and beside him like she'd been less than twenty-four hours before.

He settled for touching her cheek. "God, it's good to see you smile."

Her lips parted and the smile widened. "It's good to see you alive and in one piece."

Tory had told her what had gone down with Peter and Moira. Still, knowing her the way he did, Michael suspected she had a million questions and a few comments about the whole thing. For a second, he could see the urge behind her eyes to let them all out. However, the urge passed in a breath and she sighed. "Thank you. For everything."

Wrapping her arm around his, she snuggled up to him as much as the seat divider allowed. He shut his eyes and tucked her body against his.

The future when they got back to the States loomed like the dark outside the plane. While he would gladly testify on Tory's behalf, there was little he could do to get the charges reduced on her involvement with the kidnapping. And since he no longer had a bargaining chip for William Kent, there was little he could do there either. Brigit had held up her end of the blackmail bargain they had struck before he'd held up his, and now it looked like he would fail.

The idea that even after all he'd put her through he couldn't fulfill his promise to her made his stomach churn.

Laying his cheek over on the top of Brigit's head, he drew her closer and listened to her sigh with contentment.

"Will you do what you can for Tory?" she whispered.

He closed his eyes and told her the truth. "What I can, yes. It won't be much."

She squeezed his arm. "I've seen you work miracles. I have faith."

He checked his watch. Two and half hours until they landed. He had two and a half hours to pretend he was still the good guy. "Everything will be okay," he said, not sure if he was trying to convince her or himself.

Chapter Forty-Three

Two days later
Republic of Bolivia

The rugged interior of South America was a stark contrast to the soft green meadows of Ireland. "One minute to insertion," the pilot of the Pave Hawk helicopter announced in Michael's in-flight headset.

His chest tightened. This was it, the moment he would send a group in to back him up. President Jeffries had put his name on the line under duress from Titus Allen to authorize this exchange, but Michael was the one risking the lives of many to save one. Only a handful of people knew about this mission and most of them were on the Pave with him.

If all went according to his plans, he, Flynn and Brad would take the brunt of any fallout, but there was still the possibility something beyond his control would go wrong. Could he justify this mission when all was said and done?

The men with him had mad skills, as Del Hoffman referred to their search and rescue, infiltration and exfiltration specialties. Lawson Vaughn's Team Pegasus could do their job in any kind of weather, any type of terrain, and night conditions, which were preferred over daylight.

At thirty seconds to insertion, the door gunners opened their cabin windows and assessed treetops and hillsides over the barrels of their 7.62mm miniguns. Thanks to the Pave's mission system and GPS technology, Team Pegasus could be covertly inserted at the exact spot they wanted in case they needed to take Colonel Cortez-Uno by surprise. They could paradrop, rappel or fastrope from the helicopter.

Fastroping was dangerous even for those who trained and practiced on a regular basis. No way Michael could join them. Once a Marine, always a Marine, but those days were far behind him. Even though he'd performed plenty of special insertions and extractions during his tour of duty, trying to be a hero on this mission would only endanger the rest of the group.

Same held true for Flynn. He'd been a SEAL and could probably still do a host of stunts in his sleep, and yet he was also level-headed enough to know where to draw the line with this mission.

The two of them, plus Brad, would play a different role in this operation. An official, legitimate role.

In his ear, the pilot said, "Go."

Michael nodded at Vaughn. The commander threw a thick rope out the open slider and went out after it. The night was dark so Michael followed his descent, and the men who followed him, with night-vision binoculars.

The team members were all on the ground in seconds, disappearing into the trees.

Time to play his next card.

Washington D.C.

Michael hadn't returned one of her phone calls. Not one. He probably hadn't even listened to her voice mails. As soon as he saw who they were from, he'd probably deleted them. God, she was such a fool.

The past two days, Brigit had kept herself busy, putting her life back together while she was falling apart inside. She'd rented an efficiency apartment with Julia's help and done as many normal things as she could.

Laundry, which she could hand-wash in ten minutes since she barely had any clothes.

Grocery shopping, which also took no time because her stomach did nothing but churn with indigestion.

Buying a stack of best sellers to catch up on her reading. The pile sat on her bedside table untouched, because every time she tried to start one, the hero in the story reminded her of Michael in some way.

She knew she was projecting, but found herself incapable of stopping her own psychosis.

Picking up her new BlackBerry, she hit the redial button and waited to hear Michael's voice tell her to leave a message.

Chapter Forty-Four

"You're Butch and I'm Sundance, right?" Flynn said over the sound of the Pave's blades as they followed Brad, slightly hunched, away from the helicopter.

Michael viewed the desolate terrain, full of shadows under the waxing moon, and wondered where Vaughn and his men were hidden. The prison at the bottom of the hill showed little activity. The barely there moonlight reflected off a barbed-wire fence, and guards patrolled the perimeter with AK47s.

The majority of the prison's population was made up of murderers, drug dealers and rapists. According to the report Michael had read, a cocoa factory existed inside the prison's walls. Many of the inmates' families lived with them. For a few pesos, anyone, tourists included, could score a tour.

Outside the wash of the blades, Flynn straightened and put a pair of mini night-vision binoculars to his eyes. "Jeesh, all of Bolivia can't look like this."

The Pave's motor cut off, and the squeak and buzz of insects filled the sudden silence. Michael took the NVBs and scanned the area. "If I'm Butch, that's my line."

Flynn chuckled, his laugh tight with nerves. "I didn't even remember that *was* a line."

From the dusty road behind them, the sound of a truck engine cut through the insect noise. Michael handed the NVBs back to Flynn. "That's gotta be Cooper."

Cooper was a DEA agent working deep in the heart of cocaine country with an American taskforce. Tonight he was working alone, bringing a certain political prisoner the Bolivian government claimed they would trade just about anything, or anyone, to have handed over to them. Manny "el Rey" Sanchez was the Bolivian equivalent to the Godfather. Colonel Cortez-Uno probably wanted el Rey to expand his prison's coke production facility.

The game plan was simple. The colonel either traded Brigit's father even up for el Rey, or the U.S. government would turn el Rey free.

Of course, if the colonel refused to deal, Michael had no intention of giving the self-named king his freedom, and since the entire mission was going down under the radar, el Rey could conveniently meet with a bullet without causing an international uproar.

The old army jeep that came to a stop beside the Pave looked like it was straight out of a M*A*S*H episode. The man who extracted himself from behind the wheel was Michael's size, big and broad, dressed in desert fatigues, black boots and a cowboy hat. Michael wondered what kind of opponent he'd be in the ring.

"Cooper Harris." He held out a hand.

Michael shook first. "Uncle Sam."

"No names." Cooper shook Flynn's hand next. "Gotcha."

Flynn pointed at the bound and gagged prisoner still in the Jeep. A dirty red handkerchief covered his eyes. "This our guy?"

"The one and only." Cooper raised his own set of miniature night-vision binoculars and peered through them at the prison. "Cortez isn't expecting us for another hour. You wanna wait or crash the party early?"

Taking the only real form of Bolivian government in these parts by surprise could net you a coup or a chunk out of your ass. But keeping Cortez and his buddies off balance was probably a good thing, especially when it came to the element of surprise, and as long as Pegasus was in position, odds were in favor of a coup, no matter when the exchange went down.

Besides, Michael was anxious to get back to D.C. and a certain dark-haired woman who was all he could think about. Now that Flynn had brought up Butch and Sundance, Michael remembered another line from the movie. Sundance was talking about finding a woman. *I'm not picky. As long as she's smart, pretty, and sweet, and gentle, and tender, and refined, and lovely, and carefree...*

He started walking toward the Jeep, images of Brigit assailing him. "We go now."

Cooper drove. Michael rode shotgun. Flynn and Brad squeezed el Rey between them.

The Jeep bounced over the rocky road and Cooper took it slow. Before they were a hundred yards from the compound's gate, he said in a low voice. "We're spotted."

Adrenaline shot up Michael's spine. A second later, a spotlight rigged to the single tower in the middle of the camp flooded them with yellow light. Cooper slid a pair of sunglasses on and brought the Jeep to a stop in front of the gate.

The single guard slouched a bit, looking them over. His khaki-colored shirt was loose and his matching pants hung low on his waist. He wore a black beret over his long, dark hair. A cigarette dangled from one corner of his mouth, and his hands on the rifle he carried were short and fat.

Butch and Sundance meet Che Guevara.

The Che clone exchanged a few words with Cooper in a mixture of Spanish and some local dialect Michael didn't recognize. Cooper handed him the official papers signed by both President Jeffries and an official in the upper echelons of the Bolivian government. As the guard ignored the writing, probably because he couldn't read, Cooper pointed to el Rey in the back. El Rey's name was clear enough in the conversation. The guard spit out his cigarette and unlocked the gate.

As the Jeep entered the compound, Michael heard music coming from the prison. The deep bass thumped in a jarring rhythm and every few seconds a crowd of voices rose over the music. Cheers? Jeers? He couldn't tell.

Several men, armed and eager to escort them, crowded the Jeep. Flynn took hold of el Rey and pushed him out of the vehicle while Cooper chatted with the men. One of them shuffled away, entered the front of the jailhouse and came back several minutes later with a man dressed in desert BDUs, the official paper now in his hands.

This man was introduced as Cortez's lieutenant. Cooper shook hands with him and subsequently introduced Michael and Flynn in English as Smith and Jones.

The lieutenant gave them a sharp nod and led them into the prison's front office. They were led from the office through a locked door and down a dimly lit hallway. Another locked door was opened by guards and they entered the common area.

The music grew louder as they went deeper into the prison.

Since families were allowed to interact with their imprisoned relatives, this inner level of the building resembled a refugee camp. Women and children were everywhere. Some of the children slept on cots, some ran up to Michael and the other men with outstretched hands and pleading eyes.

It was the strangest prison Michael had ever seen. As they grew ever closer to the music, he recognized the song. AC-DC's "Thunderstruck".

One final locked gate and the lieutenant ushered them into a large common room. Cigarette smoke hung in heavy layers over the heads of several dozen men crowded into the room. As the lieutenant gained the attention of the people nearest the door, a slow, steady parting of bodies occurred.

The lieutenant led the way across the dirt floor and dozens of eyes came to rest on them. In most of the faces, heavy lids rode bloodshot eyes and Michael surmised the majority of the group was either drunk or high. Many of them crossed themselves as the blindfolded and shackled el Rey shuffled past them.

When the last of the crowd dispersed, the center of the room showed two men in shorts circling each other with fists raised. One had multiple bruises and a laceration above his eye pouring blood. The other had blood running from a broken nose.

Watching them tangle from the far side of the tent was Alejandro Cortez-Uno, the prison's warden.

He sat on a platform raised six inches off the ground. A table next to him held several bottles of amber liquid, a half-full glass and a plastic bowl piled high with cigarette butts. His face showed no surprise at seeing Michael's entourage, his glassy gaze slipping aloofly over each of them. Even when his lieutenant crossed behind the fighters and spoke into Cortez's ear, he showed nothing.

From across the room, he met Michael's gaze. The two stared at each other for a long moment, then Cortez's mouth moved and the lieutenant snapped his fingers to a woman next to the sound system. The music stopped.

Another finger snap and the fighters lowered their fists and stepped to opposite corners of the area as if the lieutenant had rung a bell.

Cortez took a sip of his drink and spoke, raising his voice to carry across the room, in the mixed dialect. Cooper responded.

They went back and forth several times. At one point, Cortez spoke to his lieutenant and the man disappeared through a side door.

"He's bringing Dr. Kent," Cooper murmured. "For the exchange."

Cortez rose, glass of alcohol in hand, and motioned for the five of them to meet him in the middle of the floor. He was short and oozing contempt as he strolled in a counterclockwise position around their group. While his aloof gaze traveled up and down each of them individually, an insistent warning bell rang like a smoke detector's alarm in Michael's head. Cortez was sizing them up.

Cortez was a psychopath.

Seeming to sense the same thing, Cooper kept talking, switching between English and the Spanish dialect, making jokes and trying to draw Cortez into conversation. The colonel stopped in front of Michael, his gaze now razor sharp and challenging. The alarm in Michael's head blared.

The far door opened and the lieutenant returned. Michael hated to break eye contact with Cortez, but his concern for Brigit's father outweighed a Mexican standoff with the prison warden. An ounce of relief hit him when he saw Dr. Kent moving on his own accord, no shackles or handcuffs. Fatigue and worry shadowed his face and he looked ten pounds thinner than his photo, yet there were no visible bruises or broken bones.

Michael grabbed el Rey and pushed him forward to stand in front of Colonel Cortez. At the same time, he crooked a finger at Dr. Kent.

Brigit's father looked surprised. Then relieved. In the next second, though, as if he remembered where he was, he cut his eyes to the colonel and back to Michael. A warning.

Cortez lifted two fingers from the glass and waved them back and forth in front of Michael's face, a smirk on his lips. Before he even spoke, Michael's gut squeezed.

"You want Dr. Kent," Cortez said in a liquor-rough, heavily accented voice. He pointed at one of the bleeding men in the corner. "You fight."

Cooper threw up his hands in a *no way* gesture, switching to English as well. "We're here for a prisoner exchange, not a fight."

Without warning, the sound of guns cocking echoed in the room. Cooper, Brad and Flynn went into fight mode, turning their backs to each other and facing out as if circling the wagons.

The colonel's cold, smug gaze did not leave Michael's. "One fight." He lifted a shoulder and took another swig of his golden tequila. "That is all. Then you can have Dr. Shit."

"Stand down," Michael murmured to Brad and the others.

Diplomacy was usually his first course of action. Unfortunately in the middle of a Bolivian prison, facing a drunken warden with a Napoleon complex and the lives of his fellow operatives riding on his shoulders, diplomacy was about as likely to work as humming "Hello, Dolly" and doing a tap dance.

Michael glanced around the throng of people crowding them, all eager for another fight. The bleeding man in the corner and his matching counterpart were both ripped, but both were lightweights at best. Plus they appeared still exhausted from their fight.

He tipped his head in the direction of the biggest one. "Rules?" he said to Cortez.

The coldness in the warden's eyes didn't change, even though he smiled. Behind him, Michael heard Flynn snort in disbelief and Brad sigh deeply. It probably took every ounce of restraint the bodyguard had to keep from saying, *Director, not advised*, as he so often did when Michael risked safety for freedom.

"One rule," Cortez said and held out a hand. "No guns."

Moving slowly, Michael removed his gun from its holster.

And handed it to Flynn.

The room seemed to take a deep breath as Cortez went back to his raised seat and Cooper, Flynn and Brad surrounded Michael. Taking off his jacket, he exchanged a knowing look with Flynn. "This goes bad, put a hole between Cortez's eyes."

Brad looked nauseated and tried to hide his *holy shit, we're fucked* expression behind a positive slap on Michael's back. "You can handle either of those guys with one punch."

"Um," Cooper said, covertly pointing to a spot behind Michael. "That's who you're fighting."

Michael turned and saw a brute of a man facing him. Shorter than him by a few inches, but built like a battleship. Steel bands of muscle ran the length of his arms, and his chest looked like it had been built from bricks. He took his two fists and pounded them together like a vise grip, his lips pulled back in a snarl as he stared Michael down.

"Okay." Michael took a deep breath and blew it out slowly. Cut his gaze to Flynn and then to Brad. "Suggestions?"

Brad spoke. "Cut him off at the legs, hit his solar plexus, elbow to the back of the neck."

Flynn studied the guy's tree-stump-sized legs. "I hope you got a chainsaw with you."

Rolling up his shirt sleeves, Michael narrowed his eyes at Flynn. "Remind me why I brought you along?"

"Don't worry, *Butch*." Flynn shot him a double wink. "I'm going to get you out of this. Do the countdown and take a swing."

Michael turned to face his competitor, natural instincts and Flynn's idea kicking in at the same moment. The big Bolivian strutted forward and did the bodybuilder thing again with his fists. The crowd cheered and Michael crooked a finger at the guy, raising his voice to be heard over them. "Someone say go."

Quick as a snap, Flynn yelled, "One, two, three, go!"

Michael stepped forward, ducked under the Bolivian's swing and cold-cocked him with an uppercut to the balls.

It was like watching Goliath fall. First his face showed surprise, then pain as he dropped like a ton of rocks to his knees. The new target was waist level and Michael used a half-spin-kick combination to clock his solar plexus.

Goliath's chest caved in and for the final touch, Michael smashed his nose with another kick of his booted foot. Blood sprayed and the man howled, grabbing at his face as he tumbled backward.

As the crowd roared, not caring who or what lost, Cortez slammed his glass down on the table. Liquid jumped. Michael danced on the balls of his feet and gave Cortez his best cold-hearted, merciless stare. *Bring it on.*

The colonel still had a few brain cells making connections. A wave of his hand told Michael to get out and take Dr. Shit with him.

Without a word, Michael accepted his jacket and gun from

Flynn, grabbed Dr. Kent by the elbow and proceeded to get the hell out of the jail.

The lieutenant seemed just as anxious for them to be gone, parting the crowd and hustling them back through the outer perimeters.

Before they crossed through the last door to the outside, AC-DC had started thumping again.

The night air hit Michael's face and a rush of sweet adrenaline raced across his skin. With one hand still on Dr. Kent's elbow, he muttered the words along with the music. "You've been...thunderstruck."

Flynn joined in, and as they reached the Jeep, Cooper, Brad and even Dr. Kent were chanting along.

Chapter Forty-Five

Washington D.C.

The next day

"Truman, I need your help." Brigit tossed another blouse on the bed and tucked her phone between her ear and her shoulder while she examined her pitiful wardrobe.

"Yes." Truman's voice did the slight cross-Atlantic delay. "Just say yes."

"Yes to what?"

"If Michael Stone asks you to marry him, just say yes."

The bruise on Brigit's heart ached at the thought and she covered it with her hand. Still no word from Michael. After all the devastating things she'd lived through in life, this one ranked up there with the worst. Unrequited love affected thousands of people, leaving a hole in their hearts and a loneliness akin to the actual loss of a loved one. Good or bad, though, it also left hope flirting around the edges of the pain. At any moment, he might realize he loved her too. At any moment, he might show up on her doorstep with a smile and an outstretched hand. He would draw her back into his world, the circle of his family and friends.

Sighing at her pathetic daydreaming, she pushed the pain away and snagged the last blouse from its hanger, throwing it on the bed next to the others. "President Jeffries has summoned me for a meeting and I don't know what to wear. My gray suit went up in the fire and all I have are casual clothes."

Truman's silence was longer than a normal long-distance delay. "You still have the Burberry?"

She'd picked the trench coat up from the dry cleaners that morning. "Yeah."

"Shoes with a heel on them?"

A pair of low-heeled black pumps sat in the closet in preparation for a job interview with a small therapist group specializing in treating children. She just hadn't found a suit to wear with it yet. "Yes."

"Wear the trench like a dress with the heels. Big sunglasses, bold earrings. Red lipstick."

"What about underneath?"

"A can of pepper spray in case the Big Bad Wolf tries to eat you."

The image made her laugh for the first time in days. Jeffries was bound to try and put the fear of the presidency in her, but she wasn't going to kowtow to him. She'd made up her mind she would do everything in her power to get her father out of the Bolivian prison, but not at the expense of Michael and his family. Even though the jerk had made it clear he didn't care about her, she loved him.

It made no sense, love. Like so many emotions, you could analyze it all you wanted and never understand it. You couldn't control who you loved or the stupid things you might do to prove it.

Like calling the Deputy Director of the CIA forty times in a seventy-two-hour time period.

Truman broke into her reverie. "How's Tory doing?"

Tory. A good subject to keep her mind off Michael. "The arraignment's tomorrow. I think I'm more nervous than she is."

"I'm sure the judge will grant a tad of leniency if Director Stone put in a word in her defense."

Brigit was sure no such word had been offered for her sister. She tried to be angry at Michael, but it didn't work. Tory had to face the music and the music wasn't pretty.

"You're staying in D.C. then for awhile?"

Brigit fingered a blouse. "At least until the trial and sentencing. I'm not sure where Tory will end up, but I plan to stay close to her so I can visit. We have a lot of catching up to do."

"Your resurrection story hasn't made the BBC yet. I've been watching."

"The FBI's been cooperative about keeping the truth under wraps for now. At least while I'm considering their job offer as a profiler."

"Sleeping with the enemy now, are you?"

"The FBI is not your enemy, and besides, I have no plans to accept the offer. I just needed a few days to get my shit together before I become a media darling again."

"Any word on your father?"

"None. That's why I agreed to meet with Jeffries."

"Still have a few tricks in your bag?"

Her bag was empty. All she had was a sincere desire to get her dad back. It was time to free him from the present and the past. "No tricks. I'm done playing political games. I might beg though."

"Well, good luck. Let me know what happens."

Brigit cut the connection and tossed the phone on the bed. Eyeing the selection of T-shirts and button-downs, she dug through the pile until she located a white tank top that matched her hip-huggers and pulled it on.

The trench coat still had the plastic bag over it from the cleaners. She ripped it off and shrugged the coat over her shoulders. The silk lining brushed against her skin, and she wondered if she really had the courage to go to the White House in such a Marilyn Monroe style.

Hell, what did she care? No one would know unless the Secret Service felt her up.

Once the buttons were secure and the belt tied in a knot, she rummaged through her purse and pulled out the single lipstick she'd bought at the local Rite Aid. Power Punch. She brought it to the bathroom and put on the only pair of earrings she had...hoops with four-leaf clovers dangling from them. Also from Rite Aid and tacky more than bold, but again, she found she could've cared less.

The bruise on her temple was all but gone. A layer of foundation dulled the yellow tinge, and she parted her hair on the opposite side so a thick curtain of waves concealed any tell-tale signs.

Just like the bruise on her heart, she was the only one who would know it was there.

She carried the pumps down to her car and threw them in the passenger seat. Double checking the trench's belt was securely knotted, she took a deep breath and put the car in gear.

Big Bad Wolf, here I come.

White House

Helena's voice over the president's intercom made Michael jump. "Doctor Kent is here, sir."

Brigit.

He checked his tie, rose from a chair across from the president's desk, and shot his cuffs before Jeffries even answered his assistant. "Show her in please, Helena."

He wasn't the only man in the room excited to see her. The elder Dr. Kent also rose from a matching chair, buttoned his suit jacket's top button and faced the door, anticipation making his aging features less noticeable.

The scar on Michael's chest tightened. Automatically, he ran his hand over it and realized it wasn't his scar bothering him. It was the hard, insistent thudding of his heart at the thought of seeing Brigit again. His voice mail box was full of Brigit's messages and it had killed him not to call her and tell her about the surprise. It had killed him to hear her voice go from bright and hopeful to disappointed to angry and finally to withdrawn.

Without a knock, she burst through the door with Helena on her heels and a set look on her face. A look Michael had seen repeatedly from Ruth's house to Ireland. The soldier was ready to take on the world.

His heart stuttered and then stopped in wonder for a split-second as he took her in from head to toe. The wavy dark curls, the baby doll eyes, the bright lipstick. The gaudy earrings, the expensive trench, the moderate heels. She was still a conundrum. Still beautiful.

The moment she saw him, she pulled up short, the determined set morphing to surprise. And then her gaze shifted to his right and landed on her father. She rocked on her heels, and Helena put out a hand to steady her.

Helena didn't need to bother. Michael was at Brigit's side in a heartbeat, his hands grabbing her around the waist.

She looked at him, her soldier's eyes softening as they filled with tears. "What have you done?"

"He saved my life," her father said, stepping toward them.

Michael didn't want to let go of her, ever, but he dutifully steered her into her father's outstretched arms. Family came first. Still, he kept his hand resting possessively on her lower back.

The two embraced and Brigit whispered, "Da."

"Well," Jeffries said, rising from his desk chair. "Good to see a family back together. I'm glad I worked this out for you two."

The elder Dr. Kent broke the hug and held Brigit away from him. "Will you forgive me?" Brigit nodded and he shot a glare at the president. "The paperwork wasn't the key to getting me released." His gaze bounced to Michael and back to Brigit. "It was your friend here. He had to fight Cortez's champion, and he laid the guy out with one punch. The whole time he was as cool and calm as a professional prizefighter."

Michael had told Dr. Kent the entire story of Ella's kidnapping, his relationship with Brigit and hunting Donovan on the flight back to the States. He'd asked for his help too, in getting back on Brigit's good side.

Apparently, it was working. Brigit glanced over her shoulder at him. "I've seen him in action. He's amazing."

Jeffries cleared his throat. "I hate to break up the family reunion, but Brigit and I have something to discuss. Would you gentlemen excuse us for a minute?"

It was not a request, but a demand.

Michael bristled.

Brigit did too. "We have nothing to discuss, Mr. President. I've turned over all my information to Deputy Director Stone here. He'll handle it from this point forward."

Jeffries blustered and turned red, but snapped his mouth shut and sat back down in his chair.

Brigit took her father's elbow and steered him toward the door, motioning at Michael to follow.

He couldn't keep the smirk off his face as he passed Helena, especially when Brigit stopped and turned back to face Jeffries. "My condolences on losing the election. I'm sure that was a major disappointment. If you need to talk to a therapist, I'd be happy to refer you to one of my colleagues."

Helena gasped. Jeffries sputtered. Michael slipped his arm around her waist and walked her out of the room. "Watch your step," he muttered in her ear. "He's still president."

She giggled. "I laugh in the face of danger, remember?"

Heat shot to his groin at the memory her words triggered, and he squeezed her waist. "I do remember."

Leaving the White House, he instructed his driver to follow Brigit and her father through D.C. and into the suburbs where Brigit now had an apartment. On the sidewalk in front of the building, he pulled her aside. "I know you need to spend some time with your dad, but I was hoping I could see you tonight. We need to talk."

A guarded expression came over her face. She slipped off her heels and bent to pick them up. "Um, sure."

She thought he meant something else. He grinned mischievously as he laid her worries to rest. "Dinner? A movie?"

Her eyes widened. "You're asking me out on a date?"

He took a deep breath and tried to align his thoughts. "We sort of skipped that part of a new relationship. We should start over. A clean slate." Reaching for her empty hand, he twined his fingers with hers. "I want to do this right."

Her fingers tightened around his. "You broke me out of jail, hunted down the terrorist who tried to kill me and rescued my father. We are way past the dating stage, Michael."

"Not to mention the stalking."

"Stalking?"

He pulled his phone out of his jacket pocket and waggled it in front of her.

Understanding lit up her face and she blushed. "Yeah, about that..."

"You never do anything half-assed. Which is pretty cool. In fact, it's damn sexy. Like I mentioned before in Ireland, you're my kind of woman."

She glanced over her shoulder at her father, who was talking to Brad. "I could say the same for you. First an Irish prison, then a Bolivian one. You got a death wish or something?"

He definitely wanted to live right now. The future stretched out in front of him with endless possibilities. Brigit understood who he was, what he did for a living, what he had survived. She could relate and love him for all his faults, for all his regrets. She gave him hope, and most of all, she gave him back his desire to live again. He couldn't, wouldn't, let her go. "Call me as soon as you can get away."

"Is that an order?"

"Yes," he said, grinning again so hard his cheeks hurt. "And wear the trench. I like it."

She squeezed his hand before pulling her own away and saluting him. "Yes, sir."

Epilogue

Two weeks later

Michael fingered the ring in his pocket. All he had to do was grab Brigit, drag her away from the spackle and propose.

She was right at home, working on their new clean slate, as she called it. The wall he'd torn down in anger was being rebuilt with love.

A ponytail stuck out of the back of the cap she was wearing and bobbed with every movement. Her coveralls were coated in drywall dust and her bare feet poked out from under the rolled-up legs. She was shirtless and bra-free. Every time she bent over to tease another chunk of spackle from the bucket on the floor, the slit in the side gave him a magnificent view of her breasts.

Day by day, hour by hour, she was helping him replace the bad memories of what had happened in this room with good ones. The ghosts were gone, and in their place, Brigit's smiling face, easy laugh and quiet determination to help him see the future as a bright opportunity full of possibilities. They'd talked for hours in front of the fireplace about their childhoods, battled over the remote for control of the flat screen, taught Pongo new tricks and played board games with Ella. They'd even confronted Ruth together about her past involvement with Peter's group, and more importantly, they'd both believed Ruth's innocence once all the facts were discussed. It wasn't the most romantic setting to propose in, but it was a meaningful one.

"Michael," she said, as if reading his mind. "The sooner we get this finished, the sooner we can go back to bed."

He smiled at her back, his heart expanding with his love for her. "Blackmailing me again?"

The flat blade of the scraper skimmed a seam of drywall and she chuckled. "Damn right. I want this wall in perfect shape by Thanksgiving."

"What's the hurry?"

She flashed him some skin as she bent to follow the seam to the edge. "I invited everyone here for dinner."

Forcing his mind to shift out of its libido-driven stupor, he leaned back against the edge of his desk. "Everyone?"

She stepped back to survey her work. "My dad, Thad, Ruth and Ella, and, well, I even invited your mom to come up from Nashville." She snuck a glance at him. Like the ghosts of his yesterdays, the hard edge to her eyes had disappeared. She'd shut the door on her past as firmly as he had. "I hope that's okay."

A traditional family Thanksgiving. In his home. With several members of his family. He swallowed the lump in his throat and pushed off the desk. Taking her by the hand, he tossed the blade into the bucket and led her over to the sofa. "Sit."

"Your house is plenty big enough, and I'll do all the cooking." She frowned up at him and crossed her arms over her chest. "I've always wanted to cook Thanksgiving for a big family. Please, Michael."

He chuckled under his breath. She didn't use the word *please* often. "Brigit, just sit."

Letting out a deep sigh, she plunked down on the couch. He sat across from her on the coffee table and leaned his elbows on his knees. "You know what I've always wanted?"

"World peace?"

"My own family. A wife, kids, the whole enchilada. I always blamed my job as the reason for not pursuing that dream. Now I know it wasn't the job keeping me from getting married and having kids." He paused, waiting for his scar to pinch at the idea he was about to announce, but nothing happened in his chest except the solid beating of his heart. "It was finding the right woman."

Her body tensed and something changed behind her eyes as she caught onto his meaning. Blood rushed to her face, coloring her ivory skin with pink. She blinked and fought a smile. "That's a big realization."

"For me, it's huge."

He was about to tell her he loved her and pull out the ring, but a loud noise that sounded like his back door slamming shut stopped him. Pongo, who'd been asleep in the hallway, jumped up and took off barking.

Conrad Flynn's voice echoed from the mudroom. "Anybody home?"

"What the hell is he doing here?" Michael muttered, rising from the table.

"I called him." Brigit cringed. "He said he'd help us prime the wall."

"Great."

Michael tromped into the kitchen to find Flynn filling the fridge with Sam Adams and Julia unpacking a grocery sack. "We brought lunch," she said.

Michael leaned into Flynn's side. "Jesus Christ, your timing sucks."

Flynn's eyes widened at Michael's death glare. "You didn't do it yet?"

Julia handed Flynn a pile of lunchmeat. "Do what?"

"Nothing," he and Flynn said at the same time.

A moment later, Zara and Lawson came through the back door with Ace and his girlfriend, Cari, tagging along behind them. Ace held up a stack of CDs. "Where's the stereo, Big Mike? Let's get this party started."

Julia and Zara started putting sandwiches together while Conrad, Lawson and Ace filed into the den. Michael looked around for Brigit, but she'd disappeared, probably upstairs to put a shirt on. He left the group and took the stairs to his bedroom two at a time, hoping she was putting on one of his shirts.

He found her sitting in the middle of his bed, fingers rubbing the gold four-leaf clover charm on the bracelet he'd given her on their first date. She glanced up at him, tears shining in her eyes, as he stopped in the doorway. "Are you sure?" she said, nearly rubbing a layer of gold off the charm.

Music began to thump downstairs as Ace took advantage of Michael's sound system. As he gazed into Brigit's eyes, his heart seemed to match the rhythm. With a steady hand, he pulled the ring from his pocket and held it out for her to see.

Her hand flew to her chest and her eyes popped off the chart. "Oh, my, God. That's one huge rock. Did you do some mining down in Bolivia too?"

He moved to sit on the bed next to her and took her left hand away from her heart. "I'm very sure this is what I want, but I can't order you to marry me."

Laughter from below rose over the music and drifted up the stairs. Brigit eyed the diamond and then locked her gaze on him, determination, mingled with youthful hope, burning in her eyes. "Try me. Right now. Give me the order to marry you."

He brushed his lips against hers, the words and the memories they conjured jacking his blood and making his voice hoarse with sudden lust. "Marry me."

"Your wish," she whispered, the tip of her tongue sliding out and teasing him, "is my command."

Slipping the ring on her finger, he kissed the tip of it. "I love you."

"I love you too."

With that, he shut the bedroom door on the party and went to work ordering Brigit out of her clothes.

About the Author

Misty lives with her real life hero and hubby, Mark, her twin sons Sam and Ben, and her big dog, Max, in a small town along the Mississippi River. She's an award-winning, multi-published author who divides her writing time between suspense and paranormal.

To learn more about Misty, please visit www.readmistyevans.com or follow her tweets at www.twitter.com/@readmistyevans. Send an email to Misty at misty@readmistyevans.com to receive her newsletter or join her Yahoo! group to join in the fun with other readers as well as Misty at http://groups.yahoo.com/group/MistyEvansSuspense.

He makes the rules. She breaks them.
This battle of wills just crossed the line...to deadly.

I'd Rather Be in Paris
© 2009 Misty Evans
Super Agent Series, Book 2

Elite CIA operative Zara Morgan has a reputation as a loose cannon with a penchant for breaking the rules. Now she's got a chance to prove she can be a competent field officer, but the test doesn't end there. She's been paired with sexy covert ops team leader Lawson Vaughn, a man who lives and breathes protocol.

Methodical is Lawson's middle name. He specializes in high-risk search and rescue, not missions that involve tracking down terrorists. Especially while trying to keep the lid on a partner who has a problem with authority and skates by on wits and bravado.

Even before they get on the plane for Paris they're under each other's skin...and fighting a scorching sexual attraction. Drawn into an unauthorized game of vengeance, Lawson is forced to dance a tightrope in order to protect his partner from their quarry—a terrorist who's about to unleash a biological nightmare on the Muslim world. And Zara is the first target.

With her life, and that of millions of innocent people, on the line, Lawson must become the one thing he despises. A renegade.

Warning: Either you're in or you're out. There's no playing it safe anymore.

Available now in ebook and print from Samhain Publishing.

GREAT CHEAP FUN

Discover eBooks!

CPSIA information can be obtained at www.ICGtesting.com
Printed in the USA
LVOW13s2017290614

392216LV00001B/156/P